Critical acclaim for

Blood Ties

'With *The French Executioner* Humphreys established himself as a quality purveyor of historical detail and vigorous action ... This unusual storyline is dispatched with consummate skill, and the conflict between father and son has an intelligence and sophistication that transcends the narrative' *Good Book Guide*

'C.C. Humphreys excels as ever in the throat-in-mouth action and knows instinctively how to keep a reader pasted to the page ... This novel shows a writer reaching ever upwards and I can't wait for Humphreys' next novel. If you like Bernard Cornwell's *Grail Quest* series, you'll love *The French Executioner* and *Blood Ties*. To my mind, Cornwell is good, but Humphreys is better' Sally Zigmond, *Historical Novels Review*

The French Executioner

'Falling somewhere between the novels of Bernard Cornwell and Wilbur Smith, C.C. Humphreys has fashioned a rollicking good yarn that keeps the pages turning from start to finish' John Daly, *Irish Examiner*

'... how he fulfills his mission is told with enormous zest in this splendid, rip-roaring story ... a fine addition to the tradition of swashbuckling costume romance of which Robert Louis Stevenson is the incomparable master' George Patrick, *Hamilton Examiner*

'Don't miss this wonderful saga of magic and heroism ... if you can find a first impression, hoard it and wait till it rises in value like a first edition of *Lord of the Rings*. This is as good. For sheer pleasure I've read nothing to match it all year' Russell James, *Crime Time magazine*

C.C. Humphreys was born in Toronto, Canada, and grew up in London. An actor, leading roles have included Hamlet and the Gladiator, Caleb in the mini-series *Anno Domini*. His plays have been produced in the UK and Canada. A schoolboy fencing champion and fight choreographer, he has turned his love of swashbuckling towards historical fiction. His first novel, *The French Executioner*, was shortlisted for the CWA Steel Dagger for Thrillers 2002. His latest novel in hardback, *Jack Absolute*, is also available from Orion. Visit his website at www.cchumphreys.com.

By C.C. Humphreys

Jack Absolute
Blood Ties
The French Executioner

BLOOD TIES

C.C. HUMPHREYS

ORION

An Orion paperback

First published in Great Britain in 2003
by Orion
This paperback edition published in 2003
by Orion Books Ltd,
Orion House 5 Upper St Martin's Lane,
London WC2H 9EA

A CIP catalogue record for this book is
available from the British Library

ISBN 0 75284 277 3

Typeset by Deltatype Ltd, Birkenhead, Merseyside
Printed and bound in Great Britain by
Clays Ltd, St Ives plc

AUTHOR'S NOTE

Whereas the genesis of my first novel, *The French Executioner*, came in a blinding flash – the swordsman, Jean Rombaud, taking Anne Boleyn's six-fingered hand as well as her head – the idea for this second arrived more stealthily. I knew I wanted to spend more time with the characters I'd already created yet the book had to stand alone. I enjoy writing action-filled adventures, but felt that this story should be more intimate, and explore further my characters' inner conflicts. The idea of a war within the family came then – father versus son, brother against sister, mother against daughter. But I still needed some historical 'pegs' to hang my fictional story upon.

When I began writing historical fiction, I thought research was about getting the details right, and indeed there is huge satisfaction in accurately describing the past. But what research *really* does is act as a stimulus. I rediscovered the old truth that fact is stranger than fiction time and again. One fact unearthed is the very seedbed of creation. And so often that fact, that date, that place, can seem an almost miraculous thing.

Some examples – I knew I wanted to involve the new as well as the old generation from the previous novel. Since I'd left my characters in the epilogue, happy and content near Siena in 1546, I wondered what was happening there, say, in 1555, when the children would be grown yet their parents not too old to have adventures. I discovered that war had once more ravaged the land and that Siena endured a terrible siege . . . that ended on 17 April 1555.

I then had the idea of transferring the threat against Anne Boleyn to her daughter. Schoolboy history told me that Elizabeth was in great danger throughout the reign of her sister – Bloody Mary. Further research told me that Elizabeth was summoned to Hampton Court, still under arrest . . . on 21 April 1555.

Across a continent, four days apart! My characters, fictional and real, in crisis. With such symmetry of dates, I felt blessed. The rest was almost easy.

Almost. There was one other aspect I felt compelled to include. Though raised in London, I was born in Canada, have often been drawn back to its stunning forests, mountains and rivers. How could I honour these two halves of myself, the Englishman and the North American? What was going on in Canada at the time that could link it to these events in Europe? I researched. I discovered, again, more amazing things than I could ever invent. Especially that in 1536, the year that Anne Boleyn was executed, a Breton explorer, Jacques Cartier made the first of three voyages to the St Lawrence. He took hostages back to France. Applying the 'what if?' of the fiction writer I wondered if a baby hostage could have survived. If so that young man would have been eighteen in 1555. The same age as Jean Rombaud's daughter, Anne.

I had my link from the Old World to the New. Hence the second half of this book. My research then disgorged facts of the native cultures of the time that almost dictated my story thereafter. Not least that the tribe Cartier encountered who, later, were dubbed 'Huron' by the Europeans, were driven away by their blood enemies, one tribe of the nations later known as the Iroquois . . .

. . . *sometime in the 1550s.*

I had my overall story and more facts gave me wonderful set pieces and characters. Several books stimulated. *The Huron: Farmers of the North* by Bruce G. Trigger, was a source of riches, as was *The League of the Iroquois* by Lewis Henry Morgan. (Written in 1851, I found a second-hand copy under strange circumstances one day while walking down the Finchley Road. It was in the window of a tatty shop that seemed to have mainly soft porn videos, with a very odd owner who tried to convince me that the Ark of the Covenant was a giant crystal CD player. Both owner and shop had disappeared when I looked a week later. Spooky!) I've taken as my Native models the Tahontaenrat, the Huron tribe that *could* have been the one driven out of the St Lawrence in 1555. I based their conquerors on their old enemies, the Seneca, an Iroquois nation who *could* have expelled them. My study of their customs and language – both tribes spoke versions of Iroquoian – are mainly drawn from written sources begun some hundred years later. But these societies, by all accounts, hadn't changed much in the previous centuries. They had their clan groupings, their councils, their ways of hunting and war, even their lacrosse. They had evolved advanced social structures and had no need to change. Until the Europeans came.

The siege of Siena is brilliantly analysed in Simon Pepper and Nicholas Adams's *Firearms and Fortifications – Military Architecture and Siege Warfare in Sixteenth-Century Siena.* The Tower of London website was a great help as was a book my brother sent me that we'd had in the family for ages: *The Tower of London* by W. H. Ainsworth. This was given to my brother by Great Aunt Ethel whose ancestor, and therefore mine, Sir Henry Bedingfield, was Princess Elizabeth's gaoler at Woodstock. (I desperately tried to get this relative into the novel as some heroic swashbuckler but he just wouldn't fit!) A retired Jesuit, Fr. Richard Foley, helped me with my Latin.

I spent a wonderful day with John Moses, a Native History Researcher at the fantastic Canadian Museum of Civilisation in Hull, Quebec. Part Iroquois himself, he talked brilliantly and had photocopied many articles that proved invaluable. Best of all, he gave me white gloves, then led me into the stacks of artefacts that the public never see. Here I hefted genuine Iroquois war clubs; one, from the early seventeenth century, especially captured me, becoming the basis for the duel fought in Part Two. I will never forget the feeling as I swung it through the air. That sort of research is beyond price – especially to a fight choreographer.

The main difficulty of writing about native affairs is the fear of stereotyping peoples every bit as complex as one's own without the innate understanding one has from growing up in their culture. There is also a great deal of controversy about certain points – for example, scalping and who actually began it. After much pondering I decided to include it as part of their way of life, while being fully prepared to admit that they may well have been taught it by early Europeans. What I was determined to avoid was the Hollywood trap of depicting all natives as 'Noble Savages'.

There is so much to admire in the proto-Huron and Iroquois societies. The richness of their myths and the sophistication of their psychology, the respect they accorded each individual. The way Huron children were treated as just other, smaller, humans and never struck, which the Jesuits could hardly believe. The honour given to women and their opinions, particularly amongst the Iroquois. Their, in my opinion, healthy attitude to sexual relations. The sharing of all things, especially food in times of hardship together with their desire to acquire status and respect rather than wealth. Their lack of a death penalty – except in rare cases of witchcraft and treason. Their command of rhetoric and their consensus politics, the elevation of leaders on merit. Friedrich Engels, for very good reasons, labelled the Iroquois a proto-Communist society, an example of one that had worked.

But . . . but . . . but . . . the native peoples of the St Lawrence in 1555 *could* be 'savage'. War, viciously conducted, was what men did. Prisoners *could* be horribly tortured before death. Their hearts *could* be eaten. In these things they were no different from those 'savages' across the Atlantic with their inquisitions, their racks, their heretic burnings, their racial slaughter. All humans have a capacity for cruelty, whatever their ethnic background; we have only to look around our world today to see that. I hope I have struck a balance, seen the good as well as the bad in all and portrayed their humanity, the dark as well as the light. For my purposes, the Huron are the good guys, the Iroquois somewhat nastier. In someone else's story, it could be the other way around.

As for the way they talk, like my sixteenth-century Europeans, I have tried to make them natural to our modern ear without being anachronistic. While working on the second draft of this novel in a cottage in Shropshire I read a wonderful novel by Rosemary Sutcliffe, *Warrior Scarlet*. Set in the Bronze Age in England, it had everyday speech referenced only by what the people would have seen around them. It was natural to them. An enviable pattern I've tried to imitate.

Some acknowledgements. As in the first book, my wife, Aletha, was a model of patience and good advice. I completed the final edit as a fellow of Hawthornden Castle so thanks to all there. Once more, I am indebted to the team at Orion. Jane Wood, Publishing Director, who wasn't sure about the word 'sequel' and then got thoroughly behind it. Jon Wood, Editorial Director, who 'inherited' me but whose love of a good swashbuckle has made him a big supporter with an excellent eye for an edit – and a fine taste in red wine. Rachel Leyshon, who edited my first novel and I hope will edit my last, and whose observations are always shrewd while she reins in my tendency to disembody ('he threw his eyes across the table' etc). My agent, Anthea Morton-Saner, whose great advice, in career and writing, I always value. My Canadian Publisher, Kim McArthur, whose enthusiasm envelopes and whose business smarts market my books in my birthplace superbly. And Alma Lee, Artistic Director of my first Writer's Festival in Vancouver – a new friend.

To these, and many others, my heartfelt thanks.

C.C. HUMPHREYS
London, March 2002

*For my parents, Peter and Ingegerd,
and the stories they told me*

PART ONE
OLD WORLD

PROLOGUE
THE EXHUMATION

Thomas stepped from light into darkness, from warmth into a chill mist. It flowed around him, probing for weakness, piercing his thick cloak, settling into the old wound rendered raw and new again by this night. The knee gave; a slight stumble forward, a hand reaching out to support him under the elbow. Shrugging it off, he lurched one step, then another, forcing the leg to its work. No one could mistake his limp, but he was the leader here and he would not be helped.

The walk was not long, a minute's stride across the Green, less. Yet the fog swallowed the path and he only knew it when he strayed from it, for the ground had a crust of frost, its crunch different than the gravel. Really, he should have let the Tower's officer go first – *what was his name? Tucknell?* – but when he'd arrived and told him the reason for his visit, the old warder's face had betrayed such horror, Thomas had thought he might actually be refused. The signature on his pass had ended any protests. The Fox's signature always did. But now they were embarked on their mission, it was important to show who was in charge. Especially as it was clear, from the plainness of his clothes, the shortness of his hair and beard, that Tucknell was a Protestant.

They had covered perhaps half the ground when a black shape burst from the mist. He had stepped off the path again and suddenly there was a blur of feathers, a carrion scent, a demonic caw. As the creature's talons reached for his face, his knee buckled again and he reeled backwards with a cry, banging hard into the man that followed close behind.

'Easy, Master Lawley. Easy.' The man – Tucknell – held him under his arm, raised a lantern. His voice was calming. 'It's one of the ravens, no more. I warned you to stick to the path.' Setting his burden upright, he added, 'Been a cruel winter for everyone, including the birds. He thought you were after his hidden food.'

At another moment, Thomas might have laughed. There was a time, in Portugal, when he'd fought for scraps with sparrows and crows. God's missions had a harsh way of testing the faithful. That was their point. And yet, if he'd had the choice between those simple days of preaching and begging through an alien countryside, and this night's work in his native land . . .

That glimpse of a memory made him think on humility, the virtue his teachers had always found hardest to instil in him, the proud ex-soldier. He had no need to dominate this man. He only needed him to do God's will. With a half-smile, he said, softly, 'Perhaps you will lead the way now, Master Warder.'

The freezing mist seemed to pool thicker about the chapel doors, yet no one seemed anxious to seek shelter from it. Tucknell fiddled with the keys in his hand, the three labourers leaned on shovels and picks, avoiding each others' eyes. Even Thomas felt a reluctance to proceed. Outside the iron-studded doors, the frigid air was at least connected to the world of the living, their footprints in the frost a trail back to light and warmth. Ahead, within the darkness, lay a deeper cold – the realm of the dead. And they were there to violate that realm.

After a few moments watching plumes of breath stripe the night, Thomas shifted, made to speak, to command. Before breath could become voice in him, the warder pulled him slightly to one side, whispered, 'Sir. Let me ask of you once more. Beg of you. Do not do this. It is a sin.'

'I have my orders, Tucknell. And you have yours. You saw the signature on the papers. This command comes from the Queen herself.'

It was not strictly true, but the officer was not to know that. He drew back, seeking Thomas's eyes.

'I know our gracious sovereign Mary has little reason to love . . . she who lies here. But to thus despoil her tomb?' His voice softened. 'You are an Englishman, sir, and a gentleman I can tell. Let us spare an English lady further humiliation.' Off Thomas's silent stare he cried, 'For Jesu's sake, man, hasn't she suffered enough?'

Thomas leaned in, so his voice, softened now, beguiling, would not carry to the waiting, shifting men.

'I do not like this either, man. But we have had reports that this woman may have taken something with her to the grave. Something that may . . . be of use to Her Majesty.'

Tucknell's face twisted, as if containing a violent struggle. 'She took nothing with her save a prayer book and the clothes she wore. I know, sir, because I was there.' The struggle overpowered him. 'I know because I helped to kill her and to bury her afterwards. May God have mercy on my soul!'

'Amen.'

Thomas watched a tear that had nothing to do with the harsh wind run from this tough soldier's eye, and wondered at the power this woman, dead nearly twenty years, still had over the living. A power to be turned into a weapon for the Catholic cause, so his superiors in the Society of Jesus believed. But only if he, Thomas Lawley, did his duty now.

'Come, Master Tucknell. You have merely to show me the way. If there is sin after that, it is I, and I alone, that will commit it.'

The soldier before him hardened, the tears withdrawn. Without another word he turned to the door and fitted into its lock the largest of the keys he carried. It grated there, with a cry like that of the raven defending its cache of food. The doors, in contrast, swung open, as silent as on any tomb.

If it's possible, thought Thomas, rubbing his knee in vain hope, *it's even colder inside than out.*

The mist may not have followed them in, but the shadows caused by their weak lanterns were nearly as thick, walls of black lining the little chapel. St Peter in Chains, it was called. He had seen it by day, knew it brought succour to the warders and their families, to prisoners on a looser leash. By night it became once more the dark centre of the fortress, the last lodging place of those who had displeased the state, who walked across the Green he had just walked across, and were carried back. By night it was a place to be avoided, for unless you desired to spend time with the unquiet dead, why would you go there?

Out of sight of the others, Thomas crossed himself, then

allowed Tucknell to pass him, to lead again, moving swiftly to the side aisle on the right. There the warder proceeded more slowly, bent at the waist, his lantern swinging close to the ground in a semi-circle before him. The labourers waited at the doorway, barely across the threshold and Thomas heard, rather than saw, a flagon being passed, a gulping. He knew he should chastise them for their irreverence, within these holy walls. But he found himself envying them their solace.

The lantern ceased its circling, was placed now on the floor. Tucknell stood, head lowered, silent, about six paces before the smaller altar on the right arm of the Transept. Thomas joined him, bent to investigate the flagstone. It looked like any other there, a pitted surface though smooth-sided, half a man's height in width and length.

'Are you sure this is it?'

Tucknell made no move to speak, gave no sign that he had even heard, his eyes gazing down as if through the stone to some private past.

Thomas pressed. 'This stone is like the rest of them, Warder. Was there no mark to distinguish her?'

Tucknell grunted. 'Distinguish? His Majesty, the late King Henry, God forgive him his sins, ordered that there be no tomb, no monument. Wanted her driven from our memory as swiftly as from his. No funeral tears to stain his wedding day the following week.' The warder made no effort to keep the contempt from his voice. 'There is a mark, if you know where to look.'

He pointed, raised the lamp. At first Thomas saw nothing unusual; then, on closer scrutiny, he made out what he'd passed over as just another scratch. A rose was etched there, in the top right corner, faint, tiny, no bigger than a little finger. Perfect. Someone had laboured with care to carve it, to make it beautiful yet inconspicuous. Thomas had heard, among the many rumours, that despite the erasing of her name, the blackening of her memory, a single white rose appeared every nineteenth of May in this chapel, on this stone floor. Someone would not forget her, nor the anniversary of her death. He looked up again, but Tucknell's face was hidden in the gloom. His voice, when it came, was brisk, uninflected.

'Shall we proceed?'

More lanterns were lit, hung from brackets on the pillars, perched on pews pushed back, a little cave of light. The scent of old incense, of polished wood and tallow candles was replaced with that of burning oil and, soon, of earth freshly dug. The flagstone, and the four nearest it, were prised up and stacked. The three men set about the earth with a speed that showed their desire to be gone from this place, the clay-rich soil a growing pile, the men sinking slowly.

'How deep must they go?' Thomas called.

Tucknell had withdrawn into the darkness and his voice came muffled, as if from afar. 'Not very.'

Despite his knee, Thomas was unable to sit. He leaned against a pillar, focusing forward, willing the men to greater exertion, to swifter result. He was tempted to leap into the widening pit, to aid them. His training had emphasized hard labour, good works, examples set . . . but he knew he would just get in the way. The shovel was not a tool that fitted easily into his hand. These days, it was the crucifix. Once, it had been the sword.

There was a crunch, different to blade on earth, a rending and splintering of wood, a cry from the workman who struck of triumph, the note of it changing swiftly to fear. The three men scrambled out, moved into the shadows, crossing themselves, mumbling prayers behind their hands cupped over nose and mouth. Thomas willed his body forward, the lantern held before him like a weapon, its frail spill of light spreading across till it touched on something white at the centre of the darkness below. As it did, the stench reached him, putrid, some sick sweetness within it, surging out as if from a bottle long corked and suddenly opened, revealing its taint. He gagged, a sleeve raised instinctively to his face. His legs froze, the weak knee locked.

'Still ripe?'

He had not heard Tucknell approach and he started at the voice.

'How can that be?' His own voice was harsh, choked. 'Has she not lain in this ground for nearly twenty years? Is it true then, all they said of her, that she would defy death?'

The warder, giving no reply, stepped past Thomas and down into the grave. Unwilling to look, unable to look away, Thomas saw what could only be the palm of a hand, bones exposed beneath rotting flesh, beneath a frantic wriggling mass, maggots squirming in unaccustomed light. The smell seemed to hit him again with double the force, yet he could not avert his eyes, despite the sweat bursting from his forehead, his body close to revolt.

Tucknell reached into the moving centre of the horror. 'Poor lady,' he murmured. Tenderly, he tucked the hand back into the splintered side of the coffin, then looked up. 'She is not the one you seek. She has lain here just a year.' Turning to the men he ordered, 'Dig deeper, this side. And dig more carefully.'

When the warder was once more beside him, Thomas, mastering his voice, said, 'Who was it?'

'Jane Grey. A simple maid, scarce seventeen. Another victim of another man's ambition.' The voice grew harsh as he gestured at the ground. 'Do you know how many headless queens jostle for precedence down there? Three. Her, whose reign was nine scant days, whose rest we have just violated. Within two arms' span lies another, Catherine Howard, a foolish, vain, girl who yet did not deserve this fate. And before them both, the first to find this false rest, the only one who deserved the title of Queen ...' He faltered, his anger no longer sustaining him. 'Well, her you shall see soon enough.'

Thomas had not yet cleared the taste of bile from his mouth when the shovel's note changed for the second time. On Tucknell's command, the men proceeded carefully, slowly clearing the earth, till a small, squarish casket was revealed, no deeper than the man's leg beside it, barely as long. Tucknell returned Thomas's querying look.

'An arrow case. That was the best that was around to bury her in.' He handed Thomas a short iron bar, flattened at one end. 'We shall withdraw, sir, as you ordered. Call us when you are done.' He looked as if he would say something more, then turned sharply away, herding the labourers outside, all soon swallowed by the mists at the door. All sound went with them and Thomas was alone, in a pool of flickering light, in the loneliness of a grave.

He thought to call out, to bring someone back, the excuse of needing a lamp held. But his orders were clear. No one was to know his true mission. Most would think he was there to put an end to the rumours that her body had been spirited away, that she'd been reburied in her native Norfolk where, it was said, a white hare made a midnight run across the fields from the churchyard on each anniversary of her death. They could believe what they wanted. No one would ever guess the truth. For he was not there to verify what was within the grave. He was there to verify what was not.

He could delay no more. Placing two lamps on the edge of the rough hole, he stiffly descended into it. He expected a struggle, but when the flat end of the bar was inserted under the lid, it gave easily, as if it had been barely nailed down. Two more positions, each with slight pressure, and the lid lifted. His fingers poised in the cracks, he uttered a swift '*Ave*', then began to breathe slowly, evenly, bringing calm into his body, his mind, as he had been taught. He had done some distasteful things in his recent life. But they had all been to the service of God, in obedience to his superiors, the interpreters of God's will. This task, however unpleasant, was just another, one more bead threaded onto the rosary of his redemption.

He lifted the lid, set it aside, his nostrils prepared for the surge of corruption they had received before. But there was nothing, no scent except . . . yes, there was something now, mere mustiness and within it something soft, almost honeyed. It was there, for a moment only, and it was gone again, as if someone had held a flower to his face and then moved away. She had lain within this casket for nineteen years. The worms he had seen moving in the dead hand of another short-lived queen, would long since have finished their feast here.

The dead hand of a queen. He had frozen there – his steady breaths, the sweet scent that had wafted away, the flickering of the lamps, all had lulled him. But the image of that hand roused him again. He had his duty to perform. All he had to do was find what should be there, and when it was found, he would make his report and return to the warmth of his lodgings, the night fading into another disagreeable task executed for the greater glory of God. His master would have to find a different method of coercion. His master was good at that.

The skull lay at the bottom of the chest, to his right, beside slippered feet. There were yet some shreds of hair, coiled up, its famed lustre long since faded. Someone had wrapped a cloak around the body, but the wool had unravelled and he was able to reach easily to the damask dress beneath, its material un-frayed by the years. Reaching up, he found the sleeve at the shoulder, traced it down to where the garment ended.

And there it was. A hand, or the bones of it, exactly where it should be. Clenched, no doubt a dying gesture, which the hardening that follows death had solidified. It was such relief to find it, his body flushing warm for the first time in an age. He was able to go back and say the strange report they had received from Rome was untrue. Thomas had no reason to love the woman within this barren chest. As an English Catholic, all the woes of his family had been caused, in a way, by the spirit once housed within these bones. But he'd seen the love she inspired in a man like Tucknell, the pain this exercise in duty was causing the warder. He was glad he would be able to end that pain, just by counting the fingers within the clenched fist.

As he reached down he noticed again that the skull was to his right. By the feet. So he was holding the right hand. The skull had confused him, because he knew, the rumours told him, he should be looking at the left. The relief he'd felt evaporated, coldness returned, squeezing his heart. Suddenly he knew. Yet knowing was not enough, he needed proof. His master would accept no less than the testament of his eyes. Leaning across, he pulled at the remains of cloak that clung there, throwing aside the clumps of wool, scrabbling at the heavy grey sleeve that was somehow rolled under the body. It was light, mere bones, yet it took an effort to pull it out. Finally, it gave with a crack, as if something had separated within the folds. Gasping, his eyes closed, he held the dress at the shoulder and ran his hand swiftly down the arm within the sleeve.

To nothing. There was nothing there. Where there should be a hand, a deformed, six-fingered hand, there was a void. He looked, though he had no need to open his eyes. His touch had told him the story, the prickle of shattered bone at the wrist digging into his questing fingers.

Somehow he forced the dress back down, the remains of cloak back over. Somehow, he reached behind him, to grasp, to slam the lid onto the arrow chest. The sound was accompanied by a sob he could not prevent, both noises echoing in the vault of the chamber.

When he opened his eyes again, feet were before him on the edge of the hole. Tucknell reached down, wordless, grasping the arm Thomas had thrust out as if to ward off evil. Pulled from the pit, his bad knee buckled again, and he slumped onto the nearest pew.

'Done your duty, sir?' Taking silence as his answer the warder went on. 'Then maybe you will be so good as to let me tend to my Queen.' He stepped down into the grave.

Thomas breathed deeply, again and again, till he gained the strength to rise and limp to the chapel door. In the entranceway he paused, looked back.

'I needn't tell you, Master Warder, of the silence we require of you.' He used the 'we'. Tucknell had seen the signature on the pass.

'You needn't. I have a wife and a family. You shall have my silence.' Tucknell paused, looking down. 'The silence of a grave.'

Thomas nodded. He thought of giving some word of comfort, some lessening of the threat he'd just made. It was still a weakness with him, wanting to be liked. But the threat was what mattered here, not his feelings.

As he turned to the door, he hardened his voice. 'See that you do, my son.'

Tucknell, watching the cloaked figure meld with mist, spat out one word. 'Jesuit!'

He didn't think he'd been heard. He didn't care, especially. Anyway, the word that had once been almost an insult was now becoming common usage for the black-robed brothers of the Society of Jesus. No, all he cared about now was the task before him.

'Oh my lady,' he whispered, looking straight into the eyeless sockets of the skull, seeing, though he knew it was impossible, a deeper darkness there, 'will they never let you rest?'

Torchlight and candlelight bounced off shield, mitre and crown, off bridles held in bared teeth, couched lances, upraised swords. Every surface reflected flame, except for the floor, so that's where

Thomas looked, as was expected of him. The contrast to the mist-flecked darkness he'd come from left him little choice.

The man he'd come to see had commanded silence with a gesture. Thomas watched the man's shadow on the floor, heard him move from chessboard to chessboard around the blazing chamber, heard the clack of piece taking piece, the soft slide of felt on polished wood as another knight or bishop slid into position. Or pawn, Thomas's role, waiting to report. It was said, by those who understood such things, that the Fox had a mastery of pawns.

'Do you play?'

The voice came so softly, Thomas was not sure he had heard. He looked up, blinking against the flames, and gazed into the only other darkness in the room. Behind the desk, the inevitable chessboard before it, a peaked night cap jutted. Within that shadow was the face of the Imperial Ambassador, Simon Renard. The Fox.

'When I have leisure, my lord. And thus, not often.'

A hand emerged, very white, very thin, the nails five perfect half moons. It floated briefly over the board, withdrew.

'Chess is not leisure. Chess is life.'

The hand came out again, striking like a cat. No, like a fox, his namesake. A knight joined his fellow on the desk's surface, a queen glided forward.

'Checkmate in three.' A dry chuckle came, a rasp like sanded paper on wood. 'I doubt the Prior of Ravenna will have seen that. He rarely looks three moves ahead.'

The beautiful fingers lingered on the queen, stroking it from crown to hip. Then the man behind the desk picked her up, leaning forward into the light. Thomas saw again the pale, long face, all planes and angles thrusting down, the eyelashes luxuriant as a veil over dark pits of eyes. His gaze met Thomas's across the room, and the voice, when it came, had none of its former languor.

'Well?'

'My lord, as we suspected. It was not there.'

'Ah!' There was a catch to that one syllable, something almost voluptuous. 'So your leaders have proved right once again. I do marvel at the Jesuitical control of information.'

'We do what is necessary, my lord. For the glory of God.'

'Of course. Always and only for the glory of God, eh?'

Thomas, hearing the mockery in the tone, breathed deeply. He had at least played enough chess to recognize so obvious a feint. The Society of Jesus had sent him to be this man's right hand because the Imperial Ambassador was the real power behind Queen Mary's throne. They and Renard wanted the same thing: England restored as a Catholic Kingdom and Imperially aligned. Compared to that great goal, the man's irreverence was as nothing, anger mere indulgence. Besides, an angry response would delay what Thomas most wanted to hear.

'What now, my lord?'

'Now, Thomas?' Renard leaned back into the shadows again. 'Now you are destined to travel, with all despatch, to Rome. To the young man who provided us with the tantalizing information you have verified tonight. That youth, according to your superiors, knows more than just what was missing from the tomb. He knows where to find it.'

Suddenly, Renard was up, and across the room, his face thrust into Thomas's, long fingers caressing him at the neck. It took an effort not to recoil from the contact, the breath that came, sickly, from between those thin lips. It was rumoured Renard suffered horribly in his stomach. It was why he never slept, spent all his nights awake among his chessboards, his spies' reports, his intrigues.

'Go,' the whisper came on tainted breath, 'fetch me back what was stolen. Fetch me that weapon of coercion. For the Glory of God. Go fetch me the six-fingered hand of Anne Boleyn.'

Thomas shuddered, even though he'd known it would come to this, shuddered as he recalled that honest warder's face, the plea to let his Queen rest in her grave. Shuddered because he, Thomas, had violated her tomb and would violate it again with his mission now. So often, the glory of God led down a hard path.

Renard was back at the table. A scratch of a quill, a paper folded, wax melted, a signet placed to seal. Another and yet another followed.

'This will get you across the sea to Antwerp. This is for the Cardinal, Carafa, in Rome. Only for his eyes, do you understand? Although I realize you will open and read it first.'

'My lord, I—'

'No protests, Thomas. I read your letters, as you read mine. Information is all that matters. Just make sure it is delivered. And this' – he held up the final, smallest packet – 'is for the Commander of the Imperial forces at Siena. It will get you, and our young informant, into the city.'

'Siena?' It was the first time Renard has taken him completely by surprise. 'But Siena withstands a siege. They say it will last as long as the siege of Troy.'

Renard looked up, smiling, weighing that surprise, delighted that his move had caught the younger man off balance.

'For once, Jesuit information is inferior to mine. Siena is no Troy. Siena ... is about to fall.'

ONE

SIENA

'Fugger? Are you there?'

Jean Rombaud had barely spoken, yet the words bounced loudly off the earth walls, echoing down the narrow, twisting passages. He had lost his way at the last crossroads, blind as a worm, his yew stick thrust out before, fingers scraping on damp mud one of his only functioning senses. That, and the way the air got staler to his tongue as he moved deeper into the labyrinth. This was not his world and he cursed again the necessity for time spent within it. Cursed silently, for any words, he now understood, were dangerous.

He walked into flesh and cried out, but a hand from the darkness pressed over his mouth. No, not a hand, for no fingers splayed across his face. A stump. He had found the man he sought.

The stump moved away and a moment later a faint trace of light peeped from a gated lantern. In the depth of that blackness, it was like looking suddenly into the sun.

Squinting, he mouthed a word: 'Fugger.'

The Fugger planted his lips next to Jean's ear. 'Rombaud. What brings you to my realm?'

The head turned away and Jean placed his own mouth to the other's ear. 'You know, Fugger. You sent word. Is it time?'

Instead of replying, the Fugger gestured with the lamp, raising it to a narrow earth shelf beside him. On it, sat a drum, a child's toy. Scattered on its surface were pebbles. As Jean watched, they vibrated across the tight skin. Something was making them move. He pressed his ear to the earth wall, heard the faintest of scratchings, like mice scrabbling behind wood panels.

Jean turned back to the Fugger, lifted his eyebrows at the wall, mouthed, 'How long?'

The man's one hand opened and closed three times.

Jean leaned in. 'Let us go back. I'll send them down.'

'I stay.'

'Fugger—'

'I stay. I know what's best for my beauty.' He patted the walls, smiling.

Jean shook his head. He had known the Fugger for nearly two decades, most of it above ground. And sometimes he forgot that when they first met, the German had lived in a cave beneath a gibbet for seven years. The man was right; no one knew a subterranean world better.

Giving him a warning look that clearly said 'get out when your work is done', Jean groped his way back, eventually emerging into the shocking brightness of a torch before a door. He rapped upon it with his knuckles, a staccato beat of three, two, three more. Bolts slid back, the door opened on an earth chamber. The next door admitted him to a chamber of stone, steps rising before him. He was out of the Fugger's dark realm, under the bastion itself now. Back within the walls of Siena.

He passed through the entrance to the countermine gallery and through the archway before him. There, gathered in the lower casemate of the Porta San Viene, leaning on its guns, spread out around its curving walls, were twenty men and one woman.

It was his wife's eyes he sought. He nodded. Beck held the look for a moment, then looked away. She always looked away first, these days.

Haakon was next, as usual. His oldest comrade straddled a gun carriage, his huge legs resting either side on its wheels. Like Jean, Haakon had lost everything when the forces of Florence, backed by the Emperor's armies, invaded the terrritory of their old rivals, the Republic of Siena. Their farms and vineyards and the Comet Inn, their home, were among the first to be pillaged and nearly destroyed. Only if Siena won this war would they get their land back.

Yet, unlike Jean, who had seen enough bloodshed for three lifetimes, Haakon did not fight only for a cause. The Norse ex-mercenary fought mainly, as always, for the pure pleasure of it.

'Well?' As he rose eagerly from the gun, a shadow rose behind him, leaner, a little taller, with as thick a beard, and eyes just as blue. Erik, Haakon's son, clutched the first of his twin scimitars in one hand, the whetstone in his other. Before a fight, he would go through the same ritual, sharpening each of them in turn, alternating, long beyond the perfect edge was obtained. Only when the actual moment of battle came would they be sheathed in the double harness on his back. Jean remembered well the young man's inspiration, the janissary Januc and his pure mastery of the weapon. Though he had died before the lad was born, the tales of Januc's valour had inspired Erik. Jean had never been able to decide who was the more deft with the curving blade.

'It is time. The Fugger says fifteen minutes, at most.'

Eric swept his shining scimitars into their sheaths, while Haakon raised his short axe and rested it in his shoulders. It was better for close work than the giant battle axe that stood now in the corner of the room. Haakon, despite his size, had become the master of fighting in close spaces.

As the men around him strapped on weapons, donned helm and breastplate, Haakon strode over to the Frenchman. 'Ah, Rombaud, what I would give to have you fighting beside me now.'

Jean put a false smile on his face into accustomed grooves. 'And I, my friend. It's been too long.'

'The wound? It still pains you?'

The look of pure concern on his friend's face almost made Jean look down in shame. His expression held, however, fingers rubbing where the sniper's bullet had passed through his side.

'It does. Jesus willing, it will not be much longer.'

'Ask Thor.' The pagan Norseman was smiling again. 'He's more likely to grant such a warrior request.'

He moved away among his men, cajoling, encouraging. Jean dropped his hand away from the scar under the doublet, from the wound only he knew had fully healed.

It was not completely true. His daughter, his darling, named for a queen, his Anne, she knew, because she had had the healing of him. And Beck suspected. But his wife, would put her suspicions down to the other anger she felt toward him.

She crossed to him and they stood side by side, watching the preparations. Glancing at her, he wondered at the years that had gone. Nineteen since he'd first seen her, disguised as a boy, fought her on that hillside outside Toulon. There was no trace of boy now, only a woman of middle years, grey throughout her thinning hair, lines on her face.

And he knew how he must look to her. No longer a warrior in his prime. No longer a hero. Far from it.

'Do you go with them, Jean?' Her voice, when it came, was flat, neutral.

'I do not.'

'Then I will see you above.'

She moved away, collecting her spanish musket before heading up the stairs. She had long since put away her preferred weapon, the slingshot, the power no longer in the arm. But she was as accurate with lead as she ever had been with stone, and had a greater range, her thirst for a target undiminished.

He wanted to say something, anything, but no words came. Then Haakon was before him, his men assembled, Erik at his right side, adjusting the sheaths of his scimitars. Jean leaned in, his words for the Norseman alone.

'It's simple, Hawk. Get in among the Florentines, drive them back, place these' – he gestured at the five kegs of gunpowder, which were being rolled out from the sealed magazine – 'where the Fugger tells you to. Then get out.'

'But Rombaud, can you not smell?' Haakon raised his nose into the air, sniffed extravagantly. 'They are roasting chickens in the trenches over there. We could all do with a late supper.'

Jean made his voice harsh. 'No risks, do your job, get out. You've heard my command, Norseman. Obey it!'

Haakon smiled, unoffended. 'You've become old, my friend. I remember a time with you and me and some chickens . . .'

'Obey me.' Jean had not meant to be so abrupt, but the memory his friend would share was connected to others. None from that time gave him pleasure now.

He turned, taking the stairs to follow Beck. Behind him, Haakon was organizing his troop, commands interspersed with encouragement. Jean knew he should have made a speech, sent his men out to die this night for the glory of Siena, for liberty, for honour. Words that would turn to dirt in his mouth.

He climbed to the top casemate, where men with musket and arquebus crowded the embrasures. He did not pick one up. Being in command he didn't have to. No one would see him fumble powder to the floor.

In the corner, Beck did not even look for him, though he could tell by the angle of her head that she knew he was there. Positioning himself where he could barely see, sheltered by the thick buttresses of the bastion, he tried to calm his breathing while he waited for the attack to begin.

It was Erik who remembered Haakon's latest carving, just as they were about to descend the stair that would lead them underground and outside the walls of Siena.

'Father? Are you not taking this?'

The boy handed him a log. It was the length of one of Haakon's arms, twice as thick, bound in coils of thick rope. It had been reamed out, from one end protruded a ball of hay, while at the other, a piece of cloth poked from a hole.

'Ah!' Haakon put his axe into its sheath and hefted his new toy with delight. 'A thing of beauty, do you not think, my son? Even the name delights: tromba di fuoco!'

'A temporary beauty. It only fires the once, doesn't it?'

'It is born, lives brightly for an instant, then dies? The best kind of beauty, to my mind.' Haakon squinted down the rough barrel, wondering if he could cram in any more loose metal. Then he thought about the effect of his words. 'But you are not a gun, boy. Remember to take no chances down there.'

The reply was all innocence. 'But, of course not, Father. I will cower with you in the rear, as always.'

Cuffing his son across the head to hide his smile, Haakon pushed him down the stair. Before he followed, he glanced up, through the open back of the upper casemate. Beck was on one side of the emplacement, Jean on the other, both turned away.

'Ah, Rombaud.' There was something between them, something wrong with his friends, some hurt Jean could never discuss and Haakon could never ask about. He'd tried, and it was like a gaol door slammed shut behind the Frenchman's eyes. The door had been in place for a while now, from before the siege. At first Haakon thought it dated from when the Florentines had come, the destruction of their homes. Later, he realized he could barely remember a time when the hurt was not there. Certainly not since Gianni, their son, had disappeared.

'Rombaud.' Shaking his head, Haakon started down the stairs. He missed having his comrade by his side, missed seeing the Frenchman's square-headed executioner's sword swinging death to their enemies. Even if Jean was a general now, Haakon would have given anything to see that blade descend once again.

His men waited for him in the narrow chamber by the well shaft. They were the usual mix, half of them Sienese patriots, half mercenaries. The latter were mainly French, for France, as always, sided with those who fought the Emperor. The rest were Scots. The patriots had the spirit, the trained warriors the skill. It was a good balance on the whole.

With Erik a shadow on his shoulder, he descended into the pit, feeling the familiar surge of battle joy. Too much of this siege had been spent watching from walls, dodging snipers' bullets, building and reinforcing walls dented by cannon. Not enough sorties, too much idle time thinking about empty stomachs. Happy now, Haakon made the sign of Thor's hammer and led his troop down into the darkness.

Haakon smelt the Fugger before he touched him, the German's life underground, digging, listening for the enemy's stealthy approach, giving him the distinctive tang of some earth-burrowing creature. The gated lantern's fragile light revealed more of the mole, a dirt-encrusted face, a shaved head plastered with mud, cobweb and timber dust.

The light passed over the drum, the pebbles on its surface bouncing hard. The Fugger whispered, 'Five, at the most!' Haakon nodded, then moved three paces back. Squatting, he placed a forked stick into the ground before him and rested the open end of the tromba onto it, embedding the other end in a rapidly scraped-up pile of earth. Blowing on the cord that hung from his belt produced the desired glow. With a sigh, he lowered himself onto the ground to wait.

The Fugger stopped by Erik, squeezing him on the arm. 'And how fares my daughter?'

He sensed, rather than saw, the young man's blush, smiled that this fiercest of warriors could so easily be embarrassed with thoughts of love. The Fugger was happy, for Erik was a good boy, if wild, and his love was clear and true. Spending his life as he did in these dark places, it was a comfort to know that his jewel, his Maria, the last light in his life, was so loved and looked after.

'She is well. She hopes to see you soon and safe.'

'After this night's work, I think.' Moving past, seeking the gunpowder, he whispered back, 'She hopes to see you safe all the more, young man. Remember that.'

Quiet came again, along with the impenetrable dark. Breathing was shallow, the air close, and if a man had to move, to unstiffen a joint or limb, he did so carefully, causing his harness to barely shift. The only regular sound was the faintest *pat pat pat* of the pebbles on the drum's taut skin. At first it was like the tapping of bees trapped behind leaded glass, then slowly it built, multiplied, until the packed earth beneath them, the rough walls, the shoring timbers, all began to vibrate with the rhythmic blows being struck barely a hand's span away. Twenty pairs of ears strained for the moment that sound would change, when a tip of metal would poke through and two pockets of fetid air would rush to meet and mingle. For at that moment, the tapping would end and men would begin to die.

It changed. A pickaxe point hit one of the stones the Fugger had embedded in the wall's surface. The *ping*, a harsh cry in a world of near silence, was lost in the roar that followed. The Fugger had gouged faultlines over his earthen barrier and along them the wall imploded.

Hush, then a harsh whisper, a single, Spanish phrase, terror, prayer.

'Mother of God!'

On his knees, Haakon's fingers circled the hole bored in the top of the tromba, the other hand bringing the glowing cord down. The searing of the gunpowder in its rough pan lit his face, illuminated, for the briefest of instances, the separate tunnels now made one. Naked to the waist, two men held pickaxes, the one buried before him where his blow and the collapse of the wall had taken it, the other man's raised high to strike. Behind them, the flash fell on faces lined with shock, glinted on the weapons slowly rising as if to ward off some invisible blow. Only these swords, these short spears and shovels moved, as if they alone had life, the humans holding them frozen in some fresco of fear.

That was the instant the powder took to reach the chamber in the tromba and then the subterranean world exploded in sound and flame and searing metal. There were torches the enemy side of the gap, thrust into embrasures in the walls and they showed men who were there and then were not, and the roar of it deafened those on both sides, those who were not already dead or dying. Thus their cries sounded faint to those that lived – though the bellow from directly behind Haakon was strong enough to reach his consciousness:

'A Haakonsson! A Haakonsson!'

Leaping over his father, lying prone where the exploding tromba had thrown him, Erik's cry preceded him down the tunnel, just ahead of his one drawn scimitar.

'Erik!' Haakon struggled onto his knees, then up. Shaking his head, still ringing from the explosion, he pulled his battle-axe from its sheath and bellowed, 'For Siena! Hoch Hoch!'

Then he chased after his son.

The Fugger, buffeted aside by the rush of men, called out, 'Haakon! Not too far. I will blow it soon.'

But the backs disappeared down the tunnel, the sound of battle joined further down his only reply. Pointing at the men with the powder kegs, he gestured for them to follow, and moved up into the enemy mine.

Erik had cleared the fallen bodies like a horse going over hedges, and it was a good twenty paces before he found someone to oppose his sword. A muzzle flashed before him, a lead ball zinged past his ear. Imagining where there was one there would be more, Erik crouched and ran crab-wise along one wall. Two more bullets testified to his caution before he was among the three shooters, their weapons raised to block, vainly, the scimitar's slicing arcs.

The torches were further spaced here, and Erik barely saw the shovel. There was not room for a full swing, but the blow caught him flat across the head with enough force to send him crashing into the wall, white spots whirling before his eyes. Through them he sensed rather than saw, the shovel pulled back, the edge of it now turned toward his face. His scimitar was pinned under him, and he could only throw up a fragile hand to defend himself.

Oh well, he thought, *the Fugger manages well enough with only one!*

The shovel hovered, then there was a crash, and it fell straight down, as its shaft splintered under the impact of an axe. A body sailed backwards into the shadows.

'Who's the leader here? Hmm? I can't hear you!'

His father's furious face was thrust an inch from his own, a massive hand coming in to grab an ear and shake the head like a rattle.

'Ow! You are, Father. You are!'

His son's ear felt sticky and, pulling his hand away, Haakon saw the blood. Anger turned to concern. 'Are you all right? Let me see the wound!'

Erik thrust his father's fussing hands aside. 'A side blow. Nothing.' Watching his comrades run past them, shouting their war cries, he grinned, said, 'I thought you said you were the leader here.'

A smile, half-anger, half-joy. Haakon grasped Erik by the collar and hauled him to his feet.

'Stay behind me!' He cuffed his son across the head in a blow nearly as powerful as the shovel's had been, and strode off down the tunnel.

'Anything you say, Father.' Erik retrieved his fallen weapon, his head ringing; after a moment's thought, he drew its twin out from behind his back. The tunnel was gradually widening as it made for the enemy trench and there would soon be room enough for two.

By the time the Norsemen caught up with their troops they were dealing with the first real sign of resistance, in the wide entrance cavern, the steps to the enemy trench directly ahead of them. Two of his men had fallen, wounded, to pistol shots, the rest were being held at bay by six mercenaries with room to swing their halberds. It was a stand-off, but Haakon could not leave these six to follow and harry them back down the tunnel, not with his wounded to evacuate. Not with the tunnel to blow.

'No chance of surrendering, I suppose,' he called, in German, across the wall of pike.

'Fuck your mother,' a heavily bearded Switzer called back. 'Like I'm going to fuck your wife when we get into your rat's nest of a city.'

His fellows laughed, added further insults. Then, above their jeering, a sharp sound rang out, as two curved blades ran off each other's perfectly sharp edges.

'I don't like it when people threaten my late mother,' said Erik. 'Or my sainted grandmother, for that matter, God rest both their souls.'

Haakon turned, though he knew it was a waste of his time, even as he raised his battle axe to take part in what was inevitably to follow.

He was halfway round, the words coming to his lips, when the flash of two scimitars flew past.

'God's blood! Erik!' The words were weary, yet not so the battle cry as he hurled himself after his son: 'Siena! Hoch, Hoch!'

Erik's attack had separated the Swiss into a four and a two and since his son had already killed one opponent and was now engaged with the second, Haakon ducked under the halberds of the larger group, dropped to his knees, and swung the axe low and level to the ground. The first Switzer managed to jump it, the second caught it in his calf with a yell of agony, falling backwards into his two comrades. Haakon's own men were among them in three heartbeats and it lasted barely three heartbeats more.

Haakon looked up to see an Erik drenched in blood, his face a mask of it, the eyes white and wild from within that mask. And, as he looked, he saw his son suddenly raise his nose into the air.

'Father! Do you smell that? Roasting chickens!' And with a crazed yelp, Erik burst up the stairs into the enemy's trenches.

Haakon had seen the young man's eyes, knew that Erik was looking out through a veil, a reddened mist that had nothing to do with the blood that covered him. Well, maybe a little, for the battle madness always tasted of iron. Words would not draw the veil; nothing could except death or victory. He could only hope, as he gathered his men to follow his son into the heart of their enemy, that the mist would descend once again for him too.

Beck had felt Jean enter the upper casemate, felt his gaze upon her, knew where he'd gone without the benefit of her eyes. She had always had a sense for him, known exactly where he was at home – in his vineyards, hunting game in their forests, tending the olive groves – but the sense had been there long before that happy time, from their very first meeting nineteen years before. She'd known where he was every day within besieged Siena, but what had been a blessing had now become a curse. She didn't want to think of him all the time. She didn't want to think of him at all.

There was no one she could tell about this. Not him, for Rombaud had never been a man to talk of feelings. Not their Anne, named after the Queen for whose cause Jean had nearly died, that name the first link in a chain that bound father and daughter so closely there was room for no one else. And not her son, her Gianni. Not any more. The man she sensed and couldn't look at had seen to that when he had driven their son away.

Beck rested the musket in the groove hollowed out in the wool sack that lay before her on the parapet, checked the glowing cord, her gunpowder flask, the lead balls in her pocket. There was still a time when she would not think of her husband – in the violence to come. Yet if Jean's plan went right, she would not get even that relief, for the brief fight would only happen underground. She half-hoped it would go wrong.

Leaning forward, she looked through the embrasure. The Florentine trench opposite, down the slope and about a hundred paces ahead was quiet, save for the odd voice raised in false normality. She knew that under the sheltering gabions filled with sand, the fascines and wicker screens, many men were crouching silently, waiting to pour into the tunnel should the opportunity arise, if their miners had stumbled upon the countermine they knew must lie ahead, which they hoped would be lightly defended. With luck, some of this enemy would soon become targets. She shifted the stock, pressing it into her shoulder, squinting down the barrel.

It had been less than ten minutes since Haakon had led his troop underground when the quiet world opposite began to fill with noise. It started with a very muffled *pop* as if someone far away had dropped a glass vessel. Then came the first of many cries, bat squeaks of fear and pain to begin, hoarse, whispered commands replaced by shouts as all need for stealth disappeared with the first casualties staggering out into the enemy emplacement. On the far side of the casemate, Beck heard Jean issuing commands on a half-breath, willing the men below to do as they had been bidden.

'Now, Haakon, lead them back. Fugger, get ready to blow it.'

Then the noise from the enemy trench multiplied by ten, as if someone had just thrown open a window on a riot. Careless of the target she made, Beck raised her head in time to see a wicker screen hurled into the air, struck by some flailing weapon or body on the other side. It fell flat to the earth and in the gap she saw two blades rise as one. They were curved and as they fell she heard the shout that always went with them.

'A Haakonsson! A Haakonsson!'

She span away, sought her husband, thinking nothing of it now. For violence had arrived to take away her pain.

'Jean! They are in the enemy trench. I saw Erik!'

'Damn! Damn them!' Jean had not looked, had no need to. He knew that war cry as well as she did.

'They will need help.'

She was moving toward him now and the last thing he needed was to see her. He pushed himself away from the wall and ran for the door. Stumbling down the stairs, cursing Haakon silently and continuously, Jean forced his legs and stick to carry him down to the lowest gun position and on to the well mouth. Looking down into the hole, he hesitated, but there was nothing for it. Ordering three arquebusiers to precede him with torches, taking a deep breath, he followed them into the pit. The light gave him no comfort, it was still a dank and dismal place, but he found his way swiftly to the main shaft, passed the Fugger's former listening post where the drum lay holed and broken and found the man himself further down, shovel in his one hand, burying gunpowder kegs against the timbers of a junction.

'Haakon is in their trenches.'

'What?' The Fugger paused in his digging, wiping a sleeve across his muddied face.

'The fool! I told him, ordered him . . .' Jean broke off, as his voice cracked. This would do him no good. With another deep breath, he said, 'How long, Fugger?'

'A few minutes only.'

'Blow it as soon as you can. We can't risk the Florentines coming through. Siena could fall.'

'And Haakon?'

Jean turned and spat. 'We'll have to find him another way home.'

The Fugger had finished packing the earth tight around the large kegs. He picked up a smaller one, tucked it under his handless arm, flicked open the plughole. A trickle of powder issued forth.

'Take the torches away, Jean. Put them all out. We don't want this to go before we are ready.'

'But how can you see to set the trail?'

The Fugger smiled. 'This is my realm. How much do you think I saw in the gibbet midden?'

'Take no chances. These men will wait with their guns, to cover you.'

With that, Jean turned and ran for the bastion, pulling torches from the walls as he went, snuffing them in the earth. He had to know what was happening in the trenches opposite.

'Damn, damn those Norsemen. I'll kill them if the Florentines don't.'

The Florentines were trying. So were the Spanish, the Swiss and a mixed bag of Germans.

At first they had thought the young man bursting from the earth was another of theirs, fleeing the fighting below. Three men had died thinking that, and three more were trying not to as they matched rapier, pike or shovel – anything with an edge – to the whirling scimitars. Then there was a battle axe there as well, another tall and blond-bearded man wielding it, then more swords borne by more of their enemy. Fearing that these were not the last, watching comrades die swiftly, the Florentines and their mercenaries fled the emplacement.

Erik saw the backs of his enemies vanish around the earthwork corner and made to follow. But a hand the size of a platter seized him by the neck, halting him where he stood, halting the flow of breath.

'Urk!' he managed to say, before Haakon had swung him around, toes trailing on the ground, red face thrust to red face.

'Enough, boy!' the elder Norseman bellowed. 'Would you take on the whole world?'

He threw his son backwards, where Erik flopped against the trench wall. There, desperate now for air, he inhaled deeply, and caught the first whiff of something glorious. Turning his head to the right, he looked at fat running down the glistening, crispy skin of a bird. It was thrust onto a spit, along with six of its fellows. In the fire pit behind, another dozen sat dripping into the coals.

'Father. Food!'

Haakon's mouth instantly flooded with saliva. Plunging his fingers into the nearest chicken, ripping hot flesh from its body, he crammed a handful into his mouth, careless of the heat. His eyes rolled up with pleasure and for a moment everything faded – the red, battle madness, the scent of blood, the fear for his boy. He was back in the courtyard of the Comet Inn with a dozen capons before him and he was going to eat them all!

A pistol shot brought him back. It was fired, hurriedly, at the edge of the trench by a Florentine officer who stepped around and stepped back as fast. He had seen what he was looking for, Haakon knew. It would be but a moment before he ordered others in.

'Erik! Take three men, hold that gap. Do not go through it!'

He looked back at the entrance to the mine. He had come too far, the Fugger would be preparing even now to blow it. It was what he would do, because the city itself could fall if the open tunnel remained. They had not fought for fifteen months to allow that to happen, not to wait for a few foolhardy comrades to return.

He peered over the parapet where Erik's initial attack had ripped the wicker screens away. Across a hundred paces of sloping ground, striped with the light of a waning moon within the clouds, loomed the walls of Siena. There, at the base of the bastion of the Porta San Viene, set into the wall, was a little door.

Angry with him though he was bound to be, surely if he went across and knocked, Jean would let his old friend in? Especially if he brought him some supper?

Raising his voice above the clash of scimitar on sword, Haakon yelled, 'Grab the chickens. We're going over.'

*

The war council, of necessity, was brief, even though they had now been joined by the overall commander of Siena, the French General, Blaise de Monluc. He'd been drawn, as ever, to the sound of the guns. Of a height with Jean, of an age, he had twice as many scars on his face. One sharp blue eye squinted over the battlements, the other a painted 'O' on an eyepatch.

'It is your command, Rombaud. Your bastion. We can help to keep their heads down, if you like.' He gestured behind him at his thirty men, some with muskets, a few with the heavier moschetti that were moved around the walls as the need arose.

Briefly, Jean wondered at being deferred to by the veteran general, before his mind swept over the options before him. But in that moment of hesitation, Beck spoke from the shadows by the wall.

'There can be no question. We must do it. We must do it now.'

To those of De Monluc's French officers who did not know her, the woman's voice seemed an affront, out of place in this business of men. The Sienese, who had seen her fight, knew differently.

Jean glanced into the gloom. 'And how many more will we lose, if we try to rescue these?'

She stepped from the shadow then, moved toward him. 'You heard what I said. There is no question. I am going out for our friends.'

She was right about the lack of question, but not in the sense she meant. Her words had put Jean in an impossible position. He could now give just the one answer, could only speak the words they all wished to hear.

'Unbar the sally port. My lord, if you will direct your men in their firing.'

'With pleasure, Rombaud. But half my men will come with you. I only wish I could.' Drawing his plumed hat from his head, Blaise de Monluc swept it to the floor. 'For France. For Siena. And for the beauty of your lady!'

Under the cheers, the men scrambled for positions. Jean caught up with Beck, turned her sharply to him.

'You should not have shamed me into that.'

'The old Jean would have needed no shaming.'

'I command here, Beck. I have to think of my men. I have to think if we can win.'

'And I have to think only of Haakon, the man who held the bridge at Pont St Just, twenty years ago, so you could fulfill your vow to Anne Boleyn. Have you forgotten him? And his son? Is he another son you have forgotten, Jean Rombaud?'

She saw the hurt, the way the words cut him, wanted them instantly back; but it was too late, and the hurt she saw was replaced by fury.

'But you do not go to fight, Beck. That is my order. I will be obeyed in that. And I'll have you put in chains if I have to.'

They stood, squared off to each other, glaring. Finally, without taking her eyes from his, she began to move past him, to the stairs.

'I will take my musket and I will watch for my friends. And we will speak further of this moment. Believe me.' Halting on the bottom step, she added, 'Do you go?'

At last, he looked away, somehow kept his voice flat. 'I do not. Cannot. I am not yet recovered. And I command.'

He heard her say, softly, 'Of course you do.' When he looked again he saw only her back, moving swiftly up the stairs.

He took a step, called, 'Beck', but she was gone. He turned away to issue his commands.

His force consisted of barely eighty men and he was lucky to have that many, the weakening defenders spread thinly around the walls of the city. He would keep De Monluc's heavily armoured French pikemen as a reserve, use his rag-bag of Sienese militia leavened with his few experienced Scottish mercenaries. They would grumble, in their impenetrable tongue, at the risk of this mission, for they hadn't been paid since the last blockade runners had broken through to Siena five months before. But they would fight, if only for their comrades out there with Haakon. They were a clannish bunch, bound by blood and strange tattoos.

He had barely marshalled them before the sally port, the last bolt shot, when the bloodied head of a Sienese burst up from below ground, an ear half off, screaming, 'They are in the tunnel! Christ, brothers, the enemy are at the door!'

If the Florentines were back in the tunnel, then where the hell was Haakon?

Cautiously raising his head above the parapet, Jean got his answer – as ten figures rose from the trench opposite and a Norse voice screamed, 'Siena!'.

The enemy *were* in the tunnels, but they were not quite at the door. The Fugger knew, because he was, along with the three arquebusiers, their weapons still undischarged. He was laying the last of the gunpowder trail that ran into the darkness ahead in a channel he'd cut only the previous night. The last twenty paces of it, by necessity, was rough hewn in the recent, scrambling minutes, being on the Florentine side of the mine.

In his battle rage, it was unlikely that Haakon had remembered to close the enemy doors. It might not matter. There might still be sufficient blast, if they shut their own doors. If he had calculated the charge right.

Poised over the gunpowder channel, the Fugger raised the glowing cord in one hand. And just as he did, three Florentines ran around the corner.

There were six flashes, from arquebus and pistol, and the explosion in that tight space blew out one of the Fugger's ears, knocking him sideways. Smoke blocked out what little light the one lantern gave; yet from where he fell, stunned though he was, he looked still for the glowing taper's end, the one he had to thrust into the gunpowder channel before him.

There was no taper. Bringing his hand close to his face he realized there was no third and little finger to pinch the taper between, just blood and shattered bone. A lead ball had carried them away.

The three men next to him were dying or dead. The Florentines ahead had disappeared but they, or some of their fellows, were still down the tunnel, rallying for an attack.

There was no time. Something had to be done, before pain made him incapable. Beside him, a pistol poked from a dead man's bandolier. It was a flintlock and he closed his remaining fingers around the stock. Primed, it needed only the flick of the thumb to turn its wheel, a spark would leap into the pan, ignite the gunpowder, fire the ball. They misfired five times out of ten, the Fugger had heard.

Blessing even half a chance, with half a hand, he lowered the gun over the channel of powder and, as the voices up ahead grew closer, flicked the wheel.

Just as the clouds parted and moonlight lanced across the ground, Haakon's men stormed out of the trenches. A dozen paces gained before an explosion of musketry from whence they'd fled and, despite the way they dodged, four were struck down immediately, one rising to stagger on alone, two of the figures, golden hair silvered in the light, stopping to aid their stricken comrades. Five more paces, and Beck felt she could get a clear shot over their heads so she fired, just ahead of the volley from De Monluc's guard. The musket balls, the heavier moschetti, tore lead into the gabions, the wicker screens of the enemy ripped away as if by an unseen hand.

It was what the enemy awaited, for even if De Monluc's reserved volley took some of them out, at least a hundred men still chose to leap the parapets and give chase. Their quarry had gained half the distance to the walls, but though some men raced further, nearer to safety, the stragglers were left behind and the gap closed rapidly. It would be but a moment and they would be overwhelmed.

'Now!' screamed Jean, and the sally port was thrown open, men pouring from it. The first of the fleeing men entered their ranks, ran on to the opening in the wall. The last five had been caught and, flinging their wounded behind them, Haakon and Erik turned with weapons raised.

'A Haakonsson!'

They were engulfed. Men swept around them, meeting those coming out from the city, like a wave crashing onto a beach colliding with the one that had crashed just before. War cries died, replaced by the grunt of blows given, blocked, struck home. The Norsemen, father and son, stood side by side, and lost count of the times they took blows meant for the other, axe and scimitars a blur of cutting edge, a space carved before them filling with bodies, soon slippery with blood.

It could not last. The waves that had clashed together had been more or less the same, stopping the other with equal force. But reinforcements kept flooding out from the Florentine trenches; someone over there had seen the tantalizing open gate in the wall they'd been trying to breach for fifteen months. As more joined, the defenders formed into a rough half circle to withstand them, giving ground, backing toward their escape, each knowing that if one broke, they would all break, to be trapped and slaughtered before that tiny entrance.

Unable to use her reloaded musket due to the press, Beck had watched the desperation build below, saw the inexorable gathering of the enemy, her friends about to be swept away by it. There was only one chance now and she took the stairs two at a time. She found Jean on the middle level, above the battle. He was pressed against the wall, his mouth working, staring into the mêlée.

'Now, Jean, now! Send in De Monluc's French. It is their only chance.'

Jean continued to stare ahead, muttering.

'What is the matter with you? Send them in.'

He turned and she recoiled from the deadness in his eyes.

'They are lost.'

Bursting past him, she ran down the remaining stairs. Leaping onto a powder barrel there she cried, 'Frenchmen! Your ancestors followed Jeanne d'Arc to glory. Will you follow me?'

A shout came from twenty throats and, pulling her short sword from her side, Beck led the pike men out the sally port. They formed up, lowered their pikes and advanced.

It made a difference, for a moment, twenty armoured men in a tight body thrusting forward. Friends dodged under their points, foes gave back before them. Disciplined, they halted at the front of their line and the Germans and Spanish there gave back a few paces, opposing pike to their pike. These soldiers, professionals all, had faced each other for fifty years across the battlefields of Italy. Each would await the other's next move.

A silence, the weird silence that sometimes descends on a combat, descended now. Men took breaths as if they'd only just learned how. Even the wounded seemed to still their moans. In this silence, Beck found the Norsemen, standing just behind the line of pike, leaning on their weapons.

'You're bleeding, Haakon.'

'Beck! I might have known I'd see you here.' He looked himself up and down. 'This? This is not my blood.' And he laughed. Loudly.

The laugh broke the silence. 'Surrender, you French and Sienese jackals. They will lock you out to die. Throw yourself on our mercy and you may be spared.'

There was a simple French word. Even in Haakon's execrable accent it was clear enough.

'Merde!'

Noise returned to the battlefield in shouts, threats, wails. And under it, there came another sound, a *crump* – it was faint, yet somehow everyone there heard it. Maybe because it was accompanied by a pulse that ran up through their boots. Flame suddenly gushed from the Florentine trench, at that point where Erik had burst through, and the killing ground around them began to buckle and shift. Furrows, as if dug by some crazed plowman, shot out between legs, knocking men aside.

'The mine! The mine is blown.'

And with that cry, a huge section of earth fell into the tunnels below. It was mainly on the Florentine side, and it dropped men thirty feet into the ground. A jagged rent appeared just before Haakon and Beck, the Norseman just managing to grab his son by the collar, dangling him over the sudden precipice for a moment before pulling him back.

Haakon yelled, 'The hand of God, Beck?'

'The one hand of the Fugger! Come on!'

The explosion had shaken Jean from his daze, preceded as it was by the Fugger bursting up from the well. Looking over, he saw, the front rank of the enemy disappear into the earth, saw reinforcements even now rushing around the flank of the hole, as his men began to squeeze through the narrow sally port.

'My lord?' he called up to the tower above.

'Seen them, Rombaud,' came a drawled response.

The volley cut down the pursuit, gave their own men a chance to withdraw. They crowded through the gate, but never blocked it and within a minute, all who could walk, crawl, or be carried were into Siena. Haakon and Beck were the last, going back for the one last wounded man of his command. Pushing him through the gate, he turned to Beck and smiled. 'After you, my lady.'

He saw the beginnings of a smile in return, then saw that smile change to surprise, as she staggered into him. Reaching around to catch her, his hand encountered something hard, feathered. It protruded a finger's length from her back.

He swept her up into his arms, moved inside. As the sally port slammed shut, he cried, 'Jean! Beck is down.'

'It's all right. I'm all right!' she said, just before she fainted.

Jean was there in a moment. 'To me! Give her to me.'

He took her, wondering at how light she had become, in the long age since he had last picked her up. Her head was rolled back, sightless eyes under her heavy lashes, and he was suddenly terrified that he would never look into those eyes again, see her love or even her fury there. The crowd of men parted before him, jubilation quelled. Above, Blaise de Monluc stepped onto the ramparts, once more slowly sweeping the plumed hat from his head. Crouched at the foot of the stairs, a bloodied Fugger raised a bandaged arm toward Jean and his burden.

There was only one place he could go, one person who could bring the flame back into Beck's black eyes. He had to find her now, and swiftly. He had to find his Anne.

TWO
INQUISITION

They began to trail him from the entrance of the ghetto. Even though they knew his destination, it was good practice to follow the old Jew through the narrow alleys, then onto the broader, crowded thoroughfares. Not only did they have to avoid his eyes – and this one was wary, stopping at street stalls, fingering a pear or a bolt of cloth while glancing the way he had come – they also had to spot and isolate his shadows. Three of them and hard to recognize in the throng, for they had eliminated all signs of their faith, dressed like any other Roman, stopping when the Jew stopped, sometimes moving past to wait, to let him pass again. They were good, but the Grey Wolves were better, soon had them isolated, cut out, two on one, within their own elaborate dance of misdirection and disguise.

Gianni Rombaud was pleased. They had learnt well, his Cubs, while his more experienced brethren – Rudolpho, Wilhelm – had assumed their role of shepherd effortlessly, restraining their own natural desire for the swift kill, in service to the plan. Wilhelm would be finding it especially hard, his hand twitching at his dagger. But meeting his eyes now, crouched over a book on the Via Gulia, haggling with the stall holder, even in the briefest of contact they allowed themselves, Gianni saw the Bavarian was poised, calm. Ahead, the Jew had lingered at a pastry cart, so Gianni grabbed an apple and threw it into the air, a coin plucked from his pocket, flicked across, before the fruit landed in his hand.

He was pleased for another reason. Three shadows meant their quarry had something valuable on him, probably rings, maybe even a necklace. The Grey Wolves hunted for the blooding, but it was always good to have a bonus for their efforts. Christ's bounty funding Christ's work.

The old man moved off rapidly, took an unforeseen turning, heading up toward the squatting mound of the Castel San Angelo. They had not been spotted, Gianni was sure, but something had spooked their quarry, some sense of danger in that old Jew head; if he was not to double back and disappear into the ghetto, where they could not follow, they would have to let him be.

Gianni began to eat the apple, not moving from where he'd bought it. It was old, had cellared the long winter, its skin mottled and streaked. *A little like the old Jew's,* Gianni thought, chewing slowly, the thought making him smile. He was aware of his men, even though he did not see them, knew they recognized the signal of the apple, and would be finding things to do, books to peruse, nuts or roasted offal to buy. The Jew's shadows flitted slowly past, one by one, slipping down the alley, soon to be lost in the maze ahead.

It did not matter. It had been a useful exercise. The Grey Wolves had stalked prey through half of Rome. Throwing the apple core into the clogged gutter at the centre of the street, Gianni turned down the alley opposite to the one the Jew had taken. He knew the rest of them would take their own routes to the rendezvous, would assemble there by the mid-morning bell. By that time, the reassured Hebrew would be inside the house in the olive grove on the edge of Trastevere. Thinking he was safe.

He passed a small chapel, erected for the working men of the neighbourhood and their families, its only outward sign a cross scored across the lintel. He paused. It would do him good to pray, to focus upon His words, to meditate as to why he was about Christ's work in this unique way. Stooping, he entered the dim and scented world. It had rough walls, a lack of any adornment, a complete contrast to the ornate palaces of worship that abounded in Rome. It reminded him of the farmers' chapels where he'd first met his Saviour, in the hills near Montepulciano.

The floor was crudely tiled, broken in places. Seeing he was alone, Gianni immediately threw himself down on the space before the altar, pressing his face to the ground, paralleling the cross above him with outstretched arms and began to recite his prayers. Usually, he could lose himself in the Latin, its comforting rhythms and familiar cadences, but today it seemed as jagged as the split tiles beneath him. At first he thought his mind was too full of the action ahead, seeking out little flaws in his plan, making adjustments. He struggled, knowing he should be able to put all that aside, to lose himself in his adoration of Christ. Struggled until he realized what was truly wrong – this chapel, so like the ones of his youth, raised memories that drove prayer from him. Even though he had not seen them in three years, his parents' sins clung to him like choke vines round the stock.

There was a cough. He stood and turned swiftly, a hand reaching to his belt and the dagger there. Behind him, Wilhelm was kneeling before the pews, his hands clasped. He glanced toward the door and Gianni nodded. Making their final kneeling tributes, crossing themselves, they stepped out into the day. Rain had come and Gianni scanned the sky for a break in it. Rain did not help his plan.

'You're bleeding.' Wilhelm ran his finger down Gianni's cheek. 'See?'

On the finger before him, a red streak. In its centre, a shard of tile.

Gianni grabbed the finger, bent it back. The big German leaned down toward him in self-protection. When he had him close, Gianni put his lips to his ear, and whispered, 'Would that I could shed all my blood in what we are to do. And yet live to do it again and again and again.'

He released the finger and Wilhelm rubbed it. The piece of tile had penetrated and there was more blood now.

'Have a care, Gianni.' He sucked at his finger.

'Oh, I do.' His dark eyes flashed. 'I have a care for the Lord's work.'

The two grey-cloaked figures shrugged into the rain, heading for Trastevere.

It fell in angled sheets, slanting into the ground, bouncing off olive trees, so heavy that the house in the centre of the grove shimmered as if insubstantial. The three shadows had gathered beneath the eaves, round a brick fire place, which they tried to stoke with a supply of sodden wood. They were having a little success, enough to keep them occupied, and the times between one of them leaving and walking around the house were growing further apart.

Gianni dropped from the wall, landing beside the two Cubs. The hulking one, Bruno, was throwing his knife into the ground between his legs, rain cascading off his cloak, oblivious to all but the way the blade dug into the mud before him. The slight one, Piccolo, was trying to light two more oil lamps from the one cradled in his lap. Each time he took a taper from its shelter, however, the rain or wind snuffed it out.

Gianni's arm snapped forward, grabbing the handle of the dagger in mid-flight. Pointing the tip at Bruno he said, 'Help him with the lamps. When they are all lit, take one to each of the others. Tell them to wait for the call. Then return.'

He threw the dagger between the spread legs, close to the groin. Bruno flinched, sheathed the weapon, and hurriedly moved to obey. Cupped hands transferred the flame and soon all three oil lumps were lit. Taking two, Bruno moved off into the rain and around the corner of the wall.

Gianni rested his back against the flaking plaster. The rain made a difference, but not that much. It might even help, concealing the Wolves' approach, even if it did mean the flames of retribution would be harder to conjure.

Raising his face to it, closing his eyes, Gianni allowed himself a smile.

Thy will be done. As always.

Then Bruno was back, a nod showing that all was prepared. Putting his foot into Bruno's joined palms Gianni carefully raised his head above the parapet. As he did, he saw one of the shadows detach himself from the fireplace at the side of the house and move around the building, out of sight of his comrades. Another ten paces would carry him around the other wall to the welcoming grasp of Wilhelm, brought running by the cry Gianni was about to order. He looked down into Piccolo's tensed face and nodded. Instantly, the boy threw back his head and let out a perfect imitation of a scavenging crow.

Looking back into the yard, Gianni saw three things happen. A large log flew over the front gate, landing with a soft but distinct crunch on the gravelled path. This brought the two guards by the fire to their feet, turning toward the sound. At the same time the other guard, stopped, hesitated, then carried on around the corner. Pulling himself over the wall, landing in the soft earth there, already running as he landed, Gianni heard the thump of Piccolo close behind, the heavier thud of Bruno following. There was a shout from the far side of the house, a cry of alarm, then of pain, turning the other sentries for a moment. He was ten paces away when the first of the men turned back and five when the guard began reaching to the wide-mouthed arquebus resting under the eaves. Gianni dropped his shoulder, put it into the man's chest at full charge, knocking him off his feet and hard against the wall. The second man swung a fist at him, but Gianni dodged, falling onto the back of the one now struggling to rise. He heard but did not see the blows as first the faster Piccolo and then the heavier Bruno caught the other man with their cudgels. Gianni found the prone guard's chin, jerked it back and swiftly to the side. There was a crack and he rode the body to the ground.

The other three Cubs from the front gate now picked up the log they'd thrown over and ran with it at the door. It splintered at the first impact, folding in on itself, the three carried through by the force of their charge to sprawl on the other side. As Wilhelm and his two Cubs joined them – one of them clutching what looked like a broken wrist – Gianni stepped through the shattered timbers into the one room beyond.

He had been there before, had anticipated the sight that would greet him. The smiling girl who had given the thirsty 'student' some water, she would be cowering there. And the Jew, of course, their quarry, finally brought to ground, he would be there. But the tall man with the pistol drawn and levelled, behind whom Jew and girl crouched, he was not meant to be there. And when he discharged the pistol and the bullet grazed Gianni's face, to bury itself in the plaster behind him, Gianni knew he must be there no longer.

'Mine!' he cried, a dagger appearing in his hand, matched by one in the hand opposite. There were few times when he did anything but curse what his father, Jean Rombaud, had given him, but lessons with a knife, he almost blessed him for those now. The man he opposed had also learned, dropping into a stance, the dagger level with the other hand that reached out, balanced, but Gianni saw he was not quite square, his right foot forward. Throwing the dagger to his left hand he thrust it toward the man's face, while his right reached up, flicked the clasp of his cloak open, swept it from around his shoulders, his hand passing over his head, carrying it down and around to the right where the rain-heavy wool wrapped around the man's leg. Stepping back, Gianni pulled hard and the cloak jerked the man's leg from underneath him, sending him crashing back onto the table, collapsing it. Dropping the cloak, stepping forward, the knife thrown back to his right hand, grabbed overhand, Gianni plunged down. With a sharp cry of agony, the man folded himself in on the blow that found his stomach, dropping his own knife, folding himself around Gianni's.

The attack had brought his face level with the old Jew's.

'What? What . . .?' was all the old man could get out and the look of pure terror, coupled with the exultation of the violence, made Gianni howl with joy, howl like the animal whose name he had taken. The wolf cry, echoed from those behind, ended when Gianni raised a hand.

'Vat? Vat?' Gianni's impersonation was exaggerated, deliberately so. 'You will find out *vat* in a moment.' He called over his shoulder. 'Take the girl outside, and the servant. And finish this . . .' He kicked at the writhing body on the floor. 'Leave the Jew with me.'

His wolves obeyed, dragging the moaning man, the whimpering girl, the pleading servant, taking them to the side of the house. The rain on the tiled roof, increasing in frenzy, swallowed all other sounds, leaving only the ragged breathing of the man before him. Gianni put his hand into the man's bony chest, pushed him gently back into the seat he'd risen from not a minute before. Setting up the other chair, Gianni sat too, arms folded, leaning on the back of it.

In the street the man's hood had been up, but the cloak was discarded now, his head bare, save for the little leather cap that clung to the crown. Thick hair radiated downward from it, streaked with grey, glossy with some rich oil, to fall onto the large lace collar. The hair and cap were his only distinguishing features. The Jew's doublet was plain but well-made, the apron such as would be worn by any artisan. Boots came halfway up the leg, meeting the thick wool leggings there.

No, Gianni thought, *aside from the head, they really don't look much different from us.*

He studied the face, the trace of greying stubble, the dark eyes under heavy brows now flicking around the room, seeking Gianni's, seeking to avoid them as well, to not antagonize with a stare. Gianni let them move around, making his own neutral, keeping them fixed on those circling before him, until, like a butterfly finally settling on a flower, the Jew was staring back at him. His lips started to move, a hum coming into his throat; finally a sound escaped.

'What . . .?' He broke off, remembering what that word had produced before.

'Please . . .' He tried again, stopping when Gianni tipped his head to the side, smiled, a parody of attention.

'No, go on. I'd like to hear what you have to say.'

'Dear sir, young master' – the words came out in a rush now, as if too long stoppered – 'I am sure we can settle this . . . this problem between us. There's no need . . . no need for anyone else to be hurt. My people will pay, they will give you anything you want, however much you want, you only need ask, you only . . .'

Gianni's hand raised slowly, politely. 'You believe we are thieves? That we want the jewels you carry?'

The Jew cleared his throat. 'Well, I know how it is. Debts, life so expensive for a young man. If you owe anything to any of my people, if the interest is too high, I . . . I feel sure we could . . .'

The hand rose again. 'Debts are owed. But not in gold. Repayment demanded. But not of interest.'

'Then what, sir? What debt do I owe? I will pay it, I assure you. I will pay.'

'Oh, I know you will.' Gianni was slowly rising from his seat. 'You will pay everything you have, for the greatest debt in the world. For did you not murder Our Lord?'

The change in the man's demeanour was not the one Gianni had expected. Instead of growing terror, a veil seemed to draw across his face.

'Ah.' The old Jew sighed.

'"Ah?" Is that all you can say? Can you deny it, Jew?'

'Would it help me if I did? Has it ever helped my people before? If we admit it, you kill us. If we deny it, you kill us. Death is the only thing we get from you.'

'Your people?' Gianni brought his face close. 'Shall I tell you something about your people? Shall I tell you a secret?' His voice dropped to a whisper and he pressed his mouth close to the other's ear. 'My mother was one of you.'

He pulled back, so he could see the reaction, the little hope that would spring up there. It was always the same. He liked it when men died with a little hope. It made it harder for them.

The hope was there, in the hand raised toward him, clutching at his doublet, in the eyes.

'Your mother's blood is your blood. Her faith is your faith. Inside here . . . here' – his fingers tapped at Gianni's chest – 'you are one of us.'

Gianni waited, savoured. When he spoke his voice was gentle.

'If you can show me where the Jew within me lives – be it in my spleen, in my liver, in my very heart – I would take this knife and I would cut it out, though I die as I cut. But I don't need to do that, because I have been saved by Christ's love. All I need do is return that love to him every day.'

In the man's eyes, the hope was replaced by something else. The younger man sensed what it was, even as the wrinkled hand dropped and grasped the handle of Gianni's knife at his belt, even as Gianni's hand closed over his. The Jew was old, but his wrists were strong and he had courage. He had pulled the knife up and out, lunged high, the point nipping Gianni's ear before he could force it up and away, bending him back over the table, using his weight, his height, his youth. He rested there with just enough pressure to hold against the old man pushing up.

'Pay the debt,' Gianni said and, twisting, he pushed the dagger home.

The old man cried out then, something Hebrew, a curse, a prayer perhaps. Then the blood rushed to his throat, choking further words.

Gianni slumped back into the chair, staring at the twitching body on the table, while the sound of the rain on the roof filled the room. It had found some crack above, because drops were beginning to fall, spattering off the table, bouncing off the body's forehead, off the bright little leather cap. Yarmulke, his grand-father had called it. His had been frayed, dull, barely clinging to the wisps of hair there, always slipping off as his grandfather pulled and twisted it, babbling his nonsense. His mother said he'd been a brilliant scientist in his day, more, an alchemist, a seeker for the Philosopher's Stone. There had been no trace of the philosopher in the drooling child Gianni had known.

There was a cry from outside, fear strong enough to pierce the pounding rain, a woman's terror. Gianni was at the door, through it, in a moment. The deluge was still so intense it took his eyes a moment to adjust. He saw the knife man first, feet hovering over the ground, swinging by his neck from one of the olive trees. Next, through the falling sheets, a huddle of bodies. Wilhelm was crouched between the writhing legs of the girl, slowly folding the skirt up. Two others held her arms, while the rest of the Cubs were scattered around, looking or not, fascinated, disgusted.

Gianni crossed the space in three strides, his hand making a fist, catching the German on his ear in a sharp blow. The men clutching the girl let her go and she scrabbled to pull down her skirts, a cornered animal, backing up against the wall.

'But, Gianni,' Wilhelm said plaintively, 'she's only a heathen whore.'

Gianni remembered when he'd scouted the house, the girl giving him some water to drink, the darkness of her eyes reminding him for a moment of his sister's, though set in a face as dull as Anne Rombaud's was lively.

'Have you forgotten your vows, Wilhelm? Do you not all know the sin that lust is?'

Wilhelm rubbed at his ear. His voice was petulant. 'I haven't taken my final vows.'

Gianni smiled. It seemed so absurd, the German sitting and sulking in the mud, in a rainstorm, the body of a man he'd killed dangling ten paces away. Smile turned to a laugh and he said, 'But Willie, look at her – she's not even Jewish.'

Then everyone was laughing, except for the German and the girl, the sudden welcome release of it, laughing as fat droplets bounced off their soaked, grey cloaks. Boys again, laughing in the rain.

Something made Gianni turn. He saw the figure, standing with his back to the gate, which was still barred and locked, as if the figure had just passed through its solidity. The hood of a cloak was thrown back, a shaven head bare to the rain. The moment Gianni looked at him, the figure slowly raised a finger, crooked it twice towards himself.

Over his shoulder, Gianni said, 'Throw the bodies into the house. Burn it.'

He had taken three steps away when Piccolo called, 'What about the girl, Gianni? She has seen us.'

She had. But if the shaven man's summons meant what Gianni thought it did, then this would be the last time he hunted with his pack. They had never left witnesses before; but if no one lived to speak of what they had done, what terror would there be for their enemies? Would not the heathens sleep untroubled by the howling of wolves in the night?

He turned back, looked at each of the boys in turn. In a way, he would miss them. Even Wilhelm.

'Tell her the name we hunt by, then release her. Let the Jews of Rome remember the Grey Wolves. Let them live with that name in fear.'

When he approached the figure at the gate, the man with the shaven head bowed once in greeting.

'He has summoned me?'

Another nod.

'Then take me to him.'

The man unbarred the gate, stepped aside to let Gianni precede him. As he stepped through, Gianni glanced back at the house, saw the first tongue of fire lick at one of the windows. The rain, fierce a moment before, suddenly slackened and, in the next instant, died. *God's blessing on God's cleansing flames*, he thought, and then he remembered the old Jew's secret, the jewels he was probably carrying. Yet the thought didn't even cause him to break step. That was part of an old life, dissolving now in smoke and fire. This mute, shaven man was leading him to a new one. Leading him to his destiny.

Thomas Lawley leaned against the oak panelling of the antechamber, desperately trying to stay awake. A chair had suddenly become vacant five paces from him, but he knew as soon as he sat down he would be gone. He had not slept at all for two nights, and in the previous three weeks had barely mustered half a dozen decent rests. Wind and tide had been against him at Dover and he had been forced to spend three days on the water, to land in Hamburg. The Jesuit system of transit was, of necessity, less developed in the Northern and Protestant German states. He'd made up for the lost time from Catholic Bavaria on, pushing each horse hard, abandoning them at the way stations, snatching both sleep and food in short bites. But time had been lost, Renard had expected him to have reached Rome a week before, to be already starting on his return, bearing the weapon of coercion.

And now he'd been standing for six hours outside Cardinal Carafa's door. It was well-known how the man inside hated the Jesuits, but he also must have known the importance of Thomas's mission. It took all of his training, meditations and prayers muttered under his breath, to calm his anger, as he watched courtier, pilgrim and priest precede him into the audience chamber. At least those around him gave him space to lean, stretch his limbs, relieve his aching knee. They would not want their exquisite robes to brush against his muddy cloak and boots.

His eyes flickered shut – and opened to the sound of the outer door, another supplicant admitted. This one was different, much younger than most of the fat prelates and courtiers gathered to pay court to the man everyone thought would be the next Pope. This youth was dressed in plain contrast to the gaudiness on display, a grey cloak over a simple black doublet, his dark hair cut short, the wisps of a young man's beard on his chin. His pale face was finely boned and, Thomas noticed, streaked with blood, probably from the scab at his ear. More blood stained his doublet and he made the occasional attempt to blend it into the dark material.

He had been abandoned by his guide, a bald-headed man who seemed to have some special privilege there, for he had swept into the audience chamber and the person who had been lately admitted, a corpulent, red-coated bishop, had been ejected, protesting vigorously. He looked like a fat and squawking pigeon, all ruffled feathers, and Thomas found himself smiling, an unaccustomed sensation in recent years. He looked at the youth to see if the amusement was shared. He found the boy staring at him, but there was no humour in his eyes.

Thomas had the sudden sensation he had seen the young man before. He looked intelligent and Thomas had taught many in Jesuit schools before his true mission began. Taking a chance now, while the other looked at him, he raised his hands to his chest, the left sheltering the right from all but a direct view. Pinching his thumb and forefinger together, he described a tiny cross in the air, the upright first, the crossbar carrying on into the curves of an 'S'. He watched the young man's eyes, saw them dart away, come back. Then saw them harden before he looked down, returning to the task of scraping the blood from his shirt front.

He recognizes me. And he rejects me, Thomas thought. *Why?*

The inner doors opened and the shaven man stood there. As the assembled company rose, to primp and prepare for their audience, the man beckoned the youth who stiffened, then strode forward. The door closed, swallowing both men, outrage and ruffled feathers returning to this side of it. Within the hubbub, Thomas made his mind still.

What, he pondered, *did the man who would be Pope want with someone so young? A boy with blood on his hands?*

Gianni knew what he wanted from Cardinal Carafa – a mission. Killing Jews was good training, but it was old sport. Besides, evil though they were, the Holy Church faced greater enemies now, greater threats, both within and without. The man he had finally got to see understood this, had led the fight against the heretic, the witch and the sinner from the very beginning. This man had founded the Inquisition in Rome, rooting out dissent wherever he discovered it, purging with flame and sword the length of Italy. Now he was preparing to take that fight to the enemy beyond, to the lands where Luther, Calvin and their ilk held sway. Even beyond them, to the new worlds opening up across the great oceans, where savages worshipped idols in the darkness of sin, in ignorance of the True Church's holy light. The Jesuits had begun such work. But even though Gianni had been educated by them, he knew them as weak, unwilling to do all that must be done. They had tried to teach him to cure with the power of love. He knew, in his own experience, how much more effective was the power of hate.

As this man knew. Gianni gazed now at the shrunken figure, swathed in red on his red throne. Carafa! Even the name made his knees go weak, so he was grateful when, before the raised dais, he was able to prostrate himself, lie spreadeagled as he had lain before the crucifix in that rough chapel earlier, while above him the shaven man showed he was not mute, leaning in to whisper secrets into the old man's ear. Secrets that had brought Gianni here.

Fingers prodded him and he looked up to meet the gaze of his hero. Long, thin fingers beckoned him forward, one with a huge emerald upon it, thrust out. Falling again to his knees, almost sighing with ecstasy, Gianni kissed it again and again.

'Enough.' The voice was soft, set at a high pitch, a quaver in it, a voice that did not need to strain to be obeyed. Instantly, Gianni laid the hand down, stepped back, knelt again at the foot of the throne.

'You have been about work for the greater glory of God, I hear.'

'*Ad Majoram Dei Gloriam.*' The Jesuits had taught him Latin with rigour, they were good for that at least. Effortlessly, Gianni slipped into the ancient tongue. 'If your Holiness deigns to think so. I do what little I can.'

There came a rasp from above, which Gianni realized was a laugh. 'And it is much. Sometimes, with all these new enemies we forget our original ones.' He paused. 'Look at me, my son.'

Gianni raised his eyes, almost expecting to be blinded. But the man who sat there was just a man, an old one, near eighty it was said, not unlike the old Jew, the same sallow skin hanging in folds down a lined face, a stray wisp of white hair peeking from beneath a cap. Under tufted white brows though, there was nothing old in the keenness of his eyes.

'And I hear you desire to be of more service. To the Faith. To me.'

His heart began to beat even faster. 'If you consider me worthy, Holy Father. If you let me, I would happily die for you.'

That rasp again. 'I am not your Holy Father yet, my son. If all goes well, I may well be Pope, within weeks. Then let my enemies fear. Let the heretic quake in his false worship, the witch cower in her coven. I will root them out, cast them into the flames, redeem their souls by the flaying of their flesh.' The voice rose in pitch, in power. 'And you would join in that crusade, my son? You would die for that?'

'Try me, Most Holy. Let me prove worthy of your trust.'

'Oh, I will.'

Carafa raised a hand and the shaven man placed a parchment into it. Squinting in the light, he read for a moment, then spoke again.

'Do you know Fra Lepidus?'

It was a name from his past, a name he tried never to recall, for it conjured a vision of a cold cell floor, of a rope biting into flesh, a falling stick.

Blinking, Gianni stuttered, 'A holy man, your eminence. The Abbot at Montecatini Alto.'

'Indeed? I know little of him. Save this ...' He waved the paper. 'It was found by someone I trust among his papers, along with certain ... implements. I dislike the indiscriminate use of pain, do you not agree? Anyway, they are irrelevant, this' – the paper again – 'is relevant. Very much so.' He paused, squinting at the parchment. 'Is it true, then, what is written here. Is it true you are the son of Anne Boleyn's executioner?'

If he had lived a thousand years, it was the last thing he expected from this man, in this place. It was all his nightmares condensed into one phrase, the yoke of shame his father had placed on him, the family sin he'd fled. No one knew this ghastly secret, no one except those who had taken part in that witch's quest. No one ...

Then the vision he struggled so hard never to see, that still woke him most nights, came back to him now, and he was there, no more than a child, at the monastery where his parents had reluctantly sent him after months of begging leave to study Christ's words. He was lying on the floor, ropes biting into his skin, a switch rising and falling, leaving horrible weals, drawing blood, Fra Lepidus, with his mad eyes, wielding it, demanding the full panoply of his sins. And an eleven-year-old boy had nothing left to confess. Nothing save one family secret, bound in a vow of silence. And he broke that vow to stop the pain, told the man with the mad eyes everything. Told him of Jean Rombaud and Anne Boleyn's six-fingered hand.

'Ah! So it is true then.'

That voice brought him back from the horror of memory, to the room where his life had just turned awry. To the wrinkled face that now smiled down on him.

'This . . . relic. It could be useful. The Imperial Ambassador in England thinks so. They are struggling to return the land to the One Church, under their good and pious Queen Mary. Her sister, daughter of that witch queen, may need . . . influencing to continue the good work.' He laid gnarled fingers on Gianni's shoulder. 'Can you bring us this witch's hand?'

The nightmare continued. He lapsed into Italian now, his Tuscan accent strong.

'Holy Fath—, uh, your eminence. It was buried before I was born. In France. I do not know where. Only three people do.'

'And they are?'

There was nowhere to hide in a nightmare.

'My mother and father. And one other man. If they are still alive.'

It sounded like the plea it was. *Leave me alone! They're dead. My past is dead!*

'And why would they not be?'

'They are in Siena. So many have died there, they . . .' He broke off. Suddenly he realized he wasn't telling this man anything he didn't know.

'Ah, yes. Siena.' The Cardinal's thin fingers dug into the flesh at Gianni's neck, forced him to take his old weight. 'Then we have found your mission, my son. You will go to Siena. You will find which of these people is alive. And you will get them to lead you to the hand. Then you will take it to England. For the greater glory of God.'

At least, even in the worst of nightmares, there was a chance of waking up. He stuttered again. 'My . . . Jean Rombaud, Most Holy. He survived terrible torture for this . . . this witch. And my mother . . . she would never betray him and his cause.'

'And the third witness? You mentioned three.'

Another image. Gianni saw again that third person, the kind and gentle Fugger, his one hand waving in the air as he declined some Latin verb, as he coached the gifted child Gianni in his studies. He remembered then a part of the saga, shaming the Fugger when it was mentioned. He had broken his vow, betrayed Jean and Anne Boleyn once, but then had redeemed himself, saving Jean's life at the last. But now, all these years later, what power of coercion could make him break his vow a second time?

For a moment, Gianni despaired. Then another vision came, clearing away all the others. A playmate sat beside him at his lessons. A playmate who did not want to learn Latin or Greek, but whose inattention only drew a caress from her indulgent father's one hand.

Maria. Daughter. Beacon in his dark. The only person the Fugger loved more than Jean Rombaud.

'I think, Holy Father, that I might have thought of a way.'

Carafa beamed. He would not correct him again on the title. It would be his soon enough, anyway.

'My son, I never doubted you that you would.'

Gianni watched the Jesuit approach the throne, bow, kiss the ring. He had recognized the Englishman as soon as he saw him in the antechamber. Thomas Lawley had taught him when he'd first come to Rome three years before. It was hardly a surprise he wasn't recognized in return; he had been one of a hundred in that intake of boys. But he remembered Thomas as being typical of his order: kind, patient, tolerant, the lessons imparted more with caresses than the beatings Gianni had been used to at Montecatini Alto. At first he had relished it and had thrived. As he grew older he recognized it for what it was: weakness. It was why he left early, seeking the more rigorous discipline of the Clerks Regular under Carafa, who was known for his loathing of the Jesuits. With them, he could think less and act more. Much more.

After the shock of Carafa's words, Gianni realized that there was no mission he would more willingly undertake. It was as if his whole life had been aimed at this point, like an arrow seeking its target. It had the inevitability of pre-destination. The sins his father had committed in his mistaken zeal for a heretic's cause had hurt the One Faith badly. He had thwarted a chance to fight back when Protestantism was still a fledgling bird. He had even killed a Prince of the Church. Who better than his son to right those wrongs? That six-fingered grip rested heavy and evil upon his whole family. He, Gianni, would remove them from its grasp. Only he could redeem the name of Rombaud.

The Cardinal's conference with Thomas was brief, swiftly reading the letter the Englishman delivered. In a moment, he was beckoning Gianni forward.

'Brother Gianlucca.' He used Gianni's full name. 'Brother Thomas.'

The two men each inclined their head.

The Cardinal continued. 'The Imperial Ambassador has spelled out here the necessity before us. There must not be any hindrance to this, for the arrival of the relic in London will greatly aid our cause there. You need not know why, merely believe it to be so.'

The two men bowed, waited.

'Our friend of the Society of Jesus' – Both could hear the distaste as Carafa spoke those words – 'has papers for the Imperial forces at Siena, power to speed you into the city. Once inside, it will be our servant here who seeks out those to fulfil our quest.'

'Once inside, your eminence? Has the city fallen then?' Thomas's tone was gentle, his eyes unfocused and aimed somewhere between the Cardinal's, his hands clasped easily before him. It was a technique all Jesuits learned, especially with men of authority.

The Cardinal recognized the manner, no softness in his voice now.

'Siena agreed terms on the seventeenth of April, yesterday. Those who wish it will be allowed to march out with full military honours on the twenty-first. Should give you time to get there and enter in triumph with the conquerors.'

He had been perched on the front of his throne. Now, he leaned back and passed a hand before his face, looking every year of his great age.

'Go now. My servant here has money, good men already hired, horses prepared. Go! And may the Lord guide you in everything.'

The shaven man barely allowed them their amens, sweeping them out of the chamber. Another flunky, to great dismay, announced the end of audiences for that day.

As angry priests and courtiers surged around them, Thomas said, 'Well, young man. Shall we be about our work?'

'God's work, Jesuit.'

Thomas merely smiled at the venom of the reply. 'Of course. *Ad Majoram Dei Gloriam.* Always.' His voice was gentle, his look unfocused somewhere between the boy's eyes. 'Shall we ride for Siena?'

THREE
HANDS OF THE HEALER

It was the realm of the dying and the dead. Of those who had fallen into the abyss and those still on its edge. Entwined on the floor, on the few stained mattresses, fevered flesh mingled with the already cold.

It was the realm of voices, pleas for cure, for husband, child, priest, prayers for confession, salvation, for the merest touch of a cool cross on a hot brow. But priests rarely came to the House of the Incurables; in a city about to die, there were plenty of excuses to be elsewhere.

It is my realm, thought Anne Rombaud. *Three floors of it and this top one the worst. Furthest from the street, from life, from hope.*

Standing in the doorway, she tried to steady her breathing, to accept the rank smells that assailed her, for they would multiply as she made her way across. She chose such path as she could see through the twisting limbs. On the far side of the room, bodies were stacked, rising to the roof, awaiting their flight through the door to the goods' yard below. Those closest to that growing pile were the ones destined next to join it. They were the ones who needed her most.

As she started across, the yelling began. A woman's hand fastened around her ankle and she bent to listen, to a list of names – saints, parents, lovers. Gently, she prised each finger away, a word of kindness for each of them, squeezed a sip of water into the mouth from the skin she carried; the woman spluttered, sank back, a momentary quiet. There were more stops, more whispers, more water to drop on swollen tongues, before she was against the far wall, turning her face away from the wall of the dead to the barely alive.

He was still there, still breathing, just, the one she looked for first. He had entered the house three weeks before, had begun lower down, where there was a little hope. But the poultices she applied to his sores had not drawn his sickness out, the fever consumed him from within and the ration allotted to the living sick, a tithe of the tiny ration that the healthy survived on, even that was soon withdrawn, on the orders of the Captain-Physician, D'Ambois. Anne knew why this prioritising had to be. But something about this old man had touched her; maybe his similarity to Grandfather Abraham, whom she had also watched die. She had tried to feed him a little of her own scraps. But he moved up the floors anyway, every day closer to the wall of death. Soon, even she saw the need to dispense the little she could not spare, but did, elsewhere. To her mother, not least, two floors below and deadly sick herself. The only thing she could do now was see that this old man, Guiseppe Toldo, carver of icons, did not die alone.

He was so near his time, his breaths a series of shallow gasps, a pause making her look to see if he had gone. Then there would be another gasp, more air sucked in, and the series would begin again. All along, his eyes would flutter, struggle to open, as if to hold onto this world by seeing it again. But they never made it wide enough.

She knelt by him, in the little space between him and the next shallow-breathing body, took one of his hands, used her other fingers to put a little moisture on his lips. The drops sat there, the effort required to take them in too much.

'It's all right, Guiseppe, I'm here. Anne is here. Be at peace.'

There was a cessation of breaths, a long, long pause, and then a mighty gasp before the breath came again. The eyelids struggled harder to open, his fingers clenching on hers. Suddenly, they fluttered up and he was staring at a point high above him, through the ceiling, beyond the room, to his native skies. Anne's eyes closed and she saw him there, not the man she had known these brief, tortured weeks, but the man she knew he'd been, the worker of wood, proud artist and artisan, husband, father, grandfather. She saw him step out of that husk he'd inhabited and gaze upwards to where she now gazed too, where a door was forming, flame-edged, solid, bright even within a cornflower Tuscan sky.

Behind her eyes, in the world they had stepped into, the world they shared, Guiseppe Toldo bowed to her and smiled. Walking with assured steps, he reached the threshold and then, even as the door was closing upon him, turned back. Something fell from his hand toward her in a shower of light. She caught it but did not look at it, preferring to watch the door flame brightly in the sky, like the silhouette of the sun disappearing behind a mountain. It vanished; her eyes opened. She was back in her own world, in the realm of the dead, holding a dead man's hands.

She didn't remember taking the second one and she looked down at it in some surprise, loosing herself from the grip. As the hands parted, she felt something roll into hers. Looking down, she saw a carving nestled there, no longer than her smallest finger, about half as wide again, yet heavy for its size. It was a falcon, wings folded, sharp beak turned to the side, hooded eyes half-open to scan from its perch on a tiny, detailed branch. It was carved from some dark wood, as if growing out of the tree it rested on.

The wailing had returned four fold and it took a while to realize that the voice beside her was not a part of it. Only an insistent shaking of her arm made look up.

Maria Fugger was there, a fair, pretty, plump girl of sixteen whose curves the privations of siege had done little to reduce. Maintained, Anne always suspected, by the half-shares taken by the two doting men in her life: her father and Erik. Even in these surroundings, Anne couldn't help but smile when she saw Maria's round and freckled face, bursting now to tell some news or gossip. And this had to be more important than most because she was struggling to contain it within lines of unused seriousness.

'Your mother, Anne. Your mother. She has woken up!'

Pausing only to close Guiseppe Toldo's eyes, Anne allowed herself to be dragged across the room of bodies and down the flight of stairs. As she came down to the lowest level, the level of some hope, Anne saw a familiar figure standing in the entrance to the building. Familiar, yet strange too, for she could never get over how changed her father was. The siege had wasted the strength of many and the weight had indeed dropped off his powerful frame – but he had lost more than that. Some part of him had been hurt inside, had not healed like the wound she'd tended nearly a year before. He leaned heavily on his stick, his gauntness accentuated by the strong sunlight that silhouetted him.

She touched his arm. The face that was raised to her was streaked with tears. Another change, for in all her life with him she'd known him cry but once – the day her brother Gianni, cursing Jean Rombaud for an atheist and a tyrant, ran away to Rome.

'Anne.' The rare smile she loved so well, the way it lit his eyes, made him seem younger again, for a moment. He sniffed, took both her hands; finding the carving, he raised it into the sunlight.

'Pretty. A present from an admirer?'

It was a game he played, for he knew she encouraged no one, never had.

'In a way.' She put the falcon away in the pouch at her waist. 'Father, she's awake.'

'I know. I was there.'

'Then let us go and—'

'You go. She'll want to see you so much.'

'And you too. Come—'

'Ah! She has seen me and that is why I am standing here.' A slight smile played again into the sadness on his face. 'She can certainly bear a grudge, your mother. One of the things I always loved about her.'

He turned back to his observation of the street. Unable to think of anything to say, she looked past and noticed all the activity. People were scurrying around, wheeling carts, carrying burdens of weapons and goods. Many were weeping openly.

'What is it, Father? A big attack?'

He did not turn around. 'You have been busy with your admirer. There'll be no more attacks. The French, and such Sienese as will join them, march out today for Montalcino. They will carry on the fight from there, so they say.'

It was true, she had been busy with her charges, her mother, Guiseppe Toldo, all the rest. The war to her was something almost distant, had just brought pain and suffering to many, including her kin. But Siena, fallen?

'What does that mean for us, Father? Do we go? Are we safe here?'

She barely heard his reply.

'I wish I knew.'

Then she remembered that beyond this uncertainty there was joy, a mother awake, returned from the border of death. She squeezed then released his arm and went back into the building.

Jean blew his nose on his sleeve, straightened as a French officer he knew made a brief salute while running by, slumped back again. The weariness he felt was nearly overpowering. He knew he should be making plans, seeking some safety for those he loved. The coming day could bring myriad new dangers. Right now, he couldn't think beyond the feeling of spring sunlight on his face. The taste of the wind reminded him of all the things he should be doing in his vineyards.

There was a man standing at the end of her mother's low cot – the cot being the privilege accorded those Incurables with at least some tiny chance of survival. He was dressed expensively, in the dark tunic and cloak of a gentleman-physician, smiling modestly, while his two, slightly less well-attired attendants were simpering their approval of everything he said.

'Ah, Mademoiselle Rombaud. I was just telling my colleagues here not to talk about miracles. Science! Pure science in the best tradition of Galen. We owe this dear lady's life to the combination of the weapon salve and the purest Theriac distilled by my own hand.'

'And the power of prayer, Monsieur D'Ambois, of course. Mother Mary has listened to our appeals and granted them.' She had found the best way to fend off the esteemed doctor's groping was to keep up the idea most men had of her anyway – that she was halfway to becoming a nun.

'Of course, of course. Prayer is some help but science ...'

Disconcerted by Anne's closeness while pushing past him to her mother's side, D'Ambois began to back away, sweeping his sycophants with him. 'I will return later, Madam, to aid your recovery further. I have a tonic that may well be of effect.'

The hand gripped Anne's with a strength surprising in one just awoken from a fever.

'If you had not driven him away,' said Beck, 'I think I would have stuck this up his pompous arse.' She raised the crossbow bolt that Anne had removed from her back. 'He said he "anointed this with a combination of purple gentian and veraine and thus the cure was effected".' Her voice had adopted the blocked nasal tone of the Frenchman, and Anne and Maria both giggled.

'Ah the weapon salve! Much beloved of these French doctors. Anoint the instrument that caused the harm with its corresponding plants and it will draw the poison from the wound.'

'And this "Theriac"?'

'A panacea containing eighty-one ingredients including grated gallstones and dog droppings.' She watched Beck shudder. 'I prefer other methods. We shall have to see if they have worked. How do you feel, Mother?'

'Like a thousand horses have ridden over me.'

'But can you move your arms and legs?'

Beck tried, moaning as she did, but each limb responded.

'Let us see if the infection has cleared. You might not want to look at this.'

Rolling her mother carefully over on her side, she unwound a bandage. As she pulled it away, a dozen, fat maggots wriggled out.

'Ugh!' Maria turned away, retching, and Beck, who had been unable not to glance, let out a cry.

'What have you done to me, girl? Am I already in my grave that I am worm's meat?'

Anne gathered the little creatures, trapping them in a piece of cloth. 'I saw a horse on the farm once whose wound healed after a week because of these creatures. And when the alternative was dog shit juice and . . .'

She stopped at Maria's pleading. She was pleased, more than that, relieved, at the pink health of Beck's skin near the wound. It had been a chance she'd had to take, for she'd long since run out of the healing herbs she might have used outside the city's walls. Maggots were plentiful in a city of the dead; especially since the spring warmth had returned to the land.

Her mother's protest had turned to a yawn. Feeling her at head and heart, she knew that what the patient needed was sleep to gather her strength. A good long sleep would require a little help so she pulled a flask from her bag and raising Beck's head, let some trickle down her throat.

'Hmm! It's good. What is it?'

'Cordial. Different herbs. It will aid you to rest.'

Another yawn, eyes flickering. Then there was a little surge of energy and Beck's dark eyes were wide.

'Tell me, child, are the others safe. Haakon? Erik? The Fugger?'

Maria spoke up. 'Father's wounds are healing, thanks to Anne.'

'Good. And the fight? How goes it?'

It was not the time for such news. 'All will be well, Mother. Rest now.'

The eyes flickered shut, then opened again. Anne anticipated the question. 'Father is well, too.'

A shadow came into the eyes. 'Oh yes. Jean Rombaud is always well.'

Then the eyes closed and she began to breathe easier.

'Can I take some of that cordial to my father, Anne? He could do with some sleep too.'

Maria's eyes shone from that open face and it was hard to deny her. But Anne needed what little opium she had left for her own causes. Besides, she knew what the Fugger really needed.

'He wants food, as do we all. Maybe the Florentines will bring some with them when they march in.'

Maria leapt up. 'Food! Of course. They are trading at the Porta Romana already. If you have something left, they will give you bread, cheese, meat. Imagine!' Her eyes lit up and she reached into her dress. 'See! I have saved this locket my mother gave me. It is gold. That should buy me some Florentine food to make my father well.'

And with that she was gone, running for the southern gate.

Anne wanted to call her back, to warn her. The city had not finally surrendered and there were still many hard and angry men around. But it was too late and Anne still had problems of her own. One lay sleeping heavily now beside her, not yet passed her crisis. The other stood at the door outside. There was something between the two of them, these two people she loved most in the world. Something none of her potions could heal. She knew Beck believed it was Jean who had driven her son away. Nothing Anne could say had ever changed that opinion.

'Oh, Gianni. Gianni,' she murmured. Sighing, she set about redressing Beck's wound.

Jean, dozing in the sun, had slipped down in the doorway, but the clatter of horses, their metal shoes ringing off the cobbled street, woke him suddenly, blinking, shielding his eyes to behold the men who had stopped before him.

'Rombaud! Giscard said he'd seen you here. Dammit, man, I've had men looking all over the city for you.'

'My lord.'

Jean moved down the stairs, bowed as Blaise de Monluc descended from his horse.

'Yes, yes, enough of that. We must have words, sir. Serious words.'

He pulled Jean into the shadow of the hospital's wall. 'God's Breath, man. This place stinks. Why do you loiter here?'

'My wife, my lord.'

De Monluc's concern was immediate and real. 'How fares she? I sent my surgeon, D'Ambois. Did he effect a cure?'

Jean restrained a smile. Anne had told him of the Frenchman's suggestions and her own actions.

'He did, my lord. She has just awakened and the danger seems passed.'

'Good, good.' De Monluc waved one of his lieutenants away. 'A brave woman. A warrior. We will need all such in the fight ahead.' He fixed that one blazing eye on Jean. 'I know you are not under my command, Rombaud, that you volunteered for Siena.'

'I lived on the edge of its territory, my lord. My farm, the inn I'd inherited, they were among the first to fall. I had little choice.'

'Indeed. Indeed.' De Monluc gestured impatiently. 'But you are a Frenchman, sir, and a leader of soldiery. The fight goes on, at Montalcino, where we are bound now, and all through the free Republic. Will you join me in that fight?'

The thought filled Jean with a revulsion he was careful not to let appear on his face. 'My lord, I am still weak from my wound. More than that, my wife lies gravely ill. She cannot be moved.'

'She will have to be, man!' Anger rose in the General's voice, then he lowered it, spoke evenly. 'You know what it is like when a siege ends and the conquerors enter a town. Despite the "honourable terms", this is still a surrender. Cosimo of Florence, with the Emperor's help, will look to crush this city once and for all, to break it so it never troubles him again. You know how it goes. Squads are waiting at the gates as we speak, armed with lists. We march out, they march in, and the leaders that remain will be snatched up in the first day.'

'I am only a leader by default, my lord. I am not a Sienese, nor is my wife.'

De Monluc laughed though there was little humour in the sound. 'Why, man, they have written ballads of you and they sing them both sides of the wall! You and your warrior wife. Not to mention those barbarian Vikings who are your shadows. You think the Florentines will care that you acted by "default"? They will care only to root out all threats. You and yours will be among the first they seek.'

It was true, and the realization filled Jean with such a weariness. He did not want to go anywhere. He could have stayed in that doorway, dozing in the spring sunshine, for a lifetime.

De Monluc's lieutenant returned. 'My lord! The hour!'

'Yes, yes, yes.' The General took a step toward his horses, turned back.

'If you will not fight for me, Rombaud, let me at least offer you and your family and friends my protection. March with us to Montalcino. Decide there.'

Montalcino! It was not far from Montepulciano, from the Comet Inn, the farm, home. The vision brought energy back into Jean's limbs, into his mind.

'We will come with you, my lord. As far as Montalcino, at least.'

'Good.' The General took off one of his rings, handed it to Jean. 'At the Porta Romana, show this to anyone who tries to stop you. You have two hours.'

He was two paces away when he halted, turned back.

'I heard another tale of you, Rombaud, just the other day. Not a ballad, though worthy of one. Is it true you are an executioner?'

Jean kept his voice even. 'Was, my lord. For a short while, a very long time ago.'

De Monluc's features twisted with curiosity. 'You killed with the sword, did you not? That takes a skilful man. Is it also true, then, the other part of the story? That you were the man who took the head of that English heretic-queen? Anne Boleyn?'

The name, all it conjured, was like a unexpected slap. Looking away, Jean forced himself to breathe. 'No, my lord. It is not true. A few heads in the army, that's all. Nothing worth the telling. The sword has long since rusted in its scabbard.'

The General studied him, disbelieving. 'Some tales I would like to hear another day. You are an interesting fellow. Yes, yes, Giscard, let us away. Two hours, Rombaud.'

The hooves struck sparks from the cobblestones, as the entourage galloped off, leaving Jean thinking about another day of spring sunshine nineteen years before. He'd lied to De Monluc. There was a tale, beyond anything the General could ever believe. He *had* taken Anne Boleyn's head. He had also taken her six-fingered hand. And the tortured path he'd trod then led here, directly to this further woe.

Once again, Jean Rombaud cursed the time he'd first heard the name of Anne Boleyn, felt weariness return to his limbs with its utterance. He didn't have time for that weakness now. He had two hours. Two! Well, they had arrived with nothing and they would leave with less. If Beck could be moved.

The only one who could know that answer appeared, just as the echo of hooves died away.

'You heard?'

'Yes, Father.'

'Can we move her?' He saw the hesitation in his daughter's eyes, those dark pools so like the woman's she was named for. Saw the sadness in them, too. He wanted more than anything to bring some light into them again.

'Can we take her home?' he said.

'But Siena's beaten. Did you not say we could only get our lands back with a victory?'

'That may still be true. Yet war moves strangely, daughter. It may have burnt the Comet and then passed by. The farm may be in ashes. But even ashes can be built on.'

'Then I think we must go to see, Father.'

'Good. Prepare her. I will arrange a cart, some bedding. I just need to find Haakon.'

Anne smiled. 'Well, you know he's never far away.'

He knew. Like an irritant in the corner of his eye, the big Norwegian had skulked near him, shadow and protector still, keeping to the windward of Jean's wrath. It had somewhat abated when Anne was hopeful of cure for her mother, when Haakon's excuse of protecting his son, mumbled to Anne and passed on, was accepted. Erik had avoided Jean's anger by keeping away, so Jean kept his glares for his old comrade.

Jean looked across to where the large figure lurked in a doorway. 'Haakon! Come here.'

Like a disobedient dog, wary of chastisement, Haakon made his way across. 'Jean. Anne. A sad day for Siena, eh?'

The mournful expression seemed so out of place on that huge and open face that Jean could not help but laugh. It was the thing with Haakon. No matter how weary he got, how desperate the situation, the Norseman had always had a way of making Jean laugh.

'We're getting out, Hawk. With De Monluc.'

Haakon beamed. 'To fight on, Jean?'

'To go home. If there's any home left to go to. To rebuild it if there's not.'

Swiftly he told Haakon what they needed. Finishing a list that already had the Norwegian scratching his head, he said, 'And keep an eye out for the Fugger. He wasn't at his lodgings, he'd gone looking for his daughter. I left him a note but ...'

Haakon smiled. 'He will have done what I will do – seek out my son, for Erik is never far from her and that great lout of a boy is hard to miss.'

With that, he was gone about their business. Jean hugged his daughter, then set out himself. There were scant goods to gather, favours to call in.

Home! The thought pushed him on. Maybe, just maybe it was possible. To go back, to make it like it was, to see his vineyards flourish, to see the light come back once more into his wife's eyes. To be reunited, all of them, once again in the courtyard of the Comet, telling the old stories!

The memory, the image, broke his stride. Some things were

possible, some were not. For there would be a ghost at any feast they held, a space between them that could not be filled.

Gianni. Somewhere out in the world his son breathed, prayed, lived. Miles from these walls, no doubt, but often the distance between two people could not be measured in miles. And Gianni was as far from him as Jean Rombaud was from the sun.

FOUR
FLIGHT

It began with the bells. The first heard was in the belfry of the Torre del Mangia, the principal and largest bell in all Siena, a deep note, single and solemn which still rung across the Campo when the second note was struck. Yet the great square remained empty, no citizen roused to answer the call, to see what the Republic required of them. For all knew that this tolling was not to summon. This tolling was to say farewell.

The soldiers massing at the Porta Romana heard that first note. Somehow it broke through the cries of the sergeants and officers trying to dress their lines, silencing even these men for a moment. Then the other towers of Siena struck up and the whole world seemed to vibrate; the nearest one to them, at the Basilica dei Servi, was a riotous medley of high and deep. With the world thus filled again with noise, the marshalling could continue, halberds used to straighten the ranks, batons to push and cajole. Banners unfurled over each company, French, Sienese and mercenary. They would march out with full honours. Arms had not defeated them, only the cruellest, most effective of old enemies – hunger and disease.

Behind the ordered ranks of soldiery, in the pell-mell of prepared flight, that first metal cry from the Tower made every one of the Sienese patriots turn and face back into the city. Many had eyes closed, some fruitlessly trying to stem tears, others as if they could trap time, hold it in the bell's note, stay for ever like this, enfolded in their city's voice. But the rest of the city's chimes, the discordancy of three hundred bells, brought them back to their present need, to the urgency of imminent exile. Those who were leaving, those to be left behind, wept, begged, prayed. Many just fought to maintain their position, their grip on their meagre possessions.

Haakon too had turned back when the bell struck, to desperately scan the surge for a shaggy blond head. Erik had gone in search of the Fuggers, father and daughter, and had not returned. Jean was looking relentlessly forward, focused on the gates ahead. When they opened, he was determined to keep his little party pressed as close as possible to the armoured French ranks, for there would be people beyond them who might not respect the truce. Sienese exiles, enemies of the republic, hated many of those who were about to leave and would seek revenge. In the end, all wars were civil wars. He had seen the aftermath of enough sieges to know that.

He looked across the little cart, across the sleeping form of Beck, to Anne. He tried to give her a smile, but it would not form, just as no moisture would relieve his mouth. She smiled at him though, then returned her attention to her mother. Whatever cordial she'd given Beck was working; she lay inert, untroubled by the tolling of bells.

'She'll need more water. There is a fountain in that side street.'

Anne was darting through the crowd before Jean could stop her. He had taken a step forward when a huge hand gripped his arm.

'Jean! There he is!'

Jean looked back. He did not have the Norseman's height, but even he could see Erik's distinctive head ploughing through the mêlée.

'Are they with him?'

'I only see Erik. And my son looks concerned.'

Erik's story was spurted out in a moment. 'We have searched everywhere. I think the whole of the Scorpion Contrada is in the streets looking for her. The Fugger leads them. I must join him.'

The boy turned back. 'Oh, I nearly forgot. I found it, Father.' Reaching into his scimitars' sling, he produced a third weapon from it. It lay in its fraying scabbard, a square-tipped edge poking through at one end, the green leather of the grip peeling off, rust around the apple-sized pommel.

'You nearly left it, Jean.' Haakon beamed, offering the sword across. 'How can you be an executioner without a sword?'

Jean looked down, looked quickly away, back to the gate. 'Oh.' His voice was flat. 'Throw it in the cart.'

'I go.' Erik was wheeling away.

'And I will go with you.' Haakon started forward.

'Haakon!' Jean's voice was sharp, commanding, and it halted the Norwegian. 'The gates will open any moment. I cannot push the cart by myself, I wouldn't make it halfway to Montalcino. And we cannot stay. De Monluc is right; our lives are in danger.'

He had managed somehow to keep the fear from his voice. Haakon paused, his son on one side, his old comrade on the other.

'Father, you should go. The Fugger and I will look. We'll find Maria and join you in Montalcino.'

Haakon's reply, when it came after a long pause, was gruff. 'See that you do, boy. And take no chances!' He cuffed his son around his head.

'Me?' There was a swift smile, a touch of a scimitar in salute, and he was gone.

To Jean's great relief, Anne was back in a moment, ladling some fresh water into her mother's mouth. On hearing that Erik had gone to look for Maria she cried out, 'But I know where she went. To the gate, to try to barter gold for food with the Florentines. This gate, the Porta Romana I think.' Seeing the looks on their faces she said, 'I should have told you before.'

Haakon started back toward the city for Erik.

'No, Haakon. We will look for her outside and we will send word. You will not find them now. And look. Look!'

Jean's panicked words brought Haakon around and, far ahead down the Via Roma, now the Sienese Republic's Via Dolorosa, he too saw the Porta Romana start to swing open. Everyone around began to lift weapons, stretchers, babies, packs, carts, anything that held their goods or their wounded, and pressed forward. Haakon, with one long last look back, bent to the handles of the cart. Beck moaned as it rose.

'Hold tight, Anne. Do not let go of the cart,' Jean ordered. He tried to breathe calmly. With a little luck, they would be out and clear soon. On their way to Montalcino and, beyond that city, maybe on their way home. His lips twisting in barely remembered prayers, he set his mind to the road ahead.

They had arrived at the gates near dawn after two day's hard riding from Rome. There, just behind the Florentine siege lines, on a scrap of barren earth, the horses were hobbled and nose-bagged before twenty exhausted men fell upon the hard ground as if it were a feathered mattress. The grey-cloaked figure who had pushed his horse the hardest, impatient with any rest, now went off to reconnoitre, to gather news of the surrender. Gianni Rombaud felt he would never sleep again. Not, at least, until this mission that was his salvation was complete.

Not so the man in the black cloak. When his head finally reached the stiff comfort of his pack, Thomas felt that he might never wake again. His body ached, his mind numb of everything except a desperate desire for oblivion. When the words reached through the cloud of his head that the French and Sienese would not march out till two bells of the afternoon, eight hours away, it was as if he'd been granted a lease on paradise.

Yet his rest was not untainted. The mustering of the Florentine forces, the cries and orders in Spanish, German, Dutch, Italian disturbed him not at all; but sometime toward midday, when the first heaviness of sleep had passed, it began to fill with images, jumbled recollections of things present and things past – a whiff of the coffin, a snatch of a rhyme, a child's hand pressed into his. This last led him on, until he was both holder and held, his father and himself, walking into the desecrated buildings of Wenlock Priory. Half the walls were down yet men still carted blocks away to the village beyond. The great rose window was a mere frame, bare of its stunning glass. On one of the few remaining leaded casements, a crow was perched, its beak upraised, cawing notes that Thomas could not hear, yet summoning fellows, until the window was filled with black feathers, and silent screams.

His father let slip his hand, and Thomas floated away from the boy on the ground, up above the sacked priory buildings, over his native village of Much Wenlock. There was his home, the comfortable brick manor house built next to the covered market, location and manner befitting the squire of the prosperous Shropshire town. But it was not his home any more, he remembered now, others lived there, others who had conformed, who had profited from those who had not. He was no longer looking down but up – now he could hear the birds, now he was a boy again, see them diving, circling, squabbling over the body swinging in their midst. It was spinning around, faster, faster, he couldn't see who it was until some unseen hand, perhaps his own, halted the whirling, scattered the birds back to their window perch. Now he could see the face, see that despite the protruding purple tongue, the rolled up whites of the eyes, it was utterly and completely his father's.

Thomas had thought his scream was silent, held within a dream. But as he sat up quickly, the looks of those around him, Carafa's men checking their arms and equipment, told him otherwise. Loosening the fold of cloak that had somehow wrapped itself too tightly around his throat, Thomas placed his forehead on his knees, began to recite his catechism, the principles of his faith, the familiar Latin words slowly having their effect. His breathing calmed, his heart steadied. He knew why he'd had the dream – the sacrilege of the sacking of Wenlock Priory, the sacrifice his father had made to oppose it, these were the goads Thomas needed to keep him on the path of righteousness. Even if he must do questionable things. And he'd never questioned anything before as he did this quest of Anne Boleyn's hand.

The man he saw striding toward him seemed to have no such qualms, no night-time terrors. Thomas watched Gianni glance neither to right or left, watched big soldiers step out of his determined path. In their brief conversations, before setting out, in hurried rests on the road, Gianni had revealed little – and Thomas had an array of methods for finding out what he needed to know. The boy was folded over some internal flame. It shone out from his dark eyes, a yearning. The man who would be Pope, the Cardinal Carafa, had said in Rome that his protégé had 'intimate' knowledge of where the hand could be found. The way he'd said 'intimate' had made Thomas shudder.

Gianni covered the last twenty paces to them at a run. 'You! Alessandro! Bring ten of your men. Armed. And follow me.' To Thomas he added, 'God has smiled upon our venture, Brother.'

'He always does. How, particularly, now?'

But Gianni did not reply. He just turned and led the assembled company swiftly away.

Thomas struggled to keep up. His knee was always at its worst after sleep.

Gianni had spent the morning moving up and down the lines, talking with soldiers and officers, gleaning information. He'd heard the snatch of a ballad sung over a breakfast fireplace, familiar names leaping from the verse. The rebel Sienese who sang, who fought against their own republic, told him the ballad was of an infamous general within the city whose balls, it seemed, were held firmly in his harridan wife's hands.

'We'll relieve her of that duty when we exiles get inside. This reckoning has been a long time a-coming. Just last week this Rombaud led the men who killed fifty of us at the Porta San Viene. Now he will pay!' The officer's eyes gleamed with vengeance as he spoke.

It was strange to hear his father and mother talked of thus. He'd left them at Montepulciano, a prosperous farmer-winemaker and his wife. Now it seemed they had returned to their former life, piling sin on sin, the subject of bawdy ballads. Well he, of all the family, would atone. He had achieved much in that line up to now, God be praised. The work he was about now would dwarf those accomplishments.

His seeking took him, near midday, down to the Porta Romana, gates he would later position himself beside to scan for his prey, to make sure they did not escape the city, but could be stalked within it. There was a crowd gathered there, for many starving citizens were testing the truce, had slipped out the sally ports to barter such treasure they had left for crusts of bread, scraps of meat. There were enough exploiters there to bargain with, not least the mercenaries who, by this honourable surrender, had been denied the looting of a captured city.

Not just looting, Gianni realized. Three soldiers, who one moment had been flirting with a ragged young girl, luring her to the side of the mêlée with promises of food, now grabbed her, a hand over her mouth, picked her up and ran her down into a little gully. He was about to walk away, to continue his explorations, when a vision of the girl's face came back to him, just before the hand went over it, cutting off the scream. It had seemed familiar in that instant, almost as if he had seen that look of terror on that very face before. Then he realized that he had, and where, and he was running back to his men the next instant.

When they reached the gully's mouth, sounds led them down the narrowing passage, sounds of terror, of laughter. As he pushed through the bushes, Gianni saw that Maria Fugger was lying, spreadeagled, pinned by two of them at arms and legs, the squat, bald sergeant crouched before her, pulling at the straps around his waist.

The sergeant, hearing them, turned and snarled, his face contorted into the grimace of an animal interrupted with its prey.

'We found her first. You can fuck off and wait. There'll be some left over when we're done.'

Gianni paused. He had no particular regard for Maria, a stupid girl he'd enjoyed tormenting sometimes, who had early formed an alliance against him with the equally bovine Erik. She had probably brought this on herself with her sluttish, sinful ways. This was not like Wilhelm, these soldiers were not in training to be priests. As long as they didn't kill her . . .

As he considered, a black-cloaked figure pushed past him.

'What is happening here?'

Thomas had been a soldier himself, had turned away from such desecrations before. What he didn't know was why Gianni was here watching it.

The young man told him. 'God's smile, Brother. She is the one we seek, whose father will lead us to our goal.'

'And you would see her raped first?'

When he saw the young man shrug, anger surged through him, bile burning his throat. With it came the memory of his dream, the questionable decisions that must be taken for the greater glory of God. This Gianni was a part of all that, a weapon in his own right, part of what had to be tolerated. But there were other things that needn't be.

'Let her go.'

The sergeant's hands held his belt, which he was about to discard. Instead, he reached down toward his sheath.

'You'll wait your turn like a good boy.'

Thomas was a soldier of Christ now, but he had been a soldier of England once. There were rules he had lived by then, rules he had not forgotten. So he acted on one of them – strike before you are struck.

He bent down, turning half away from the man before him, his body and cloak hiding his left hand until it was too late for it to be stopped. He used the heel of his palm, striking upwards and across, snapping the man's nose, reeling him back against the gully wall. Both soldiers dropped the girl's arms, reaching toward a pike and sword resting upright against a bush behind them. The sword was sheathed and buckled so Thomas went for the man with the pike, seizing it as the soldier was trying to bring its point down, driving the shaft back and up into the man's neck, collapsing him. He swung it around toward the man who had unsheathed half the blade of his sword, who stopped when he saw the cutting edge in Thomas's hand, dropped his sword, stepped back with arms upraised.

Gianni only had time to say, 'You surprise me, Jesuit,' when a cry cut across his words, and the sergeant, blood pouring down his face, knife in hand, ran at Thomas's exposed back. The blade was a hand's length away when it halted, seeming to hover there a moment, pointing like an accusation into the Englishman's black cloak. Sounds emerged, but no words – blocked, no doubt, by the dagger that had appeared in his throat. The man dropped to his knees, his own knife still held before him, plunging it into the ground as he slowly sank forward, his forehead coming to rest on the ground almost between the terrified girl's legs.

For a moment there was silence, save for the gasps of Maria Fugger, the deep inhalations of the Jesuit, the gurglings of the man whose neck held a blade. Gianni stepped forward, gently pushed the sergeant's body with his toe until it keeled over onto its side. Then he bent and retrieved his dagger from the throat, wiping it on the man's jerkin before straightening up again.

'Did you have to take his life?' Thomas threw the pike down as he spoke.

'Now,' asked Gianni, smiling, 'is that gratitude?'

It was then that Maria's tears, long held back, began to flow down her cheeks. She was staring at Gianni, disbelief mingling with the horror, words choked in water.

'Hallo, Maria.' Gianni's voice was pleasant. 'How's your father?'

Sobs cut off any reply. Turning to the men behind him he barked, 'Bind and gag her.'

There was a rush to obey. The men who followed him were Carafa's and the Cardinal's orders had been to do as this man bid them. Any question they might have had about doing that had ended when a thrown dagger had entered a throat.

When they began to truss the sobbing girl, the locket fell from her clothes. It was handed to Gianni, who opened it and nodded, showing the miniatures inside to Thomas.

'The girl's parents. This is the man we seek.'

As he spoke, the great bell in the Torre del Mangia sounded its first sad note. Gianni looked up. 'Ah! Shall we see if we can find him?'

Thomas let all the others leave, Gianni at the head of his men, the girl pushed before him. The two soldiers had fled the other way, deeper into the gully, leaving the body of their comrade in the dust. Thomas bent over it now. The blood had pooled, forming a great circle, a halo of red around the head. Grasping even this small symbol of grace, Thomas swiftly genuflected, touching his fingers to his lips. The prayers had, of necessity, to be short, for all the bells of Siena were tolling in mad carillons and, under them, he could hear the beat of the French drums.

He found Gianni again as the first regiments, under their swirling banners, were already sweeping by their vantage point a few hundred paces before the Porta Romana. Blaise de Monluc rode at their head, glancing neither right nor left, his one eye fixed ahead as if on future battles. The soldiers that followed did not look as if they had withstood fifteen months of privation and siege, for the spring sunshine dazzled as it bounced from burnished armour and helm, from pikes proudly raised, swords swept up in salute. The French, and the mercenary companies among them, were birds of prey still, united in the glitter of their plumage, with their puffed and blistered sleeves, the linings pulled through the cuttes in a rainbow of colour, extravagant doublets of crimson or eggshell blue surmounting the clashing ochre or gold breeches, the black and silver hose. Thomas shuddered as he remembered the profits of his first sacked city in Flanders spent on just such finery. Putting it aside to don the sackcloth and rough wool of the noviciate had been like a second birth to him.

The Spanish lining the road jeered the French, who returned the favour, the mercenaries of both sides exchanging greetings and abuse with present enemies, past comrades, future allies. They took half of one hour to pass, the soldier in Thomas calculating their number to be about five thousand, each regiment accompanied by its goods and wounded in large wagons. When the last of these had passed there was a pause, as drumbeats receded down the road, the dust hanging thick in the air. Then there came through the gate a shrill cry of command followed by the roar of one word, the name of their city. Then the warriors of Siena marched forth.

The contrast to those who had gone before was marked. There were drums still, a few, and banners sporting both the city's symbols, of wolf and founding fathers, and the mark of several of the Contradas – the Lion, the Unicorn, the Scorpion, the Broadsword. Beneath them, though, Thomas saw men and women in plain garb and practical armour, starved faces trying to stave off tears, failing, their bodies savaged by hunger and wound yet forced to march proudly from homes they might never see again. Their leaders marched among their people, distinguished only by their plumed hats, alike in the tears that flowed, in their bandages and their limps. Though it was clear the majority were not professional soldiers, yet they contrived to march in step, their footfalls stirring up more dust from the roadway. The drum, the heavy breaths of exertion, were all the noise that accompanied their sad exit. Their enemies watched in silence, save for the occasional exile who stepped forward to spit at some old rival's feet, to receive not even a glance in response.

In their midst, in marked contrast to the huge wagons of the French, small dog carts were heaved, piled with groaning bodies, meagre goods. Thomas sensed the tension in the young man at his side, for Gianni had craned forward at the first sad beat of the Sienese drum, wrapping the hood of his cloak about his face despite the warmth of the sun, one hand holding an edge so that only his dark eyes were clear, studying the throng. Gazing at him, Thomas decided he would be better served watching this boy to whom he had been shackled like a slave on an oar bank. To better know this enigma, who lived in a monk's habit yet killed like a street assassin.

Gianni saw Haakon first, of course, even though the Norseman was bent before a small cart, his huge hands gripping its two handles. His eyes immediately swept around the cart, missing what he sought, looking around, looking back, settling finally in a sort of wonder, for his father had changed in the three years since he had last seen him, changed mightily. It was not that he had shrunk, as Gianni knew parents did when sons grew older. It was more as if something had been cut from him, thus reducing him in size to this small, limping man struggling to push a dog cart. Something misted in his eyes and he reached a hand up, stunned to encounter moisture there. He wiped it away, sought his ready anger, forced the water down. He had vowed long before that he had shed his last tears for his family. Sinners were not worth the salt!

His sister walked on the other side of the cart in that calm gait he had so loved to mock, to imitate; yet he had never quite got right the way she seemed to hover over the ground. One of her hands was placed within the cart, he thought at first almost to tether her, to prevent her floating away. Then he realized that Anne's hand held another, one that emerged from what he'd assumed was a stack of rags and blankets. Then Gianni saw the high forehead, the greying-black hair of his mother. Her eyes, the twins of his own, were hidden beneath her closed lids. He could see that she was alive and he could see that it was only just.

He did not know he had taken a step forward, that a word had escaped his lips, until the Jesuit had spoken beside him:

'What? Do you see him? Shall I gather the men?'

Gianni raised a hand, stepped back, made sure that, as his family passed, no one else passed behind them. At last, when he was sure his voice was his own again, he spoke.

'He is not with them. He would be, if he were leaving. He is still in the city looking for this.' He toed the girl lying in a bundle at his feet, who moaned through her gag. 'She's told me their address. Shall we enter?'

Thomas let Gianni order the men, tried to settle his impressions of the last few minutes. He had been right to watch for he knew now that the calm young man he'd just met was capable of emotion – and emotion was always a useful tool. He had also seen what the young man had looked at, or rather whom, knew that his reactions could only have been provoked by people he loved or hated. Perhaps both, for sometimes the line between the two was hair thin. But then Thomas had become distracted by the girl walking beside the cart. No, not walking, floating somehow, as if allowing the cart to pull her along. She was air, translucent, a mote hovering in the sunbeams that streamed in the road dust, passing through the veil of her black, black hair.

It was only the young man starting forward that brought Thomas back from this vision, had him scrabbling for words. In action there was a course out of this confusion.

Though there was a scramble at the gates, the main conquering army would enter from the north-east, through the Porta Camollia, so it took them only a little time to force their way in. The gag was dropped long enough for the directions to the Fugger residence to be ascertained. It was as good a place to begin as any.

Gianni called to Alessandro, one of the troop leaders. 'Take her to Rome, to the Lateran prison. She is to be released only when this locket is brought for her. Understand?'

Maria was thrown across one of their horses, and half his force accompanied her back out the gate. Gianni led Thomas and the remaining ten men away from the main Via Roma, where soldiers streamed toward the Campo, and up a narrow side street, the Via Valdimontone. He'd quite recovered from his strange reactions at the roadside, determined now to atone for even so slight a display of weakness. Ahead was a man who would help him in that atonement. A one-handed man who would help him atone for everything.

For the Fugger, searching frantically through the falling city, the bells were terrible goads pricking him on. Without his Maria there was no life, she was the last memory of her beloved mother, also called Maria, his wife's shy smile, quick laugh, gentle touch still alive in those of his daughter. He had talked to his wife every day of the five years since the flux had taken her. He talked to her now, even after the last of the drum beats had faded, running down the side street that led to the ruin he had called their home for the last fifteen months.

'You've taken her there, haven't you, my love? Guided her back, away from all the evil of this day. She's there waiting for me now, there's still time, we have nothing to carry, just ourselves, down to the Porta Romana, out, they won't have gone far. Jean, Haakon, Beck, Anne . . .'

Anne would be angry with him. The bandage she'd so carefully wound around his hand, over the stump of his two fingers, had unravelled, was trailing now as he ran. He could see the shattered flesh beneath a final layer of cloth.

'They've chopped more bits off me, Maria. They'll be nothing left soon. What life will there be for a one-handed, three-fingered man on a farm?'

The farm! Jean had written in his note that they would try to return there, to start again in the place all of them had known their only true happiness. There, he had invented all sorts of devices to aid in the pressing of olive and grape. Surely, he could invent something that could be worked with a thumb and two fingers. His daughter would help him. She always liked to help him in his work.

'If she is there, wife. If she is waiting for me just around the next corner, like any sensible girl would.'

She wasn't. Armed men stood in front of his doorway, and he ran into one of them, into hard breastplate sheathed in black cloak, the pace of his run knocking the unprepared soldier back into a comrade.

'Heh, you stupid . . .'

The voice was rough, the dialect Roman. The Fugger, knowing his late enemies instantly, adopted the accent of the Sienese, along with a servile attitude.

'Sorry, Master, sorry. A thousand apologies.' He was backing away slowly the way he had come, glancing past the soldiers into his lodgings, hoping for a glimpse of his daughter, hoping she was not there in this new danger. So focused was he on this hope, he did not see the one guard nudge his fellow and point at the Fugger's puckered stump. The men lunged for him, holding him beyond hope of escape, before running him through the doorway.

Inside it was dark, except for bars of light which dropped through the broken roof, showing the meagre furniture and the two men, one sitting on the table's edge, the other standing, his hooded face in a shadow, turning Jean's note over and over in a sunbeam. This hood raised toward the Fugger, who was thrust onto his knees, his face in a patch of sunshine, dazzled, blinking up. Strangely, his first thought was of roofing materials.

'Ah! The Lord continues to smile upon us.'

That voice! The Fugger knew it, yet could not place it at first, the calmness of it, within that calm an energy barely contained. Then the face moved forward into the light.

'Gianni!'

Along with his gasp, the Fugger's mind filled with contrary images, flashes of memory. The quick boy who soaked up all the Latin and Greek the Fugger could teach him. The sad boy who came back from the mountains. The cruel boy whose tricks drove his Maria to frequent tears. The angry boy who'd stolen away into the night. The boy in the man's face that looked down at him now.

'But ... how ... why are you ... what are you ...?'

A simple question cut off the stuttering. 'Do you know where your daughter is, Fugger?'

The tension held within the voice wrapped around his fear, doubling its intensity.

'My daughter. My Maria. I ...'

'Because I do. I know where she is, I know where she is going and I know what is going to happen to her there. All the terrible things that will happen to her there.' The words were said so calmly, as if they were of no matter at all and the Fugger felt his heart like a creature, flapping at the bars of his chest. 'Unless ...'

A hand went into the cloak, emerged with a glitter that dangled at the end of a chain. It swung back and forth there, a pendulum of light, trapping the Fugger's eyes.

'Unless, Gianni?'

'Unless you do exactly what I ask of you. Exactly. And if you do, I will give you this. This will free her. Save her.' The locket stilled, spinning slowly now in its one position. The clasp had opened and the Fugger could see inside, to the two tiny portraits there, his wife, himself, his wife, himself, revolving before him, blending, until it was his daughter spinning there, the melding of these two halves.

He raised his trembling half-hand toward the locket, which withdrew at the approach, dangled and spun just beyond the outreached fingers.

'Not yet. First you have to do what I ask of you. Don't you want to know what that is?'

It could be anything and the Fugger knew he would do it. Any crime he was asked to commit, any sin, to have this locket in his hands. To fulfil the promise in those words. To free. To save.

'Yes,' he said. 'Yes, Gianni, tell me what I must do.'

And Gianni told him and the glitter disappeared from his sight, swallowed by the black pit of his horror, the black pit just like the one where he had lived, if life it could be called, in a midden beneath a gibbet cage at a crossroads in the Loire. He had been delivered from that pit by Jean Rombaud, a man whose cause he had followed and later betrayed, who had nonetheless raised him up a second time, given him again his friendship, another chance, the joy in the day's light he had had in all the years since. He owed the man everything. And that man's son was now urging him to a second betrayal, a worse betrayal than before, to destroy a man's life work even near its end. And the tears that now forced their way from the Fugger's eyes, as his wife, and his own and his daughter's image revolved before them, were tears of a bitter certainty. She was all the joy he had left, all that remained of the only woman he had ever loved. What were friendship, loyalty and a dead queen's bones, compared to that?

He fell onto the floor, a shadow passing before his eyes, as if some black bird had squatted over the hole in the roof and blotted out the sun. His voice had just such a carrion croak.

'Jesus save me.'

Only one man there said, 'Amen.' Hitherto silent, he sat at the table. Gianni Rombaud jerked the chain, catching the locket in his hand, and looked up, triumph in his eyes.

It was no bird that had shut away the sun. Erik had hidden in the street when he'd found the soldiers there, had watched the Fugger taken into the house. Not knowing if his Maria was within as well, he'd scrambled onto the roof from the adjoining building.

As stealthy as any big cat, he'd worked his way around shattered tiles and exposed beams to the largest hole, wedging himself into the chimney breast just beside it. He had not been able to hear, what with the noise of the fallen city all around him, the wailing and drums and bells. But he had seen the Fugger kneeling before the hooded figure, had seen something tiny glitter between them, had caught the upsurge of despair that came from the man he'd known all his life. Then he'd seen him fall down, and he'd moved across the hole as the man who had just been the crown of a hood before, now looked up. Erik had frozen, both because movement would betray him and because he recognized another face he had known all his life. The boy he'd grown up with, the boy he'd learned to loathe, was below him, and no longer a boy. And he did not need the Fugger's despair to tell him that if Gianni Rombaud was involved, something bad had just begun.

FIVE
ROYAL PRISONER

Elizabeth had never been in this part of the palace, not when she'd visited her father in the easy days of childhood, not now when her movements were restricted to the west suite and its little walled garden on the river. If she had more liberty she would not have come here anyway, for you had to walk through the kitchens, where scullions stopped their business to point and mutter, then on through a disused stable yard, her escort's one torch failing to disperse the night gloom. Up a narrow stair, through a low doorway. The oak-panelled room itself was comfortable enough, if spare; the door by which she'd entered was seamless within the panels, no handle, no keyhole, though she had heard the key turned in the lock by the silent, hooded man who had led her there. A table stood at its centre, two high-backed chairs behind it, one stool before, a lamp the only light in the windowless space, leaving the corners of the room to the shadows. Beside the lamp was an inkwell, three quills, a penknife and a sheaf of blank parchment.

She might never have been there before, but she knew the room at a glance. Rooms of interrogation were always the same. She had been in enough of them to know.

There was one difference here. She discovered it on her first turn about, on the back wall, behind the interrogators' chairs. It was a mirror, circular, slightly concave, its age showing in the flaking gold frame. The glass was exquisite though; even in such poor light it revealed her to herself clearly. It was not meant for this room, but for some richer place and she wondered how it had made the journey here to confront her with her own imperfections. Wondered, as she always did with mirrors, at the

82

faces that it must have held and lost before. Faces she would recognize instantly, others she would half-remember. Her father had certainly looked in it, never a man to pass a mirror, and she saw him now reflected in her own strong jaw, in the high forehead and its framing of thick red-gold hair. Her mother was such a faded memory and the few portraits that had survived her failed to do her justice, it was said. However, what little she knew and remembered she saw now, in the sharp cheekbones, the arrow straight nose, mostly in the deep caverns of her eyes. Hers were not the fathomless pools, which, it was said, her mother had used to lure and tantalize, but they were considered as fine in their setting. Those, and her delicate hands, her inheritance from the woman she'd never truly known. She raised one now, held the palm to the side of her face, then the back. Recalling the difference between her hand and her mother's, she swiftly lowered it. It had looked strange to her anyway, even without the extra finger so-called friends teased her about; bony fingers, not fine, the skin as sallow as her face, both drawn by the long years of watchfulness, of suspicion, of . . . *waiting in rooms like this!*

She did not know who had summoned her to this midnight meeting, her first since they'd brought her from Woodstock the week before, to the Queen's palace if not her presence. Her sister would still not see her, despite Elizabeth's entreaties to be seen. She had hoped that the summons to Hampton Court would mean her imprisonment was coming to an end, but even if the chains were looser here, she was still not free of them. Meetings like this could be preliminaries to journeys she did not want to take. Back to the boredom, the petty tyrannies of Sir Henry Bedingfield, at Woodstock. Or back to something far worse, the river journey that had begun from this place a year and a month before, downstream to the Tower.

No! It would not, could not lead there. They had tried to trip her, catch her in conspiracies and lies before and they had failed. She had survived that black prison, survived the attempts to link her to those who would harm the Queen and overthrow her Church, to Wyatt and the rest. She would survive still, as long as her nerve held, as long as she could outface whoever walked through the door now. It was intolerable that they kept her waiting in this gloomy chamber and they would know her displeasure; if she had inherited her father's colouring and jaw-line, she had his temper too.

And the room was hers. Disdaining the stool, she sat on a high-backed chair, focusing her attention on the door before her and the unknown opponent who would walk through it. It was as if her concentration was a summons, because almost instantly she heard the scrape of metal in metal. The door unfolded from the panelling.

'Princess Elizabeth.'

The tall figure stooped in the entrance, a gesture of a bow with the head.

Renard! Of course it would be him, could be no one else. Only the Fox does his scavenging at night.

Elizabeth laid her arms out along the chair's, relaxed them, aiming her anger forward.

'Ambassador. Do you consider this an appropriate hour for an interview?'

'Alas!' He turned and pushed the door to, an unseen hand beyond fitting key to lock. 'My labours suck away my daylight hours. It's late in the day when can I look to my own pleasure.'

'Pleasure?'

'Oh yes, my lady. For this is more in the nature of a personal visit. To welcome you back to court from your exile. To hope that this is the beginning of happier times for you, as they are happier for the kingdom and all its subjects.'

Elizabeth bit back the retort that surged within her – that the martyrs who were being burnt by the score for their Protestant faith were hardly happy. But she had spent the better part of two years trying to convince this man, among others, that she was a loyal daughter of the Catholic Church and rejoiced in its glorious restoration. This man had tried everything within his consider-able means to have her condemned as a heretic or a traitor and killed as either by flame or axe. She would not give him anything that might help him pursue that cause anew. So she said nothing, gripped the arms of the chair, waited.

Renard eyed the seating arrangements with amusement and instead of taking the stool, he walked forward and placed a package, wrapped in red velvet, on the table beside the lamp.

'A present, for you, my lady. To welcome you back.'

Elizabeth made no move toward the object. 'What is this kindness, my lord?'

'You will have to open it to see.'

'I would prefer if you opened it for me.'

Another smile. 'As my lady wishes.'

Long fingers untied the loose cord, slipping a small wooden box from out the velvet cover. It was slightly larger than the width, and of the length, of one hand, the depth of two hands joined in prayer. Designs were carved into the walnut – the coat of arms of the Emperor. When Elizabeth still did not move, Renard lifted the lid off, placed it to the side, stood back, clasping his hands before him.

Lamplight glowed on a chess set, tiny figures exquisitely carved, ivory white facing ebony black. Bending forward, Elizabeth lifted a knight past its initial resistance, to reveal the little peg that had held it.

'It is beautiful.'

'The craftsmen of Modena have excelled themselves indeed. You do play?'

'I am a novice in the art, but yes, I play.'

'I believe my lady is being modest. I hear you surpass your tutors in this as you do in most of your studies.'

'And I have heard you are unmatched in Europe.'

There was no denial, merely an incline of the head, another slight smile. 'Would you play with me?'

'Is it not a little late for games?'

'It is never too late for games. Or for chess. Indulge me.'

The Princess glanced away from those sharp dark eyes, back to the board. The pieces waited, but not in their opening ranks.

'But this game is already advanced.'

'I have taken the liberty.' Renard's voice was gentle. 'Between skilled players, the opening stages of any game are so predictable. We have played them often, you and I. It's the endgame that intrigues, do you not think? You may choose either colour.'

'I do not like my moves being made for me.'

'But there are certain moves you are powerless to make otherwise.'

Elizabeth allowed a smile to come. 'Are we still talking about chess, my lord?'

There was a shrug, a hint of hardness now in the voice. 'Choose – white or black?'

The game was seven moves in and white had already seized the middle ground. Black was in a good defensive position though and, despite a sudden urge to carry the attack to the enemy, Elizabeth knew that her survival depended, as always, on caution. Especially against an opponent such as Renard.

'I will play black.'

'A wise choice. You have the next move. My last was there, my knight to the centre.' Renard moved away from the table. 'You will not mind if I do not sit. Hard stools do not agree with me.'

Resisting the impulse to give up her own, leather-cushioned chair – she had gained that position and would not surrender it – Elizabeth concentrated on the board. Her own knight was under threat. Should she move up her queen or bishop? As she studied, she was aware of Renard drifting up to the mirror, aware of his reflected eyes upon her. She rolled her shoulders, planned her move, awaited his. It came.

'Have you seen Her Majesty, your sister yet?'

'I am sure you know I have not. My entreaties to be allowed into her presence have been denied. So far.'

'Ah yes. Sad that sisters should be so sundered. Especially at this time.'

'This time?'

He had turned to her now. 'To succour her in her pregnancy. You know she is not far from her term.'

Elizabeth kept her voice even. 'I had heard, my lord, and I rejoice in it.'

'You . . . rejoice?'

'Of course, my lord. I know how my sister longs for a child.'

'"Rejoice" – a curious word.' Renard had moved, was still behind her but to the other side. 'You rejoice at a birth that will deprive you of the crown? That will guarantee the Catholic succession you deplore? Wouldn't you rather rejoice if the Queen was to die in childbirth and the Spanish brat with her?'

It was a sudden attack and she swivelled in her chair to meet it. 'I desire no such thing. And you are a brute and a slanderer to suggest I do. The Queen will hear of this.'

Instead of meeting her anger with anger, Renard laughed, a sound devoid of any humour.

'Come, Elizabeth. The Queen will hear nothing of you, save what is ill. Last week she called you, when I and others stood by ... let me see, oh yes, it was a bastard, a heretic and a hypocrite. And she prayed again for the fruit of her womb to deliver the country from you.'

Elizabeth rose slowly, the anger tight in her chest. 'It is by listening to men like you that my loving sister has been poisoned against me. Yet she is the Queen and may call me what she likes, however false those titles may be. You, Ambassador, may not call me anything but "Your grace" or "My lady". And I will not stay to be so abused.'

She moved to the door, waited there, her back a barrier to the man who began now to applaud.

'I had heard that you delight in masques and revels. I did not know you had absorbed so much of the player's skill.' Receiving no reply, no turn of her body he went on. 'Come, my lady. Shall we stop this game?'

'Isn't that why we are here – to play?'

'Perhaps. But I have a proposition for you, a secret to tell you, better than any game. Would you hear it? Come, return to your seat. Come. Let me share a secret known to maybe five people in this whole kingdom.'

The door would not open until he commanded it. She had made her point, won it even. She sat again, as Renard moved around before the table.

'*You* would share a secret, my lord?'

The Ambassador leaned forward, fingertips resting on the table edge, his eyes beneath the heavy veil of his lashes fixed upon her.

'The Queen's pregnancy is false. Her desire for Philip's child, for the heir to a Catholic throne, for the sign of God's Blessing so long withheld in her years of hardship, this desire is so strong that she has conjured herself a phantom baby – a shade so powerful it brings her a swollen belly and milk to her dugs.'

Elizabeth's first thought, heaved with sadness into her heart, was, *Oh, poor Mary.* But she would not reveal that emotion to this man.

'And how do you know this? How do you know for false what so many others believe to be true?'

'Her closest lady-in-waiting is my ... confidant, herself the mother of three. Her doctor tells the Queen what she wants to hear and then tells me the truth.'

'And what of this? If it is true my sister will learn the sadness of it eventually. Within two months it is said.'

'What of it, indeed. That is where my proposition comes in. Though now I think on it, maybe "ultimatum" is the better word.'

'It is not a word I respond to, Ambassador.'

Renard went on as if he had not heard her. 'All that matters to the Queen is her belief in this answer to all her prayers. She is convinced she will deliver a healthy child. What would she do to the person who would harm that beautiful baby? If she believed, say, that witchcraft was being practised against her and her innocent unborn? Would anything save that person, no matter who?'

Elizabeth almost laughed. 'I have been accused of almost everything in my twenty-two years, Renard. But I have never been known as a witch!'

'No,' the Fox replied, 'but your mother was.'

It was as if those words stopped air from entering her body. She could not breathe in for a moment, and the words that forced themselves out seemed as if they were the last she would ever be able to speak.

'My ... mother?'

He saw her pain, leaned in to savour it, his voice low and hard. 'Anne Boleyn. A whore, certainly. A heretic, undoubtedly. The woman who stole Mary's father's love from her mother, breaking her heart, breaking the Church. You wonder that she will not see you? Every time she looks in your face she sees the cause of all her woes imprinted there. Sees that bewitcher in you.'

Somehow, air came in again, and she used it, and the next breath to muster her defence. There had never been proof against her. No one had ever proved anything, it was why her head still sat on her body. This ... absurdity could likewise not be proved.

'What will you do? Take a poppet with "Boleyn" smeared in goat's blood and a pin through its belly? Place it under the

Queen's birthing bed wrapped in my kerchief? My sister may have her great desire but she will not be blind to cozenry of that sort. She will not condemn a sister on such a falsehood.'

Renard's eyes had grown large as she spoke. 'They say you have a good eye for archery, my lady, and you are so near the mark. But a poppet? Oh, I think we can do a little better than that. Something that can be placed there, under that bed, something so distinctive it could only have come from that whore, that heretic, that witch, your mother.'

'What object so distinctive that it could condemn one of the Blood Royal?' Elizabeth's voice was strong again.

The dark eyes gleamed. 'Why, the very symbol of her magic. Her six-fingered hand.'

Her stomach threatened to void through her parched throat. With it came disgust, outrage. Once more they were trying to use her mother, the woman she hardly knew, who yet lived in every pore of her body, filling now with fury.

'You have violated my mother's tomb, stolen her bones, to threaten me with this?' She was out of the chair now, her face thrust up into Renard's. Surprisingly, he leaned away.

'The hand was not there. It confirmed a strange story we'd heard. Men have been dispatched to find the resting place of this unique . . . relic. As we speak, it is probably on its way to us. We hope to have it within the month. Within the time span of your sister's remaining hope, anyway. And then, we can use it or . . .'

'Or?'

'You can agree, with oaths and papers signed, to prior contract to marry your sister's husband, Philip of Spain, on the sad circumstance of the Queen's death.'

And there it was. A simple sentence, simply spoken, the core of the complex web. Strangely, instead of being more enmeshed, Elizabeth felt almost free. She had plucked out the heart of the mystery. England, her England, locked through her in the Imperial-Spanish embrace, within the bosom of the Holy Church. This was the ultimate. There was no greater danger to be faced. Her breathing began to grow normal, a trace of a smile appearing, as it often did, when the mask returned to her face.

'Well, Ambassador, you would have me think on this?'

If Renard was disconcerted by the change in her, he did not

show it. 'Of course, my lady. You have a little time. As I said, the relic should be with us soon. And your sister still has her hope. The game, for the moment is paused. It is your move.'

Elizabeth looked down then, to the tiny warriors below in their ivory and black ranks. 'Of course it is. And I may take this board away with me?'

'It is my present to you, my lady, as I said. I have this game on another board at my lodgings.'

Elizabeth reached down, moved a piece to cover her knight.

Renard leaned forward. 'Your queen? Is it wise to bring her out so early?'

Elizabeth smiled. 'As you said, I only have a little time. And the queen is the most powerful piece on the board, is she not?'

The door opened to three raps of Renard's hand, her hooded guide beyond, beckoning her to follow. She kept her eyes fixed ahead, her head high, ignoring the stares of the kitchen lackeys. When they reached the dark stable yard she clutched the chess box tight to her bosom, as if to ward off the night breeze. Yet the cold was not outside her but within, where Renard had laid it. She felt it spreading, pulled the wood even harder into herself, so that a sharp corner gouged through her dress and marked her skin there. Focusing on that pain helped her stave off the other that threatened to overwhelm her. If she was in her quarters she might have let it burst from her, where others would not see her weakness, report it. She had between there and the west wing to master herself, to begin to plan. The game was not yet over.

After Renard had closed the door, he went immediately to the opposite wall. Running his hand down the panelling his fingers encountered a catch which he flicked. A door swung open and a man stepped out, short of stature, richly dressed, pulling at the small white ruff around his neck that hung over the gold brocade doublet.

'Christ's Wounds, Renard. We cannot breathe in there any longer.'

The man fell gasping onto a chair, while Renard stooped into the little chamber and pulled the door partly to, just enough so that he could look out through the mirror. The room seen, from that side, through slightly convex glass, spread away from him, outer objects blurry, the King at the table perfectly clear.

'A marvellous device is it not, Majesty?'

'Yes, yes.' Philip had regained his breath, moved back to stare into the mirror, scratching at his trimmed, pointed red beard. 'It's remarkable. One really can see nothing from this side. She was looking straight into our eyes. It was . . . disconcerting!' The series of 'esses' came out on that Castillian lisp that Renard found 'dithconterting' himself. The English mocked their 'Thovereign' relentlessly for it behind his back.

'Italian, you say.'

'Venetian, Majesty. Though it is said they learned the craft from the Turk.'

'Really.' The King moved around to look out through it again. 'We tell you what else disconcerted. Her eyes! Extraordinarily fine, eh? And her skin – like a milk maid's, is it not? Eh? Eh?'

'Indeed. So your Majesty will not find his part in the game too tedious?'

There was no hint of mockery in the voice, but Philip of Spain looked at Renard sharply before moving back into the room.

'We wish you would stop referring to it as a game. We are dealing here with affairs of the highest order. The preservation of the Faith in this island. An alliance against the treacherous French. And we do not like the way you speak to . . . to our future consort. We still think that our wooing would be enough. We do not think these threats made against her, with their taint of sorcery, are necessary. She is a princess, my future Queen. You must remember this.'

Renard made an elaborate bow. 'Your Highness is right in this as in all things. The one sister, your sad Queen, dotes on you as on some Greek hero. How can the other sister resist you?'

Philip, King of Spain, heir to the Holy Roman Empire, uncrowned King of England, again looked for something behind the words. In his entire time in this rough kingdom, he and his court had been subjected to the barbarous native 'wit', and he was sensitive to it. But Renard was his ally here, his subject and servant. Someone he had to trust, even if he didn't particularly like the man from Franche-Comte.

'Well, we shall see. We will do our duty.'

Renard saw the smile come again into the Spaniard's brown eyes. Philip was nobility incarnate, courteous, charming and, to a woman, not unhandsome. He could see why poor Mary so adored him. He could see Elizabeth, beset so with her enemies, desperate for any friend, falling too. Goaded on with a push from a six-fingered skeleton.

Bowing to usher the king out, Renard lingered on that image and smiled. The game was advancing, with pieces of power nearly ready to be brought into play. He just had to clear a few pawns out of the way first. Yet pawns, as every chess master knew, were important. Vital even. Following Philip from the chamber, he wondered where some of his pawns were now.

SIX
BROTHER SILENCE

In the walled garden of the Jesuits, scents assaulted the Fugger's nostrils like waves of soldiers storming a breech. His back was against one of the dozen cherry trees, blossom heavy, thick bulbs of petals shedding some of their number to float by his face, settle on his hair, his clothes. In the earth beds before him, herbs released their unique fragrance, each struggling to outdo its neighbour. On one gentle breeze, lavender would predominate, the swathes purple and prominent; then would come the softness of camomile or the barest hint of clary sage. There was tangy citrus, a bergamot tree in bloom. Nearer the house, all he could see were the bushes of rosemary, their delicate pink flowers bursting forth and when that savour reached him he turned his face away again, tried to resist his overwhelmed sense. Rosemary was for remembrance and, if he and his were going to survive, he had to force himself to forget.

Suddenly, the wind changed, swept now from the town below, bearing its different aromas, more fitted to the cast of his mind; for under the salt of the sea was the corruption of the harbour, rotted wharves, rotting fish, rotten humanity. He had arrived in Tuscany here, at the harbour of Livorno, nearly twenty years before. It had been a fetid stew then and was still despite this demi-Eden hidden behind its Jesuit walls.

Nothing changed. He'd arrived then in search of Anne Boleyn's hand, and he was leaving on the same quest. When the tide turned, in a few hours, they would be sailing for France.

They let him sit there, no manacles to hold him, one soldier dozing in the shade of the doorway the only precaution against a man with barely half a hand climbing the high walls. Gianni had come out just once in the afternoon, glanced at him, said something to the guard and gone back inside, busy with his preparations. He had his father's certainty, that was clear, and he had decided that the Fugger was barely worth the watching. And he was right – for as long as that locket swung at Gianni's neck, Maria faced terrible harm and the Fugger was as powerless as he had ever been in his life.

He had attempted to talk to the boy he'd once taught Latin and Greek, but Gianni had walked away, wanting no news of his family, giving no reason for his actions. Only his other captor, the Jesuit, Thomas, would listen and the Fugger had poured out much of what he'd wanted to say to Gianni, about family, about loyalty and love, until he came to the story of the hand and he realized that the Englishman's smiles and his eyes focused softly ahead, were weapons and the listener was on the side of the enemy.

As the sun finally dipped below the wall, a bell sounded in the little tower. The gardeners laid down hoe, fork and spade and made toward the house. Thomas appeared in the doorway, sought the Fugger, beckoned.

'I know you have little appetite, friend, but eat you must. We will sail with the night tide and I think our days at sea will not be so well-fed.' He took the Fugger's mangled half-hand. 'But let me first change this bandage. The herbalist here has distilled a new compound from a plant sent from our missionaries in India, blessed by the hand of Francis Xavier himself. He says this "jasmine" has a beneficial effect on the blood. We need to get more into your hand if we are to save it.'

The Fugger allowed himself to be led away from the stream of people moving into the food hall, to a little table where a tincture was applied to his wound, the whole wrapped in fresh linen. Thomas's gentle questions he ignored. The bandaging done he followed the black-cloaked figure into the hall.

Though their men ate with the rest of the Brothers and their lay counterparts, Gianni, Thomas and the Fugger joined the leader of these Jesuits, Nicholas, a garrulous Neapolitan, large of body, short of hair, at the small separate table reserved for honoured guests. Thomas's papers, from the Emperor and the high offices of the Society of Jesus, granted them this special favour. One that Thomas felt he could have done without as Brother Nicholas was starved of conversation, far from the intrigues of Rome, and wanted to give his opinions on all that was wrong, all that should be done. Thomas would have preferred to listen to the lessons from the Bible being read at a lectern at the room's end, but out of politeness he nodded in agreement, made the occasional comment. Gianni ate sparingly, drank little, said nothing, listened to everything. The Fugger merely stared at the plate before him, until admonished in a whisper to eat by Gianni.

'You won't cheat us that way, Fugger. If you die from lack of food, who will take the locket to Rome to free Maria from those guards who must be so amusing her by now?'

Brother Nicholas had despaired of stimulating conversation. 'I was in a silent order once.' His voice was plaintive. 'Three years, on the coast of Denmark – of all the places I have visited in this world the most barren and isolated. The ignorance of the people there was astounding, in everything, that is, except fleshly sin. Even within the monastery. No, especially within the monastery. I've disapproved of mute observation ever since. With words, at least you can accuse people of their sinful acts. That's why here, I encourage talk, debate, discussion. We need words. Do you not agree?' He was speaking, pointedly, straight at Thomas.

The younger Jesuit smiled. 'I think there is a time for words, certainly. How else are we to spread the knowledge of God's love, of his forgiveness of humanity, demonstrated in the sacrifice of his only Son, the Redeemer?'

'With actions.' Gianni's voice was quiet, intense. 'Words are weak tools, too easily misinterpreted. Actions – decisive, bold, true – they are unmistakable. The sinner ignores the words that urge him to repent his sin. He can't ignore the firebrand thrust into the pyre at his feet.'

Brother Nicholas was surprised at the torrent his own words had produced and not displeased. *Debate at last!*

'Well, Pope Innocent the Third agreed with you, young man. "Action ranks higher than contemplation," he said.'

Thomas's eyes had not left those of the young man opposite, for the cleansing fire Gianni talked of burnt there, the first time he'd revealed any such flame.

'Forgiveness is an action too, is it not?'

'Forgiveness ... is a word.'

The fire had disappeared, eyelids snuffing it. Thomas noticed that the Fugger had looked up from pushing food around his plate, was now staring at Gianni intently. Behind him, behind Brother Nicholas, one of the lay brothers was reaching forward to refill his master's wine goblet. Thomas had noticed this man in the simple wool cassock before, among the herbs, a hood pulled down well over his face. Noticed him because he seemed not to want to be noticed ... no, desire was not part of it, he simply wasn't present unless you chose to single him out with a look. It was the sort of oddity Thomas noted, a large man who moved like a small and stealthy one. He'd tried to speak to him, to question him about the jasminè. A finger had pointed an answer, the only reply he received. To forestall the next esoteric point bound to be coming from their talkative host, Thomas gestured to the man pouring the wine.

'And yet within your domain some have chosen a wordless world, Brother Nicholas.'

The Neapolitan looked around, started a little. 'Ah, he always does that to me. You can be quite certain you are alone in a room, maybe testing out its acoustics, eh? And he is standing there like that. Yes, yes, pour my wine.' He held up the goblet. 'He has earned his name well, for in my five years here and, I am told, in the fifteen before that, he has never uttered a single sound. He hears, he obeys, he ... treads around. Softly. But he does not speak. Can't, probably.'

'And his name?'

'Not very original, I'm afraid. They call him Brother Silence.'

The goblet rose beside the Fugger and his eyes rose with it to the hood that had opened somewhat so that the face within was partially exposed. Not much of it, the right side, and he thought, at first, not even that because it did not seem to bare any aspect of man. Where the eye should have measured the pouring, there was a puckered depression, a socket of old scar tissue with a darker red slash from the missing eyebrow to the top of the cheekbone. The nose looked as if it has been partly burned off, a nostril that was little more than a flap of skin resting atop a gash of a mouth. As the man bent, the hood opened to the other side and a solitary eye gleamed there, as blue and pale as ice on a carp pond. It was a ruin of a face and in a moment, the Fugger saw again another face, laughing in a roadside tavern in Bavaria as he chopped off the Fugger's hand, howling in a dungeon within a kaleidoscope in a palace in Siena, finally shrieking his death agony at a crossroads in the Loire – the same crossroads that the Fugger was leading these men to now. At each encounter there had been terrible pain and it had ended only when that ruined face was punctured by the Fugger's dagger. He had killed a man called Heinrich von Solingen at that crossroads, finally, certainly, nineteen years before. But gazing at this silent brother's hideous scars and the blue eye, he could almost believe he hadn't. That thought, of nightmare beyond words, brought him to his feet, crashing the chair to the floor behind him, had him running for the door before the meagre contents of his stomach could void his body.

His guard followed him, stood in the doorway, as the Fugger vomited again and again, long after all that came was bitterest bile. In a bed of lavender, pressing his face into the sweet-scented herb, pressing through the branches to the earth below, he sought to hide his own face and the ruined face, deep in the Tuscan earth, as he had once hidden just these horrors in a gibbet midden. Buried there, somehow his breathing came back to near normal, his eyes focusing on the purple stems he'd crushed beneath him, his nostrils filling with their fragrance, clearing the vision from his head. Another came, from that same time, when his mind had been taken over by savage secret potions, and a Black Mage called Giancarlo Cibo had tried to raise the spirit of a dead queen using that queen's six-fingered hand. Anne Boleyn *had* come but only to the Fugger, she had saved him, given him the courage he needed to fight, to help Jean Rombaud, in the fulfilment of his quest.

As he lay there breathing in the scent of purity, he saw her again as she had appeared to him, in the whitest of robes, thick black hair cascading down onto her bare shoulders. The spirit of a Queen giving him the power to act as he never had before – with courage. He had betrayed her once, for his family, betraying his best, his only friend, Jean Rombaud, with a Judas kiss.

'No!'

He buried the silent scream in the herbal bed. He could not

betray them again. Not even for the daughter he loved beyond life. There had to be another way.

Groping forward with his bandaged hand, the Fugger encountered the first step of that way. His back to the guard who had followed him out, he raised himself up from the lavender bed onto his knees.

'Help me, friend, for mercy's sake,' he cried.

The guard came forward, muttering. When he was about a pace away, the Fugger gripped the shovel handle as best he could, supported it with the stump of the other hand and swung up and over. The metal plate caught the man on top of the head, but the Fugger didn't wait to see how good the blow had been. Not very, he suspected. Enough, perhaps, to see him into the cherry tree and over the wall.

Erik had circled the Jesuit compound a dozen times, always ending up beneath a blossom-heavy tree, whose overhanging branches allowed him a perch to sometimes study the house within. As he leaned against the wall, he was feeling quite pleased with himself.

'You see, Father,' he muttered, 'I have followed, waited, watched. I have not stormed the house. I have not killed anybody. Yet.'

He hoped the waiting would not go on much longer. For one thing, he was starving and if there was no movement from his quarry soon he would have to leave his post and steal some food. For another, the longer he lingered there, idle, the more his thoughts turned on Maria, and the only fear he'd ever known. He had followed the Fugger because he was the only connection to his missing love he could find in the falling city. He was the father of the woman he loved and, if Gianni Rombaud was involved, the Fugger was in terrible danger. Erik had grown up with Gianni, knew better than any of the parents the darkness that had taken over the boy's soul. He also knew his intelligence. That's why he was so pleased he was waiting outside the compound, under clouds of cherry blossom. He had out-thought Gianni Rombaud! He would wait for him to make the first move that night – then take him in the dark.

A sharp *clang* brought him from this reverie, and the groan that followed it had Erik leaping from his squat and up into the branches, pushing through the petals. There was enough light left to see the two shadows running to the tree, his tree, both stumbling through the herb beds. There, the first figure tried to leap up, but failed to get a grasp, a bandaged hand flailing as he fell back to where the second man was even now reaching for him, with curses and outstretched arms, a step away.

A step he never took. It had taken Erik one second to leap up into the tree. It took him just another to drop down from it. The reaching hands of the guard found a huge and solid chest. The eyes came up in shock and Erik headbutted the man between them, at the bridge of the nose. He fell like a tile from a tower, instantly silenced. The other man had jumped again, even managed to get one arm around a tree branch before he slid back down, moaning.

'Fugger! Fugger!'

He raised his bandaged hand to ward off this new threat, then lowered it when he recognized the voice. 'Erik? By all that's holy, how . . .'

'Time to go now. Time to talk later.'

He hoisted the Fugger up onto the lower branch, climbed up beside him, straddled from tree to wall, then lowered the Fugger down the other side, dropping him into the soft earth there, where he began to scramble away. Erik caught him, held him.

'Fugger. Where is Maria?'

'Rome.'

'Rome?'

'Come, I will explain. We must get away. They will be after us and I cannot run fast.'

'You do not have to. I have a horse. There.'

The two men ran to where the animal was tied and the Fugger was lifted up again. Erik mounted behind, gently nudging the reluctant beast with his heels. They had gone a mere hundred paces, walking on the sandy verge till they were out of hearing of the Jesuit house, when the Fugger let out a groan.

'Are you in pain?'

'Yes! What have I done? My daughter! Oh, my Maria!'

'What of her? Tell me.' Erik jerked the reins, halting the horse. 'We do not move until you tell me.'

In jerky sentences, the Fugger recounted what had happened, all Gianni had said and done. It didn't take long and when he was done, Erik said, 'And this locket? The one that will free her. He has it?'

'He wears it round his neck.'

'Then I must take it from him.'

Erik slipped off the horse as he spoke. The Fugger reached down an arm.

'No, Erik. There are too many of them. And they will be doubly on guard now. We need help if we are to stop them in what they are planning. It is a great evil.'

'I do not care about that. Maria's in danger.'

'Erik . . .'

'There is a barn just as you leave the town to the south. Hide there. I will return with this locket by dawn. If I am not there by then . . .'

'Wait!'

It was no good; the youth had disappeared into the gloom. The Fugger almost followed, until he remembered how crippled he was. He would only hinder. Cursing his helpless state, he prodded the animal toward the south.

When the guard was found, they didn't know how long he'd been unconscious but it had taken less than a minute to muster and dispatch the rest. It took less than thirty for the first of them to return, reporting failure in a mumble, avoiding the young man's furious eyes. An hour later all the men had drifted back and 'nothing' was still all they could report.

'It would be difficult enough, in a harbour town, at night, with fleets preparing to sail. But now we know he has help . . .' Thomas looked across at the guard, just conscious, still trying to stem the blood flowing from his broken nose.

'And what do you suggest we do, Jesuit?' Gianni made no attempt to keep the acid from his voice. 'Give up? Soothe the situation with *words*?'

Thomas felt his own anger rise, took a deep breath to quell it. 'I suggest we look to where he will go. Anticipate his actions before we take any of our own. He is not a well man. We still have his daughter. I think he will enlist help and then go for her.'

Gianni was pacing around the small table where Thomas sat. The refectory hall was empty save for their party, Carafa's men, at the large table, muttering in low voices, drinking the wine that Brother Silence dispensed. They were all booted, spurred and cloaked for travel.

'So what are you suggesting? That we go to Montalcino where his "friends" are and wait for *that* siege to end? Then break people who have never been broken? Or make for Rome, stake out the prison, hope the Fugger decides to drop into our web?' Gianni leaned on the table, bringing his face close to the Englishman's. 'I will not return to tell Cardinal Carafa of failure in the first task he has entrusted to me. I have waited too long for him to notice me.'

Thomas stretched his leg out, rubbed at his knee. 'I do not know we have many other options. He must learn of this, as must the Ambassador in London. This . . . relic. It would have been a useful point in the tennis match, but it is not the whole game.'

'But it is. It is!' Gianni thumped the table hard. 'You speak of games? You do not know the curse that was laid on my father by that witch of England.'

'And "the sins of the father are visited upon the son". So it is revenge you seek? Or atonement?'

'I seek the glory of God, Jesuit.' Gianni held Thomas's stare. 'And believe me, I would rather go to France and dig up every crossroads outside every village, beneath every gibbet in the Loire, than kneel before Christ's representative on earth and tell him that the guilt of the Rombauds still lives in this world.'

'Carafa is not Pope yet.'

'He will be. And the gift I was to lay before St Peter's throne was the six-fingered hand of that great heretic, Anne Boleyn. I will descend to the lowest reaches of Hades to find it.'

In the silence that opened between them, a voice entered. It was a voice that none of them had heard before. Indeed, it had not been used for nearly twenty years. There had been nothing in all that time the speaker considered worth saying. He was not sure this was either. But he said it anyway.

'The village is called Pont St Just, a day's ride from Tours. To the south, there is a crossroads. A gibbet stands there. Four paces from its base, where the four roads meet, a casket is buried. Within it rests the hand of Anne Boleyn.'

While the voice spoke, for a little after, no one moved, as if the sound held them in some binding spell. Gianni and Thomas's eyes remained fixed on each other, the guards' goblets of wine frozen where they had been when the voice reached them. It was croaky from disuse, yet it had carried into every part of the hall, each word clear as if it hung in the air like smoke from the fire, drifting, like that same smoke, to the open window where it reached a man perched outside and above it on the stone lintel. But Erik, like everyone else, did not move. 'How do you know this, Brother Silence?' asked Thomas, gently.

He considered. *Did he need to add any more to what had been said?*

'I was there. I saw it buried.'

He hadn't thought about that night at the crossroads in nineteen years. But now, in the question of their stares, he did – and remembered everything. How the one-handed man, that same man he had served wine to this evening, had leapt from a gibbet midden and plunged a dagger through his eye. How he'd fallen but not lost consciousness, his other eye open, unpierced, so he had not lost all his sight. All he had lost, in one moment of terrible pain, was his discrimination, his ability to care about anything he saw, or felt, or heard. One agonized moment, and all the events of his life, the triumphs, the cruelties, the men he'd killed, the women he'd taken, all turned into shadows dancing on a wall. Nothing worth talking about.

He remembered everything from that moment on. Saw again the head of Giancarlo Cibo, his master, severed by the flying sword. Saw the French executioner, Jean Rombaud, take the witch's hand and bury it in the centre of the crossroads by the light of a full moon.

The silence extended so, in it, he remembered everything thereafter. How Rombaud and the others left, and the villagers came, thought him dead, took him when they realized he wasn't and might be worth a ransom because of his rich clothes. A barber-surgeon removed the dagger lodged in his head. Somehow, to everyone's surprise, it didn't kill him, though death came close in the weeks that followed. But when he'd recovered and still wouldn't speak, when they couldn't find out how to profit by him, they turned him out onto the road. It led south, by diverse paths and ways, till one of them crossed that of a monk returning from pilgrimage, a kind man, who took him for charity and because his size was some protection on the road, taking him all the way to his order's house in Livorno. He stayed on when the order was abolished and the Jesuits took over the house, and he had just carried on silently doing what he had done ever since a dagger had entered his eye and changed his world. He tended to the gardens, and served the travellers and pilgrims who rested there. If their plates needed food, he piled food onto them. If their goblets were empty, he filled them with wine. And if they needed to know where Anne Boleyn's hand was buried, he told them.

He bent forward, poured wine, waited. He assumed that more words were coming, now he'd decided to speak. He didn't mind waiting for them, he was comfortable with silence. It was the name he'd lived by for nearly twenty years, once he'd stopped being Heinrich von Solingen.

There was nothing Erik could do. The Fugger had been right, there were too many of them; Gianni, and the locket, always in the thick of his men. He'd clung to the lintel and listened to the extraordinary tale. He'd followed them to the harbour and right up to the ship, considered stowing aboard. No opportunities came and, anyway, a voice began to work in his head, an unfamiliar voice speaking of caution rather than immediate attack, telling him of a better way than discovery at sea and a watery grave.

So he watched the ship sail on the night tide, then rode for the barn on the outskirts of Livorno. Briefly, he told what had passed.

'Then hell has broken its bounds.'

The Fugger sank down into the stale hay, his legs losing their ability to support him. The glimpse that had merely reminded him of his old enemy had been enough to spur him, vomiting, into the night. The thought that Heinrich von Solingen had triumphed over death – for it could only be him – took away all the little courage he had mustered. Erik, on learning who it was, merely whistled.

'So I have seen the Bogey-Man.' Von Solingen had been the stuff of nightmare in all their childhoods, a goad to good behaviour. 'Well, I am glad I saw him leave on a ship.' He leaned down to the Fugger, his face flushed with his excitement. 'They all left, Fugger. Every man including that German monster. Do you know what that means?'

The Fugger barely shook his head.

'It means they sent no message to Rome. No punishment for your escape. Gianni must be too busy with his great work. It means Maria will still be alive, till their return. It means we have time to break her out of this prison.'

Erik smiled. This was the thought that had occurred to him at the docks, why he had let the ship sail without him. Action delayed could lead to more glorious action.

The name of his daughter seemed to revive the Fugger. He struggled to his feet.

'First, Jean must know of this, that the evil he nearly died to oppose is again upon the earth, incarnate in its most awful servant. Poor man, all he wants to do is have the rest he has earned. Yet I fear his sword must wake again in his quest.'

When the young man had helped him onto the horse then mounted behind him, he spoke one word.

'Montalcino.'

SEVEN

THE RUIN OF ALL HOPE

They came through the woods just after dawn, for though the spring foliage was not yet far advanced, the trees would still shelter their approach. The rigour of a night spent in a ditch had stiffened Jean's body, and each step was a jolt through his sinews, no matter the softness of the forest floor.

The track widened into a small clearing, the trees around it mainly sweet chestnut. The ground was covered in last year's husks, the once green-furred shells now brown and cracked.

Anne paused, looked around them, smiled. 'You were ambushed here once. We pelted you with chestnuts till you surrendered to us. Do you remember?'

Jean turned, dug the point of his stick in anew, leaned again. 'I don't. Who was "us"?'

'All of us.' Anne took the rope-wrapped bottle from around her neck, uncorked it, handed it to her father to drink. The morning air was chilly, but the sweat still showed on his face. 'Erik, Maria . . . Jojo.' She used Gianni's childhood name, but it did not keep the shadow from her father's eyes. She continued hurriedly. 'You made us gather all our "weapons", and Mother made them into a pie. Remember?'

'Your mother used to make wondrous pies.'

Jean turned back to the path. He didn't remember, didn't really want to. More and more, it seemed impossible to separate the good memories from the bad.

'Let's rest here a little, Father. I'm tired.'

He didn't look back this time, no smile for her caring lie. 'No.' He drank, handed back the bottle. 'We go on. Whoever's there may still be asleep and that will give us our chance. I'd like to be back in Montalcino by midnight.'

Midnight! They had set out late and it had taken a day and a part of both nights to arrive here. And he wanted to be back inside the day!

He still calculates distances like a mercenary, by forced march, she thought, as she watched him limp on down the path.

He moved quickly now, spurred on by the closeness of the goal, and it was not till the edge of the forest, under a copper beech that had once been one of her thrones, that she caught up with him. He had rested his shoulder against the trunk, his head angled around it. She knew his eyes were not for the long sight, that the building he stared at on the next rise was more blur than structure.

'The Comet,' he said, and the hope in his voice made her throat tighten.

Let it be as he wants, she prayed, *Holy Mary, let him have his reward.*

She did not usually conjure the names of the Church. She knew so little about it, despite all her brother's efforts to save her. But a mother and her suffering son she understood.

They left the shelter of the wood and began to move cautiously into the vineyard. The light was still pale but it was enough for Jean to see what was wrong.

'Look at the roses, Anne. They have not cut them back. How will they give warning of disease?' He pulled at one, sucked at the finger that bled. 'And look at the vines. Unpruned, since we left. And the weeds!' He swished at some with his stick and she could see his excitement. 'Lots of work when we get back. Come, let us see what they have done to the Inn. If it is as neglected as the fields, then no one will be there. We can move straight back in.'

They had covered half the ground, were fifty paces from the building when the side gate banged open. They froze, had not even the time to sink into the red earth, before a man emerged and began relieving himself against the wall. He was singing and even though Jean could see the gawdy clothes he was wearing he didn't need his eyes to tell him what the man was. The tune was familiar, even if the words had changed a little since Jean's day.

The farm lass, the weaver's trull
They both will bend for me.
For I am he, who's fit for she
Who craves the Mer-cen-ree.

A mongrel dog began barking an accompaniment to the song and ran from the gate, pulled up a pace out of it by the chain around its neck. He continued barking, his muzzle toward the watchers, until the soldier voided himself on its head. It yelped and ran back inside, to be followed by the laughing, yawning man fumbling at the ties of his breeches.

When she turned back to him, Jean's eyes were downcast, his body shaking slightly. 'We have seen enough.' His tone was flat, dead. 'Let us return to the city.'

'Father, we don't know how many of them there are. He may be alone.'

'Mercenaries are never alone.'

'You were.' She put a hand on his arm, felt the shudder within it. 'Father, rest by that broken wall, by the pine there. I will take a closer look.'

'You will not.' The voice quavered. 'I forbid it. These are dangerous men.'

'And we live in dangerous times.' She squeezed his arm. 'Wait for me over there, Father. I will not be long.'

And she was gone, walking swiftly around the corner of the outer wall. Jean took a step after her, cursing. But his legs did not seem to want to work properly and it took an effort to make his way even the short distance to the broken wall. Falling behind it, he wondered for a moment why he had never knocked it down. Crouching, his heart seemed to beat loud enough to echo around the crumbling brick, the sound bringing another echo, a memory, called up by the resiney scent of the overhanging pine. For the flash of that moment, the dawn light faded, the moon came up, he was gazing down at Beck's naked body, striped by silver beams and realizing he had never seen anything more beautiful in his whole life. They had made love here the first time and later, when his vow to Anne Boleyn had been fulfilled and they came back here to live, when his body had recovered from all the torments it had been put through, they had made love here again, often. That was why he had never knocked down or rebuilt this wall, never altered any part of it. Their love had been moulded here, of pine needles and brick dust. Their children were conceived here, form of their joined forms.

And as he thought on them, the memory flashed away, replaced by his concern for one of them. Raising his head cautiously, he stared at the corner she'd disappeared around, and tried to draw his daughter back.

They'd approached from the rear of the inn, so Anne now moved to its front, facing the road that led to Montepulciano. Half the gate hung by one hinge, while all that remained of the other were the brackets that had held it. Peeking round, Anne could see up the drive to the house. It was unrecognizable from the gravelled path that had welcomed travellers to what had reputedly been the finest tavern in Tuscany. The small cypresses that had lined the path were gone, mere hollows in the ground now. Lemon, bergamot and olive had filled the yard with their fragrance, but these too had been torn up, fed to the insatiable flame of the fires that smouldered all around. Bodies sprawled before these blackened patches, heads resting on saddles or field packs, plumed hats covering faces, hands stretched toward the flagons and cups that had rolled away from them. In this, the dawn hour, the soldiers' sleep was heavy with snores and the occasional muttered phrase.

There were fifty at least and that meant there were even more within the house, though looking up, Anne realized that the roof would not give better protection than the sky, as most of it was gone. So a hundred men – and their camp followers, for skirts were dotted among the breeches – now called the Comet home, though no one would do to their own home what these scavengers had done to hers.

She began to turn away from this desecration, tears in her eyes, when something made her pause. It sounded like a voice, though she was sure it did not come from one of the soldiers or their concubines. No more than a whisper, yet it carried from beyond the yard. The voice was sexless, timeless and it said, distinctly, 'Come.'

There was no reason for her to enter. There were perhaps a hundred and more reasons why she should not. She had seen all she needed, a ravaging of her childhood home, the end of her father's hope. Only further despair awaited within the danger. Yet the voice was compelling and somehow did not seem to threaten her. Taking a deep breath, she entered.

The path was as occupied with bodies as the lawn and she picked a wandering path between the clumps. When she was halfway across, a soldier, younger than the rest, threw aside the thin jacket spread to part cover him, grabbing at her ankle with a little cry.

She froze there, waited. He held her, squeezing tight, muttering some plea or prayer and so she bent down to him, drew the jacket back up to his neck, touched his hot forehead with her cool hand. She whispered, 'Sleep, child. Be at peace.' The boy calmed, a smile came, and he released his grip on her. She moved on. When she reached the main door, she hesitated. The courtyard was to her left, the place where she had first heard the tale of the woman, the Queen, for whom she was named.

It drew her. She moved inside, passed more bodies to the entrance there. The door to the courtyard was gone, taken to feed some soldier's fire. As she stepped through the gap she saw the magnificent chestnut tree had gone the same way, whittled down to a stump that reached blackened spars waist high from the cracked tiled floor. It was like a broken barrel, could only be empty, yet she stepped forward to look within it.

Something glinted in the charred depths. She stretched a finger to it, rubbed the ash away. A tiny cross lay there, but she did not pick it up immediately. She knew it, though it was grimy now, its silver tarnished with the years, blackened with the smoke which must have passed over it as they burnt the tree around it. Its twin cross struts made it unique, something their father had brought from France. He had given it to Gianni one day, and the boy had loved it wholly and utterly from the first moment.

It had been hard between them for a while, as she knew it often was between fathers and sons. Erik had chafed under Haakon's strict rule. But between Gianni and Jean it was different; especially after Gianni had returned from the monastery where Jean and Beck had reluctantly allowed the God-loving boy to go and study. He brought back not only an increased, almost fanatical devotion to God, but a pain lodged in his eyes. And his father's godlessness now obsessed him. The cross had been Jean's last attempt to reach his son with love.

She touched it now, let her fingers close over it, and the night filled with blossom and old smoke, the tiles under her feet became whole, and her mother was preparing food in the kitchen as Anne laid out the platters and knives on the table. But her mother was not singing and her father had gone to town, to trade he said, to hide, she'd said. And Gianni came to her, crying, the first time she'd seen that in years for he was near a man now. And he took her hand and pulled her up into the tree, leading her, climbing with one hand, holding her with the other, as if the two of them were one person, climbing like they used to, like they hadn't done since Gianni came back from the monastery.

High up the branches, they heard their mother call them and he begged her with his eyes to stay silent. When Beck went inside again, he held the cross up before his tear-run face and said, 'This will wait for me, Anne. I will come back for it one day. To prove that once he loved me.' With swift strokes from a little hammer, he tacked the cross to the tree. And then he was gone, the supper growing cold for him, the cold spreading between her parents. And there was nothing Anne could do to warm it.

As the memory faded, she gasped. The cross was burning the centre of her palm, but she could not let it go, for the pain brought a vision of her brother, as he was now, the boy's face hardened into a man's. Determination was there, as it had always been, but cruelty was there too and something else – a zealot's desire. She cried out as the metal scorched her but more because she looked into the vision's eyes, her brother's dark eyes, and knew he was about a great evil.

Then a voice suddenly spoke from beside her, the vision was snatched away and the cross slipped to the ground. Anne started, blinked and the voice spoke again.

'There's not enough work for us. We don't need no new recruits.'

Anne turned to a woman, her skirt torn, its rear muddied, a ragged shawl around bony shoulders.

'What?' she whispered.

'You heard!' The woman's voice was as hard as metal, the eyes dull and dead, the pox scars livid on her cheek. 'Pretty thing like you? Think they'll look at us after? Thought you'd cash in, eh? Leave now. Or I'll do for you myself.'

The woman lifted her skirt, fingers moving to where steel gleamed. Anne stepped around her, bending to scoop up the cross from the ground. As she brushed past, the woman reached out, gripped the wrist that held it.

'Heh, what's this? What do you have here?'

The voice was louder now, and it brought mutterings from within, so Anne hit the woman as her mother had taught her to hit men, with the heel of her hand, striking up to the point of the chin. The woman's head snapped back and Anne caught her before she fell, their faces close, sour breath from the woman's lips, lowering her to the ground. Since voices came from the house now, she turned away, brushed past the stump, leapt and scrambled up and over the wall of the inner courtyard. The soldiers still slept beyond it and she threaded between them, leaving at the side gate, joining her father who rose anxiously from his hiding place.

'By the Wounds, Anne, you were so long. I heard noise . . .'

'Come. They have woken up.'

As she led him at a run through the vineyards, she heard a screech and then shouting from the house. They would be awake soon, all save the woman who could tell them what had happened. She would be unconscious a little longer, long enough for them to be deep within the forest.

As she ran, Anne opened her pouch and dropped the cross into it. She heard a clink as it nestled next to Guiseppe Toldo's falcon.

Oh Gianni, she thought, *what deeds are you about now?*

They made Montalcino just after midnight, for Jean would barely rest and it was now Anne who struggled to match his stride. She had told him only a little of what she'd seen but it was enough to drive him forward, widening the distance between himself and his shattered dream. It had been such a little hope and, now it was crushed, there was only movement, pushing through his constant pain, the journey from despair to desired oblivion.

The gates were barred and the guards there did not recognize him, would not let him in. Fortunately, Giscard, Blaise de

Monluc's adjutant, was making his rounds, heard the argument, and intervened.

'You must forgive them,' the young officer drawled, 'they are of this town and have not yet heard the story of the last triumph of Siena before its fall. The defence of the bastion at the Porta San Viene, the blowing of the tunnel, your sally to rescue your men! Quite brilliant, Monsieur. It was an honour to be there.'

He had climbed the steep streets with them, the final stretch to his billet sapping the last of Jean's strength. For his status, he had been given a singular privilege – a whole room for himself and his family, in a house next to the monastery of San' Agostino. He leaned against its door now, as the officer removed his plumed hat to bow.

'The General expects you at the war council tomorrow. The call has gone throughout the land and men will soon be gathering around our standard. Siena may have fallen but the Republic lives on. We will need your skills and courage again. Captain Rombaud. Mademoiselle.'

He bowed, reserving an especially gallant smile for Anne, and departed.

Jean did not even have the will to mutter a curse. 'Get me in, child,' he said.

But there was no rest beyond the door that Haakon flung open.

'Rombaud!' he bellowed, enveloping the Frenchman in his huge arms, lifting him across the threshold. 'You made good time, man. And you arrive just when the action begins, as always. Come, they have wine here, real wine, not like that vinegar we were drinking in Siena. Montalcino won its siege, so they have wine!'

Anne went straight to the back of the room, where blankets served as curtains over a bed. She did not even pause when she saw a bright-eyed Erik and the Fugger sat at the table. There was a more important question to ask first.

'Mother, how are you?'

Beck's eyes were open, if somewhat dull, her head was cool enough, her heartbeat steady. There was no mistaking the firmness in the hand that gripped Anne's.

'Well, child. Better than I have been in an age.' She nodded past Anne to the room beyond. 'They have brought me news of my Gianni.'

Anne started when she heard her brother's name, felt a burning in her hand. She looked down. The outline of a cross was still there, its twin crossbeams clear.

Beck struggled to raise herself, Anne placing rolled blankets behind her. 'Open the curtains. I need to hear what they are saying there. So do you.'

The Comet was disposed of in a few sad sentences, Jean summing up what Anne had told him. She had not mentioned her encounter in the courtyard. She had not been able to find words to describe it.

'Well,' Haakon grunted, 'if the Sienese and French can win their fight, they will kick those Florentines out for us and we can go back.'

'Is that the action you are so excited about, Haakon?' Jean asked wearily, gulping wine. 'Haven't you had enough of this war?'

The Norseman's eyes gleamed. 'I have. They don't pay enough. No, the action I speak of is more personal. You will think so too, when you hear what the Fugger has to say.'

Jean was tired. He hadn't even noticed the fact that the companion he'd mislaid in the fall of Siena had returned. He looked at him now through drooping eyes. He thought he would fall asleep at the Fugger's first words, sleep and never wake. *What sort of bliss would that be, an endless, dreamless sleep?*

But the Fugger's speech woke him in an instant.

'I have seen your son, Jean. More, I have seen the evil he is about. Such evil that it has raised the dead.'

The Fugger told the story swiftly, sparely. Beck, who had only been told that her son was alive, slipped back lower onto the bed as she listened. Anne sat unmoving beside her, rigid, as the vision of Gianni returned, stronger now his purpose was revealed. Jean stared, first at the speaker, then above him, finally across the room at Beck, whose eyes would not meet his.

It was Haakon who spoke next. 'This is the action I spoke of, Jean. The two actions, though they are linked. Fighting on two fronts is never good strategy but I believe there is no choice. We' – he gestured to his son and the Fugger – 'are going to Rome. We will swiftly find a way into the Lateran prison and we will free Maria. Then we'll come after you, to aid you on your front.'

Jean's mouth seemed unable to make enough spit to speak. He took a sip of wine, said, 'And where will I be?'

Haakon laughed, his son echoing him. 'On the trail of your son, of course. You heard, Anne Boleyn's hand will be unearthed. Why, man, do you not see?' The Norseman thumped the table. 'The quest begins anew.'

In the silence then, Beck finally met his eyes. Held them, while she made one clear motion of her head. *No.*

Haakon didn't see it, went on with the same enthusiasm in his voice. 'It should not take us long. With the Fugger's mind and our strong arms, what chance do these Roman dogs have? But while you wait for us, you won't be alone.' His voice deepened, some emotion quivering there. 'You will have another old friend to look after you. Erik?'

He gestured and, with a shy smile, the young man reached behind him, picked something up, placed it on the table before Jean.

'I was doing mine anyway,' he said. It was no trouble.'

Jean's sword lay on the table before him, the pommel toward him, the bottom third of the blade protruding from a new soft leather sheath, a different weapon than the one Jean had seen, ragged with un-care, as they fled Siena. The grip was once again wrapped tight with green leather straps, as good a binding as Jean had ever done. The guard and apple-sized pommel both gleamed with the lamplight bouncing off their polished surfaces. And he could see, even before he leaned forward and ran his finger over the bright cutting edge, feeling the slightest of cuts there, how keen the blade was.

'It's as sharp as my scimitars. Sharper! It's a fine weapon!'

'Toledo steel,' Jean said softly, 'the finest there is.'

He looked again to Beck. And she spoke. 'You will not use it. Not in this cause. Not against your own son.'

Haakon blustered, 'I did not mean that, Beck, of course. It's for the German, Von Solingen. Gianni will see reason, he'll . . .'

She had waited for an answer. Haakon's words she ignored. When Jean stayed silent, she went on. 'You fulfilled your vow. I helped you do it, though you and I, the Fugger and Haakon so nearly died in its doing. Januc did die. It's over. Leave it be.'

Jean still would not speak, just stared back at his wife, so Anne did.

'Mother, I saw Gianni, here,' she touched the side of her head, 'in the courtyard of the Comet. The Fugger is right . . . he is about evil. I do not know the extent of it. But evil it is and we have to try to stop it.'

Beck laughed, a sound of bitterness. 'You want to stop evil, daughter? Then do not go to France to seek it out. It begins at our front door and it runs from there through all the world.'

Beck raised herself from the bed, her feet reached the floor and somehow she was standing. Not even Anne moved to help her as she shuffled to the table's end and looked down at her husband.

'What do you care about the destiny of queens and countries? They have destroyed your home, broken your body, killed your friends. What do you care which faith rules? You are the most godless man I know.' He shuddered then, made to look away, but she leaned down, holding him. 'You drove your son away. Now he is about his own quest, one he believes in as much as you ever did in yours. It is the same story spun in the beginning of the world – fathers age and sons grow bold. Leave. It. Be.'

She sank then, finally, the last of her strength used. Haakon put a stool under her; Anne came to hold her arm. Five heads faced Jean from the end of the table, questions on every face.

His finger had stayed pressed against Toledo steel. Looking down now he noticed that the blade was as true as its promise, for blood flowed there, dripping onto the table. In it he saw his answer.

She was right. He had shed enough in this cause, could shed no more. And in his heart of hearts, he knew this truth – even if he had still been strong, he had no courage left to shed blood with.

'My wife is right. I have done enough. My duty now is here. To her. And to Anne . . .' He faltered on the name. 'My daughter, Anne.'

No one spoke again, and in the silence his weariness returned five-fold. Rising he shuffled past them to the bed and turned his face to the wall, away from their demands, away from the concern and the disappointment in their eyes.

EIGHT
RUNE CAST

It was the middle of the afternoon before Haakon returned from organizing his journey and Anne was able to take his arm and lead him outside the door. The Norseman was distracted – he needed horses and horses were at a premium in a town preparing for war. His eyes were focused over her head, musing on theft, so he did not hear her clearly when she whispered her request.

'Runes?' She shooshed him and he went on more quietly. 'Child, I have taught you all I know. You have the meanings as well, probably even better than I, for age is robbing me of memory.'

'But I do not have the sight. Without that, they are like letters in a language that is dead to me. I cannot read them. You have to teach me.'

Haakon sighed, as the bell of the monastery struck three above them. 'It cannot be . . . taught. It is a path that you must walk alone.'

'And I will. But someone must lead me to where the path begins. My desire is not enough. Someone led you.'

It was true. For a moment Haakon saw his mother again, taking the frightened yet curious boy to the forest, giving him his murdered father's legacy, twenty-four disks carved from a narwhal's tusk. Leaving him there alone for three days and three nights.

He sighed again. 'Anne, this takes time, which we haven't got. It also takes a forest or some other still place and none are near.'

'Then we must make time.' She almost hit the big man in her frustration. 'Haakon, I cannot see what it is that threatens us. I just know it is a terrible thing and my brother is at its dark heart.

And I can see this also: if my father does not try to prevent it, he will waste and die here, where his sword sleeps.'

Haakon was silent, these words taking away any he might have.

Seeing his face soften, she added, 'And I know a still place, close by. Will you help me place my foot upon the path?'

Despite his need, he could see that hers was as great. His too, for he loved Jean Rombaud beyond all men.

'I will.'

It was not a forest. Any trees near Montalcino had long since been chopped down to feed the furnaces of war. But Anne led Haakon out of the north gate, where the land was gouged with a series of little streams running through the vales they had carved, steep-sided, barren of any path save those made by rabbit or fox. A scrambling route took them beyond the sight of the walls, through thick bushes sharp with thorn, down to a stretch of running water that they could only walk down by straddling the flow. Gradually the stream widened, forcing them onto a narrow path along one bank. Eventually they came to a small pool, sheltered by seven silver birch.

Lowering himself upon a stone, Haakon gasped, 'How did you ever find this place?'

'Father brought Gianni and me to Montalcino when he came to sell his wine. We escaped his watchfulness, ran outside the city, came here. Will it serve?'

Haakon looked around, listening to the wind moving through the young leaves. 'It may. The birch is a tree of great power, none is better for our purpose.' Seeing her smile, he cautioned, 'But this is a difficult art we attempt, Anne. Do not hope for too much.'

She came to him, offered her hand. 'Shall we begin?'

Haakon allowed her to help lift him. Pulling a knife from his belt, he went to a tree, ran his fingers down one of the black patches that lay under the scaly, pale bark.

'This one is older, in her prime. She may not mind sparing us a small part of herself.' He beckoned. 'Here. I will lift you up. Cut that branch off, close to the trunk.' He placed his cupped hands so she could stand in them, and when she was balanced against the tree, he added, 'And ask the spirit of the tree permission before you take one of her little fingers.'

Closing her eyes, Anne uttered a short prayer, stating her need. Her forefinger and thumb, circled, could meet around the branch and the sharp blade sawed through in less than a minute. She descended, handed knife and her prize back to Haakon. He turned the pale wand, twice the length of one of his arms, over and over in his hands.

'It is even for most of its length, see? You could carve a set of runes from it, if you had the time.' He looked up into the sky, sniffed. 'We don't. We have time for just one.' He handed her the branch. 'Hold it and seek the rune of your need.'

She began to look around her, at tree and water. He reached forward. 'No. Not out there. Seek in here.' And he pressed the branch's cut end into her forehead.

She closed her eyes, the peeling bark edge digging into her skin, and she began to think of all the runes, of all the stories connected with them, hearing Haakon's voice back in the courtyard of the Comet, as he spoke of saga and legend, of heroes and giants, endless winters of ice and night, brilliant, brief summers. Some stories she had loved and their symbols crowded forward, offering themselves, yet she knew memory would not serve her; this was new land, not to be read by old signs. Breathing deeper, she settled within herself and a shape came to her. She opened her eyes. Haakon crouched before her.

'You have one?'

'Yes, but it is strange – I cannot remember its name.'

Haakon frowned. 'Then draw it for me. Here in the mud beside the stream. Use the wand.'

It took but a moment, a slash down straight, then a diagonal from its top to the right.

'Do you remember it now?'

She stared at the mud glyph. The slashes were beginning to fill with water. 'It's water, isn't it?'

He nodded. 'Lagu, in old Norse. All fluids, not just water. That which pours out of a woman at birth. The sea, rain falling. Beer.' He smiled. 'It's good for intuition and for love. For following your heart.'

She felt strangely empty. 'But what does that tell me? I cannot see into my heart. I sometimes feel there's nothing there to see. I watch Erik and Maria, you with your Michaela, may her soul rest in peace. Even Mother and Father . . . before. I have never had that in my heart for any man. Maybe that's why I cannot see with it, cannot read these omens that frighten me. Because I cannot open myself up here.' She struck herself in the chest with the butt end of the wand.

Haakon sucked at his lower lip. After a moment, he said, 'You're wrong. I have seen you love. In the way you heal, the way you touch. Perhaps you need to clear what's ahead. Perhaps it is this dread that is blocking it.' When she did not respond, he took the end of the stick, pulled it away from her chest. 'Come, shall we try to see if we can find your path?'

Her voice was small. 'How?'

He pulled her by the stick to the rock he had sat on.

'Here. Use the knife again, cut a disk about the thickness of my thumb.'

She did so. The scent of sap filled her. He took the stick, leaned it against the tree.

'Now, you are going to cut Lagu into this disk. Just two strokes, like you did in the mud, but before you do, clear your mind. Put me, this place, the world of woe, put them beyond you. There are no omens to frighten you here, no past or future. There is only this moment. Time that is and time that is becoming. Water flowing, life proceeding from that flow. Speak the words that speak to that.' He took her hand, laid the blade upon her palm.

At first, it seemed that Haakon's words grew louder, echoed around her distorted, the reverse of what he'd asked for, mocking any effort to be calm. Coldness seized her, hands became so clammy she nearly lost her grip on the knife. Her need, all her desires, her terrors crowded into the air around her like carrion birds descending on a corpse. She saw a leering Gianni, a weeping Beck, Jean Rombaud turning his face to the wall. Then she saw another man, a grotesque, a gargoyle, features eaten away as if by burning pitch. She wanted to run from them all, to use the knife to cut her way past them. But then she heard the sound of water again and knew that the only escape lay in diving deep.

It wasn't water, it was blood, blood that was to come. Haakon had said that Lagu was all liquid and she held onto that, clutched the knife by the blade to use its point and it was as sharp as all Haakon's weapons were, cutting the thumb that balanced it to the bone. Blood dripped then upon the wood, that was the sound she'd heard and she bent to it, made two slashes in the young, reddened disk, one vertical, one diagonal and as she made them she intoned, 'Life flows. Fall into its flood.'

It took a thought, no more.

She was before a hut. In the centre of its door the rune, Lagu, was inverted, vulnerable as a wounded creature with legs thrust into the air. All that could be good in it was stagnant, full of ill omen.

But I know that.

With her thought, the rune began to shimmer, dissolve, vanish. As it went, she noticed tendrils of smoke rising from the sod roof of the hut toward a black sky. Someone was inside. She rapped on the door, once, twice and again.

A voice that seemed familiar spoke a word she'd heard before, at the Comet, only the day before. 'Come,' it said, and she pressed against the door which gave grudgingly, dragging across the rough earthen floor of the entrance. As soon as she was inside the door, it vanished in a soundless instant, along with all walls, all structure, swallowed by gloom. The dark was like a weight pressing her and she raised her hands to ward off its threat. She was lost in it, floating, for the ground was not solid, the roof immeasurable, the walls a distant hope of solidity. She screamed then, though no sound came, or if it did it was sucked into darkness, feeding it, making it grow denser.

There was a choice – to surrender to this darkness and let it take her where it willed, or to move forward in whatever direction that might be. She only knew that her hands were before her face and with an effort she stepped after them. Instantly, if faintly, a light shone far away, a flicker in a fog. She had a direction now and she moved towards it.

The light came from the flames of a fire. They licked at the side of a great cauldron suspended over them. When she was close she saw a hand reach over the cauldron, releasing something into it. The mist cleared completely then, the air filling with a sweet savour, like incense but lighter, floral. Anne saw that a woman crouched there, feeding the pot.

'Welcome,' she said, and stood. She was as tall as Anne, though as light as Anne was dark, golden hair falling in thick waves upon her shoulders, upon the richest of gowns the green of apples, studded with cornflowers, like a meadow in summer. Her eyes changed colour in the light, now a deep green, now an ethereal blue, couching and reflecting back the flames.

The voice was calm, light. 'What is it that you seek?'

Anne felt what was in her hand, held it out. It was the birch disk, the symbol on it etched in blood.

'Lagu.' The woman reached forward. 'Life-Bringer, rune of rain, oaths, hope.' She touched the disk and Anne saw that it was now reversed, as it had been on the door. 'Lagu, rune of treachery and despair.'

'Which is it for me?'

'What will you give me to see?' The voice had changed to a lower note, not as dulcet in tone. Around the now grey eyes, little lines had appeared.

Anne thought, *I have nothing to give*, then realized her pouch was still at her side. Reaching into it, she felt Gianni's cross. Next to it was a wooden shape.

She pulled out Guiseppe Toldo's falcon. 'This.'

The woman nodded, though the hair that once had swung on her shoulders now hung limp around a pallid face. She said, 'Throw it in.'

Shuddering, Anne did as she was bid. The falcon tumbled from her fingers, head first as if it stooped to the depths below, seeking prey . . .

A shrill note, piercing. A feathered blur shot across the sky clutching an awful prize, not caught according to its nature, hit on the wing, but stolen from a grave, plucked rotten from the earth as if by any carrion vulture. The bird flew high, seeking a perch to feast, but even at that great distance Anne could see, with eyes as keen as any falcon's, what it held there in bloodied talons. She could even make out the tiny sixth finger . . .

And where the bird passed, where the grave-flesh fell, the land blistered. A cloud blotted out the sun, and iron-tasting rain stung her face. Sickly calves wandered orphaned next to a choked and bloated river that had flooded the fields, mud churned across to the village where a church bell struck a single note again and again, while rag-clad people scurried from building to burnt building. One fire raged in the centre of the village, a pyre, a cross in its middle, something struggling to escape. The falcon swooped over it, cried again, stooping for yet more easy prey, a blur of feathers falling onto her from the sky, talons reaching for her eyes . . .

Anne swayed before a cauldron, in a dream within a dream, where a toothless crone in shredded finery fed a fire with foul-smelling dung. Anne gasped, almost pitching into the pot, 'Is this the choice of worlds that will be?'

The crone chuckled. 'What business do I have with your visions? There are many worlds, many paths leading to them. Nothing is written till the pen meets the parchment. Nothing set in motion till the rune is carved and thrown.'

Anne looked down to the disk of birch in her right hand. Suddenly she saw, in the red-lined slashes, in the straight and the diagonal, the flow of water there, feeding the world. She turned it and saw that water pool, grow stagnant, because she'd failed to keep it upright. And as that thought came, the room around her began to dissolve, to shrink, the roof pressing down, the cauldron turning to a pot, the flames beneath mere flickers with no heat. The crone was poking at its contents with a stick, looking up suddenly as if she only just realized that Anne was there.

'Go,' she croaked, 'find your own. There's not enough here for two.'

Anne turned, pushed through darkness . . .

She opened her eyes, closed them against the rain, breathing in the scent of flowing water, hearing a breeze riffle through the branches of seven silver birches. She opened them again, to a night sky and Haakon's wide face above her.

'You have returned. I was concerned that you might not.'

He helped her sit up, fetched water from the stream. She drank carefully, savouring its sweetness, while he squatted patiently by. Then she told him what she had seen. He listened, silent. When she began to tell him what it meant to her, he raised a huge hand.

'I do not need to hear. Words cannot tell this, for speaking them will change what you have felt, as the telling always does. I only need to know what you will do with what you have seen.'

'I have to speak to my father. I have to change his mind.'

Haakon nodded. 'Then let us return and begin. I think you have as grave a task ahead as the one you have faced here. For Beck will not like your vision.'

It was a city heady with freedom. Spring sunshine dappled every cobbled street, red-tiled roof, and church basilica with a brightness that matched the citizens' hopes. The exiles from Siena had been met by their cousins of Montalcino with the best of food and wine, with new clothes, an abundance of weaponry, shelter, a chance to heal, to rest, to not wake each night with the terror that the Florentines had breached the walls and were storming through their streets bent on rapine and revenge. Soldiers greeted old comrades with a firm handshake and the kiss of brotherhood. Children mingled and played on the streets. In the loggias, under the porticoes, the men and women gathered to talk of freedom, of the proclamation of defiance sent to their recent conquerors, of the reinforcements sailing from France and the volunteers marching from all over to join the crusade against the usurpers. The Republic of Siena was still free, and rallying to its banners.

Jean walked through this joy like a phantom, unseen, unseeing. He had attended the war council earlier that day, where 150 men had crowded into a small room in the Palazzo Publico, listened to the speeches, the plans to take the fight back to the enemy. He had kept silent throughout, his head bent, even when his name was mentioned and Blaise de Monluc designated him a commander. He would take the title, because with it came a greater share of the Republic's bounty and the ability to feed his own. He would find ways to avoid acting his role, in his wife's sickness and the wound all knew he had sustained. Mostly in his reputation, glossed by his 'victory' at Porta San Viene, the Republic's final defiance in the siege, the story blown like glass, puffed up with the need for good news within the fall.

He knew he was a straw man, without substance, reduced to caring about nothing more than survival. The news of his son's betrayal, of both himself and the cause of his life, had confirmed that, for in the terrible moment when the Fugger's words came out, it was not the violation of Anne Boleyn, his Queen he thought about, only the threat to himself. It was Beck's eyes he sought because he knew he would find his escape in them, his excuse. Some vestige of him, some husk, still wanted his friends' good opinion, and his love for wife and daughter was the only reason he need give them for not pursuing his cause again.

Now though, walking streets filled with men and women who still believed in something, the memories he'd tried to shove aside came jostling back, fresh-minted through the gap of time. There were years he had felt like this before, straw filled, using his sword to take heads, gain rich purses, only to buy himself yet another flagon of the best wine, another woman, to forget, for a moment of lonely release, his precious first wife and child, his Lysette and Ariel and their plague-smitten bodies laid in the ground. Anne Boleyn had ended that life that was not a life, given him a vision of heaven, a cause, the quest to regain and bury her hand leading him through extraordinary hardship to extraordinary happiness. In the end, he had triumphed, taken his reward of Beck, his children, his life at the Comet. But maybe his son was right, maybe the sins of his life had weighed too heavily in the scales. Torment had followed too brief a joy and he was a straw man again.

When darkness came to the streets, he felt no urge to return to his lodgings, though abundant food awaited him, befitting his new title of Commander. Beck awaited him there too and that was no lure. She might not want him to go, but neither did she especially want him to stay, for when he lay beside her on the bed, Gianni lay between them. Haakon, the Fugger, Erik would be there as full of hope as any Sienese Republican. Anne would have returned, but he knew what he would see in her eyes and he had had enough of disappointment. So he slipped into a crowded tavern, took a flagon of the heavy wine of the region to the darkest corner, away from the boasting and the martial songs and began to drink. Maybe solace could be found near the bottom of his bottle.

It wasn't there, and only a single gulp had passed in his search through a second when a large shape appeared before his table.

'Haakon.' He nodded at an empty chair. 'Sit, there's wine enough for both of us.'

The Norseman sniffed at the flagon, shook his head. 'I'll wager

there's better at your lodgings, newly delivered ... Commander.'
He leaned down. 'Can I escort your eminence there?'

'Eminent arseholes. Let's finish this one first, eh Hawk? And
maybe its twin?'

Jean made to pour but a large hand delayed him. 'It's our last
night, Jean. We leave for Rome at dawn. And Anne ...' He
hesitated then went on. 'Anne has something to tell you.
Something of importance.'

Such little effect as the wine had had left him in that instant
and he stood, followed Haakon out onto the street. Dread grew
with every step he took.

The room was filled with the savour of roasted meat. Erik had
turned the hearth's spit industriously and the results lay on the
table: two partridges, a grouse, three pigeons, a skewer of
starlings, a brace of rabbits. In the centre, four capons, breast to
breast. There was a rib of Chiana beef, glistening with juices, pink
meat, thick fat golden around it. A wheel of dense bread that
could have supported a cart lay at the table end, bowls of olive oil,
thick and green beside it, next to a slab of goat's cheese, its
whiteness bursting through a coat of fine ash.

Five people sat around the table. All of them had spent the last
months living on a handful of barley floating in thin gruel,
flavoured with whatever rank and salted meat had survived the
winter. Their mouths filled and emptied with saliva as the scents
assailed them, yet not one reached forward to the feast. Their
hands lay idle in their laps, their eyes fixed on a sixth person
standing there, their minds filled only with her visions.

Anne related what she had seen in the world beyond the world,
told it simply, neither dwelling on nor diminishing any part of it.
She had begun with eyes closed, partly back in that land of
memory, but found that she needed sight as she went on, that
seeing was part of the way forward. She needed the eyes of the
listener, to search them for understanding. Yet only one of the
people she most needed returned her gaze and the strength
challenging her almost caused her to falter. She stuck to her tale,
however, concluding it with simple words.

'That is all I saw, the first to the last of it. Help me with it now.'

They all waited. All knew to whom the appeal was directed and it was he who had to answer. He knew too, and the man who had avoided her eyes finally looked up and met them.

'There is no other interpretation?'

'I can see no other, Father. The sixth-fingered hand, if it remains unburied, will bring this harm.'

There was a harsh intake of breath.

'Well, I am no visionary, but even I can see another here.' Beck's wound pallor was stark in the candlelight as she leaned into it. 'Maybe the land will be all the fairer for its purging, as woods are cleared of their dead timber by a gale, only for the whole to grow stronger. As a sick body mends when it is purged of blood – even if you don't even believe in that, daughter, though all the world does.'

'I don't. But, Mother, it is the feeling behind the vision that is as important. When have I ever got that wrong?' Off her mother's silence she continued. 'When I saw the failure of the harvest, we husbanded our plenty for the next year, saved ourselves and many others. When the plague was far off, I took us to the hills. And when Gianni was sick, I already had the herbs planted that kept him alive.'

'So your vision is limited!' Beck's voice was bitter. 'Why save he who will be about such evil? Surely better for all to have let him die then.'

'No. Because this story was not written then. It is made by everything that has happened since. Every path chosen.'

'And Gianni's path? Do you deny him his choice?'

'No.' Anne's voice was as calm as her mother's was harsh. 'But I know I have to try to stop him on mine.'

'You? A girl of eighteen?'

'The daughter of a woman who, at eighteen, rescued her father from a sorcerer's cell, her husband from a torturer, who married him even when her father forbade it. The daughter of a man who followed his own vision to the borders of death and back.' She smiled. 'Would you have me deny my lineage?'

Erik thumped the table, said, 'Well-spoken, Anne.' He had always been a little afraid of her, her certainty, her far-seeing eyes. But he had always admired her courage.

Beck went on as if no one had interrupted. 'I would have you obey us. I forbid you to journey into such great danger for a cause long dead, one that has nothing to do with you. Your father forbids it. If he will not pick up his sword for this cause, then you will not. And as we all know – Jean Rombaud's sword sleeps in its scabbard.'

They were out, the words no one wanted to hear, and Beck wanted them back the moment they were gone. Not only for their cruelty, retaliation for his words at the bastion in Siena, but also for the challenge implicit in them. Haakon and the Fugger shifted uneasily; Erik turned away, poked at the embers in the hearth. Jean flushed, the heat bringing sweat to his forehead, chilling the moment it appeared.

'Does it, Father?' Anne's soft voice felt like a stick beating him. 'Even after all I have told you, will you let it sleep still?'

He had to look at her. 'If I forbid you to go, will you obey me?'

There was only a flicker of hesitation. 'I have never gone against your wishes. Yet I cannot deny my vision. I was raised by people who never denied theirs.'

'Then it seems I have no choice.' He forced his voice to go hard, somehow stopped the shaking in his hand enough to touch the hilt of his sword at the table's end. 'Time to awake, old friend.'

There was instantly a lot of noise. The other three men exhaled as one, and Haakon was up in an instant, slapping his friend on his back. Erik took the opportunity to grab a rabbit, his teeth swiftly severing the meat from the bone. Anne simply closed her eyes and smiled. It was a moment before anyone realized that Beck was speaking.

'So you have chosen once again. Your cause over your family. This queen, whom you barely knew, who nearly robbed you of your life, over me. You have chosen not only to drive our son away, but to pursue him with your enmity.'

Jean said, 'Beck . . .'

'My name is Rebecca bat Abraham. And I was told what would happen when I married outside my people. My father begged me to think on our traditions, but my love for you blinded me. For a while we were happy, for a while . . .' Her voice cracked and they could all see the struggle as she tried to centre it again. 'No matter. Now I am punished for my sins.'

She was moving toward the door now, every step painful.

'Mother, where are you going?'

'There are members of my tribe here, even in this place. I know some of them, have always denied them my greeting. Maybe I can begin to atone.'

Anne was beside her, a hand placed on Beck's arm. 'You can't . . .'

'Can't?' Beck rounded in fury. 'You try to command me? You have proved you can disobey, but I think commands are yet beyond even you. Let me go!'

The hand dropped and Beck, after a struggle, opened the door. On the threshold, she paused, looked back.

'I do not need Anne's gifts to see this future, Jean Rombaud. It is clear as if the hand of God had written it on the sky. If you try to thwart him in this, our son will kill you – and I will not wait here for that news. I will not . . .'

Finally her voice did break, and she was gone, leaving curse and prophecy hovering in the air. It was the Fugger who finally cut through it.

'I will see her safe.'

Anne gathered some things, though she was having difficulty seeing. A cloak, the last of her cordial, some of the food were all shoved into a sack and the Fugger departed. Closing the door behind him, Anne turned back.

'Father . . .' she began, but Jean held up a hand. Silently, stiffly, he rose from his seat, shuffled over to the bed.

'We leave with the others at dawn, Anne. Will you see to it?'

Haakon stood at the table end, his face contorted with emotion. 'Jean,' he said, 'she will not keep to this. She'll understand that this is what you must do. She . . .'

The gruff voice trailed off as Jean passed close to the Norseman, giving no indication that he heard him. Lying on the bed, he drew the blankets around him. Beck's scent, her sickness, herself, entered him. He turned his face to the wall, so no one could see his tears.

NINE
CROSSROADS

Rain fell in huge drops, thudding into cloaks long since saturated, deafening within the hoods. Streams found gaps, carving channels over chilled skin. Thick mud sucked at their boots, a sticky bond formed with every step, and wind drove against them. Jean longed to mount the horse he led forward, but they had ridden all day and he'd need the horse's strength to ride away from whatever lay ahead. The final stage of any journey always seemed the longest, but never had it proved itself more so than this evening's march toward the crossroads at Pont St Just.

He'd been thinking of the last time he had approached it, how then he'd had hope, broken in body though he'd been. An end was promised, at least, either in the fulfilment of his vow, or in his death. This time his hope was confined to such a tiny chance, that the hand was still there, they had somehow travelled the faster and his son had not violated its resting place. Then it could be buried again somewhere safe and he could turn back. Yet he did not need Anne's long sight to sense that even such a little hope was futile, that the crossroads ahead held no end for him, only the beginning of another, even harder journey. A crossroads of the mind as of the earth.

He turned to the figure beside him, cloaked and bent just as he was, pushing into the water and wind. Anne had tried to keep his spirits up in the two weeks they had been on this chase, through storms at sea, fleeing brigand ambush in the mountains, via all the flea-infested inns if they were lucky, the roadside ditches if they were not. Now, he could see that even her store of faith was nearly spent, her body sustained only by her will, driven by the visions that tormented her.

As he studied her weariness she looked up, summoned by his gaze. She raised eyebrows and he glanced around, mouthed, 'Not far,' though his glance had told him nothing; the weather and the dark wiped out even the edges of the forest to his poor eyesight. There was mud a pace ahead of him and the pace after that. They could be hours from their goal or one minute away.

Then, as if an unseen hand had suddenly stopped pumping, the rain slackened and, in the next instant, ceased. A little light came upon them, as the waxing moon peeked through shreds of cloud. They halted, threw their hoods back, their horses nudging into them. The wind had changed, blowing a little warmer from behind them now, up from the sea they'd long left behind. They turned their faces to it, grateful to absorb it for a moment.

Without opening his eyes, Jean said, 'Shall we rest here, beneath the trees? Dry out and then go on at dawn?'

He hoped she'd say yes, delay the inevitable that awaited them. He knew she wouldn't.

'I think we should keep going, Father. And did you not say there was an inn at Pont St Just?'

'There was.' A memory came, of wielded blades, men dying, a first glimpse of a dangerous enemy. 'It may not still be there.'

'Let us hope it is. A double reason to go on, then.'

'Aye. But let's ride at the least. These horses have rested enough.'

The mud sucked at their hooves, but the rain had stopped and the wind now pushed them forward. The forest started to thin, some trees were coppiced, or had been reduced to stumps, the trunks for building or fuel. They passed a rough hut, its side walls bulging outwards, a thin straw roof that must have been less protection even than his hood. There was movement from the side of it, and a pig rose from the mud within its pen, sniffed at them, lay down again. Jean thought he saw human eyes peer at them from a doorway, only to dart swiftly away. He had been raised in similar country himself, also in the Loire, knew the terror their passing such a lonely place would have caused. Travellers were rare at the best of times there. On such a foul night, they could only be the Devil's messengers.

The road twisted between two banks, curved around almost on itself, then broke sharply northwards again. Within the glimpses of the moon he was able to see up ahead, to a line of blackthorn at his left, another at his right. The road led to the gap between them, a last twist and corner concealing that gap until they were upon it.

Jean was not sure if he reined in or his horse halted of its own will, but they stopped just as the moon cleared a bank of cloud, dappling the crossroads, glinting off the gibbet beam and the scrap of metal that swung from it. The cage of his memory was mostly gone; only the headpiece remained, rusted, split, yet still retaining the vague form of a man's face, curved out for nose, lips, chin; hanging like heads that had hung from his hands on scaffolds across Europe, raised by the hair to screaming crowds.

'By the wounds!' Jean swayed, felt a hand reach out to steady him, too late, as he slipped from the horse, sliding down its flanks, his legs giving way and dropping him onto the ground. He sat there, in the red mud, and stared up at the mask he'd once stared out from and the years collapsed in on themselves, he looked again through slats, tasted again of that horror, felt, in every tortured bone and ravaged joint, the hurts inflicted on him since the time he last fell to this ground from that cage, each of them flaring within him.

Anne was beside him in a moment, supporting him, helping him to stand and lean against his horse, pressing a rope-wrapped bottle of wine against his lips. He drank, choked, drank again, his eyes gradually clearing till they could focus on the face before him. Strangely, she was smiling.

'Wrong crossroads then?' She spoke like a child and as if she had been promised some treat at their destination. She had that from him, the scaffold humour.

'Happily not.' He managed a half-smile, shook his head, trying to clear it, looked down – and all humour was snatched away. Where he'd landed, at the very centre of the crossroads, there was a pile of disturbed earth, crumbling into a shallow pool. Someone had dug there and recently, for not even the rain had managed to obliterate the trace of it.

He fell again, thrust one arm into the dank water, up to the shoulder, fingers flailing at the edges of the hole. He couldn't believe he encountered the bottom of it so soon. The casket, with its treasure, had been buried far deeper, deep as any grave. Here, there was nothing but mud, water, loose stones. No hardness to give him hope.

He felt Anne's hands on him again, under his shoulders, and he let himself be lifted till he was once more leaning against his horse.

'It is gone, Anne,' he whispered. He was not sure if he spoke to the woman who was there or the one who was not.

She held him there against the horse, feeling his heart shudder, his shallow breaths. She knew he had been sustained by his little hope, that somehow the hand would still be here, undisturbed in its meagre tomb, that his son had not violated his life's faith, that a monster had not risen from the dead. If all that were true and the quest of the hand over, he could return to Tuscany, try to make amends to Beck, seek the rest that, surely, he had earned. She had hoped for it, prayed, in her own way. Yet in her mind she knew Gianni had too great a start on them and in her heart she held the vision of the tormented land.

But which of the four ways do we now take? she thought. Neither the Fugger nor Erik had overheard the grave robbers' destination. Closing her eyes did not help – her visions took in the consequence but did not extend to the practicality of tracking their quarry. In the sky, between tatters of cloud, she could see Polaris, the North star, that they had followed up from the coast. Should they take that road, continue north? Without knowing her brother's intentions, any direction they took could be opposite to the one they needed. She could get no sense of where Gianni was in the world. Back? They would have met him on the road south. East, where a gradual lightening finally showed the approach of day? Down to the coast by the mountains, over the next range and the next and finally into the Italian States, thence back to the heart of his beloved Church? Or . . .

It was when she turned to the west that she saw the figure, a shape she'd taken to be just part of the midden, emerging from the shadows beneath the gibbet, as if drawn by the moon. A hood was bent over, hands tightly clasped against a stomach, the back leant into the wooden upright.

'Father!'

Her gasp brought Jean away from the horse, which, spooked, skittered away with its companion to the field's edge. He looked at her, followed the direction of her hand, froze. At last, when there was no movement from any of them, he whispered, 'Was he here when we arrived or is he newly conjured from the earth? Hell's spawn or human?'

She whispered back, 'I do not know.'

They waited, watched, holding each other. They could see the apparition's cloak was brown, his feet bare in sandals, that a puddle of rain water had gathered in the lap.

'I will go and see.' She took a step forward.

'No.' Jean's throat was dry, the word came out in a rustle. Clearing it, he said, 'I will.'

First, he went to his horse, calming it with gentle sounds, reaching up to the pack. His hand touched the hard outline of a sword hilt beneath some sacking, but he wasn't ready for that. In a saddle holster lay a powderhorn and a pistol, a wheelock. He carefully poured a little fresh powder into the pan, lowered the serrated edge onto the flint. With the weapon held before him he moved cautiously toward the gibbet.

He was a step away when the hood lifted. He thought about firing, put pressure on the trigger, felt it give slightly. A swift pull and the spark would fly, a lead ball would send this demon back to whatever hell it had come from. Then the demon spoke, a single word.

'Rombaud,' it said, and Jean saw within the brown folds of cloth, the face within the shadows. Though it was a face from any nightmare, he knew it had not come fresh from hell. For he had seen it many times, under swung blades, through a sheen of blood, within the walls of agony. Nineteen years before he thought he had seen the last of this face as it fell to this same ground, pierced through the eye by the Fugger's dagger, and though he'd been told this corpse yet walked the earth, Heinrich von Solingen speaking his name froze him where he stood, his useless finger struggling to pull the trigger.

They remained like that until a woman's voice ended the silence.

'Is this him, Father? Is this your tormentor?'

'Tormentor.' The word came to the scarred lips as if they tasted it, the voice without colour. 'I tormented you. I thought to watch you die.'

'By what pact with Satan are you yet living, Heinrich von Solingen? Here, upon this ground, nineteen years ago, I thought I *had* watched you die.'

'Well, you can watch me die now.'

As he spoke the hands clasped in his lap parted and the puddle there Anne had assumed was rainwater suddenly filled with entrails and more blood. The face whitened, the one eye closed.

'No!'

Anne's cry took her forward before Jean could stop her, hands reaching out to push back the awful flow, the remorseless rush of death. And a hand, slick with blood, closed over Anne's there, the grip unbreakable.

It was Jean who cried out now, stepped forward with pistol levelled, and it was Anne's other hand that halted him.

'No, Father.'

She had never been able to bear any suffering, be it a rat in a snare, a rabid dog. Now she held the hand of the man she knew had inflicted such pain on one she loved. Yet her voice, when it came, was gentle.

'Be at peace, friend.'

'Peace. Friend.' Once more he sampled words, the strangeness of them in his mouth. 'I have not known either of these things.'

'You will soon perhaps.'

He looked through her, past her in distance and time, then settled back. 'I have been told I am a sinful man. I can remember the reasons why I am called that. Rombaud bears scars that prove it. But . . .' There was a shudder, a grimace of pain. 'Something happened to me here when that knife entered my head, when I should indeed have died. It cut the cord between the sins and their reasons. I feel neither guilt nor joy in them. They just are.'

His voice faded as he spoke, the eye fluttered as if to close. Then it fixed on hers.

'You have the same eyes as your brother.'

Anne leant in closer to hear, to speak. 'You know him?'

'I led him here. He took what was buried here. He put a knife into me here.' His hands parted to another run of blood.

'You lie.' Jean came forward, the pistol before him. 'Do not believe him. You know your brother. He is many things, but he is no killer. He is training to be a priest.'

The voice came again, a whisper now. 'He is as good with a blade as you are, Rombaud. Maybe better. Hard to tell, as I offered no resistance. He came back for me, when the other, the Englishman, rode off, content to leave me here, since I wouldn't leave. So you have your wish. You can watch me die, upon this ground, and blood of your blood the cause of my death.'

Anne took again the hand that had loosened in hers, placed the other to his head, warmth to its ice.

'Friend, can you help us? Where has he . . .' She flinched as she thought of her brother, the havoc he had wrought here, havoc that was beyond even her skill to heal. 'Where has he taken what was buried?'

She thought she was too late, felt the pulse fade within his hand, sensed the door opening above her as it had for Guiseppe Toldo, as it would for everyone. Murmuring words to smooth the passage, she suddenly felt her grip returned, lips moved.

She leaned in. 'What is it, friend? What?'

Words came. Only a few. Then he was gone. Beyond any doubt, Heinrich von Solingen was finally dead.

She folded his hands back into his lap. Standing, she looked at her father.

'London,' she stated, brushing past him, moving to the horses. 'Gianni's taken the hand to the Tower of London.'

The words sliced through him, severing the vague hope that here would be an ending, that he'd done all he could, that he could not chase the chimera if he had no notion of the direction it had taken. He was at the crossroads again and the way had been chosen.

'London,' he said, as simply as Heinrich von Solingen would have done.

Where it all began. London.

TEN

LONDON

The peril was clear. If Elizabeth didn't take immediate action her defences would be overrun. Yet what could she do? Hope was dwindling, each sacrifice costing her more, him less. On her left side, Renard's white queen had advanced, threatening her king. Now the Fox strove to support the assault with mastery of the middle ground. It could only be a matter of time.

Renard was dictating the game, as he always knew he would. Playing white, he acted and she reacted, it was the nature of chess. Yet he was only playing this game to emphasize his dominance in their other, more vital struggle. Renard's queen, England's queen, threatened to end Elizabeth's game, her very life. And as on the board so in the world, for Elizabeth could not reach her sister. Mary continued to deny her an audience where she might plead her cause. The struggle seemed hopeless.

No! She banged her hand down hard upon the table. Surrender was not in her nature. There had to be another way.

Rising, Elizabeth crossed to her window, seeking an escape through the thick, leaded glass. Above the brick wall a dozen paces away, the tops of the willows on the Surrey bank of the Thames swayed in a gentle spring breeze. They seemed so close, as if she could reach out and touch them . . . were her windows not barred against opening, were the gate in the wall below not locked and patrolled, were she not still a prisoner here at Hampton Court, able to leave her chambers only when some higher authority bid that she must or could. Only three people had that authority: Mary, whose thoughts were poisoned against her; Renard, who liked to keep her close; and . . .

The thought of that one other made her turn to study the

board anew. After a moment, she laughed bitterly. 'Yes,' she said out loud, 'in this, alone, does chess not parallel my life, Renard.'

On the board, she could not reach Renard's king. Yet in the two weeks since the game had begun, scarcely a day passed without seeing him.

Philip. The thought of the Spanish King turned her back to the warmth outside that beckoned her from her cage. Just the day before he had taken her once again into Bushey Park, opposite the palace gates, a walled area her father had established for his hunting pleasure while in residence at Hampton; though yesterday they had exchanged the hounds and spear of the stag chase for the jesses of the hawk. Philip had presented her with a falcon, a young male, newly trained and untested by royalty, and she had been delighted when her gift soared to his great height, then stooped to take a pigeon on his first assay. Her heart had soared with him, her mind and body flying as free as him for his one glorious escape. Philip had sensed her sadness when the bird was held and hooded again. In an aside that none but she could hear, he had whispered, 'He will fly again soon, my lady. As you will.'

Philip! She pictured him now, his slight stature, refined features, reddish beard. The vision made her smile. She knew she should not like him as she did. She knew her people hated the very idea of him and the Spanish match. She had tried to remain aloof, treating him with little more than a cool courtesy when he came to see her the day after her interview with Renard. Yet he was not the arrogant Castillian his unwilling subjects supposed him, but a cultured and sensitive man, full of charm and humour, and he showed her the first kindnesses in a long ago. He promised to speak to the Queen on her behalf, he took her out of her cramped rooms and into the fresh air of spring, her England's most glorious season. That first day, when he discovered she delighted in the chase, he lent her his favourite mare, took her into Bushey Park, demonstrated his skill in single-handedly killing a fiercesome stag they had chased down, displaying a courage of which even her father would have approved.

She found her thumb and forefinger resting on the white king and she quickly withdrew them, rubbing them on her skirt as if to remove some taint. The idea of Philip was different from his reality, for he was part of Renard's scheme against her, indeed the ultimate goal of it. She had never mentioned it to the King or questioned him about it. It would have seemed a breach of etiquette somehow for all he would be able to do was deny. And Philip was always absolutely proper in his attentions to her, speaking of his admiration for the Queen his wife, his respect for her courage and her faith. Yet, despite all the correctness, when they were out on horseback, or walking beneath the avenue of elms that swept to the east of the palace, in the silence that followed laughter or the ending of some heated Classical debate – for he was as well-read in Latin or Greek as she – Elizabeth would sometimes catch him glancing at her and there was a passion in the look she had seen before when men looked at her, a passion that made her both excited and afraid.

Well, thoughts of Philip would not help her in the game, in either game! Renard would be expecting her next move by nightfall. She had not seen the Ambassador since that last disagreeable meeting, had received nothing more by way of contact than written responses to her moves. Concentrating now, breathing deeply, she sought a way to thwart him.

There was one move, almost her only option, which would protect her for a while. Dipping her quill in the inkwell, she was just bending over the table to scratch it down on some parchment, when she heard the key in the door behind her turn. It was about the time that Kat, her servant, should be returning with her noonday meal.

'Set it down there, Kat, by the window. I can at least gaze out of my prison bars. And then you can take this to the poxy Fox, may God rot him further every day.'

'You'll forgive me if I don't say, "Amen".'

She rose from her bent position, took time to blot the parchment, replace the quill in the inkwell. When she was ready, she turned to face him, smiling.

'Ambassador. Are you yet living?'

'No thanks to your good wishes, I am.' Renard stooped in the low doorway. 'May I enter?'

'You don't usually ask permission for anything, do you? Please.'

'Ah well, you see, the King tells me that I must mend my ways.'

Renard entered, a smile on his thin lips. 'After all, you may be his Queen one day.'

Elizabeth stiffened. 'I may be . . . Queen, it is true, though God preserve my sister and her throne. I am grateful though to his Majesty for this lesson to you in etiquette. I expected no less from him. Would that he heard all my thoughts on you.'

Renard ignored the barb, moving past Elizabeth to study the chessboard. After a moment he said, 'So you still threaten. That is good. No, I do not think I will let you have my knight.' His long fingers closed over a rook, lifted it from the board, set it down in a new hole. 'Checkmate in about seven or eight, I fear.'

'Oh, was my move that good?' said Elizabeth, moving up beside the Ambassador who glowered, then forced a smile.

'Speaking of knights, I should introduce you to one of mine. Enter, sir!' he called, turning. 'Oh, you already have! So silent, these Jesuits.'

Elizabeth looked to the door where a man of some thirty years now stood, black-cloaked, the hood thrown back, dark hair streaked with grey, his pale face composed of features that showed some breeding. The man bowed.

'Thomas Lawley, your Highness. Your servant.'

'I am grateful you address me with that title, sir. Few around here do.'

'My loyal servant has been away on an errand for me. No, errand is too small a word. A mission? Well, almost a crusade, wouldn't you say, Thomas?'

The Jesuit glanced at Renard, returned his gaze to the Princess. Now he was before her, Thomas felt a pang again, similar to the one he'd felt in the chapel in the Tower, down in the grave of this woman's mother. Yet he kept his face impassive.

'I believe I have been about God's work, yes. I could not have done what I have done otherwise.'

There was something in what he said, the tone in which he said it, that hinted of regret. Elizabeth saw the apology there, saw the troubled decency of the man, and her fear grew as she saw it.

Renard continued. 'Oh yes, a crusade, I think. And with better results than some of our illustrious ancestors had on theirs. Tell her *Highness* what you found in France, Thomas?'

She knew before he spoke and the knowledge caused her legs

to weaken. She felt she might have fallen so decided to step forward instead, toward the man who was regarding her with something close to sadness in his gaze.

'Yes, tell me, Master Lawley. What evil thing have you found to help my enemies practise upon me?' She was pleased how firm her voice sounded.

His reply came evenly, uninflected. 'We found the skeleton of a hand, my lady. It was buried in a casket in the middle of a crossroads in the Loire, beneath a gibbet beam.'

'And what has this to do with us?'

'The hand had – has – six fingers.'

There it was, as clear on the man's honest face as if it was laid before her, as if she felt again a strange touch she'd forgotten, except in a dream of happiness from a distant past. She did stumble now, toward the man and he caught her, supported her, and she hated the weakness in her that needed his arm to help her to a chair. Hated above all the triumph that her weakness provoked in the Ambassador. She sensed his smile, his fox eyes fixed upon his prey.

Still, she was Harry's daughter, and if her legs betrayed her, her mind would not.

'Well, Renard, what are you waiting for? Why do you not produce this . . . this blasphemy, and have done?'

'My lady! Has our game taught you nothing? I do not run with all my forces at my enemy. I come to them in stealth, square by square, until success is certain. Unlike you, I do not bring my queen forward until I am sure of victory.'

She saw an opening. 'You have not seen this . . . desecration, have you? You cannot know its effect.'

'I have not seen it, no. But my trusted friend here has.' He put his hand on Thomas's shoulder. 'It is now in the safest place in the kingdom – the Tower. And timing is everything. The Queen, poor lady, as you know, is not yet come to her crisis. Your mother's hand will have its best – or worst – effect when she has just lost all hope. Nothing would save you then.' He leaned in, his voice losing its venom, gaining a honeyed quality that Elizabeth found even more distasteful. 'But why should we talk of such unpleasant outcomes? Perhaps I am deceived and the Queen will be delivered of a healthy child, a Catholic heir to a Catholic throne. And then your promise to marry Philip – such a noble, handsome Prince, is he not? – will not matter. It is so little a thing we ask of you, a signature no bigger than the scrawled chess moves we have been exchanging.' He moved to the table, dipped the quill in ink, bent over a blank parchment. 'Why not sign here, let us fill in the details later?'

Elizabeth rose, found her legs were steady again, walked across to the table where she took the quill and set it down again on its stand.

'You know I put my signature to nothing that may be misconstrued. You could write treason here and have my name attached.'

Renard looked wounded. 'My lady! Would I do such a thing?'

'You would sell your mother to a whorehouse if the purse were heavy enough. And if you could discover her name.'

It was the noise like a suppressed sneeze that turned them both around. But Thomas Lawley's face was as blank as ever, even if something twinkled in his eyes.

'Well, lady.' Renard's tone had regained its former fury. 'We shall see how this progresses. The Queen shall hear of your continual stubbornness, even if we will not yet reveal this part of it. She shall know how you still refuse to admit your treasonous plans and will not throw yourself on her mercy!' He made for the door.

'If I could but see my loving sister, she would quickly learn how innocent I am.'

Renard pivoted, snarling. 'She will believe nothing good of you, daughter of the heretic-witch who ruined her life. The stars will fall before she will see you.' He paused on a thought. 'But you would see her, would you?'

'It is my dearest wish!'

'Then let us fulfil it. Come!' He beckoned. 'Come, do not fear! I shall take you to where you can observe your sister. But beware! She has forbidden you her society. Watch but do not try to force yourself into her presence or worse than further exile might await you!'

As the two antagonists swept from the room, each as determined as the other, Thomas sank gratefully onto the chair at the window. He couldn't remember the last time he'd slept for more than an hour. The boat from Tuscany, probably. Since then it had been endless days on horses, his young companion setting a relentless pace, to the crossroads, beyond it. Sleep had become an impossible dream. They had arrived at the Tower near dawn and he had immediately to set out with the tide for Hampton, leaving Gianni to guard their prize. That was Renard's order, to keep the relic safe in the strongest fortress in the land. At least he would not be able to return there until the evening tide, might have some chance of snatching a few hours of rest. He wouldn't even need a bed. Just the back of this chair would do.

As his eyes closed, he smiled, thinking of the Princess's rejoinder to Renard, her allusion to his bastardy. He felt sorry for her, so young, so beset with enemies. He himself was one, he supposed, and he was sorry for that in many ways. Yet she, as heir, represented a return to the land of the Protestant faith he abhorred, that his father had died trying to oppose. Renard's ways might be devious but, like the Jesuits, he knew that the ends justified the means.

Such means, such ends. He shivered, tried to rise. *Just one more second of rest*, he thought as his head slipped onto the back of the chair. Just one mo. . .

The Ambassador knew passages around the palace that Elizabeth, in a hundred childhood explorations, had never discovered. His anger swept him forward at great pace and though she would have preferred a more dignified step, she was determined not to lose this chance. When he finally stopped before a painting of a lady, some unrecognizable ancestor in the Long Gallery, she was right behind him.

'Wait here,' he said curtly. 'Listen and do not think to speak. This is not advice to serve my ends. You shall hear how the Queen thinks of you and discovering you spying here would not serve her temper, your purposes or mine.'

With that, he pressed a panel and a door swung open on a cramped chamber behind the painting. He gestured her inside and when she was reluctantly within, pressed the door upon her. At first, she thought he meant to suffocate her, for there was little air within her confines. But then she saw a chink of light and, moving a cloth aside, was able to place her eye against a hole the size of a farthing. She had a strange feeling that her own eye was within the eye of the painted lady. Shivering, she prayed she would not be kept waiting there long.

She was unused to prayers being answered at all, let alone with such rapidity. Voices carried from beyond the room, footsteps entered it, and to her eye, pressed to the hole, was revealed what looked like a procession. A series of servants were carrying what appeared, at first, to be large wooden boxes. When they set them down on the floor, however, Elizabeth saw that each rocked back and forth after the servant had moved away and she realized they were cradles, each beautifully carved in woods of varied hue. Then she heard a voice she recognized and had long yearned to hear again. The voice of a sister. The voice of a Queen.

'My Lord, come, help me choose, for I fear choice will be too hard for me alone among these riches.'

Elizabeth tried to peer around to the source of the voice, but Mary was just out of her sight to the left. Someone came into her vision though, she saw the back of the head, an edge of beard.

'They are each miraculous, each worthy of our saviour himself.' Renard bent out of her sight, straightened into it again.

'Do you truly think so? Let me look closer.'

It was nearly two years since she'd heard her sister's voice, yet Elizabeth could hear the change in it. But it was not preparation enough for the sight of Mary as she appeared, a lady-in-waiting supporting her under each arm. She gasped, saw Renard's head flick toward her in irritation.

Mary had never been pretty, but her features had been small and delicate, her hair thick, her skin rosy. Now her pale cheeks were puffed, her face blotchy and bloated, her hair thin and unkempt. Her eyes, her best feature, were glazed, a darkness under each matching a greater one within. Though she seemed to be trying to put some light and life into them, to lighten them with a smile, the effect merely served to highlight the strain as she bent, with help, to rock one of the cradles back and forth.

If she is with child, all this could be explained. If Renard is right in his assumption . . . oh, how horrible! Elizabeth barely managed to restrain another sigh. She watched as Renard leaned in and whispered something into the Queen's ear.

Mary said, 'Affairs of State, Ambassador?'

'I am sorry to burden your Majesty but . . .'

Mary raised a hand. 'It is a burden that a queen must carry. You may put me in this chair and leave me now.'

The servants did her bidding, bowed their way out of the room. The Queen sat, facing the painting and Elizabeth's hiding hole. For a moment, she felt almost as if their eyes met. She dared not look away, dared not let the cloth fall. Then Renard stepped in and Mary's sad eyes raised to him.

'It is to do, once again, with your sister, Majesty. She requests to be admitted to your presence.'

'I will not see her.'

'She has been told so, Majesty. Still, she entreats a reason.'

'A reason? She demands a reason from me?' Elizabeth saw her sister's face set into bitter lines. 'Tell her to look into a mirror. The reason is there.'

'A mirror, Majesty?'

'Her face will be there and on it her whore mother's face is plain, conjoined with the man she bewitched, my poor father of blessed memory.'

'Do you think that magick was truly practised upon him?'

'How else could it be?' Mary's voice lost its strained quality, filled with passion. 'He loved my noble mother, his poems, his songs to her still speak to that. He loved the Church – did he not write against Luther and was named "Defender of the Faith" for it? Yet he forsook them both – Virtuous Queen, Holy Church – for that . . . heretic Anne Boleyn! How else could she have prevailed upon such nobility except by witchcraft?'

Renard looked at the painting, at Elizabeth, turned back to murmur, 'You do not think . . . you would not believe it possible that her daughter has inherited more than a face from her mother?'

It appeared that the two sisters both paused for breath, but it was Mary who regained hers first. In a lower voice she said, 'Do you suspect that, Ambassador?'

'I . . . I am not certain. It was just that your husband seems so taken with her of late. I merely wondered if the daughter could have inherited some power from the mother, that was all.'

Mary tried to move in her chair, writhed, returned as

uncomfortable to her former position, her hands clutching at her breast.

'He says it is best to be her friend, to reconcile the kingdom, that is all there is between them; yet he takes her to hunt, to hawk. He spends more time outside with her than he does inside with me.' The hurt within the words was clear to the listener, and Elizabeth instantly regretted her falcon's flight.

'I am sure my noble master intends no ill by it. Unless . . . no, it cannot be.'

'What, man?' Mary leaned forward impatiently. 'Unless, what?'

'Unless, your Majesty's fears are well-founded. That the daughter has inherited the talent of the mother, as witches always pass on their skills. Skills of a dark allurement beyond her youth, the comeliness of her figure and face – which alone could not be enough to draw so noble, so religious, so dutiful a prince as your father . . . oh, excuse me, I meant your husband, away from your side.'

The dart was well-placed and Elizabeth saw it hit the mark. Mary's cheeks burned as she said, 'Oh, get me the proof of that, Renard. Show me that she intends to replace me in my husband's bed, beside him on my throne, using his seed to create another line of Royal bastards to make my realm Protestant for ever and I will . . .'

Mary gave a cry and suddenly leaned forward, hands clutched to her stomach. 'My baby surges within me at the thought. Call my ladies, quick!'

'Help, here, you there! The Queen is sick!'

Her attendants rushed into the room. 'Take me to my bedchamber,' Mary gasped as they lifted her from the chair. Passing Renard where he stood directly to the side of the painting, she stopped, whispered, 'I want that proof, Renard. I would not execute her as a traitor, as you wished me to at the time of Wyatt's rebellion. But I will burn her as a witch if she practises sorcery against my husband, my baby, myself.'

With that, bent in pain, the Queen allowed herself to be helped from the room. Elizabeth resisted the urge to burst from her hiding place and throw herself at her sister's feet, cry for mercy. The hatred in Mary's eyes held her there, sucked all breath away; the space was suddenly too small, as if the walls and roof pressed in upon her. Yet she couldn't remove her eye from the hole, couldn't stop looking at Renard, alone now, frozen in a deep bow as the Queen was carried from the gallery. When the door shut behind her he slowly straightened, then moved, his back still to Elizabeth, toward the cradles. One by one he nudged them with his feet, till all five were rocking. Only when the last one was moving did he look at the painting, at Elizabeth. She wanted so much to look down, away, anywhere; but she could not take her eyes from the room, from the only movement there. Up and down they went, back and forth; empty, like little wooden coffins. Up and down. Back and forth.

ELEVEN

REUNIONS

'The Bridge! London Bridge! Anyone who's goin', for fuck's sake, go!'

It would take more than the wherryman's bawling to wake Jean. Anne wished she could have left him alone, wished too that she could have joined him in oblivion. Never had she felt more tired. The journey from the crossroads had been harder than the one to it. Days on an open boat, blown astray on the English Channel. Sway-backed nags hobbling from Dover to Gravesend. Then this boat ride upriver, the ripple of wind on the moonlit Thames a lulling torment. Her eyes had closed so many times and each time had sprung open to see a fellow passenger moving stealthily toward their bags.

She'd wanted to join Jean and sleep for ever. But they couldn't.

'Father? We are here. Father?'

Jean jerked awake, a hand flung out to ward the blow descending from the blue sky of his dream.

'We are here.'

He managed to keep hold of his bag before the boatman flung it onto the docks and, helping each other, they clambered ashore. As the wherry pulled away, heading for the other side of the river, Anne's eyes preceded it.

'Is that it?' she said softly, pointing through the mist.

Jean did not need Anne's keen sight to know what she looked at. Lights floated there, dotted around squat shapes that loomed within the shadows.

'Aye. The Tower of London.'

They went up the stairs, onto the wharf. Though it was late in the night, even shading to morning, there was a bustle there, reed torches lighting the goods unloaded onto waiting carts, drawn by horse or man. As soon as they appeared, three ragged boys ran at them, screeching.

''Ere, miss, master, 'ere, let me 'elp, I'll carry 'em, no, I will. Leave off, Jackson, you whelp, I sees 'em first.'

Anne had learnt English from her mother, but Beck's Yorkshire tongue had not sounded anything like the wailing of these youths. She recognized the word 'Tavern' amidst the torrent and, raising her hand, managed to get a degree of silence.

'We need a tavern.' Incomprehensible words burst forth again. Over them she shouted, 'And we have no money.'

It was not true, but it had the effect desired because each boy looked at the others, then two ran off to confront another passenger, a fat monk who had just made it up the steps and who began beating at them as if they were fleas. The third boy, the smallest and dirtiest of the three, stayed staring at Anne with huge eyes, the only bright thing in the grime of his face. One bare foot rested on top of the other, and his hands darted in and out of the rags he wore, scratching at skin that Anne could see was welted and sore.

'No money, miss? Nobody 'as no money. I even 'ave a farthing.' A tiny coin appeared for an instant in one hand, flashed in the half-light as he flicked it into the air. The other hand grabbed it, disappearing it once again into the rags.

'A man of substance, Anne.'

She turned to him, catching the faint smile on his face, wondering how long it had been since she had seen one there.

The boy chirped, 'That's me, sumtance, lots of it. Can always do with more.' He tipped his head to the side. 'So 'ow much is no money? I can get ya straw for a farthing, but you wouldn't like it much. 'A'penny will buy y'a bed and only five to share it with. Penny'll get ya straw to yesself, though not really fresh, like. A groat – well, you could 'ave a room for that. 'An' for a shilling . . .'

'What would this buy me, friend.'

Jean had worked his fingers into the split in the seam of his doublet as the boy chattered. What emerged from it he palmed and then seemed to pull from behind the boy's ear.

The flash of gold stunned the boy, but no more than Anne, for her father had taken not a single risk on this entire journey, maintaining that only under the guise of poverty was there protection. To produce one of their store of ten florins, on a ill-lit street in a strange city, to an urchin of a boy? She wondered if a fever had seized him.

The coin had come and gone, but the flash of it lingered in the boy's wide eyes. His voice was almost sombre when it came.

'Reckon ya could buy a palace for that, mister.'

Jean smiled again. 'Not necessary. But an inn that has a small private room and food, yes.'

The boy seemed frightened of Jean now, as if he were some magician, but he took Anne's hand and led them from the wharves, into the alleys behind, a honeycomb of little passage-ways, with no light to see by, treading on things that they could only choose not to guess at. Still, the boy progressed at a good pace, and soon they emerged into a wider street where a faint light shone from a lantern that dangled over a swinging sign. As they approached the door beneath it, a church bell began to toll close by, striking five times.

'Southwark Minster,' the boy said. 'The Ram's in its lee.'

He rapped on the door, and after a moment there was shuffling of steps within, a bolt drawn, a muttering.

'Guests!' said the boy proudly, pushing past a toothless old man in nightcap and gown. 'I'll take 'em.'

A corridor led to the main room of the inn, around whose hearth sprawled bodies, lying on every available table, chair and piece of floor. A large man with jet black hair and head slumped on his arms straddled the bare counter, a spilled pewter goblet at his side. He swatted at the boy when he tried to wake him, but when his eyes opened and he saw his visitors, he awoke instantly. Boy and suddenly friendly potman led them further into the dark recesses of the inn. A door was opened, there was an angry exchange, and a man was ejected from within.

The potman's Irish accent was as thick as the boy's London one. 'Dere y'are, sorr, madam. Best da Ram can offer.'

It was tiny with a low ceiling and a cloth pinned over a window hole. But the straw on the raised dais looked reasonably fresh, and they would be the sole occupants. Food was promised, most of their English coins handed over in exchange. Jean kept two, a farthing and a groat, and waited till the innkeeper had closed the door behind him.

'What's your name, lad?'

'Jackson, sir.' He stared at Jean's hands, each, he knew, containing one coin.

'Well, Jackson. This' – he handed the boy the farthing – 'is match for the coin you have. This doubles your wealth, for your services so far. While this' – he waved the groat above the boy's head, his eyes following it back and forth in the pale lamplight – 'this is for your silence and your future service. You know the city well, I trust? Good, then come back tomorrow – today – at noon. We will make use of your knowledge.'

As the boy left, too stunned to speak, Anne turned to Jean. 'Was that wise, Father? This boy knows we have gold. Might he not share that knowledge?'

Jean lay down, his sack for a pillow. 'Wisdom? I gave up all claim to that when I agreed to this journey. Now we are here, let us do what we can, and do it quickly. I know no one and nothing here. This boy has been sent to us, somehow, to be our eyes and ears. Sleep now, and let us think no more on it till tomorrow.'

It was the first time in her life she'd ever heard her father talk about any form of destiny. He was not that sort of man, nor one to take the chances he just had. Pondering this, she was about to fall asleep, when her father spoke once more.

'Besides – did he not remind you of Gianni at that age?'

Jean slept, but, despite her exhaustion, Anne lay awake a little longer. Her brother's name had conjured his image and she bent her mind to seeking him out, to see if she could get a sense of him within this strange city. But either she was too exhausted, or Gianni lay within walls made up both of stone and his own resistance. She could not find him.

Finally, she tumbled into a dream-strewn sleep.

A crow could have flown the distance with one snap of wings and a single glide. For Jackson, the journey was more tortuous, for the way wound through the filthy stews of Southwark and even at this early hour, threat waited in the shadows – men and women with nothing, willing to attack anyone who might have just a little more. Even a ragged street boy like him could tempt the hopeless, so he moved slowly, scanning each fetid lane before he moved down it, walking in the centre of each where the sewer ran and the rats nuzzled the garbage. It was only when he was close that he sped up, covering the last part of the journey at a sprint, for he didn't want to be observed on the open ground just before the bear pit. He leant against the whitewashed walls that rose three storeys above him and curved away from him on either side, breathing heavily. The man he sought had rooms within the structure he owned, but Jackson had no idea where they lay.

Another roar, just the other side of the wall made him jump, spring away. It was followed by a howling of dogs, the sound of chains being run out and snapping at their limit. Growls and barks alternated until a human voice intervened, a string of oaths followed by the crack of a whip, the dogs tailing off in whimpers, the bear giving a last growl before also falling silent. The man's final curses drew Jackson to the large wooden gates. They were barred, but beside them was a smaller door, half ajar. Cautiously, the boy thrust his head through the gap . . .

'Gotcha!'

The hand descended on his neck, grabbing at his rags, which tore in his struggles but did not give, not before another hand clamped upon his arm, pulling him into the darkness.

'I wondered why me animals was awake.' The voice was harsh. 'Now I know – they smelled breakfast!'

Jackson's cry of fear met the laugh that came, but there was no wriggling free from the grip. Instead, he was dragged through an archway, past rows of benches, out into a roofless space with straw scattered over the ground. The dogs howled again, as he was thrown onto the ground, a shape looming above him, a fist silhouetted against the sky.

'Lemme get a look at ya. Move, and by my whore's crotch, I'll kill ya where ya lie.'

Jackson gazed on a nightmare. Such light as there was gleamed off a bald pate, four scars that ran in parallel lines the length of one side of the face, an eye whose lid was torn and puckered, a beard that grizzled the chin. Rolls of flesh encased the neck, spreading into the huge body below, the bare chest traced in other scars, some faded, some fresh. Jackson would have done anything to be able to escape from this vision. But he found that no part of his body answered his urgings. All he could do was lie back on the straw.

'Shuddup!' The face turned away toward the dogs who, on the instant, ceased their yelping. He bent again to the prone boy.

'Thief, are ya? Scout for a mob come to rob me? Which one ya with, then? Dempseys? The Flems?'

The toe of a boot accompanied the last words, jabbed hard into thin ribs. Jackson squirmed away, scrabbling legs finally working, propelling him back toward the centre of the arena.

'No, no no no. No one. I've come ... I've come ...'

The huge man followed, toe prodding. 'Yes? Why? Why? On your own, to steal? Think the old man sleeps, do ya? I never sleep!'

With a thump, Jackson hit the wooden barrier. 'Please, no. I've come to see Uriah.'

The boot that was raised, now slowly lowered to the ground. 'And what makes ya think Uriah would want to see a little rat like you?'

''Cos ...' Jackson wiped the snot away that had mingled with his tears. ''Cos I got information for him, that's why!'

'Information!' The big man laughed, then bent his twisted face till it nearly touched the boy's shaking knees. 'And you think that Uriah doesn't know everything you could possibly know – and more? That 'e doesn't have men out on the street – men, not snot-nosed boys – in every tavern, every whore 'ouse, every stall, who tell 'im everything that's worth knowing?'

''E couldn't know this, 'cos they just arrived.'

'Who did?'

'The Frog and 'is daughter. They give me a groat.'

'A groat?' It was a large sum for a boy like this and it made the man pause. 'Show it me.'

'I've 'idden it, sir, back on the street.'

'Wise lad. Or a liar. Shall I turn you upside down and see which?'

A huge hand reached for him and Jackson leaned as far back as the wooden wall allowed. 'A groat's nothing, sir,' he said desperately. 'Froggies got gold. Lots of gold.'

The fat fingers halted an inch from his face. 'Gold, is it?' The eye appraised him. 'So why do you want to tell Uriah this?'

Jackson's breath had evened a little. He could see he had this man's attention. 'Because I wants to work for 'im. Even a groat won't last me long. But a share of Froggie gold . . .' He even tried a smile. 'That could be the beginning of an apprenticeship.'

'Well, well,' the big man said, 'you've just begun to interest me, boy.'

Jackson rose slowly, scraping straw and shit from his rags. 'So, uh, will ya take me to meet Uriah, like?'

'Y'already have.' The big man lowered his face. 'I'm Uriah Makepeace.'

Six of the noon-hour bells had tolled when the door flew inwards.

Jean had no moment to pause, to fear, to wonder if it was still a dream. A man was leaping at him, so he took the attacker on both feet, brought his legs to his chest, turned his face out of the path of the blade that skittered down the plaster wall, kicked out, sailing the first man back into the second in the low doorway.

Now the terror came, but his cry was lost in the yelling from the attackers, in the shriek of defiance from his daughter. Anne seized the wine jug on the floor, hurled it at a third man leaping over his sprawled fellows, catching him in the face, smashing there. He fell over the first assailant trying to get up.

'Father!' Anne screamed, in one movement grabbing the sheathed sword and throwing it across to Jean. He caught it, by hilt and end, parrying the thrust that came at him, deflecting the man's lunge to the side. The man fell onto the bed and Jean struck down with the pommel, missing the first two times, blows glancing off wriggling shoulder and back. Then it connected with the man's skull, once, twice, again and the body went still, a dead weight pinning Jean's legs to the bed. Anne was on her feet, swinging a knife that she'd pulled from her sack as the next man came off the ground and opposed her blade with his, crouching to attack.

'No!' Jean screamed, raising his sword back over his head, hurling it forward so that the stiff leathern sheath shot from the steel, striking the man on the side of his head. The square-tipped sword was bare now and the odds in the cramped room had changed in their favour, even if no one saw how much the weapon shook in the Frenchman's hand.

A rough voice broke the silence, coming from the figure that was making the doorway look small.

'Send boys to do the work of a man!'

The figure stepped through, moving the other two assailants out of the way with the short barrel of the arquebus he carried.

'Now, do I 'ave to use this, Froggie?' The barrel's end tipped toward Jean and he could see the glowing cord poised above the pan beyond it. 'Or do ya want to put down that . . .' The voice broke off with an oath. 'Where d'ya get an executioner's sword? Eh?' A heavily scarred face leaned into the light from the window hole. 'Only man I know who 'ad one like that . . . by all that's . . . can't be!' The barrel wavered, lowered. 'Rombaud?'

Jean could hardly take his eyes off the death that threatened from the metal hole ahead of him. The use of his name seemed to come as if from a far off place, unconnected with the world he knew now, this world of terror. Blankly, he sought within the tracery of scars, above his wavering blade.

'It's me . . . I don't believe this! Oy, lower your blades, you scum.' He turned back. 'Rombaud. It's Uriah. Uriah Makepeace.'

The name brought a flash of memory, of a city in flames. 'Uriah?'

'The very same.' There was a hint of a bow, then the scarred head turned to his two men, who were regarding him with wonder. 'Out. And take this fool with ya.' As they rushed to comply, to pick up the prone body of Jean's victim and drag him to the door, he added, 'And send us up a flagon of wine. Let the boy bring it. Tell Magonnagal, the good stuff too.' He turned back, smiling. 'For this is a special occasion.'

As the men left, Anne lowered her knife, while the two men regarded each other in silent amazement. Bending, she picked up the sword sheath from the floor, slipped it over the end of Jean's sword lying in his inert hands. Uriah appraised her dark hair, her eyes, her shape.

'Found yessself a nice little companion, Rombaud. My congratulations. Pretty girl for an old sod like you.'

The lechery in the Englishman's eyes brought Jean fully back to the room. 'She's my daughter. Anne, this is Uriah Makepeace. He's . . . an old colleague.'

'I remember the name.' She looked unflinchingly into the

scarred face. 'You were the Executioner of Munster. You tried to help my father escape. Gave him an assassin's knife.'

'What knife?' The Englishman's face crinkled in concentration. 'Oh, I remember. A Pistoia. Useful little shive that, wished for it many times since. Munster eh?' He shook his head. "Ow d'you ever survive that? And wait ... wait, now I remember! You arrived carting that dead queen's hand. Anne Boleyn's fucking six-fingered hand!' He collapsed onto the bed beside Jean. 'Rombaud, you have some stories to tell me and no mistake. Not least, what, by the useless balls of a Jesuit, you're doin' back 'ere in London?'

Jean looked into the eyes, the one distorted by its scars, the other bright. Everything about the man spoke of old comradeship – except for those eyes. In them, Jean saw calculation, as if his neck was being measured for a noose. He remembered then that though Makepeace had helped him at Munster, it was at no risk to himself. And he had just tried to rob and kill him.

Looking down, beginning to weigh his words – for Makepeace would be useful for information – Jean saw a strange figure on the back of the huge hand.

'What's this, Makepeace? An "M" tattooed to help you remember your name?'

'This?' Uriah raised the hand so that Anne too could see the letter that covered half the back of it. ' 'S'not a tattoo, 's a brand.' He chuckled. 'This signifies that I am a man of God. A priest, no less.'

'A priest?' It was Jean's turn to laugh. 'You've changed your trade! Did you come tonight to bring us to salvation?'

"Ardly. But this shows that I am a priest who, alas, strayed into sinfulness. The "M" does not signify my name. It stands for "Murderer" and tells that I murdered once. If I do so again, I will not be so lightly forgiven.'

'I think this is something you will have to explain.'

Makepeace sighed. 'It is not the prettiest of stories. Perhaps your lovely daughter ...'

'I have just spent fifteen months in a siege, caring for men and women who ... well, if I ever did, I no longer need stories to be pretty.'

'I can see the cub is as fierce as the sire! Very well, I'll tell my tale, maybe still leaving out some of the more, er, grisly, details. Ah wine!' he said, as the door was pushed open and a shaking Jackson carried in a flagon. 'And 'ere we 'ave the reason for our reunion, Rombaud. The latest recruit to my enterprises.'

The boy avoided all eyes, placed the tray on the floor, then scuttled out the door.

'Seems to feel guilty about something. 'Ave to knock that out of him if 'e's to work for me. Terrible thing, guilt. No use at all, eh Rombaud?' He poured the wine, passed the goblets around. 'A pox on guilt, eh? If we was guilty about all the 'eads we'd taken . . .' He drank deeply, refilled his cup as the others sipped.

'You don't get branded as a murderer for taking a head, Makepeace.' Jean swirled the wine in his goblet.

'No. Nor if you don't get caught. I was unlucky, that's all. You see, it 'appened like this.' He looked around, lowered his voice. 'I 'ad a partner. Samuel Braithewaite. Sam 'ad fingers in lots of pies. Owned the Bear gardens just down from 'ere, very profitable that, a couple of inns beside, two, uh . . .' He glanced at Anne. 'Two 'ouses for ladies of the night. 'E was also supplying for the Tower. Most profitable bit of all. It's like a little city over there, all the palace servants, the garrison. The prisoners. Need lots of food, beer, wine. Oh yes, 'e 'ad a nice thing going all round. But 'e got greedy, careless. Too much water in the wine, too much sour beer, not enough of the right palms being greased. That's what really cost us, 'cos there were lots of others who wanted that contract. We lost it. And I wasn't very 'appy.'

'So you killed him?'

Uriah returned Anne's questioning gaze with a sad smile. 'I did.' He shrugged. 'But not in anger, you understand. It was just business.' He sighed, emptied the flagon into the goblets. 'Problem was, I didn't have that little knife I lent you, Rombaud, what would have done the job properly. This dagger was clumsy and it skittered off his bones. Took him two days to die and in the meantime he tells the Watch who done it. First time in their lives those bastards were efficient. They caught me in one of me own brothels and 'auled me before the court. Looked like I was for the Hemp Drop. But then' – a grin spread across the scarred face – 'then I remembered a very useful piece of church law – if you can prove you're a priest, you can escape punishment for your crime.'

Jean smiled. 'I don't think anyone would believe you were a priest, Uriah.'

The Englishman leaned down, his fat fingers going round his throat. 'But that's just it. I could prove it. I don't know what it's like elsewhere but 'ere in England, if you can read, you must be a priest. Then you can claim what they call "benefit of clergy".'

'But can you read?'

Uriah guffawed. ''Course not! But that's the beauty of it, Rombaud. You don't 'ave to! As long as you can remember. Because they always ask you to read the same thing. Psalm Fifty-One, verse one. Recite that with the book open before you and you're a free man. Well, a little branding to make sure you can't use it again.' He waved his hand. 'A small price, I say. They call it the Neck Verse. You should learn it.'

Uriah stood and declaimed, 'Have mercy upon me, O God, according to thy loving kindness, according unto the multitude of thy tender mercies, blot out my transgressions.' He lowered his head. 'Brings tears to me eyes, it is so beautiful.

'So I was free. And Braithewaite and me 'ad a contract between us, in another of me names, of course. All properly drawn up with a little clause in it what said that if either died first, the other got the lot – stews, inns, bear garden. I was now sole owner. Did very well, apart from this little mishap with a bear when my bearward went sick.' He rubbed the scars on his face. 'Still, life's better without a partner. More profit to me. I even got part of the Tower contract back. I go in and supply all the food and drink for special events. Now I watch executions rather than do 'em. Got a burning tomorrow in fact. More heretics.'

He smiled down at his two listeners, then sat between them, the branded hand moving to Jean's leg.

'And now, Rombaud, favour for favour, story for story. 'Ere you are in London, you and your sword. Must be another commission, eh? Though these days they prefer butchery to your artistry. Must be someone royal then?' He scratched at his beard. 'You missed Jane Grey by a year, can't think of anyone worthy of your talents ... or your price, unless ...' He leaned into Jean, suddenly excited. 'Unless you come for the daughter like you did for the mother? Princess Elizabeth's for the chop, is she? We've been expecting that for a while.'

Jean looked beyond the eager face to the one beyond. Anne shook her head just slightly. She did not trust this man any more than he did. Still, he had access to the very place to which they sought entry, where Heinrich von Solingen had declared that Gianni was headed – the Tower. So Jean began a tale of a son gone bad; worse, one lost to the fanaticism of faith. Of how they'd tracked him to London, where they hoped to confront him, kidnap him if necessary, remove the shackles that the Roman Church had placed around his heart.

'A sad story indeed, Rombaud.' Makepeace ran his fingers down the scars of his face, contemplating. 'Never had children myself . . . well, none that I acknowledge. But I understand how much woe they can cause.' He looked at Anne. 'And pleasure too, of course.' He scratched at his beard. 'So am I right? You'll be needing some 'elp, eh?'

'Can you get us into the Tower?'

Makepeace clambered off the bed, opened the door and shouted 'Wine!' down the stairs, turned back. 'You're an old comrade, Rombaud, and I would do anything to help you – you and your fair daughter. But what you ask means risk; to me, to my livelihood. I don't take risks, unless . . .'

'Unless there is profit in it.' Jean nodded. 'You already know we have some gold – it's why you visited us this morning, is it not? You can have . . . most of it, if you help us reach my son. Five gold florins of the seven I have left.'

'Five florins, eh?' Makepeace had waited at the door, received the flagon that was hastily shoved in. He went to pour it into Jean's goblet and his gaze flicked to the bed beside him.

'Rombaud's sword,' he said. 'May I?' Putting down the flagon, he picked the weapon up, unsheathed it. 'Still a beauty, isn't it? Feel that weight.' He made a cut through the air, whistled. 'And the shame is that in this whole kingdom there's probably only you and me that knows how to use it. No call for such quality these days.' He made another cut just above Jean's head, who tried not to flinch. 'Do you know, miss, your father traded me this weapon once for that knife you mentioned, oh, nigh on twenty years ago now. Then a Turk, a janissary, bought it back off me. And somehow it got back to you again.' He made another cut. 'I regretted selling, later. Money's money, but this ... I always thought how good it would look on the wall of my inn.'

'Take it.'

'Father!'

'No, child.' Jean turned to her. 'This sword led me to the Tower once, and now it leads me back. Both times have meant sorrow for me and for those I love. I have had enough of sorrow.' He turned back to Uriah. 'I will not use it again. Take it.'

Makepeace sheathed the sword, spat in his hand, held it out. Jean spat, clasped. They shook.

'A compact made! And I'm off to the Tower tonight, where I supply a dinner on the eve of this execution. I'll find out if your son is indeed within and if he is, we'll get you in tomorrow for the burnin'. Who knows? Under the cover of all that smoke, you should be able to smuggle him out. You stole an 'and from there once, the most famous in the kingdom. You should be able to steal a boy.'

Jean looked down, to where their own hands met. His thumb curled over the back of the other, reaching down into the letter there, into the heart of the 'M'.

Holding the murderer's right hand, he looked to the man's left one, still waving the square-headed sword through the air. He had seen it rise and fall a thousand times. Now he prayed he never would again.

TWELVE
INTO THE BELLY
OF THE BEAST

Gianni Rombaud pushed the unidentifiable lump of meat around his plate, making cruciform shapes in the grease-rich gravy. He tried to use the images created to stimulate prayer, to narrow his mind down to the comfort of familiar Latin phrases, but his concentration was broken each time by that intrusive nasal voice.

Simon Renard! How could this man be the main pillar of the Church in London? A braggart, testifying to nothing but his own genius. And what did this Defender of the Faith want to know most from Gianni? Not his desire to root out heresy, not his dreams of martyrdom. No! All he'd wanted was the story of the six-fingered hand. He'd been as eager as any court gossip, especially desirous to know of Jean Rombaud's role, Jean Rombaud's actions, Jean Rombaud's sins. It was only when Gianni's replies became terse to the point of rudeness that the Ambassador grew bored, turned to the only other diner, Thomas Lawley.

As a servant loomed over him to take his barely touched food, a bell tolled midnight from a nearby tower. It was the hour Gianni had appointed as the limit of his politeness. He stood.

'If you'll excuse me ...'

'Young men need their sleep, I suppose.'

'I have two hours of prayer ahead of me, my lord Renard. Then I must be awake with the dawn. The chaplain has asked me to seek the condemned's repentance one last time.'

'Ah yes.' Renard turned to Thomas. 'I hear you succeeded in bringing one of these unfortunate Protestants back to the light.

Do you join our enthusiastic young friend again in that good work?'

The Jesuit murmured, 'I do not. The boy was young, suggestible. The others are too locked in their faith.'

Gianni glared down at him. 'Their heresy. Faith is what we have, remember?'

Thomas raised his calm face to the boy's angry one. 'Of course. I merely meant that they will not bend. All I can do now is pray for their souls.'

But that is not all I can do, Gianni thought excitedly, as he bowed and moved away. He would pray first and then he would sleep. He wanted to be well-rested for the morning's ceremony. For he had been promised a special role.

As the door closed behind him, Renard said, 'I heard that you wept when the sinner repented, Thomas. *You* displayed an emotion. Can this miracle be true?'

'A soul was saved as well as a young man's life. Yes, I found it moving.' Thomas smiled. 'And it is said in Rome that our beloved founder, Ignatius Loyola, weeps three times a day. He calls it "the gift of tears". Should I disdain his example?'

'It is also said in Rome that Jesuit weakness is due to its Spanish roots. Doesn't Cardinal Carafa call Spain "a mongrel nation of Jews mixed with Moors"?'

The calm tone of voice belied the light in the Ambassador's eyes, made up of both challenge and wine.

Thomas would certainly show no emotion to the Fox. 'I am English born and bred, my lord. And do you not yourself serve the King of Spain?'

'So the Jesuit can find a mark? At last we have a game. Excellent!'

Renard leaned forward to fill Thomas's cup with wine. A hand prevented him.

'But you have barely drunk tonight, Thomas. Neither you nor our young friend.' Renard emptied the flagon into his own goblet, drank deeply.

'Maybe, like me, he fears a loosening of his tongue, my lord.'

The words were accompanied by a little glance around the room, at the servants who moved about, attending to plates, wine, fire.

'Is that . . . criticism I hear in your voice – Jesuit!' Renard spat out the last word, his voice suddenly sharp. Raising his goblet, he added, 'Do you imply that this makes me careless?'

'I would not presume to criticize you, my lord.'

'Of course you wouldn't! Direct attack is not your way. You sit back with your observation, your judgements, your unfocused stare . . .' He thrust his heated face close to Thomas's. 'I let my tongue loosen only when it is safe to do so. You think any of these peasants' – he waved at the servants – 'can speak even one word of the French or Italian we have been using? You have forgotten your countrymen's inordinate capacity for ignorance. These animals can barely speak their own language.'

He turned to the table's end, where one of the servants was stacking platters. 'You see that one! The big one, too stupid to have removed his fat face from some beast only slightly dumber than himself. Heh, you, Ox!' he called down the table. 'Do you know of anything beyond the sewer, the filth of your daily life? Eh?'

The servant finally raised his head at the end of the torrent of French, realizing it was aimed at him, incomprehension on his face. He muttered, in English. 'More wine, sir?'

Renard smiled, replied in the same language. 'Yes, why not? More wine. My tongue needs loosening.'

He looked at Thomas, who bowed his head slightly, as he was required to do. Victory achieved, Renard's face folded once more into its customary lines of calm disdain.

'Now, where were we? Ah yes – the similarity in my two servants. A desire for a clear head, a rigid tongue.'

'It may be the only trait we share, my lord.'

'Criticism again, Thomas?

'A comment, merely.'

'But you disapprove of this Italian? Why? He seems as devout even as yourself.'

'I am certain he is. But his devotion is dark. It seems founded on . . .' Thomas hesitated, then said, 'hate.'

'And yours is based on . . . what, love? Was it love, then, that saved that young heretic today?'

'I believe so, yes. But not mine. I am a mere conduit for Our Saviour's love.'

'And the burnings tomorrow? You disapprove?'

'No ... my lord. I can't ... disapprove. It is unfortunate, but ... sometimes the sword is necessary. And the flame.'

'And this boy, this Gianni, he is sharp, an unsheathed sword, eh? While you, Thomas, you are a blade veiled in velvet.' Renard laughed, leaned back, letting the servant who'd returned with the wine, fill his cup. 'Gianni ... Rombaud. Did you see how reluctant he was to talk of his father?'

'I saw how interested you were in that subject, my lord.'

'Oh yes, I am interested in this executioner. I am always interested in puzzles. When small men interfere in great events. This brute of a man took the Queen's hand – more than a queen and more than a hand, by all reports – took it and buried it at a crossroads in France! Why? Are you not consumed by the mystery of that? And that was not the whole of the story, not close to it, even our monosyllabic friend implied there was much more to it. No, any knowledge I can gain of that tale can only help me in my ... my game with the Princess Elizabeth.'

His slender fingers ran up and down the fine bones of his sharp face. The Fox's dark eyes gazed into the fire, its light reflected in their depths.

'Oh yes. I would give much to meet Anne Boleyn's executioner.'

How much? Uriah Makepeace thought, as he followed the Imperial Ambassador along the inner wall of the fortress. Despite his size, he moved delicately, flush to the wall, in contrast to the man ahead whose high-heeled shoes, tipped in metal, clicked off the cobblestones in the very centre of the way. Feeling no need for silence, Renard was even humming some Spanish ballad as he walked. For what harm could befall him here, in the stony heart of the kingdom?

Uriah knew his destination, indeed, knew every lodging of each 'guest', willing or unwilling in the fortress. Until recently, he had supplied provisions to them all. He knew where Renard kept his rooms, and that, as one of the Queen's chief advisers, the Fox's attendance was often required at council meetings in the upper level of the White Tower, at torturings in the same tower's depths, at executions before it on the Green, like the one on the morrow.

Uriah looked up to the roof of the Garden Tower, where three cloaked figures huddled beside a brazier. He raised a hand, received an acknowledgement – he was a familiar sight within these walls. But the guards' presence confirmed his plans. Best not to approach Renard beneath their gaze, but wait for him to reach the Salt Tower. Uriah knew a secret stair that would take him, unseen, right to the Ambassador's bedroom door.

His plan was quickly jettisoned when he looked back along the shadowed cobbles. For his quarry had vanished in the moment he'd taken to look up and wave. Moving swiftly, Uriah paused at the edge of the Wakefield Tower. He could hear the gurgling of the Thames as it surged through Traitor's Gate and was about to move on, when two other sounds reached him. The first brought relief, the second made him smile. Peering around the corner of the wall, sight confirmed sound. The singing Ambassador, whose cup Uriah had kept full all night, was standing at the top of the stone staircase, relieving himself into the incoming tide.

'And a fine night for it, is it not, my lord?' Uriah said, stepping away from the wall.

'Son of a whore!' Renard spluttered, one hand reaching for his sword, the other trying to put himself away though it was clear he was not yet finished. 'Who's there? I will call the guard!'

'No need for alarm, my lord. 'Tis only I, Uriah Makepeace. Excuse the interruption.'

And he stepped forward again, raising the lantern he'd kept hidden till that moment under his cloak, holding it up to his face.

Renard, having partially succeeded with his buttons, now withdrew his sword, levelling it before him. He squinted over the blade.

'Do I know you, fellow?'

'I hope so, sir. I served you wine all night.'

Uriah could not decide if the Ambassador's expression was more comical now than it had been a few moments before.

'But you speak French!'

'And some Italian, though that's gone a little rusty. German too. Useful for a mercenary to speak a few tongues other than his own.'

Renard had regained some of his calm. 'So you were a mercenary and now you are a spy. And what's this?' The sword flicked to Uriah's hand that held the lantern. Its point nicked, drawing blood from the centre of the branded 'M'. 'A murderer too! I think I will call for those guards.'

Uriah sucked at his hand. 'If I spy, my lord, it is only to do you service.'

'Indeed!' Renard took a step forward, the sword steady, forcing Uriah to give ground. 'And what was this service you were thinking of rendering me?'

'Your Excellency expressed a desire at supper to meet a certain Queen's executioner.'

'Yes?' Another step taken forward, another one back.

'He's a friend of mine.'

'Really? How good a friend?'

The blade reached out to rest on Uriah's doublet. He didn't even look at it.

'Well, not one beyond price, my lord. Certainly not beyond price.'

Though it was less than an hour after sunrise, London Bridge was already crowded. Yet it was not the impediment of jostling, shouting humanity that slowed Jean's feet, nor was it the weight of the cart he pushed, piled high with barrels of Uriah's ale, that caused his breath to come short. It was the barest glimpse through a gap between buildings. He'd looked away again as swiftly, too late. The Tower's battlements now loomed in his memory as they loomed over the river, grim and grey, and he struggled to move forward, flushing cold despite his efforts. Finally, it was a sudden, terrible thought that had him lowering the cart's end to the ground.

'What day is this?'

His raspy voice carried to the black-browed man ahead, the Ram's Irish landlord and Uriah's lieutenant, Magonnagal.

'Eh?' he grunted. 'Some saint, isn't it? Always some bloody saint. Clear the way there!' he bellowed ahead, then, turning back, he added, 'Saint Experious, patron of the plough and bloody planting. Nineteenth of May.'

He'd known. Of course he'd known. But something inside him had tried to force that knowledge away.

'Father! What is it?'

The concern on Anne's face showed him the anguish that must be on his.

'Nothing, child, it's nothing. Help him push. I'll catch up.'

The nineteenth of May! The day itself? How was that possible?

Nineteen years to the very day when last he'd been in the fortress he approached now. Nineteen years since he'd taken Anne Boleyn's head, more, sworn a vow, taken her fabled hand, begun that journey. How many lives had that vow affected, how many deaths had it brought? As well as the birth of the girl now looking back anxiously along the bridge and of the boy Uriah had told them awaited ahead. Nineteen years and the circle complete, the journey back at its beginning, the hand returned. All that suffering – in vain.

Frozen there, as the crowds cursed and surged around him, his whole life suddenly seemed to him mere mockery, a hideous masque performed for random and capricious gods. He was their puppet, a plaything. And of this, above all else, he was suddenly certain – the masque approached its climax. He had been summoned back to this stage to die.

Jostled and knocked, he lurched forward, took one step and then another. The cart had been held in a duel for the roadspace, Jean catching up as Magonnagal threatened another carter with a whip. The man conceded the way to the huge Irishman, and they moved on.

Anne touched her father's arm. 'Are you all right? Should we rest, go back?' The greyness of his face frightened her. 'Maybe we should return another day?'

'This is the day, child. The only day.'

She turned away, couldn't look at him any longer. Not when she couldn't separate his fears of what lay ahead from her own.

As they left the bridge, the crowds got denser, as ways merged, and all headed to the fortress. Uriah had told them that there had been disturbances when burnings were held the week before on the hill outside the Tower's walls. Sympathizers had almost freed the heretics, so the authorities had decided not to take that chance again.

'So they'll burn 'em inside, before an invited audience,' the Englishman had said. 'Which is better for me. Outside, it's like a fairground, anyone can set up a food stall. Within the walls, that's my little manor, with a richer crowd who will pay well for their pleasures. Know the funny thing?' His smile grew. 'I have to cater to different tastes each time. At a beheading, they want pastries, sweetmeats, all manner of sugared goods. At a burning, now, all they crave is roasted meat! The blacker the better. Must be the savour in the air, eh?'

Anne hadn't liked the man, was glad when he went ahead long before the dawn 'to get the spits turning'. Still, they had no choice but to trust him. Her father was determined that it must end now, this day, that they had to get to Gianni, get the hand if possible, flee again. It was as if he sensed the limits of what he could do and knew they fast approached.

The crowd was thickest at the first gate, where warders turned many away. Magonnagal showed them the barrels on the cart, passed one over and they were admitted, following others of the privileged across a small drawbridge to another gateway. Beyond this, a larger drawbridge led to a much larger Tower.

'The Byward,' Magonnagal muttered. 'Through that, and we're a short push to the Green. Then I can rest my bloody shoulders.'

While most of the crowd surged forward, parallel with the river, the Irishman led them left, bringing the cart to a small wooden door set in the wall beside a large rectangular tower.

'The Beauchamp,' he said, rapping three times on the wood. 'Brings us out beside the Green and we don't have to shove through the bloody crowd.'

Bolts slid within, two of Uriah's men appeared and immediately began rolling the barrels into the darkness ahead. Jean, who'd paused in the doorway at Magonnagal's words, now grabbed a barrel and followed the men into the tower.

'Too many ghosts,' he muttered as he entered. 'I can't stop and acknowledge every one!' Nevertheless, as he followed the men down the flagstoned corridor, he could not help but remember. Anne Boleyn had spent her last night in the Beauchamp. He had sworn his vow to her within these flagstone walls.

The view, nineteen years on, as he emerged into the light again, was different. Then, there had been a bare hundred people, the elect of the elect, who had fought to be present at the killing of the Queen. Now, at least five hundred heads bobbed on the Green, between the south wall and the squat, massive White Tower opposite. His view was different too, for then he'd stood with his back to the chapel, on a straw-strewn scaffold, the small crowd reaching right up to it. Now, the chapel was to his left with no wooden stage before it, just four stakes thrust into the grass in a rough semi-circle, a huge pile of chopped wood at their centre, warded by a double line of soldiers that stretched all the way across to the White Tower. Beside three of the stakes stood men in besmirched leathern aprons, crude, sack-like masks over their heads, oval slashes for their eyes. Each held a hammer, nails, and a hoop of iron.

'Now where's that bloody man at, then?' Magonnagal peered over the crowd, shading his eyes from the morning sun. 'Ah!' he cried and Jean followed his outstretched arm to the corner of the White Tower, where smoke was already rising, blown across the crowd by a strong easterly, carrying the first scent of roasted flesh. At the centre of the swirl, he could see the huge figure of Makepeace, stripped of his doublet, moving between two spits, cajoling the spit boys, larding the sheep carcasses, the fat lifted from a trough within the fires with a large ladle. He saw Uriah see them, see Magonnagal anyway, who was waving a scarlet cloth on a pole above his head. Raising the ladle in acknowledgement, Uriah turned to talk to someone beside him, but Jean could not see who it was through the smoke.

'Ale!' bellowed the Irishman, rapping the pole on a hogshead. 'Finest sweet ale from the Ram, in Southwark.' Those nearest began to press upon them, waving wooden cups and small coin. Jean and Anne, squeezed to the side, mounted the stairs that led to the upper level.

He had just turned to her to say, in vain hope, 'Do you see Gianni?' when a blast of trumpets overcame his words. It issued from the White Tower, whose massive, iron-studded doors swung open to the sound, as if the braying had hitherto been contained within them. The single blast still bounced off the walls when another sound joined it, the deep trump of a single drum. All eyes, including theirs, fixed upon the dark entranceway, as the head of the procession emerged. It was led by pikemen, dressed in the scarlet doublets and black hose of the Tower guard, advancing in four ranks of five, their weapons lowered so that the crowd parted before the points, forming an avenue as wide as the squad's front. To their rear, the single drummer walked alone, his beat dictating the procession's pace. Behind him came five trumpeters, their instruments now at rest to their sides. These were followed by the priests, six of them, in white surplices, three carrying banners of black silk split with a white cross, the lamb of Christ couched in the top right quarter. One waved a censer that issued forth clouds of fragrant sandalwood smoke, two clutched huge altar candles with sheltered flames, a fourth tolled a heavy bell; each of the six chanted, as they walked, the Latin *Misere* in harmony and dirge-like solemnity.

The crowd began to shout, for behind the priests emerged those they had come to see die. The four prisoners were dressed in simple contrast, like pilgrims in their plain smocks, barefoot; three had their hands bound before them, one huge man and two women, while the fourth, a youth, the only one of them who wept, clutched a piece of firewood in his un-yoked hands. Beside each of them a cowled figure held a book of prayer, their hooded faces leaning in, lips moving in the shadows. Only the man in the black cloak beside the weeping boy did not speak, a hand resting on his shoulder.

'Why does he carry wood, Father? What does it mean?'

'He has repented. So he "carries his faggot" as a sign. The boy will not burn today.'

As the end of the procession emerged – a company of archers following a few richly dressed men, members of the council – the head of it reached the rank of soldiers before the execution ground. They parted to admit them and warders and priests spread out among the stakes. The weeping youth threw down his wood and was led away by his black-cloaked comforter. The remaining three prisoners were seized by the masked men, who girdled them with the iron hoops, fastening these with rivets to the centre of the stakes. They began to build a rough pyramid of logs around each stake over a core of dried bracken while the trumpets sounded. As their call died away, as the priests ended their dirge, the drum struck, once, twice, again.

Two of the cowled companions who had prayed and exhorted

beside the sinners until that moment now moved to places behind the council. The third, who had stood beside the huge heretic, went the opposite way, toward the brazier, where a torch was lit and passed into his hand. Raising it high above him, he picked up the drum's beat and walked slowly toward the first stake, the man he'd just left, whose lips moved in ceaseless prayer. A silence now gripped the throng, one so profound that all that could be heard beyond the drumbeat, beyond the snapping of silk banners in the breeze, beyond the whisper of the martyrs, was the crackling of flames.

It was when the torchbearer threw back his cowl that Anne gripped Jean's arm, crying out as if she had been stabbed. He could not penetrate the smoke that swirled between him and the killing ground, could not see what she had just seen. But there was no mistaking the voice he next heard, though he had not heard it in three years, though it had deepened and lost its Tuscan coarseness.

'Observe the justice of the Lord!' cried Gianni Rombaud as he thrust the flames into the pyre.

That voice took away all other sounds, those words breaking something inside Jean. Time slowed, as it always had at Death's approach, but now he was no longer at the centre of that vortex of power, he was at its edge, unable to channel it, scarcely able to move, only able to watch as his daughter went past him, lifting one foot, setting it down, lifting the other, setting it down, lips forming a name, her brother's name, as if his name, screamed out, would be enough to stop the horror. He knew that in her world sounds existed, exploding from a frenzied crowd moving forward for a better view, that in her world the hand he raised – too slowly, too late – might stop her. Yet even though she seemed to barely move she was gone, the black hair glimpsed now and then as she somehow passed through the throng.

'No!'

It was Jean's turn to scream, for once more a Rombaud stood at the darkest centre of this dark realm, wielding death. Yet all that despair was a whisper in a storm, snatched up, blown away, by the noise of the crowd returning in full fury. He turned to his right, to where Uriah was forging, as if through a sea of caps, toward him. He turned left, to see Magonnagal pick up a club from behind a hogshead and take the first step his way. Suddenly, he knew, he recognized his betrayal and he turned away; but his children were before him and, at just that moment, another surge in the crowd pushed those behind Jean forward. Somehow, the shadow of the gap Anne had opened was still there. He let himself be swept into it, people flooding behind him into the channel, like the tide carving into a cliff face.

'Anne!' he screamed, to no avail.

Each step was harder, the wall of flesh ahead of her denser, but she had to break through. For it was not her brother who stood there exalting death. It was not he who pushed the brand into the wood, nor he who had stabbed the German at the crossroads. A demon possessed him, that was clear, and she only had to part this crowd, to reach the centre of the swirling smoke, to wrench that demon from Gianni's soul.

Gianni prayed for the wind to return and clear the smoke away. He had heard that heretics would choke and faint, that they were smoked to death rather than burned. That seemed like an evasion of God's will, for only in fire was that will made manifest, representing both the purging of all impure elements, the scouring away of these heretics' dreadful sins and the awful warning of what awaited such sinners in the eternity of hell. He had himself pulled the sacks of gunpowder from around their necks that some kind or bribed person had tied there to end their pain more swiftly. God would not be so cheated! The flames felt like an extension of himself. They did not start when he pushed the brand into the brazier, they ran from within him, his holy spirit flowing from his heart, transforming wood into tongues of fire.

It is all so simple, he thought, *As simple as faith. These sinners would bring the Antichrist. These sinners must die.*

Jean saw the torch raised in triumph, then thrust into the last of the pyres, just as the smoke from the first, fast billowing now, snatched away his view both of his daughter pushing through the dense crowd and his son aglow with the ecstasy of sacrifice. Sounds were clear within the smoke, the coughing of both victims and spectators, frantic prayers turning to shrieks as the heat reached the heretics' bare feet, the beat of the drum, the tolling of the bell, the dirge of the *Misere* all undernotes to the baying of the crowd. Somehow he had closed the gap to his daughter, she was two arm's lengths ahead of him, five people between, the rank of soldiers buckling as far ahead again. Jean knew that his pursuers were not much further behind.

'Anne!' he screamed again, knowing it was futile.

He'd all but reached her when she hit the line of breastplated guardsman, ducked down, disappeared into the thrust of legs. He saw her again as she appeared on the other side, running the short distance now between the soldiers and the last of the pyres.

Hands wrapped around the arm that clutched fire. Gianni looked into a face that couldn't be there.

'Stop this!' Anne cried, the suddenness of her assault wresting the brand from him. She threw it aside, took his head in both her hands.

'Gianni, oh child, oh my brother! What sins do you commit here?'

The words, the hands, the black eyes. His whole family in them, everything he had escaped from, all that was wrong with the world. He looked away from her to the backs of soldiers struggling to contain a crowd. To one man standing before them. To his father.

Jean Rombaud was close enough now to hear the words that went with the slap, as Gianni backhanded Anne, crashing her onto smoking wood.

'I do God's work here, *sister*. And the only sinner is . . . him!'

And just as Gianni pointed directly at him, Jean felt fingers dig into his shoulder.

'Nothing personal, Rombaud,' came a familiar voice. 'Just business, you understand.'

He squirmed in Uriah's grip, but the hand held him firmly, joined by others as Magonnagal arrived.

'Club the bloody man, shall I?' the Irishman said.

'No need.' Makepeace looked like he was bestowing a great favour. 'Rombaud's a man who knows when a game's up.'

Jean sagged, would have fallen if the press of the crowd and the hands had not held him.

It was at that moment that the first pyre truly caught and the giant heretic left his prayers to scream. All eyes were drawn by the dreadful wail of agony. The man tried to escape the heat, raising his legs from the ground, his body contorting. But the iron girdle around his waist held him and he sank down again, his brown shift catching, encasing him in crimson and yellow, his hair smouldering. Then, just as it seemed as if his agony could go on no longer, as if the martyrdom he'd sought would take him, his huge body bent, dipped into the heart of the fire and, uttering his most terrifying groan, he stood up. The stake that had held him was wrenched from the ground.

The sight took away the crowd's voice, halted the drum, stopped the bell, suspended the dirge mid-note. The burning figure took one step, another, began to totter forward. Then, with the scattering of the embers at his feet, as flaming logs cascaded off the pyre, the burning man burst from the middle of his own execution, bent and ran straight into the line of soldiers.

The top of the stake drove into a guardsman's head, snapping the neck, knocking him forward. The blade of his halberd sliced into a man to Jean's left, one of Uriah's who held him. The crowd exploded away from the burning man. As the stake went over his head, Jean ducked, was singed as the human torch flared by him, separating him from Uriah, who had no choice but to leave his grip or burn. In the space that had cleared, the martyr now began whirling, as if in movement there would be relief, instead of the increase in flame, in agony. The people scattered, trying to avoid the sparks that showered off him, several caught by the ends of the stake as it swept by. Free, Jean saw a gap, and dived into the crowd. He didn't look back until he had reached its extremity, until he could raise himself onto the lowest step of the Beauchamp Tower.

The whirling figure finally stopped, staggered, fell in a flash of flames. Lit by them, Uriah was casting about, shouting, seeking. Jean ducked, but not so low that he could not see to the centre of the Green. See his daughter, lying at his son's feet where his son's blow had thrown her.

Anne! He took a step, just the one, back toward her, his hand clutching the emptiness at his side. Once there would have been a sword there. Once he wouldn't have thought, just drawn Toledo steel, thrust its square tip ahead of him, used it and the chaos around him to get in, seize his child, get out. *Once.*

Turning his back, Jean Rombaud crouched low and ran.

THIRTEEN
TARTARUS

'Something's happening!'

'Oh yes?'

'The gate.'

'Ah, the gate.' There was a yawn. 'Anyone come out?'

'Not yet. Wait, there's someone, it's . . .'

'Another guard?'

'Two. And the gates haven't closed behind them.'

'Really.' Haakon yawned again. He hadn't even opened his eyes so he didn't need to reclose them. When they'd first found this perch opposite the prison, in the barn beside the tavern, he'd reacted almost as swiftly as Erik to every action at the gate opposite, hoping for a pattern to emerge there or some moment of carelessness, anything that might give them their chance. Three weeks of such reacting had worn away his edge. Three weeks of plans, from the abduction of guards to tunnelling from where they watched, each one feverishly thought through, then painfully abandoned. It drained him; so, latterly, he had limited his efforts to restraining Erik from charging the gates.

'They look different, Father, these two. And they're pacing as if they're expecting someone.'

'It's a prison, boy. People come and go every day.'

'Look! Two more have joined them. They're pointing back into the yard. Look!'

With a groan, Haakon rolled over and put his eye to a gap in the rough loam wall. Four guards were indeed standing there.

'So? Waiting for the rest of their shift so they can go and get drunk next door. I wish I could join them.' Haakon dropped back, closed his eyes again, ran his tongue around the dryness of

174

his mouth. Their remaining coin bought them the right to sleep in the stable and just enough food for each day. He hadn't tasted wine in a week.

The door creaked, and the third of their number appeared. 'Something's happening,' the Fugger said.

'That's what I've been trying to tell him!' Erik was already reaching for his weapons, as he had one hundred times since their arrival. 'It's those guards, isn't it?'

'Guards?' The Fugger looked out, then back. 'I don't know about them. But something is happening in Rome.' He squatted down beside Haakon. 'The Pope is dead.'

Again, Haakon didn't bother to open his eyes, just sighed. Between his lovelorn son and the anxious father he seemed to be the only one whose brains were not addled.

'Fugger, the Pope died three weeks ago, the day after we arrived. Why are you excited by such old news?'

'Because I'm not talking about Paul the Third. I'm talking about Marcellus the Second.'

Haakon finally opened one eye. 'But wasn't he just elected?'

'Yes. And now he's just dead. But there's much more than that. The man who succeeds him? Who is already issuing his orders from the Vatican? It's Carafa.'

This brought the other eye wide open as Haakon leaned forward. 'That Neapolitan bastard? The Head of the Inquisition? But he's mad!'

'That never disqualified anyone from being Pope, Haakon.' The Fugger spoke with a contempt born in his Protestant youth. 'No one cares, because his madness is directed against the Church's enemies – and Carafa has a long list. Anyone who strays one fingernail from the Orthodox is in grave danger. The rumours I have heard say that squads of soldiers are already spreading out through the city, arresting heretics, witches, Jews, anyone who carries the Lutheran taint. You know what that will mean?'

'What?' Erik said, when his father merely nodded.

'The prisons will be crammed full, boy. Lots of to-ings and fro-ings, lots of activity, which is good for us. In fact . . .' Haakon put his eye again to the gap. 'By a whore's weary back, you were both right. Something is indeed happening.'

They all went to the entrance of the stable. Across from it, the prison gates still stood open, but there were twenty guards now, soldiers in helm and breastplate, pikes at port, forming a corridor out into the street. As they watched, there was a stirring within the yard and a man put his head out, blinking into the sunlight. He looked around in panic, tried to withdraw but was shoved forward by someone behind him. A soldier raised his pike, struck him with the butt end in his side. The man ran forward, receiving blows left and right, falling once. He reached the end of the line and ran, down the street, round the corner. He'd just cleared it and disappeared when a group of five ran from the gates, followed by ten more, some clutching little sacks, most empty handed, raising them to ward off such blows as they could.

'What is this?' Erik winced as he saw kicks connect.

'A little last punishment, a warning.' The Fugger's voice was grim. 'They're clearing the cells to make room for the new Pope's enemies. These are the unimportant prisoners – thieves, murderers, rapists. Far better they are free so a woman who wants to read the Bible in her own tongue can be locked away.'

'Maybe they'll free Maria!' Erik was studying the crowd outside closely.

'Alas! Since Gianni works for him now, I think Maria's name will be on Carafa's list.'

As they watched, the guards suddenly seemed to lose interest in their exertions. A last, large group of men, a few women, fled with little more than a boot aimed at their backsides. Most of these headed straight for the tavern beside the stable.

'Come on,' said the Fugger, 'we haven't had a chance to speak to a woman inmate yet. Maybe they'll have news of my child.'

It was an ugly crew that filled the tavern, large men with brandings and tattoos, reed-thin women with sallow skin and steel-hard eyes. The innkeeper seemed to know a few and was advancing cheap wine on credit. There seemed little doubt as to the type of profession most of them followed; little doubt too that the landlord saw future profit in his generosity.

They split up, listened to conversations, spent some of their precious coin on loosening tongues. Erik found favour with one woman. Though three times as old as he, she was nearly as tall, and her prison-shrunken frame must once have been as wide, for her skirt, shift and cloak swamped her in excess cloth.

'Want to get into the women's cells, do you, sweet boy? A lusty lad like you needn't go so far to find his pleasure. Why not just give yourself to Long Margaretha, eh? Come! Come outside now.'

A gnarled hand reached out from within the tattered garments, running swiftly down below his belt. He intercepted it, placed a cup, poured some wine. She drank deep, sought a refill, drank again, smiled. 'No? You're one of them, eh? Only like them if they're captive?' She let out a loud cackle. 'Well, some advice then, young pretty. If you do get in, stay on the main floor for your jigging. Nice girls like me up there, good daughters of the Church, all. Slip the guard a florin and he'll leave you alone with us. Slip us another and you can slip us what you want – we'll bless you as we take you in!'

She drank hard again, then leaned into him. He forced himself not to withdraw from the foul scent of the cell that clung to her.

'But here's some other advice – don't descend the stairs, for they lead straight to hell. No, they pass by hell. They finish . . . in Tartarus.'

She shuddered, some memory suddenly sobering her, her voice dropping. 'You can hear them wail down there, just sometimes, if the night is very still,' she continued in a whisper. 'Once I heard them singing, a hymn it was, but in Italian, not Latin! Protestants, you see! No wonder they are condemned to the foulest vault!' The eyes, that had cleared in the recollection, glazed again and she belched extravagantly. 'So don't go there, my lover. Not unless you likes to stick it into skeletons! And I've met some who do!' Her laughter rolled over him. 'Heretic skeletons at that!'

Erik felt a chill. He was suddenly certain where his Maria was held. He swiftly rejoined the others.

'New sweetheart, boy? Little big for you, wasn't she?'

His father could find humour in situations where there was none. 'A woman from the prison. She told me they put the heretics in some sort of vault on the lower floor. She called it Tartarus!' He burst out, 'I fear my Maria is there.'

'Tartarus?'

'You know it, Fugger?' said Haakon.

The question was unnecessary, for the man's face had turned

white. 'I know it. Sometimes, in my despair, I called my midden chamber by that accursed name. I sought to glorify my paltry suffering but I was barely in hell, while Tartarus is seven leagues below the deepest level of Hades.' He let out a cry. 'And they keep my daughter there? Oh Merciful Christ!'

'Then why do you stay?' Erik was more terrified by the shadows in the Fugger's eyes than anything he had heard so far. He was on his feet, his hands reaching below his cloak to his weapons. 'I will try my scimitars against those Roman dogs at the gate right now.' He stepped toward the door.

'And you will die for nothing.' Haakon grabbed his son by the shoulder, pulled him close. 'We know now that more prisoners will be going in than have been released. The gates will open and close often, day and night. There's our chance, perhaps. Fugger, tell the boy!'

But the German's eyes were still focused inward, gazing on horrors.

As Erik began to argue, the main door of the tavern swung open. In the entrance stood a tall officer, dressed in the uniform of the Vatican guards. This Pope's policeman brought instant silence to a room filled with some of the Pontiff's recent, reluctant guests.

'Scum of the earth!' the man boomed. 'Just who I'm looking for.'

He mounted a chair in the centre of the room, swept a plumed hat from long, beautifully coifed red hair and shouted, 'So, you dogs, I'm recruiting. We have a lot of work to do tonight and not enough men to do it. This gives you a chance to redeem yourselves for your miserable sins . . . and to earn good coin into the bargain! Buy yourselves a few more nights of drinking and whoring before you sin again and we throw you back inside those walls.'

Some of his audience, wine bold, jeered, some slunk away, most stayed silent and stared.

'It's very simple, even to donkeys like yourselves.' He reached into his cloak, pulled out sheaves of parchment. 'These are lists of people we want. One list, one officer. Three of you go with each of my men and bring these villains back to the prison. For each one brought back, there's a ducat. For a family, you'll get a piece of gold.'

There were cheers at this. He continued, 'And what's more, there's no danger. Those we want you to arrest are not scum like you . . .' More cheers. 'They're scum like Luther, Calvin and such folk. Religious scum. Jewish scum. And witches, too. So you'll make gold on earth while you store up treasure in heaven.'

This was greeted by the largest burst of cheering so far, and men began to crowd around his chair. He descended, before he fell, and led a party of them outside. Through the open doorway, he could be seen issuing arms, assigning men to his officers, sending them on their way.

'Are you thinking what I'm thinking, Haakon?'

'Yes,' said the Norseman. 'We sign up for one of his squads, and escort prisoners right through that gate.'

'And leave my daughter in Tartarus for another night? No. I was thinking of something a little less complicated.' Red spots glowed on the Fugger's cheeks. 'Why don't we just stove this bastard's head in and steal his pass?'

Captain Lucius Heltzinger stroked his magnificent red-gold beard, well satisfied. He had got so many volunteers he was able to select the pick of the crop, the murderers rather than the rapists, thugs who had already killed and who would happily kill again if it was required. Sometimes it was. He'd lied when he said there was no danger, for these Jews and heretics put up a surprising resistance on occasion. Hence these sheep for the sacrifice! If he lost a few of this prison scum in taking his quarry, well, that was more of Carafa's gold that could find its way into his own pocket! He had plenty of gold, it was said, this new Pope. And he wasn't like his predecessors with their talk of reconciliation and reform. Reconciliation never bought new armour, as Lucius's father used to say. There was no profit in peace. Carafa, the Inquisitor General himself, had sent them back to war!

Feeling so pleased with himself, he was even indulgent to the one-handed beggar who approached him, just as he'd handed his final list to his last subordinate and had watched the mix of soldiers and criminals march away. Instead of the tip of his boot placed in the dog's backside, he just barked at him, 'We have all we need, turd. And we wouldn't take cripples anyway!'

He was turning back to give orders to the two soldiers he'd retained with him, when he felt a tug at his sleeve. He raised his hand to strike the impudent cur, but he had scuttled back, stump of hand held up, words spilling out.

'There are people hiding nearby. Heretics! I can take you to them.'

'There are heretic pigs rooting everywhere. I have enough on my list to deal with.'

'But these are heretic sows, master. In the stable, right here, kind lord. Two girls, left by their merchant father these three days.'

'Girls?' Both the officer's head and those of his soldiers now swung fully to the informant. 'How old?'

'Not very, master. Fourteen, perhaps.'

'Well, it is our duty to root out heresy, wherever we find it, is it not?' The Captain stroked his moustache. 'Lead us to them and there will be a ducat in it for you.'

'Kind master!' said the Fugger, limping toward the stable.

It was dark in there after the brightness of daylight. Lucius and his two men stood blinking into the gloom.

'Where are they, dog?' Lucius whispered.

'There, master.' The Fugger, who had withdrawn into further shadow, whispered back. 'The left stall, under that old blanket there. There! See how they shiver!'

Lucius could now indeed make out a shaking under the straw. 'Drag them out,' he mouthed, drawing his sword.

His two men moved forward. They could see the blanket quivering for themselves, even hear a high-pitched whimpering coming from within it. Smirking, one of them leaned down and grabbed a frayed end, the other poised with arms spread wide to stoop and snatch.

The blanket rose into the air, dust exploding into the sunbeams, a man exploding up from within the cloud, a man with a piece of wood in each hand. They were stretched out, then crossed before him, catching the light as they went, passing from flame to shadow to flame again. When they stopped moving, there was a loud thump and the two guards seemed to meld together before, joined, they sank unconscious to the floor.

Lucius shrieked, wheeling back toward the door. But someone stood now between him and escape, as tall as he, wider. Haakon bent under a desperate sword slash, drove his shoulder into the officer's stomach, running him back into the central post of the barn, which cracked, shaking the whole structure. There was a brief scuffle, till a huge fist rose and fell. Then there was just heavy breathing.

'Fugger, the doors! Erik, help me get this bastard's clothes off before there's too much blood on them. And bring the ropes.'

The Fugger slammed the stable gates closed, barring them. 'Find his authority, Haakon. His papers. They should be in that satchel.'

Haakon threw the bag across, while he and his son began to strip the body.

'Haakon!' The Fugger held up his stump of a hand, beside the half hand barely healed from Siena.

'Sorry, Fugger.' He left Erik to his task, came across, opened the strap on the case. 'Is this what we seek?'

The Fugger flicked his three fingers through the oiled parchment. 'Yes. He's wasted no time, this Carafa. His crest is already encircled by the Papal. This will get one of us into the prison.'

'Let it be me.' Erik had just finished undoing the laces where the doublet attached to the hose. Slipping it off, he held it up. 'He's about my size.'

'He's more like mine,' said Haakon. 'You are not going, boy!'

'I am.' Erik stood to face Haakon, eyes ablaze. 'She's my love.'

'And you are my son. And I know you. You'll start laying about you with your swords, you'll get nowhere near to freeing her, you'll—'

'And you?' Erik was almost shouting now. 'What good will you do, old man? I have the strength, and the swords and the cause and—'

'And I have my axe!' Haakon bent and swept the weapon up now. 'It has seen more blood than you, or your scimitars, could ever dream of. And as for strength . . .'

Their heads were almost conjoined now and the Fugger had to push hard to get between them.

'Listen to me! Stop shoving and listen!' The two big men took a pace back, breathing heavily. 'I think you should both go in. I think it would be better.'

'But we only have a pass for one.'

'One soldier, yes. But it also speaks of prisoners. This officer could bring prisoners in.'

Haakon whistled. 'So I could take Erik in as my prisoner!'

'Or I could take you in as mine!' The younger man glared.

Before Haakon could answer, the Fugger raised his three-fingered hand.

'There's more to it than that. There's no point just getting inside. We need to get to the women's cells. We need a woman prisoner.'

Erik laughed. 'And where will we find a woman's clothes to fit one of us? It's impossible.'

The Fugger scratched his head for a moment. Suddenly, he smiled. 'Who was your large girlfriend in the tavern, Erik? The one who told you about Tartarus?'

'Long Margaretha? Well, she, she . . . why are you looking at me like that, Fugger?'

Instead of replying, he turned to Haakon. 'You always wanted a daughter, did you not, Haakon?'

'No!' Erik's words came out like prayer. 'You didn't see her properly, smell her, oh, she . . . she . . .'

'She'd be more than willing to shed a few clothes,' Haakon said, winking, 'for a lusty lad like you.'

It all took longer than they'd expected. The guards had to be stripped, trussed, gagged, then placed in three of the old wine butts that were stacked in the rear of the barn. Erik had to shave. Then Long Margaretha had to be fetched. The Fugger's entreaties proved no use and she was only pried away from the escalating debauchery of the inn by Erik, who lured her with soft words, smiles, a glimpse of coin. When they finally had her in the stable, she was initially frightened by the three men, then could not stop laughing when they explained what they wanted. More wine, their last florin, and the quality of the guard's clothing she would get as temporary replacement convinced her. She made a great show of teasing as she removed her clothing. She also talked continuously about the prison, adding to their store of knowledge. By the time Erik was dressed in skirt and bodice, a shawl over his head, they had a good knowledge of the layout beyond the prison walls. Their last fear, that the woman would insist on rejoining her companions in the inn, was allayed when the quantity of wine took its effect and Long Margaretha sank gracefully into the straw, snoring gently. No shaking would rouse her.

They left by the rear door, went down the alley and around to the corner of the street that led to the prison. A prisoner and escort emerging from the barn might have caused some suspicion. Even though the gate guards were fully occupied, as they could see as soon as they peered around the building.

'It has begun, then. The new and glorious Papacy of Carafa.' The Fugger spoke softly as he watched a family being dragged by thugs towards the gates. The father was barely conscious, blood caking his face, his stockinged feet scraping the cobbles as two men ran him along by his arms. Two more held a daughter apiece, young faces averted from the grizzled beards that were thrust at them, the whispering of some crudity. A boy was carried in another's arms, barely seven, kicking wildly until a blow made him go limp.

'Come then,' said Haakon grimly, 'let us join this merry throng. They might not notice us.'

He pulled at the Switzer's doublet, tight around his throat, undid another of the buttons that constricted his chest.

'Haakon, you are the officer, remember? Do not slink to the rear, a leader does not try to slip in. Boldness now, my friend. Hide in plain sight.'

Haakon nodded once, then breathed deep, snapping another button.

'Come on then, you trollop.' He gave his son a mighty shove, the boy staggering forward, tripping over unfamiliar layers of skirt. The bell began to toll seven as they moved out of the shadows and Haakon called over his shoulder, 'We will be coming out of that gateway before eight bells, Fugger. Be ready!'

'I will be.' The Fugger watched them cross the street, cursing the one-handed state that meant he stayed behind. Near the gate, Haakon stooped and flung his son across his shoulders, skirts flapping around his face. 'May Jesus Christ protect you both. Bring my child back to me.'

Then he set about his own preparations. There was so little time till eight bells. But if they did not emerge then, there was an eternity of sorrow before him.

'Mind the way there!' Haakon shoved against the clamouring group at the gateway, one arm under his son who hung limply, the other shoving aside men who snarled and shoved back. 'Move aside, I say! I have a queen of sinners here!' He reached the officer at the gate. 'Tried to escape dressed as a whore, she did.' He turned, flashing Erik's face.

The harassed gate commander snatched the papers Haakon proffered, glanced at them, then squinted at the Norseman.

'I've never seen you before. What squadron are you with?'

Haakon stepped close to the man, forcing him to step back a pace.

'If it's any of your business, friend, I've just arrived from Naples. Ordered from his home by his Holiness himself. Just take your time and read the whole document, why don't you? I'll be sure to tell Carafa how helpful you've been!'

The officer lowered his eyes, mumbled, 'No need for that tone,' the words barely carrying above a burst of shouting, the noise of blows, of wails that doubled with the arrival of more prisoners to the horde outside the gates.

'Go through.' The papers were handed back. 'Women's cells to your right across the yard. Stop shoving there!'

He turned away, aiming blows, while Haakon marched Erik through the archway. On the other side he set him on his feet where, for a moment, they contemplated the mayhem before them.

The prison yard was filled with a crowd four times as big as that before the gate. The majority of the seething mass was to their left, where the men were being selected, searched, shoved through a dark doorway. Thugs with cudgels struck out, driving the herd forward, dragging any rendered insensible by the blows. Most went meekly to the table where men sat with lists, checking off the names of the new Pope's enemies. A few, drawn by the cries of their women and children, tried to resist, even when the clubs fell, when their blood ran.

'This is hell, Father!' Erik muttered, bent still, trying to diminish his size.

'And we are bound for its lowest level. Come, over there.'

Reaching the table of parchments, Haakon threw his son down before it.

'Captain and prisoner!' he said loudly, dropping his pass onto the table, praying to both Odin and Christ that no one here knew the man whose name was on the papers. When no one reacted, and the clerk to the officer's left picked up the piece of parchment, he added, 'And a special prisoner it is too. This is the Witch of Trastevere.'

He kicked at the prone body and Erik gave a convincing female groan.

'I have not heard of her.' The clerk's voice was nasal, high-pitched. He began flicking through his lists.

'Not heard of the Witch of Trastevere?' Erik noted his father's voice drop into a familiar register, one he had heard all his life as Haakon wove his dazzling tales. It was barely above a whisper, designed to draw an audience in. The clerk and officer leaned forward.

'Not heard of the hag who pulls unwanted babies from careless girls' stomachs, who uses the flesh of the unborn to curse the father, wither his flesh, ravage his manhood with carbuncles and boils?'

Both men shifted in their seats, crossed their legs, crossed themselves.

'When I went to her hovel, candles were set in skulls and flayed skins hung from the rafters. I killed twenty cats, her familiars, that snarled, bit, scratched at me, barring my way to her dank bed.'

Erik let out what he thought was a cackle, swiftly cut off by the toe of Haakon's boot.

The clerk swallowed. 'Speed her inside then, just beyond this doorway. We'll keep her nearby, for she sounds like one of the first for the flames.'

'Oh no, friend.' Haakon's voice maintained its timbre. 'When the sun is fully gone, she can turn into a bat. Those barred windows will not hold her. There is only one place for the likes of her: Tartarus!'

'Aye,' said the officer. 'We'll send her there. Guard?' He called over his shoulder.

'I must take her, friend.' Haakon leaned closer. 'One look at her face and she has you in her power. It was only that I killed her familiars, took their power, that I can control her. Their blood has dried on my skin. See!' He thrust out a wrist, scratch marks there from the struggle in the barn.

Clerk and officer looked at the wounds, at each other, the latter nodded, and a seal was dipped in ink and banged down on the parchment.

'Through that door on the left, the low one. There is only one stairwell.' The officer crossed himself again, added, 'But do not linger down there long, Captain. Dump her and leave. And may Christ protect you!'

'Amen, friend. I will stay only till my holy duty is done.' Haakon smiled briefly, then kicked the figure at his feet. 'Come, whore of Babylon. To your fate!'

Erik struggled to keep the headcloth in place as he got up. It slipped a little but the men's eyes were averted, heeding the warning, choosing to focus on the heretic families behind him. Haakon's hand in his back shoved him forward.

'Lucky so far,' his father whispered as they climbed the stairs to the doorway.

'Do you have to keep kicking me to make your points?' Erik hissed.

'Suppose not. But why deny myself the pleasure?'

They were at the door, the parchment raised to the grate there causing bolts to be withdrawn. They stepped into the gloom.

Maria Fugger waited, the bone clutched in her right hand, her left fingers checking and re-checking the saw-toothed, sharpened point. She had cut herself upon it ... when? An hour before? A day? It didn't matter. It was the moment she'd tasted her own blood and liked it, its warmth, its iron tang. She had been tempted to cut herself again, in a place where the blood might flow more readily, flow longer. Her own blood had been the first food, the first liquid, that had passed her lips in ... three days? A week? She was hungry and she needed to eat. If she didn't eat she would sleep and if she slept she would never wake again, that was clear. Then she considered that blood alone, however salty-delicious, would not sustain her long. It was not an unlimited resource. But there was other blood near, an endless supply. If she was clever.

She had heard them move about, listened to their snuffling, felt gossamer whiskers flick her face, kicked out again and again against the prying snout, the scrabbling claw. She had always thought to drive the rats away. Until now. Now she prayed for them to come, prayed hard, waiting in her straw cave, bent over the little space she'd cleared before her. She was ready. This was her realm; for she was a Fugger, after all, and her family ruled the dark, cramped places.

Sounds came. But not the ones she expected, no scratching, no high-pitched squeak. Instead there was a scraping of a key, a shooting of bolts and then . . . then the most wondrous sound of all – the voice of her love, shouting her name.

'Maria!' Erik stood, a silhouette against the torch his father held behind him, reeling from the stench of corruption that he had unleashed in pulling back the door.

She had seen and heard such glorious phantoms before in the month? The lifetime? – she had been in this place. She knew better than to answer them for she would drive them away with attention. If she lay back and kept her silence, maybe the spirit would speak more.

Erik grabbed the torch from his father. Haakon reached back, over the prone body of the gaoler unconscious at his feet, and took another from its bracket on the wall. Flinging their arms across their mouths, trying not to breathe in the stench that assailed them, the Norsemen entered Tartarus.

Hummocks of straw lay scattered before them, like the seed pods of giant plants, random clumps disappearing into the gloom beyond the torch-spill, whose light failed to reach any boundary of wall or ceiling. Where it did fall there was an instant rustle, as if each cave was alive, a creature folding in on itself, shrinking from the glare.

'Maria?' Erik called again, almost slipping down the slick two steps that led to the dungeon floor.

'Maria?' a man's voice answered him, calling back in just his tone. He spun towards it.

'Maria?' cried another, a woman, from the opposite side. He spun back. Then the shrieking began, voice after voice crying out the one word, from all directions, a hideous cacophony building to a peak and then suddenly dying, as if choked off by a single hand.

'Father . . .' His next words were lost in the babble of voices that rose again.

'Father? Father! Father! Father?' Echoing against the walls, dying just as suddenly as the word before had. And in the silence that followed there was now a palpable anticipation. Somewhere in the darkness someone giggled.

Haakon, joining his son on the floor, pointed to himself, mouthed, 'I'll try.'

'Friends . . .'

'Friends, friends, friends, friends.'

Rolling over them, waves of sound, the glee in the game clear. Erik cursed, a Tuscan farm curse and some heard it and repeated it and that word then swept around, alternating with, finally subduing 'Father'. He was about to curse again when that father's hand clamped over his mouth.

'Freedom,' cried Haakon, the word instantly picked up, passed around, crescendoing. This one didn't die, though some ceased, some carried on using it. One voice finally spoke, a man's voice.

'Freedom?' he said, and the tone was questioning.

As soon as it was uttered, Haakon shouted, 'You're all free!' He got the words out before some picked it up, echoed it, while others began crying other words in response. Where before there was uniformity now there was chaos, voices seeking to overrule, to dominate. As the babble built, Haakon took a step deeper into the prison, wondering what to say next. He had no sooner planted his foot when something shot out from a hummock and grabbed it, nearly bringing him down. Haakon lowered the torch till he could see what held him. It was barely a hand, five stumps projecting from a blistered palm. Yet the grip was strong and, as Haakon bent, the voices died around him, allowing him to hear the cracked whisper rising from the centre of the straw.

'You offer those who have nothing the one thing they desire.

But because we have nothing, we have nothing to lose. So beware, if you torment us for your pleasure!'

'I have opened the door,' Haakon said. 'I am going to walk through it once I have found whom I seek. I will leave it open, if you will help me.'

These words were not echoed. Instead, it felt as if the whole cell, every cave creature, the very walls were leaning in, listening, waiting. Silence pressed until finally, that dry voice whispered again.

'Then speak. No one will mock you now.'

Haakon turned and nodded to his son.

'I seek Maria-Carmine Fugger,' Erik declared in a loud voice. 'Can any here tell me where she lies?'

In her cave, Maria smiled. Of all the dreams she'd had since her imprisonment began this was the best. The words she most desired to hear spoken by the voice she most missed. There was no point speaking back though. Phantoms were so easily scared away. She would answer in her head though.

'I am here, Erik, my lover, my only. Lying back in the straw as you like me to!'

She couldn't understand the giggling that rose all round her. She was sure she had not spoken aloud, though it was strange that heavy boots seemed now to be marching toward her. She nestled further in, hiding in her cave.

'Speak again, my love.'

His voice came from quite close, over to her left. Soon her phantom lover would be there. He would take her in his phantom arms, lay the length of his phantom body beside her, then . . .

She let out a little moan. Almost instantly, hands were burrowing at the frail roof above her. Others had tried this before, when they suspected that she had bones to suck. Well, she had a bone now, a special bone, ready to stop any thief by the drawing of his blood.

The hand reached in to her and she jabbed it with the sharpened bone. The cry of pain had a familiar tone, she had heard something like it before – Erik cried like that when she raked her nails down his back.

A hand reached again, grabbed and she was being dragged up,

out. She raised the bone knife high to drive it down into this violator's neck . . .

'Maria!' Erik cried, holding her above him, looking up in wonder, tears beginning to track down his face.

'No!' The weapon dropped and she shook her head violently from side to side, tried to twist from his grip, to fall, to scuttle back to safety. Phantoms shouldn't pick you up, hold you in the air, stare at you with love.

He held her, despite her wriggling, despite the torch in his other hand.

'Oh my Maria, I have found you.'

He brought her down, her chest across his shoulder. Suddenly all her struggles ceased.

'The best dream yet,' she thought, snuggling into him. 'Might as well enjoy it.'

'Come, Erik, bring her. Her father waits.' Haakon was back on the steps. He turned, raised his torch into the darkness. The hummocks of straw moved as if drawn to the flame. 'And for any who wish to leave Tartarus, the gate is open.'

It was the sight of Captain Lucius Heltzinger in his underclothes running to the prison gates, Long Margaretha at his heels, that finally drove the Fugger to action. Till then he had been content to wait beside the horses, knowing that he could only act when Haakon and Erik appeared. And pray. But the sight of the Captain, trailing his bonds, changed that. The Fugger left the lee of the wall and ran after him.

'Let me through, let me through! I am a Captain of the Guard.' Lucius was trying to force his way into the dense throng at the gate many of whom resisted being jostled by the nearly naked man.

'They are trying to break out of the prison! Vassari!' he screamed, seeing a guard he knew. 'It's me, Heltzinger. Let me through!'

'By the cross, Captain.' The soldier looked him up and down in wonder. 'What has happened to your clothes?'

'Give me your cloak, dolt!' He ripped the covering from the man's back. 'Bruno and Guiseppe are back there, in the stable, trussed in barrels. Send someone. The rest of you, follow, swiftly.'

The Fugger arrived as Heltzinger grabbed a pike and led a group of men, both soldiers and recently conscripted criminals, through the gate. The Fugger, awkwardly pulling a pistol from within his cloak and yelling as loudly as any, followed.

The yard within was packed with prisoners and guards, wailing children, angry men, shouting women; the sudden insertion of Heltzinger's dozen men, shoving and striking out, only raised the temperature. They pushed their way through to the table set before the women's cells where the officer rose from his seat behind the table.

'You can't be Lucius Heltzinger,' he said, concern on his face, trying to be bold. 'Lucius Heltzinger is inside. He had just taken a prisoner in, not five minutes since. The Witch of Trastevere.'

'The Witch of Trastevere? The Witch of . . . Christ, you fool!' It was all Lucius could do not to strike the man. 'He has hoodwinked you. He goes to free some female traitor. Come on, men! And you, get more guards and block all the gates.'

'No, Captain, not that way! He didn't go to the women's prison. He went down there.' The guard, anxious to redeem himself, had grabbed Heltzinger's arm. 'To Tartarus.'

Using the pike butt, the Captain pushed the low door open but it caught on something just the other side. Two of his men shoved hard, and forced the door. The body of another guard rolled a few steps down, settled.

'Onward, men.' Lucius decided to lead from the rear. The man he'd wrestled with briefly in the barn was a man he had no desire to meet first.

The Fugger watched the dozen men go through the low archway. He almost followed, till he realized how little use he would be down there. That was the Norsemen's province. But if they made it to the top of the stair they would need help.

He looked around the yard. Many guards had joined the Captain in his descent, leaving less than a dozen now trying to marshall the horde, a frightened, angry mob of at least eighty of Carafa's enemies. As he watched, a man resisted, struck back, was beaten down with pike butts while others glowered, surged forward in anger.

The whole place reminded him of the tunnel under the walls of

Siena. A well-placed flash of gunpowder could collapse everything.

Checking that his powder was dry under the wheelock of his pistol, the Fugger moved into the mêlée.

They were halfway back up the stairwell, when they heard muffled shouting ahead. Haakon raised a hand. Erik, holding Maria against his chest, halted. Behind them, out of sight, there came a faint whispering.

Then the door above must have opened because there was a blast of noise, a gust of fresher air and, a moment later, the sound of boots descending the circular stair.

'Back!' Haakon hissed, dashing his torch against the wall. They'd passed a small alcove on either side, six steps below. It wasn't much, but with walls closer than the span of his arms it was something. He pulled his short battle axe out from the folds of his stolen cloak. From the darkness opposite him, he heard a whispered 'Can you walk?', a simple 'Yes', the scrape of scimitar on scimitar.

'On, men, on!' yelled a voice from above and almost immediately there were flickers of light. Torches, thrust forward, preceded the footfall of iron-shod boots.

When the first flames drew level with his eyes, Haakon screamed, 'Now!' and swept his blade above the light.

The cry of fear that greeted his shout was cut off by the blow, but another followed swiftly.

'Help! We have found th—'

Erik struck, though the low roof meant that he could not swing, just use the point, the least effective part of his curved weapons. Nevertheless this cry too was choked in blood, replaced instantly by his yell of, 'Haakonsson!'

The fall of the torchbearers meant instant darkness, men scrambling up and away above him before the sudden assault, panicked feet slipping on the stair.

'Go!' yelled Haakon, but his son needed no bidding. Haakon trying to follow, tripped over a body. Above him there came a clash, cries in the dark. He was up and on.

There was some light here, torches waving behind the front rank of men. At the back of them Haakon recognized the officer he'd left tied up in a barrel and cursed his previous haste. Then he was among them, dodging a pike thrust, moving his chest away from the jab of a sword. He struck back, using the butt of the axe like a pole into someone's face. The man fell, but there was another behind him, and another behind him. Unable to use their weapons effectively, father and son blocked the thrusts that came at them, blades locked and the shoving began. Strong though they both were, they were just two. And the ten or more above had the height.

'Yes! Drive them back to hell!' shouted Lucius Heltzinger, looking to thrust his pike point over the head of his men. Then he changed his grip, placed the length of the shaft against the back of those nearest him, shoved hard. The extra weight caused a bowing and first Haakon, then Erik tumbled back.

The ground they had gained was lost. Pikes drove at them and they reeled back, parrying desperately. Maria screamed and pulled Erik away from a sword aimed at his face, into the alcove where she had remained. Haakon collapsed into the other one, his axe cutting down on the pike pole, snapping it.

They were trapped. There was a moment of silence. The men above had halted, a hedge of sharp points now pointing into the alcoves.

'Keep herding them back!' cried Lucius Heltzinger. 'We'll pen these sheep into the foulest region of hell.'

Haakon looked across, found his son's eyes. In them he saw what must be within his own. An acknowledgement that this was the end.

He was about to say it, to yell 'Farewell' and throw himself onto the pikes, when a sound came from behind them, from down the stairs. It started low, one word on a single whisper, taken up by a voice, then another, another, building, till a score of voices spoke, more, and it was no longer a whisper but a roar. Bodies in rags, straw-strewn and filth-encrusted, swept up the stairs, screaming out that word now, transformed from the label of their degradation to the banner of their hope.

'Tartarus!'

Its legions poured from their prison. Bone knives thrust before them, they ducked under the pike blades, stabbed upwards. The soldiers on the stair stumbled, fell, cursed, tried to avoid the shards of bone jabbed at their faces. Those that had not fallen broke and ran, wraiths a step behind.

Those within the alcoves needed no second bidding. 'Come!' shouted Haakon, and they trailed the last moving pile of rags up toward the light.

The Fugger knew he was looking at a powderkeg. The heretics, the Jews, all the fearful prisoners of the new Pope, they had all but given up in their despair. But the brutality of their treatment, and the diminishing number of the guards, was instilling some courage. They would follow someone who took a lead, he felt sure. They would heed a sign.

As he drew close to the officer in charge, he drew the pistol from within the folds of his cloak. Then, as he stepped forward, screams erupted from the gateway to Tartarus.

Lucius emerged first, his cloak abandoned, once more clad only in his undershirt.

'Guns, here!' he screamed, and four guards with muskets moved to obey him, to encircle the tiny entrance.

This was the moment and the Fugger recognized it. As he pulled the trigger, saw the wheel strike the flint and drop sparks into the pan, he cried, 'Death to tyranny!'

The gun exploded and a guard died. Beaten prisoners saw their chance of vengeance, turning on the thugs that had molested them. The yard convulsed in a frenzy of separate battles. Only before the women's prison did the Fugger see any ordered resistance, where Heltzinger stood with his men and their half dozen muskets. Then, just as these were primed and lowered to fire into the mêlée, grey bodies burst from the building, bone knives in their hands. The last semblance of order dissolved.

Behind him someone had opened the gates of the men's prison and the Fugger was nearly swept away, buffeted about by the surging, screaming mob, the pistol ripped from his half-hand. Over the heads he saw a familiar figure in the doorway.

'Haakon! Over here!' he yelled, to no avail. He saw the Norseman scan the crowd, then gesture behind him. Erik stepped out, a bundle of rags held in his arms. It took the Fugger more than a moment to realize what he held there, tears arriving with the realization.

'My daughter! Oh, my child!'

Haakon began to push through toward the gate. The fight was over, revenge just begun. Passages opened within the surging crowd, and the Fugger struggled to the gate. He arrived at the same time as the others.

Barely able to form the words, he asked, 'Is she alive?'

A hand came out from the rags, bloodied and begrimed, gripping his arm. 'Don't go, Father!' Maria said softly. 'Tell me another story.'

The gates had already been breached; two dead guards lay in the mud. The Fugger led them swiftly to their horses. They mounted and spurred into the crowd that ran from the broken gates. Through them Haakon glimpsed a writhing, half-naked body hoisted on pike points, red-gold hair waving, an undershirt staining in blood. Flames had sprung up in one of the buildings there, and above their crackling could be heard the ugly chanting of a mob united in vengeance.

Haakon shook his head. 'Is this what you had in mind, Fugger, when you said we should hide in plain sight.'

The Fugger returned his grin. 'Not exactly. Montalcino?'

'Aye, Montalcino. As swift as these nags can carry us. Right, boy?'

But Erik had no ear for his father's words. He was too occupied hearing everything that issued from his love's ragged, beautiful lips.

' "They make haste to shed innocent blood." Isaiah, I think.'

'Isaiah? What the hell has Isaiah got to do with the price of pork, Fugger? Anyway, it's not innocent blood I desire to shed, but the guilty.'

'But you'll drag my Maria with you, risk her blood.'

'Hell's teeth! She can stay here! I've said!'

'I will not be separated from my Erik again!'

'It will only be for a little while, love.'

'No! Besides, it was Gianni Rombaud who condemned me to that hell. I look forward to meeting him again. I'll have his eyes on my fingernails!'

A huge fist thumped a table. 'Then, by the wounds of Christ, let's all go!'

'But where, Norseman?'

'To France. We agreed with Jean and Anne that we would rendezvous in Paris—'

'From the third day after St Aloyisius and on, outside Notre Dame between noon and three bells.' The Fugger huffed. 'I always thought it was a crazed plan. If Gianni beat them to the crossroads, as seems probable, he could be on the way back to Rome with his prize. Or returning it to London. Jean and Anne could be anywhere in pursuit.'

Haakon smiled grimly. 'Rendezvous, however crazed, must be kept. France is the last place we know they were, for Jean will have followed Gianni to the crossroads for the hand. And Paris is as good a place as any to gather information as well as being three days' ride from the Loire. Or from London. So unless anyone has a better plan . . .'

One by one each shook their heads, even, finally, the Fugger. At his sigh, Haakon rose, held out a hand. Each there laid a hand on top. 'Then the quest is reformed. Most of it, anyway. Through the ogres of hell, or a thousand French swords, we will find Jean and Anne again. Four against the world, if need be.'

'Five.'

They had not heard her come, for she had not wanted to be heard. She had stood in the shadows near the door and listened, tears in her eyes, her face red with the struggle between heart and mind.

'Five,' she said again, coming forward to where they had frozen at the sound of her voice. She laid her hand on top of those already there.

'Beck.' Haakon's voice was troubled. 'Are you well enough to travel?'

'I am. My daughter healed me well. I will not hold you up, Norseman, and I am still better with a musket than any of you. Besides, I need to be there to stop this one ripping my son's eyes out.' She laid her other hand on Maria's shoulder, stopping the girl's protest with a squeeze.

The feel of their hands under hers. The power of their friendship in the circle. She had missed that in the weeks of rejection while she had tried to return to her Jewish faith, to the tribe she had rejected so long ago when she took Jean Rombaud as her man. Now, hearing them, feeling that power, she knew where she had to be.

'So I will come with you to Paris, to London. To the end of the world. I will try to stop my men killing each other, my strong, proud men. I will try to do what is right.'

Now it was Haakon's eyes that filled with tears, but his voice was strong. 'Truly, the quest *is* reformed. Let them feel, wherever they are now, whatever peril they are facing, that we are coming to their aid.'

As one voice they said it.

'Amen.'

FOURTEEN
SINS OF THE FATHER

'*Benedic me, Domine, quia peccavi in cogitatione, verbo et opere. Mea . . .*'

'Forgive me, my son, for I speak only the language of this land. I am a poor priest of this parish and have little Latin.'

Gianni glanced at the grille that separated the cubicles. Behind it, a darker shadow showed where the priest leaned in to listen. Sighing, Gianni thought of the walk here from the Tower, by-passing church after church in order to reach this cathedral of St Paul's. He'd reasoned that at the centre of worship in this realm, surely there would be someone of both intelligence and rigour to hear his confession, then apply a suitably harsh penance for his sins? Yet even here, all he encountered was ignorance. No wonder this kingdom had strayed so far from the light when even its priests could not speak the holy tongue.

Of the four languages he spoke, English was his least favourite; and this priest, by the roughness of his voice, spoke one of the strange, guttural dialects that seemed to change every second street! He was tempted to leave, but it had been some time since his last confession in Rome, when he had been absolved for the murder of the old Jew. There was fresh blood on his hands – enemy blood, heretic blood it was true, but blood nonetheless. Yet to speak of all that to someone who had probably never left the cloisters of St Paul's?

Still, perhaps this was all part of the penance. Leaning closer to the wooden slats, Gianni said the same words again, in English. 'Then, forgive me, Father, who have sinned in thought, word and deed. It is four weeks since my last confession.'

'What sins have you committed since then, my son?'

This lack of subtlety. This directness. So very English.

'The first is pride. I have achieved much for the Holy Cause and I glory in it.'

'So you regret what you have done?'

'Of course not. I have shed the blood of Christ's Enemies alone. But I should not take pride in their deaths, I should be merely the Lord's humble vessel.'

'I see. Is pride your only sin?'

'It is the greatest.'

There was a pause, then that strange voice rasped again. 'And what of wrath?'

'Wrath?'

'You say you have shed the blood of Christ's enemies. Do they stir you to anger?'

'Of course. I could not kill them otherwise.' What was this ignorant man talking about?

'Would you like to punish all the sinners of the world? Here, in London? Perhaps your family?'

'My family?' The conversation had taken an odd turn. 'These are my sins we are discussing, Father, not theirs.'

'And have theirs not come down to you?'

Gianni withheld a gasp. This English directness again! He avoided talking of his family, especially in confession. He couldn't frame the words, even his confessors in Rome had never been able to understand the depth of those sins. Yet this ignorant Englishman, who spoke no Latin, who barely seemed to speak his own language, spoke of his familial guilt?

The priest's voice had lowered, forcing Gianni to lean in closer to the grille.

'Come! You know about the sins of the father. Have they not been visited upon you?'

Gianni shook his head, sat back, anger flooding him. This was not what he wanted to talk about. 'Perhaps. But you cannot grant me absolution for them. Only God can.'

'Maybe if I understood what they were . . .'

'That's simple. My father serves Satan.'

A longer silence. Then. 'How?'

'Why must we talk about him, Priest?'

'How?'

Gianni's jaw clenched. Words came through his teeth. 'He raised me in ignorance of Christ's glory.'

'Many men are ignorant of it. Is ignorance a sin?'

'Yes! It is sinful to be ignorant of God's commandments. And by that ignorance to seek to harm the Church. He sinned with one of Satan's strumpets!' Gianni's voice burst through the grille as if he would shatter it. 'He was her champion, this whore, this heretic, this witch who led your land away from the light of Rome.'

'Calmly, my son, calmly.'

There was silence again, while each man listened to the other's breaths. In the end, it was Gianni who broke it.

'But I have atoned for my father's sin. I have brought back what was stolen. I have undone all his works and I rejoice in that.'

The voice came back in a whisper. 'Pride again?'

'Yes!' Gianni said savagely. 'In undoing his evil I take great pride!'

He had grown tired of all this. This stupid priest had wearied him. He made ready to leave without absolution.

Then the voice came again. 'And have you also atoned for others in your family?'

Gianni peered through the wooden web that separated the two cubicles. 'I would atone for them. But my mother was born of sin, being of the tribe of Christ's murderers. And my sister . . .'

A vision of Anne came to him, of the last time he'd seen her. Renard before them both, raging that he had been cheated of the prize of the executioner, their father. When she wouldn't speak, he had vowed to obtain the Council's order for her torture. The thought made Gianni go weak in the stomach, so he forced himself back to harshness.

'My sister must atone. And she will, soon.'

'How?'

He didn't know why he told this priest. Perhaps he wanted just to be gone. Perhaps he only wanted to get the visions that had been haunting him out into the air.

'A Jesuit examines her first. Jesuit techniques of gentleness to persuade her of her errors. They will never work with her.'

'And when this Jesuit fails?'

It was then Gianni felt the strange sensation on his cheek. He reached up and touched the tears, wondering. The weakness caused him to sin again, as fury overtook him.

'Then, the day after tomorrow, another man will come and wed her to the rack.' His lips were at the grille. 'He will stretch and break her body. And he will fail too, for Anne will betray nothing. Nothing! Nothing!' His voice cracked. 'By Christ's wounds, Father, give me absolution for myself and let my family be!'

Gianni pressed his face hard against the grille till the webbing marked his skin, became wet with his tears, listening to the silence from the other side.

'Father?'

It was the word that did it. Suddenly, he knew. He ripped down the curtain in his haste.

The next cubicle was empty though the seat he ran his hand over was still warm. Behind him, down at the far end of the nave, he heard the small door, set within the cathedral's huge oaken one, open and close. He ran to it, fumbled with the latch, burst out, knocking aside those who wished to enter. It was early evening and many people were about. Whoever he sought, was lost among them.

'Father!' he screamed, differently than he'd said it inside and men and women shied from his anguish.

It was hopeless. Jean Rombaud was gone. Sinking down on the stone step, careless of those around him, more tears came soundlessly.

In the mouth of an alley, peering over the crowd from its shadows, Jean watched his son. He wanted to go, take Gianni in his arms, try to reach across the chasm between them, but he knew it would be in vain. Compassion would turn his son swiftly to rage, back to his 'mission'. The confession had told him that. When he'd followed Gianni from the Tower, where he'd kept constant watch since he had fled it the day before, he was hoping that maybe he could persuade him to help free Anne. When he'd seen him enter the confessional, it seemed like a chance to talk. But hearing his son call him 'Father', however it was meant, had stayed his tongue, had given him a way of seeing into the young man's heart. And all he saw there was horror.

Gianni would not get him into the Tower. Yet, within its walls, Anne awaited the torment of the rack.

It was a place Jean dreaded above all others. He had no choice but to go there. And watching his son weeping before the huge wooden edifice of St Paul's, a vision came to him of another parent, another child. That child was probably the only person in the entire kingdom who could help him now.

'Forgive me, my son!' he whispered into the night, across the measureless chasm between them. Then he turned down the alley toward the Thames, walking swiftly to a pier where wherrymen jostled for custom.

The cold of the flagstones had long since numbed his body. Though Thomas's superiors no longer advocated pain to concentrate the mind, he felt this paltry discomfort helped. He had even chosen the most uncomfortable room in this half-repaired tower, the Martin, where no one else stayed, because it reminded him of the harsh monastic cells where he had learned to love Christ.

It had been hard to reach any clarity today. Injunctions of duty were sucked into a whirlpool, there to meld with long black hair, black eyes, with a woman floating clear of the road outside Siena. He had recognized Anne the moment he'd seen her at the burnings. And it was only after these long hours of meditation and prayer that he'd disentangled her from his answer. It lay in the weakness of his spirit, as usual, his former life of sin. When he had been a soldier, women were around, available, fought over; he had even believed he was in love once. All delusion, the Devil's temptings. Ten years now he had shunned them, ten years as Christ's Soldier in the Society of Jesus. This one, this Anne, was just a reminder of former days. Finally, he separated out his reaction to her flesh, and her undoubted spirit, from his desire to save her soul. By the time he heard the footsteps coming up the crumbling stair of the tower toward his chamber, he was ready for her.

She does not float so much now, he thought.

Anne stood with her head turned to the side, her hair a dark veil over her face. Traces of dirt and straw were in it, matching the marks that discoloured her blouse and shift. Her arms were folded across her chest, the fists clenched.

'Will you sit?' he said, gesturing to where two chairs faced each other the same side of the small table.

She did not acknowledge that she had heard. Only when he repeated the question, made a small stiff move toward her, did she raise a face to him as dirty as her clothes. There was a bruise on her right cheek bone, livid, swelling.

He gestured toward it. 'You have been mistreated. I am sorry. Please sit. Please.'

This is how it begins, she thought. *I have heard of the ways of torturers. The foul cell. The guards, cruel, lustful. Then a gentler man, offering kindnesses. Finally, the man who so raged yesterday, returning with his order to hurt.*

Anne sat. Wine was poured, bread offered. She began to chew on the hard crusts, drank but only a little. She had not eaten in a day and a night.

Thomas watched her. When the second of the hard rolls had been consumed, he spoke.

'Do you know why you are here, child?'

The food had restored her. 'To continue my torment. To weaken me for what is to come.'

'Do you think so ill of me?'

'I do not think of you at all, sir. I do not know you.'

'My name is Thomas Lawley. I am a member of the Society of Jesus. Does that mean anything to you?'

There were crumbs on the plate and she picked at them. 'Yes. My brother studied with your order in Rome. You are the Pope's janissaries.'

It took him by surprise, the old insult from her mouth. He laughed. 'We may indeed be warriors for Christ, lady. Yet your remarkable brother is not of our order because, I think, he finds our methods not militant enough. He would burn the heretic to save them from their sin. We seek to persuade, not coerce.'

She looked him directly in the eyes for the first time. 'So you would save me from sin?'

'It would be a great joy to me.'

'But I am not a heretic.'

'Yet you are about heresy's cause.'

'I am about the cause of my family, sir, that is all. And how can I be a heretic if I was never a Catholic?'

'You were not baptized?'

'I was not. My father did not like what had been done in the name of religion. And my mother ...' She hesitated for a moment then went on boldly. 'My mother is Jewish. She says that makes me one. So now you can hate me for that as well.'

'Hate you?' It was stunning news. This woman's brother was the most virulent Jew hater he had ever met. And he had met many. Yet Gianni, through his mother, was himself a Jew.

He moved away from the table, looked at the bare wooden crucifix that hung upon the wall. With his back turned to her, he said, 'Do you know what our dear leader, Ignatius Loyola, says about the Jews? "What! To be related to Christ our Lord and to Our Lady the glorious Virgin Mary!"' He turned back to her. 'No, I do not hate you for this. I honour you.'

Anne searched the man's face. She knew she was there to be examined. Wasn't this the way, to treat her well, entice her, feed her? Yet he seemed genuine. All the more reason to be on her guard. She couldn't help her tongue though, for she had always found the certainty of religious men aggravating.

'Yet I love the story of Christ, too. Not what the Church has made it. His story in his words!'

'Child, it is not for you to interpret his words. That is the Holy Church's task. Anything else is heresy. Do you not realize, a woman burned here yesterday for that sin?'

'There you are,' she said. 'It seems I am a heretic after all.'

It was not going the way Thomas had hoped. It was time to change his approach.

'I wish I had the time to loose you from your error. Alas, those hours are not there for us. My master here in England is an impatient man. He seeks information from you. His methods of obtaining it are very different from mine.'

Her voice came in a whisper. 'Is it noble of you to threaten me, sir?'

'I do not threaten, child. I tell you what will be, what I am powerless to alter. Unless ...'

'Yes?'

'Unless you tell me now what we need to know. If you do, not only will your life be spared, but we may then get the time I'd need to save your soul as well.'

She could not tell if his honesty was mere deceit. With her eyes still downcast, she murmured, 'What do you need to know?'

Thomas sighed. It was a beginning. 'We must know everything about the hand of Anne Boleyn. Everything about its magical properties, its power to curse, to heal. Everything about the headsman, Jean Rombaud; what your father has told you of the hand, of his dealings with this queen of heresy and witchcraft. Open your heart to me – and, believe it, I will know if you withhold one jot of knowledge – be open and plain, and I will put myself between you and your fate.'

She didn't know what she could tell him. What did she know after all? She would try to give him something. But not about her father.

'I have never seen the hand but . . .'

'Would you like to see it now?'

He realized he also wanted to see it again, now, here, for he had merely glanced at it once, when they first dug it up at the crossroads in France. It was a relic to him, nothing more, and he had his own unvoiced doubts about the collections of saints' bones that filled the cathedrals of Europe, traded for piles of gold. He had no doubt though about the power of this symbol over the credulous. That was what men paid for. That power.

He went to the corner of the room to a bare oak chest. Opening it, he pulled a small casket from within and brought it back to the table. The key to it lay on a chain around his neck. He fitted it to the lock and opened the lid.

'Here, child,' he said, stepping back so he could watch her face. 'Here is the source of so much effort and pain.'

With trembling fingers she drew back the velvet cloth. Then she cried out in pain.

It was nothing. The bones of a hand long since picked clean by the processes of decay.

It was everything. It wasn't a skeleton or a symbol and it wasn't the extra finger nestled in small beside what should have been the smallest. It was the instant blind-flash-touch of it, as flesh connected to bone and both Annes were suddenly there, joined across the years, across what was not possible and what could not be denied. A queen grasped her, black hair and blacker eyes, not frozen, not a portrait on a wall, but living, breathing . . . dying, a line ripped across the slender throat, a fracture spread across the bone-wrist she held, a cry cut off from two decades before.

To Thomas, her yelp of pain was the beginning and the end. She fell forward across the table, her hair covering her face. Beneath it he heard a sob.

'What is it, Anne? Do you feel the evil there? Does the Witch-Queen seek your soul? Christ will protect you, child, have faith only in him. Here, I will hide it away from you. Here!'

He stretched over her to the box, managed to shut the lid, though the angle his body made in trying not to touch hers was awkward. It was when he tried to lift the oaken casket from the table that his knee, wound weakened and now cold from its long exposure to the floor, gave way. He heard the pop, cried out as he collapsed onto her.

She had not heard his words, still reeling as she was with her vision. She felt his weight on her suddenly, pressing her face down onto the table. She slipped from under him, rolled across the floor, came up in the defensive stance her parents had taught her, a leg braced back to kick, hands low, ready to strike. But Thomas lay where he had fallen, half on the table, a hand reaching down one leg, agony creasing his face.

'Do not fear!' he gasped. 'It's my knee. I . . . aah! I need to get to the bed.'

He tried to raise himself, to lean on the chair for support, but it slipped, drawing forth another cry. She knew his suffering was real. No matter that he was the enemy. He was in pain. She moved across the room to him.

'Come,' she said, 'let me aid you.'

He grasped the outstretched hand. There was surprising strength behind it and he pulled himself up. Leaning on her, they made the short stagger across to his cot.

'You see the sort of interrogator I make!' His face was contorted by agony and the effort to smile.

She had placed a hand against his knee and he felt the first warmth there he had in an age.

'What have you done to it? Come, tell me. I have some history of healing.'

He was about to protest, to reassert who was in charge. But her strong hands were moving around his injury and where they touched, though he could not believe it, there seemed to come some relief.

'I was a soldier. It was broken at a siege, and never reset properly. I . . .'

'Ssh!' She laid a finger to his lip then resumed her probing. Twice she made him jump in sudden spasm. Gradually, though, he eased back, letting her fingers work. At last she sat back on the cot end and looked at him.

'I have seen this sort of injury before. The bone of the knee is out, there is little to hold it in place. I can put it back but it will hurt.'

'One doctor laid me on the rack while the pulleys tried to re-align it. I am not afraid of pain.'

'Good then. Lie still. And think holy things.'

He heard the smile as she said it and he smiled too as he lay back. It was not a smile that could last; sudden torment shot through him, turning all thought to mist, bringing oblivion.

She laid the leg down and looked up at the unconscious man. She would need to wind cloth tight around the knee if it was not to give again. One of the bedsheets was frayed and she swiftly ripped long strips out of it. As she raised the limb to slip the material under, Thomas gave out a groan. She was at his head in a second, a hand stroking gently.

'Peace!' she whispered softly, as she had to the boy soldier in the yard of the Comet, as she had to Guiseppe Toldo and a thousand more of the sick and the dying during the siege of Siena. And just like all of them, Thomas Lawley sank back into sleep at her touch, at the soft urgings of her voice.

The knee strapped tight, Anne sat back at the table. He would not sleep for long. And anyway, the door had been locked behind her.

She looked again at the casket that the Jesuit had knocked over in his agony. She set it upright but did not open it. She had seen all that she needed to see of the hand of Anne Boleyn. There was only one small hope for both Annes now. And only one bringer of that hope.

Elizabeth threaded through the thicket of ferns, her soft-soled shoes silent on the tiny, narrow track. The plants were taller than her by a good head, reducing vision to what her weapon could touch. Nonetheless, she moved swiftly, reading the signs as her father had taught her, here a broken stem, there the imprint of hoof in the mulch. The boar had crossed here, crossed back. When she came to some droppings that were still warm, she knew how close she must be.

She was still hot from that last wild gallop across the open field, overtaking the hounds halfway to this fern sea. Their handlers had halted them, their frustrated yelps and snarls pursuing her as she went where they were not allowed. There were human cries too, fearful voices trying to restrain her as the chains had the dogs. But she would not be so bidden, no command could leash her in, and no one would catch up with her here. She knew this land better than any of them, for had her father not created this whole chase?

She thrust the boar spear ahead of her, using it to part the fern that had overgrown the deer track, her left hand holding it in an overgrip halfway up the oak shaft, her right couching it to her side. It was time to move more slowly, for the boar would have paused somewhere just ahead, now that the dogs had halted. This was when the animal was at its most dangerous. Its instinct had caused it to run so far, to out-distance the baying pursuit. Now it would be listening for her just as she listened for it.

A voice called out, about a hundred paces to her left, she reckoned. Philip! His stallion had almost been at her shoulder when she spurred her mare for that final dash, the smaller horse's nimbleness giving her the edge over the short distance. He'd probably had a glimpse of her when she dismounted to enter the ferns, but she had cut sharp right and right again down the little paths.

Philip. He had teased her, in his courteous way, when she took a boar spear from the rack. 'A warrior queen – like your Boudicca!' he had called her, before gently reminding her that it was the men who did the killing, the women who sat back and admired them. He wanted to preen for her, as he had done the week before with that handsome stag.

Well, she was tired of men strutting before her, leaving her the role of simpering adoration. This was not the dry plains of Castile but her green England. She was Harry's daughter – and her father had taught her how to use a spear.

She paused, her eyes sweeping the track ahead, her own breath suspended as she listened for other breath from heaving, furred flanks.

There! Was that a creature shifting on dried leaves, rising slowly to its hooves, crouching again, preparing to charge, lowering dagger-pointed tusks toward the fern she was just about to part . . .

She was hit from the side, the little breath she'd held expelled from her, spear dashed to the ground. No chance to cry out, instant terror, anticipating the bone blades slicing into her. Her face down into fern, one hand pinned under her as she fell, though the other reached across, stretching toward the dagger at her belt.

A hand met her hand, another covered her mouth. Relief at the human touch, then outrage. No one touched a princess in this way! Not even a prince. She bit down, tasted blood, heard a muted but satisfying yelp of pain. But the hand did not leave her mouth, no matter that she bit harder. Instead, a mouth was at her ear and a voice whispered urgently, 'My lady, do not scream, I beg of you. I am a friend and I bring you news.'

Friends did not press her body to the ground. She bit on.

There was more whispered anguish. 'Highness! I am Jean Rombaud. I was . . . your mother's executioner.'

Elizabeth ceased biting, tried to breathe.

'It is true, Princess, I swear it. I did . . . some service to your mother. And now you, her daughter, are in grave danger.'

She turned her mouth away from his smothering hand and he let her.

'Get off me,' were the words that came, yet she whispered them and he did. She scrambled away from him, to the far side of what she now saw was a small cave of fern. The scent of boar in it was unmistakable. She had found the lair but of a far more dangerous animal. Her hand reached the dagger now, drew it from its sheath. The man squatting opposite showed his empty hands.

'Jean Rombaud was a giant. Young, powerful. You—'

'I have heard ballads, Princess, that make me full seven feet tall and almost as wide. And as for youth . . . well, it was almost twenty years ago.'

There was something in his eyes, beneath the greying hair, a smile there, a sadness too. She had become good at discerning lies from truth. Her life depended on it. The blade lowered slightly, didn't quite drop. In the world beyond, she heard someone calling her again.

'Jean Rombaud,' she said, 'is a name from a nightmare.' She felt the tears come. 'You took my mother's head.'

Jean nodded. 'I did, my lady. I killed her who I loved because I had no choice.'

'Who you . . . loved?'

'Aye, my lady. And for that love I swore an oath to do something your mother asked of me.'

The knife fell from her hand. 'And what did you do?' she said softly, although she knew the answer.

'You mother feared the harm that would be done in her name. The harm that could come to you, among others. So she begged me to . . . to take her hand, *that* hand, and bury it in a land where once she had been happy.'

Happy? It was not a word that she had ever associated with the mother she could not remember. No one told her happy tales of Anne Boleyn. No one spoke of her at all.

More cries, Philip and others now, concerned, drawing nearer.

Jean looked around anxiously. But he had to wait for her to speak.

Her voice came harsh, the tone set by the emotions surging inside her. 'And you failed to do this. To keep your oath. For this hand is a great danger to me now.'

'I succeeded for a time. The hand remained buried until . . .' He could not talk about it. There was no point in excuses, in actions by others he still didn't understand. And the voices were getting nearer. He continued. 'It does not matter. But the hand is here again. I believe it will be used to threaten you just as your mother feared.'

'It already has been. Such a threat as I have never faced before.'

She had not admitted that to anyone. But here, with this man, there was no time for games.

'What do you want of me, Jean Rombaud?'

It was her voice, the way she said his name. Time dissolving, collapsing twenty years, and a queen asking him for a boon. He was asking one of that queen's daughter now, offering to her great need something he could not deliver. But his own daughter was in peril now and that was all that mattered.

'I have to get into the Tower, my lady.'

'You would try to steal the hand again?'

He lied. He had no choice. 'I have to. For all of us.'

She was versed in reading men's lies. But her great need, this sudden slight hope, overcame her discernment. Besides, there was no time to consider, as cries of 'Elizabeth! Princess!' drew ever closer.

She pulled a heavy bloodstone signet from her finger. 'Take this. There is an officer serving at the Tower who loved my mother and, during my late imprisonment there, proved that he loves me as well. His name is Tucknell.'

Voices so close now. 'Princess! My lady!'

'Give it to him. He will do whatever the bearer desires. For my mother was not the only woman men swear vows to.'

Jean pocketed the ring. A stem cracked and they heard footsteps. Someone had found the little track they lay just off.

He bowed as well as he could from his crouched position, then made to slip through the foliage. A hand on his sleeve stayed him.

'Tell me, Jean Rombaud – how did my mother die?'

He looked into those eyes, her mother's legacy. He might not be able to save her but he could give her this much. His hand closed over hers.

'She died like a queen. And, at the very last, she spoke your name.'

He squeezed her hand and was gone. He did not stay to see her tears; it was Philip of Spain who beheld them as he stumbled upon her.

'My lady Elizabeth! Are you hurt?'

'No, my lord,' she said, wiping her eyes. 'I tripped, is all.'

He helped her rise. 'Why did you not answer our calls?'

The mask was back in place, just where it had to be. 'What, my lord? And have you mock your Boudicca, who falls over her own spear?'

She laughed and he joined her.

'Do you wish to see me kill the beast, Elizabeth? My men have it cornered up ahead.'

He gestured the way Jean had gone. She sighed, leaned into him a little, their faces close.

'I feel a little faint, my brave prince. Could we not sit awhile and talk?'

His face flushed above the beard, his voice came huskily as he pressed back into her. 'Anything for my princess,' he said. 'Let me take your weight.'

As he led her to the track, she glanced back. When she spoke, it was inside her head.

Godspeed, Jean Rombaud. The tide is turning. At least, I pray it is.

At the water's edge, Jean sat in a boat, the same one that had brought him down. The wherryman had asked him to drink in the bankside inn while they waited for the tide, but he needed, more than ever, to be alone. The ring lay heavy in his pocket. The tide would turn and he was several hours from the Tower. Once within, he knew what he would do, and what he would not. Reach his daughter, named for a queen, inside the place where he had taken that queen's life. Free her. He might just have the courage for that, but for no more. He would have nothing else to do with oaths and queens.

FIFTEEN

ENDGAME

In this hour before the dawn, mist rose from the river and frigid vapour fingers pushed beneath his insubstantial clothes. Yet he knew that his shivering did not come solely from the morning's chill. For he was stood where the wherryman had dropped him, on the dock beneath the Traitor's Gate.

The guard had been reluctant to wake his officer, had only gone to do so under threat of the consequences should he not. The producing of the ring had made his decision for him, sending him off grumbling. Jean had not wanted to let it out of his keep but he'd been given little choice. Now, as the minutes lengthened and the faintest hint of light reached into the sky downriver, he began to fear that he would never see it again.

'Where is this man who disturbs my rest?'

The voice made him jump, echoing loudly through the vaulted dock.

'Here, sir.'

'Then come up, fellow.'

He climbed the slippery steps carefully. A tall man stood alone in the darkness at the top of them. Jean could not see his face but words came in a whisper from the shadows.

'How came you by this ring, sir?'

'You know it?'

'I know it. And I wonder that you have it. Did you steal it?'

'I did not. I was given it from . . . the lady's hand.'

'Were you indeed?' The suspicious voice lowered still further. 'This . . . lady told me she would never send this to me except in her direst need.'

Jean kept his silence. After a long pause the man spoke again. 'What is your name, sir?'

There didn't seem any point in lying now. 'My name is Jean Rombaud.'

A whispered obscenity, a snatching of a torch from the wall. The man brought it close, lighting both their faces. Jean saw someone maybe a little younger than himself, though as grey of beard and hair, strong features creased now in wonder. And rage.

'Rombaud! A curse of a name.' The torch moved up and down as the man surveyed him. 'It is you, indeed. We have met before. Do you not remember me . . . Executioner?'

'I am sorry, I . . .'

'Tucknell.' He pushed his face closer. 'I was there when you killed her. I raised her bloodied head, may God forgive me.'

Jean could see the power of the memory take the man. It came back to him now, a little. This man had loved her. One of many.

'I remember you, sir.'

'Then maybe you remember . . . sir,' Tucknell was struggling to control his temper, 'that I had no reason to love you. You butchered her.'

'I rendered her a service.'

'A service?' The laugh was strained, false. 'And do you offer the same service to my Queen's daughter? Are you measuring the Princess's neck for your sword, as has so long been threatened?'

Tucknell's voice had grown loud with his anger. One of the guards drew nearer from his place in the tower above. Jean stepped closer to Tucknell, looking up into the taller man's face, forcing his voice to calmness.

'Sir, I think you know that the Princess would not have given me that ring for such a purpose. The service I rendered her mother was greater than you witnessed. Far greater. The Princess understands that. That's why she sends me to you now.'

He saw the deep suspicion still there on the Englishman's face.

'Come, man,' he said. 'I loved Anne Boleyn as much as you. I only seek to show that love to her daughter now.'

Tucknell stared at him, shaking his head. Finally, he said, 'And how will you show it, Rombaud?'

Jean drew breath. Now he had to be most careful. 'There is a prisoner here, a young woman. She has . . . information that the

Imperial Ambassador desires. He has a warrant to examine her this morning. If he gets the information, it will not just harm the Princess. It will condemn her.'

'So you are here to end that threat? To add "assassin" to your list of honourable titles?'

'No. I am here to free the girl. To get her away from here. Out of the kingdom.'

Tucknell studied Jean who stared back, his face betraying nothing. At last the Englishman spoke. 'What you ask is nearly impossible. If she is to wed the rack then she will be closely watched. It will be a great danger to me to help you.'

'It is not me you help. It is the owner of that ring. And it is the last hour of the night. Even watchful guards grow weary.'

Tucknell pulled the ring from his pocket, stared at it for a long moment. 'I swore a vow to her, when she was imprisoned here last year, that I would do everything in my power for her, and for the love I bore her mother.' He put the ring back in his pocket. 'It seems I have no choice.'

He turned and walked rapidly away from Jean, who stood for a moment, uttering a short prayer of thanks to the love that princesses inspired. Then he followed.

Though dawn barely glimmered in the east, enough light showed Jean the Green, bare of people yet crowded still with the vestiges of execution. The reek of burnt flesh clung to the walls of the towers. Circular scorched patches showed where the martyrs had been burnt, two at the site before the chapel, one further on, where the giant heretic had rushed and flamed and died. Ravens hopped about, seeking bits of flesh unconsumed by fire, squabbling when one was discovered with cries like the wails of the damned. Shuddering, Jean fixed his gaze on the cloak ahead of him, willing the man to move faster. It was not merely the danger to his daughter that urged him on; all his ghosts gathered on that scrap of grass.

They passed close to the eastern wall of the chapel and soon stood before a squat, battlemented tower.

'The Flint,' muttered Tucknell. Taking Jean's arm, he twisted it up behind his back, feigning little. 'You are my prisoner. Do not speak.'

The first guard merely nodded at the officer; the next, at an iron-studded door, was pacified with the watchword. Bolts were thrown, they entered and immediately began to descend the steps in a circular stair, winding deep into the earth. The torches guttering in brackets on the walls were spaced far apart. At last they halted before a door, a rusted grille set in its centre. Three raps upon it brought a face, bearded and bleary-eyed to the gap.

'Prisoner!' Tucknell barked. 'Another cursed traitor to her Majesty.'

'It's damned early, Tucknell,' grunted the guard, stooping to his bolts. The door creaked open.

'Aye, man,' said Tucknell, stepping past. 'But treason never sleeps. No, William,' he added as the man tried to move by, 'I'll take him. A few questions to ask, if you know what I mean. You go back to your cot.'

Grumbling still, the man did as he was bid, first handing the officer a bunch of his keys.

'Now, Rombaud, we must be swift. This way!'

If the stairwell above had been dank and dark, it was as nothing to these catacombs below. Tucknell led him down the twisting corridors, the only light now the paltry one from his lantern, spilling over the straw-strewn floor that tilted and caught at Jean's feet with unexpected projections, his hand saving himself from falling against walls rough and wet. It sloped downwards and every few paces his fingers ran over the roughness of a door. He touched one and something stirred the other side. He heard a muffled cry, a body thumping against thick wood, a sob.

At last, deep down, they stood before the lowest doorway yet. A rusted key slid into a lock and after much twisting the lock gave. With his boot, Tucknell pushed the door open. Stale air released outwards and Jean almost choked. At a nod from Tucknell, Jean thrust his head into the foul darkness.

'Anne?'

Held in dreams she moaned, hit out, resisting the grip that would drag her to her doom. Then she heard the voice, the voice from a dream, and she fell into her father's arms.

'I knew you would come.'

'Hush! Hush! No words.'

Tucknell shook the lantern from the doorway. 'And if you would leave, you must go now and swiftly.'

Outside the cell, Tucknell led them the opposite way to the one they had come, deeper into the labyrinth.

At Jean's first question, Tucknell said roughly, 'I cannot take you back, or I am ruined in your escape. There is another way. Here!'

They halted. Above them, Jean and Anne felt a flow of fresher air. The lantern raised to the ceiling revealed a grille.

'Your hands.'

Jean intertwined his fingers and the Englishman stepped up, grabbing the bars above, twisting them hard. The grille loosened and he forced it up into the opening.

Stepping down, he said, 'This vent winds to the surface. You brace yourself to the top. It can be done, because a prisoner once did it. It comes up beside the Martin Tower, flush to the inner wall at Brass Mount. The tower is in bad repair and little guarded, for few stay there. Can you swim?'

They both nodded.

'A stair to the side of the tower leads down to the moat. Swim straight across. A hawthorn hides a tiny gate there in the outer wall. This key' – he pulled an ancient piece of metal from his pocket – 'opens that gate. Lock it again, throw the key away – for if you were caught with it, it would go ill with me – and run. God speed.'

He turned but Anne's hand delayed him. 'Thank you, sir.'

'I do not do this for you, but for the lady I pray to my Saviour in heaven will soon be Queen.'

'Will you be in peril when it is discovered I am gone?'

'Perhaps. But I will go back and break your door now. And as I told you, a prisoner once took this passage before. I just hope you are luckier than he was. Fare you well.'

'What do you mean?' Jean said, but Tucknell was already off, lantern light receding into the gloom.

There was no choice. Fresher air and freedom awaited them above. Anne placed her hands this time and Jean rose to her groans. He scrabbled into the narrow gap, braced himself, reached down. She grabbed at his dangling arm and he pulled her to where she could get a purchase. Soon they were wedged together in a hole no more than their conjoined bodies in width.

'Does the lady precede, Father?'

Jean smiled and hugged his daughter. 'I think youth precedes, Anne. You were always the best climber in the family. Anyway, you do not want my old limbs tumbling onto you from the darkness above.'

A returned hug and she was gone. He gave her a few seconds then reached up to follow.

The walls were narrow and rough, outcrops that jabbed into the back also providing handholds. Anne moved swiftly up, Jean following more slowly, making sure of his bracing each time. The tunnel twisted, almost levelling at one point before heading up again. The air got fresher and soon Anne detected the glimmer of a lighter darkness.

'Father! I am at the surface, I . . . I cannot move the bars!'

Jean squeezed in beside her, they both pushed hard and eventually there was a giving. Carefully, they moved the grille to one side. Jean thrust his head up, sensing the air around him.

'Come,' he said, and hoisted himself from the hole.

They were flush to the wall of a tower. Scaffolding stood against it, repairs underway to its crumbling stone. Jean moved to the edge of the battlements; a stair did indeed wind down to the dull waters of the moat. He shivered, turned back.

'Anne,' he said, then realized she was no longer behind him. He ran back and found her, staring up at the precarious wooden platforms that girded the tower.

'Child! We must go. A cold swim awaits us before we gain our freedom.'

'I have been here before.' Anne continued to gaze upwards. 'This is where I was brought for that Jesuit to examine me. Father!' She turned excitedly to him. 'This is where I saw it!'

'Where you saw what? Come, we must leave! Now!'

'The hand. Anne Boleyn's hand. It is in this tower.'

He said, 'No'. He even reached for her. But she was quick, tucked in her shift, swung up on the nearest wooden beam. It shook, but took her weight.

'Anne!' Jean hissed. 'We have done enough. We must escape. It is a slow death for both of us if we stay.'

She looked down. Her voice was soft and clear. 'It is a lingering death for this land and a curse that will pursue our family for ever if we leave without what we came for. Wait for me.'

His whispered cry of 'Anne!' went unheeded. Hand over hand, she disappeared up into the wooden structure. She reached planks, these leading her to the lip of a wall. Slipping over it, she found she was on the first level battlements. An archway opened onto an inner stair and, realizing that it could be the sole one within the tower, she began to climb.

His cell door was ajar. Peering around it, she sought his shape on the cot where she had last seen him. But he lay on the floor before the table, before the rough hewn crucifix, his arms spread wide and parallel to its crossbeams. Behind it, lay the casket.

She waited for him to shift, for his lips to move in the prayers indicated by his attitude of supplication. It was only after she had watched him for some little while that she realized his breath was shallow and regular. The Jesuit, despite the hardness of his bed, slept.

Placing each foot lightly down, she moved into the room. It was small, and the prone man took up most of the space. She stepped up to his left arm and carefully leaned over to the table. The casket was heavy but, bracing herself, she managed to heave it toward her.

Thomas Lawley cried out. In wakefulness his prayers calmed. In sleep, his dreams tormented. Both concerned the woman he had examined the previous day. In his prayers he saw her repenting her sin, coming gently, beatifically, back to Christ the Redeemer. But in this dream he saw her coming to him, and she was naked. He wept, in terrible desire, in rejection. Then, the rejected, so beautiful body that once had floated, now lay broken on the rack and he cried out, 'No!' screaming the word again and again . . . until a hand descended from the heavens, to caress his forehead and a voice whispered, 'Peace' softly in his ear.

The horror faded, dreams vanishing into a serenity indistinguishable from prayer. Pulling his outstretched arms in, he curled into himself and slept on.

Anne left her hand upon his forehead for a moment, marvelling at the calm that had come to the man below her. A younger, almost handsome face she decided, when the lines of etched pain relaxed.

This is the real him, she thought, stroking, soothing still, *behind his rigid faith. This is the man before the hurt.*

Then she straightened, picked up the casket once again, and crept from the chamber.

When Jean heard the scaffolding creak, he stepped into the still thick shadow that girded the wall. But his daughter's voice drew him out.

'Anne! What are you about?'

'This!'

She held the casket toward him, made to open the lid, for the key was in it. He laid one hand on hers.

'No. I do not want to see it. I never wanted to see it again. What it has done to me, to my family . . .' His voice shook. 'If we must bring it, then we must. But do not show it to me. And, for the love of Christ, hurry!'

He pulled her toward the moat. They'd nearly reached it when the voice halted them.

'You can show it to me, girl. I'm afire to see what so many 'ave desired, so many died for.'

Uriah Makepeace rose from the water stair before them. The pale dawn light glinted off the sword that rested on shoulders. 'Especially since what has ruined your family could be the making of mine, Rombaud, old comrade! So show me.'

Uriah moved a pace toward them; they stepped back.

'I'd almost given up on you. No one could find you nowhere and I 'ad men all over the streets. I thought, 'e's not going to leave his pretty daughter to be stretched, is 'e? Not the fearless Jean Rombaud. So I thought I'd keep a personal watch at the dock. And there you came. I lost you underground but then I wondered if you knew about the gate behind the 'awthorn? Seems you did.'

It was the apple-sized pommel that Jean recognized. Uriah saw his eyes widen. 'Yes, Rombaud, it's your old friend. See what good care I'm taking of it?'

He lifted it and they saw the short, heavy blade, the distinctive square end silhouetted against the dawn sky. The Englishman kept it up on high, where the killing strokes begin.

'Why?' was all Jean's dry throat could manage.

'Why . . . betray you?' Uriah looked sad. 'Alas! But I told you about how me and my late partner lost the Tower concession, right? Feeding the prisoners, doing the banquets, all that? My lord Renard has promised me them all back. That's a lot of silver, my friend. So my conscience didn't come cheap, I can assure you. And what with stopping you escaping, and retrieving the Witch's 'and and all, well . . .' The grin returned. 'Got to be worth a few guineas on top, don't it? Eh, far enough, you!'

It was Anne who had moved. The casket thrust before her, she said, 'But didn't you want to look inside?'

Jean recognized the tone of the voice. It was the way Beck spoke, just before she struck.

'Anne! Stop!'

Uriah raised the weapon, his shoulders tensed. 'You listen to your father, girlie. I may not be Jean Rombaud, but he knows I can use this sword. Put the 'and down and move back.'

Reluctantly, she placed the casket on the ground, rejoined her father.

There were half a dozen paces between them. In a sudden movement, Uriah flicked the catch of the casket with the blade. The lid swung up, the interior facing him.

'Well, well, well.' Wonder spread over the scarred face. 'So she really did 'ave six fingers. No wonder his late Majesty loved that whore's caress. 'E liked the unusual, I'd 'eard.' He chuckled, then his eyes hardened. 'So much death, Rombaud, come from you taking what you oughtn't 'ave. They do say, one man's death is another man's fortune, though, don't they?'

He took a pace forward. They retreated another. 'You would murder us here?' Anne's voice had lost none of its edge.

'Not you, missie. Not unless you force me too. I think his eminence 'as plans for you and 'e'll be ever so grateful that I prevented your escape. But you, Rombaud . . . I just can't take the risk with you. You've got some pact with the Devil going. You've survived what would kill a 'undred men. You'd survive this and come back for me. I know you would.'

Moving toward them slowly, Uriah continued, his voice low, calming. 'And as for murder . . .' He laughed, and for a moment used his nose to nuzzle the branded 'M' on his left hand. 'Well, it's not like I 'aven't done it before.'

His slow steps closed the distance between them. Their backs pressed against the stone of the tower. He halted, a sword's reach away from them, his knuckles whitening on the grip.

'Anyway, it's fitting, don't you think? A sort of justice? Jean

Rombaud, Anne Boleyn's Executioner, executed. Making his end, right here, right where it all began.'

Jean suddenly felt an enormous weariness. There was a sword raised on high once more in the Tower of London. There was the hand it had taken, the hand of a dead queen, returned, as if his vow, all the suffering, was for nothing. Uriah was right. He, who had been the very cutting edge of justice, now faced justice of his own. It was . . . fitting. And he was so very tired.

He yawned. It was the yawn that delayed Uriah, just for a moment, just at that moment when he bent his legs for the strike, as his shoulders tensed and his wrists tightened. And it was just at that moment that he died, more or less, the point of a rapier bursting through his throat, severing an artery there, ribbons of blood hitting the wall above their heads. He fell forward and Jean, weary though he was, reached up and caught the pommel of the sword as it came down.

Uriah's eyes were open as he died. As his head passed Jean, he looked as if he would speak. But he was a big man and he fell fast, his head striking the stone beside Jean as the Frenchman stepped away.

Tucknell had withdrawn the rapier as the man fell.

'I had misgivings,' he said calmly, wiping the blade on his cloak. 'And I wanted to make sure the grille was replaced properly. Ways of escape from this place are few and who knows when one might need them?'

He had moved back to see if the noise had drawn anyone to them and his glance fell into the open casket.

'Jesu save me!' he cried, a hand rising to his mouth. 'Is this . . . this . . . Holy God, what horror is here?'

Anne bent and closed the lid. Jean took the officer by the arm. 'It is too long a story for now, Tucknell. Know only that the queen we both loved wanted this hidden for ever. But her enemies would misuse her still and have thus disturbed her rest.'

'I knew it!' Tucknell's voice shook. 'When that Jesuit dug her up, I knew he was about some evil!' He gestured to Anne. 'Give me the hand, lady. I will restore it to her violated grave.'

'It would not rest there,' she said. 'I truly fear it will not be safe anywhere in this world. But we must take it and try again to fulfil the vow my father made to her.'

He looked at them both, nodded. 'Then go! Go now and go swiftly. For the dawn overtakes you, and Simon Renard and his torturers will soon be here.'

Anne looked to her father, the executioner, to the sword in his hand. She looked down at the casket. Then she looked at the dead murderer sprawled in his blood at the base of the tower.

'Father, there is something we must do first, before we go.'

Jean heard that tone again in the voice and he sighed – for he knew when he heard it, that there would be no opposing his wife's child.

She continued. 'You must use your sword within this place one last time.'

Thomas's sleep had latterly been free of nightmares but he awoke in horror when Renard burst through his door.

'She has gone, Jesuit! Fled! These fools have let her escape!'

'Who, my lord?' Thomas raised himself from the floor, biting back the groan that came as his bound knee took weight.

'Who, my lord?' Renard's sharp face was thrust into his, close enough to scent the rank breath. 'The girl, Rombaud's daughter. She whom you failed to get information from. Here's James Woolston from the Council with the order for her examination. But there's no one to examine. The witch has vanished.'

Thomas felt nothing but relief. He kept it from his face, though and studied the other men who had crowded into his cell. The fat and florid councillor. The Tower guard who had first helped him dig up Anne Boleyn's grave, Tucknell. And Gianni Rombaud.

With a shout of fury, Renard dashed almost everything from the table, even the crucifix, glaring at each of the discomfited men in turn, daring them to challenge him. Then the hand came back to rest on the casket.

'Well, at least we still have this,' he said, striking it. 'I have been denied one pleasure today, but I will not be denied my triumph. You . . .!' He gestured at Gianni. 'Bring it. Come, Lawley. Queen Mary's crisis is almost upon her. She has taken to her birthing bed. It is time we confronted the Princess Elizabeth with the proof of her satanic legacy! It is time we bent her to our will!'

He marched from the room, the councillor in his wake.

Tucknell glanced expressionlessly at him before following, leaving the two men.

Gianni moved first, picking up the casket. 'Well, Jesuit,' he said, 'all our efforts have come to this moment. Praise God and Carafa, for making us the instruments of Christ's triumph.'

As the younger man left the room, the box tucked under his arm, Thomas bent painfully to the floor and picked up the crucifix, setting it once more in the centre of the table. He genuflected, his fingers pausing at his lips. Behind them, he mouthed, 'And praise him for leading his child Anne from the darkness, like the first Pope, Holy Peter, from his prison. Guide her still, Lord, wherever she may be.'

She had expected the summons. The rumours had spread swiftly around Hampton Court that the Queen had taken to her birthing bed. And though the final crisis might be delayed a week, even longer, Elizabeth knew her opponent would not wait so long. As with the contest in chess, Renard was preparing his endgame.

She had not expected to be taken to his chamber. They had not met there before, only in the bare room with the convex mirror, or in her own apartments.

The light, contrasting with the wet darkness outside, dazzled her; so she paused in the doorway, till her eyes were more accustomed to the brightness of the clusters of candles. Between their banks of light she saw the chessboards, all in play, on every available surface. There was just one on the main table that faced her though, and even if her eyes were still adjusting to the light she saw immediately that it was their game, identical to the one that lay on the tiny board in her room. These pieces, by contrast, were huge, beautifully carved, as tall as a man's hand. On these squares, too, white knights, bishops and pawns hemmed in her black queen.

Hovering over them was Simon Renard.

She spoke from the doorway. 'Do you always need to play your games so late, my lord?'

He gestured her into the room, sitting as he did. His voice was brisk.

'We conclude a bigger game tonight, lady. And its triumph will surpass anything that can happen on this board.'

She came into the room. She could see now into the shadows behind the table. Two men stood back there. One was the Jesuit she had met before. The other was a dark young man with a face that seemed familiar, yet she knew she had never seen before. The way he regarded her, the mixture of hatred and a strange joy in his eyes, made her shiver. Yet she spoke out boldly. 'And is a princess not to be given a chair?'

The Jesuit made to move, was waved back with one gesture from Renard. 'You do not have time to sit, lady,' he hissed. 'You have time to make a decision, and that is all.'

Her look of disdain led him on.

'You have heard that the Queen is come to what she believes is her crisis.'

A nod. It was all she could give him. She suddenly didn't trust her voice in the face of these men's certainty.

'She will lie there a week, maybe two. By then, even she will have come to know her mistake. Even her great hope will have ended.'

She found a voice from somewhere. Anger, probably. 'And you call this "triumph"? Are you not ashamed to glory when the Queen, my sister, is to be so desolated? Do you not pity her?'

'I pity no one. I care only to keep this country in the Holy Faith and Imperially aligned and I will do anything to achieve this. Anything!'

His hunger was clear. It silenced her, that naked desire lit by candles. He pulled up a parchment and held it toward her.

'Will you sign this, lady? Will you agree to marry King Philip in the event of your sister's death should she die childless? As she will.'

She could only shake her head. He reached behind him and placed upon the table a small walnut casket to the side of the chessboard. Its lid was down.

'Perhaps this will change your mind.' His long fingers stroked the wood almost languorously. 'For if you do not sign, be assured that what lies within here will be placed under the Queen's bed. It will only be discovered at the moment of her greatest sadness, when all hope is finally gone, when she is asking that question we all ask when our greatest longing has been lost.' His voice rose to a shrill, whining imitation. 'Why? Why have I been cursed? Holy Me? Good Me? Mary, namesake, mother of God, why me?'

Flickering candlelight danced on his face. 'What lies within this box will give her that answer. When she sees it she'll know who cursed her. She'll see again the woman whose memory she hates above all others. The woman whose daughter wants to make heretics of her people, steal her crown, bed her husband.' His voice dropped to a whisper. 'For what lies within this box is nothing less than the six-fingered hand of your mother – Anne Boleyn!'

He threw back the lid, raised a candelabra above it, triumphant.

She staggered then, thought that her legs would not hold her. Despite the light, it was as if she could not penetrate the mist that descended between her and the table. Yet she knew she had to know the extent of what opposed her. So planting her legs square, her father's daughter, breathing deep, she looked into the casket.

At first, there was revulsion, an instant of terrible shock. But she took a breath again, another, kept her gaze fixed on the horror within the box. Long moments passed, in breaths and guttering candles. Finally, when she felt she once more had control of her voice, she spoke.

'It is said I have inherited some things from the mother I barely knew. An aspect of face, a cast of eye and brow. Mostly, they say, a certain daintiness . . . of hand.'

She raised one, moved it gracefully before her face, drawing all eyes to it before she continued, her voice growing ever stronger.

'They also say my mother had six fingers. But try as I might I can only see five before me. Five! And though I barely knew her, I do believe these two things of her. She was not a man. And she was not a murderer.'

Silence in the room, silence so deep only the candles could be heard in their burning. The look of triumph did not alter on the Ambassador's face for it seemed he had not heard Elizabeth's words, was still listening to those he'd expected to hear, those that announced her complete surrender to his will. It took Thomas, limping forward to look into the casket, to end the silence.

'Holy Father,' he said simply. 'Holy Father in heaven.'

Only then did Renard move, seizing the casket, spinning it

round to face him. He tipped it, and what lay within fell onto the table before him. He staggered away from it, collapsing onto his chair.

'What . . . what?' was all he could manage.

A silence again, but a shorter one, and it was the Princess who broke it. She stepped up to the table and looked down at the chessboard there, at her queen, surrounded, hemmed in by Renard's men.

'It *was* checkmate in three, wasn't it, Ambassador?'

She waited for his glazed eyes to meet hers. Held them there but for a moment. Then she bent, placed her fingers under the board's varnished edge where it overlapped the table and threw it high up into the air. Black and white shapes spun through the candlelight, fell into Renard's lap, onto the floor, rolled across the table to nestle against the 'M' branded onto Uriah Makepeace's severed hand. And only when the last piece had stopped moving did Princess Elizabeth turn and walk, very slowly, from the room.

SIXTEEN
THE HOSTAGE

From the buttresses of Notre Dame, stone demons shrieked rainwater across the great square. He had thought he was tracking a bear, which had made as much sense as anything within this dream. The huge black animal, the sign of his clan, had beckoned him with his grunts, the *hmm hmm hmm* drawing him from the forests of the homeland he could only imagine into the familiar stone canyons of Paris.

Now Tagay stared at the great church. The bear's call had faded away, leaving only the soughing of the wind through the eaves. That made him look up to them, to see a woman standing there, her long, long black hair coiling around her. No, she did not stand, she floated, one foot loosely tethered to the stonework.

He had never seen her. He knew her.

'Ataentsic! Great Mother!' he called.

The Goddess looked down and her foot slipped. As she started to fall, the bear Tagay had tracked and lost emerged from the shadows at the great wooden doors. He knew the bear must catch her, for his people believed that only if the Great Mother reached the earth safely could the world be formed. He ran forward, becoming the bear, becoming the Goddess falling faster now, harder now . . .

Tagay tumbled from the bed, his knee, elbow and hip striking the floor, waking him to pain. His head hurt the worst, as if it were filled with boiling oil, although that had nothing to do with the fall. That was all the wine he had consumed the night before.

He had cried out when he fell, and he cried again now as nausea swept him. There was an echo from the bed, a rebuke, some muttering. Raising himself carefully, he looked at the woman sprawled among the dishevelled bedclothes. He didn't recognize the blonde, matted hair, the smeared, powdered face. The woman was as naked as he was, and it was the rolls of pallid flesh beneath the sheets that reminded him. She was a cousin from the country, come to Paris for the King's birthday. The Marquise had pushed them together at the dinner last night. This cousin was at least twice his age – and weight. But after the usual night of drinking Tagay went where he was told.

He crept back onto the bed. He wanted to consider the dream as his mother had always taught him to. But the spinning returned, worse than before. He rose, steadied himself against one of the bedposts. On the armoire under the window, there was a basin of water. He plunged his face into it, held it under. Then, with droplets running off him, he raised his eyes to the mirror that hung there.

His face was puffy, the whites of his narrow, dark eyes a tracery of red lines. His long, black hair was flattened, oil and night sweat pinning it to his scalp. His brown skin looked almost pale, its sallowness emphasized by the wisp of beard that clung unconvincingly to his jaw. His mother had always told him not to grow a beard, said that among their people it was a sign of low intelligence. But his mother was long dead, and the men who had looked after him since her death all had beards. Even the Marquise had one, though she would not have been flattered if he said he was imitating hers.

The thought made him laugh and realize that he was still a little drunk. He turned back to the bed, ignoring its occupant, searching the floor nearby. A flagon was on its side, yet suckling produced little more than a thirst-inducing drop. He was reaching under the bed frame when he heard scratching at the door. It opened, and the Marquise thrust her head into the gap. He was naked, but didn't bother covering himself up.

'Well, well!' The older woman took in the scene with satisfaction. 'Did you give my cousin something pleasant to remember when she returns to her decrepit husband and rotting castle?'

He ignored her, continued his hunt for wine. Another flagon produced only a sip. Frustrated, he sat on the bed's edge and groaned.

'Come, Tagay.' Her voice was gentle, which surprised him so he looked up. She had come part way into the room and was beckoning him. 'Let us away before she wakes. Your beauty is too tempting and you both will need some rest before tonight.'

'Tonight?' His voice was raspy. 'And what is tonight?'

'How could you forget, you silly boy?' She was moving round the room, gathering discarded items of clothing. 'Tonight is the feast for the King's birthday. Henri will want his "Little Bear" beside him.' She stooped, and pinched his cheek. 'And I have someone very special for you to be nice to. Very special – and very rich.'

Anger rose in bile to his throat. 'Wine,' he said. 'I want wine.' He tried to squeeze another drop from the flagon.

Hardness took over the wrinkled face. Snatching the bottle from him, she said, 'You'll drink wine when I let you, you Indian dog. I want you sober tonight which you won't be if you start drinking now. I told you, we've a rich one. The richest yet.'

She thrust his clothes at him and he slid, with some difficulty, into the doublet and breeches, holding them at his waist, not even bothering with the strings to tie them to each other. He could do that in his attic at the top of the house, later. The Marquise was limping about the room, searching. Under a jumble of discarded stays she found her desire.

'Ah!' She weighed the bag and they heard the satisfying clink of coin on coin. She opened it and ran the contents through her fingers, nodding in satisfaction. He reached out toward her.

'What do you want money for, Little Bear? Don't I take care of all your needs?'

'New sword,' he grunted. 'Broke mine yesterday.'

'You've not been fighting again? I won't allow it.'

He said nothing, held out his hand still. Reluctantly, she reached into the purse, pulled out one small gold coin.

'Just you be careful. We don't want the merchandise marked, do we?'

She placed the florin in his outstretched palm, running a cracked nail along his brown inner arm. She chuckled as he withdrew his hand, hid the coin in his clothes.

She slid out the door, beckoning him to follow. He glanced around the room once more, looking for a bottle he could conceal but found none. His eyes, finally resting again on the mirror, encountered his own gazing back.

'Dog,' he said, sticking out his tongue. 'Indian!'

The great bell of Notre Dame struck, and at its toll the roaring began. Anne had first heard it in Southwark, from Uriah's bear gardens, and thought she must be back there now, this conviction curling her up on the bed in fear; for if she was in London still, heretics were yet to burn, the rack was being prepared and Jean Rombaud would never come.

The animal cries drew her, the shouts of a crowd, and she was walking into the arena. But it changed as she looked; no longer circles of seats filled with jeering drunkards, she moved now through a masque, interlocking couples weaving in dance, their faces concealed in leather and lace. Glimpsed through joined palms, beyond rich hooped dresses and sword hilts encrusted with jewels, something dark flitted. She had to reach it, thread through this maze of elegance. Yet it remained elusive, beyond sight and touch. Finally, as if they'd planned the move all along, the dancers cleared and she was alone in the centre of a circle of silent, masked nobility. Then she heard a whimper and there was a bear, attached by golden chains to a post. The animal raised his sad eyes to her, lifted paws from which the claws had been cruelly gouged. She took a step toward him, then another, raising her own hand as she went, reaching toward the bloodied paw. Finger and fur were a handspan apart when she heard the slipping of the leashes, the snarling, saw the blur of teeth as the first hound leapt past her.

'Free him! Free the bear!' she cried as the bell tolled the seventh hour of the evening in the tower of Notre Dame and her father rose from his chair and took Anne in his arms. He parted the veil of her black hair and looked into her face, into the starting eyes. Then he cradled her head to his chest.

'Hush! Hush now, child!' He rocked her as she straddled the land between sleep and wakefulness.

'We must free the bear, Father!'

'Of course we must. Shh! Shh, child!'

He held his daughter close to him and listened both to her wild heartbeat and to the bell's deep echo dying away.

Why were they in Paris?

For a rendezvous only a fool would try to keep! Who knew where Haakon and the Fugger were now? Almost certainly still stuck outside the gates of a Roman prison. And if they weren't in Paris, how long could he and Anne wait? He had agreed to come because such a vast city seemed a good place to hide ... and because he seemed to have lost all capacity to make decisions. But he had no illusions – his son would be close behind them, days, if not hours away. He had seen Gianni's fanaticism at the burnings, heard it in the confessional. He would not give up, as Jean would not have given up at his age. Not only the sins of the father are visited upon the son.

Above all, Anne had insisted on Paris, with that look of total certainty. He had learned that he could not oppose that look, not after all that had happened in the Tower; not when the shape he was feeling as he comforted his daughter, nestled in its bandage prison at the base of her back, was the skeleton of a six-fingered hand. Her look, that certainty, had brought the hand to them, had governed their escape. She would choose what should be done with it now. And she had not decided yet, that much he knew.

She pulled back from his embrace. 'How long have I slept?'

'From dawn till now and I only a little less. Your cries woke me. You had a nightmare.'

She looked beyond him, back into the vision of her dream. 'It was not a nightmare, Father. I think it was a prophecy.'

He smiled. 'To free a bear? For that is what you were calling out.'

'To free ...' She paused, her brow wrinkling. 'I don't know if I can explain it but ... I think there is a bear ... beyond the bear. Some creature, a person. And that person is tied to a post, in chains, even if they are not real. And they are golden.'

'The chains?'

'Yes!' Anne gripped his arm excitedly. 'This bear is one that lives among nobility. I saw them dance!'

Jean shook his head. 'I do not understand. Do you wish to go to a bear baiting, is that it? I thought you abhorred them?'

'I do. But this is no ordinary baiting. No ordinary bear.'

She got up, walked to the window, looked out. When she looked back her face was flushed with excitement.

'Father,' she said, 'where is the King's Palace in Paris?'

He was about to deny her, to caution and oppose, when he saw that look, the certainty. He sighed and began to tell her.

In the gardens of the Louvre, torches lit a scene of carnage. Amidst the carcasses, unsated scavengers stalked, ripping at any overlooked roasted flesh. All that remained of the ox that had stood centre in the tableau were its spreadeagled ribs, thrust up like the spars of a beached ship. Stuffed within the beast had been a whole lamb, which had contained a hare whose remains were still being poked by questing fingers searching for one more puzzle box to open, one last tender surprise.

Swans' feathers had settled like a snowstorm, for the three birds had been roasted then sewn back into their finery and pieces of down still clung to many a bloodied face; while the walls of the pastry Notre Dame were quite overthrown, eager hands having long since ripped the choir stalls apart where choristers of sparrow, thrush, starling and quail had revolved on iron spits.

The glazed eyes of the insatiable now turned to the final offering of the feast. It sat on the high table directly behind the King and flush to the walls of the palace, thrusting spun sugar towers twice a man's height into the air, its flaked pastry and cream battlements perfectly reproducing his Majesty's newly commissioned fortress at Aix-en-Provence in a sublime combination of the architect's and the confectioner's art.

Tagay looked down from the high table upon the besmeared faces of the subjects that watched the King, awaiting his signal; no one could begin the final assault until he did. And since Henri was in heated debate with the Papal legate, Borromeo, it did not look as if the feasters would be storming the sugar battlements any time soon.

Tagay gnawed half-heartedly at an ox rib. He had neither eaten nor drunk much. Partly it was the warning look from the Marquise, shot from her position beside a sumptuously dressed Duchess, whose plentiful jewels over her revealing bosom highlighted both her wealth and her age. The Marquise had shown her to Tagay before as his mark for the evening.

233

'She's very refined, the Duchess of Epais-Rouland. So watch your drinking!'

They are all very refined, Tagay had thought sourly, *until the doors of their boudoirs close.*

The expectations of the evening were not all that kept him from the wine he yet craved. His dream still hovered at the edges of his mind. He had been unable to shake it all day. It was as if, from the corner of his eyes, he still saw a bear stretching out his arms.

'My Little Bear is distracted tonight, is he not?'

All within earshot immediately ceased their own conversations to listen. It was always thus, when Henri of France spoke.

Tagay looked up at the King from his stool. He inclined his head but did not reply.

'And who is this pretty little brown fellow?'

The Papal legate had leaned down, his fat and florid face heated with food and conversation. Tagay had heard the words 'war' and 'Spain', common words lately around the King's table. Before he had returned to his own thoughts he had gathered that this representative of the new Pope in Rome was trying to persuade his master into another conflict. He also realized he was being used now as an interlude in this debate.

Henri also leaned down, his fine-boned features and trimmed beard a contrast to the ruddy Italian.

'This is my pet bear, your eminence. The only representative at my court of my colonies in New France. Or Can-a-da, as he calls it. Is that not right, Tagay?'

Tagay nodded, kept his silence.

'Ah, yes, another one of your possessions yet threatened by our mutual enemy of Spain.' The Italian made his point then returned to his study. 'He looks like one of those Asiatics who come with Russian delegations to the Holy Court. And yet he comes from the Americas?'

Henri nodded. 'My good and loyal Breton servant, Jaques Cartier, brought him back on his first voyage, oh, twenty years ago. Or rather brought his mother, for this rascal was a stowaway . . . in her womb!' The King laughed as did all within hearing. 'Alas, his mother and all my other Indians died. Only my Little Bear proved hardy. Everyone loves him here – is that not true, ladies?' Another laugh, sycophantically echoed. 'Tagay, speak some of your language for the legate. Really, it is marvellously strange. Speak, Tagay. Give his eminence his full title in your tongue.'

Tagay stood and bowed, then spoke in the language of his tribe, the Tahontaenrat. 'Your ugliness informs me that your mother was a beaver who was sodomised by a moose.'

The legate clapped his hands, delighted. 'We must send for more of these Little Bears, Majesty.'

'I desire it too. But a colony we tried to start there failed. We will commission another expedition, and soon. It is our Christian duty, for they are devil-worshipping heathens to a man. Yes, French government and Catholic morals. That's what my Little Bear's people need, eh Tagay?'

Tagay bowed. 'You would honour us, Mighty Father.'

'He calls you "Father"! How enchanting! And his French is enchanting too.' Borromeo clapped his hands. 'A worthy crusade, Majesty, to bring his people the language and the cross. Perhaps after our Spanish problem is solved?'

With these words, the two men renewed their former conversation. Tagay reached for wine to pour over his anger, soothe his sadness, but it gave no comfort. Though she had been dead two years, the thought of his mother always hurt him. And he was hurt every day.

He looked down, saw the Marquise glower at him so he raised the wine and toasted her, then drained the glass in one.

'Now!'

They had waited for the patrols to turn each their respective corners, the one onto the embankment of the Seine, the second to the Louvre's front wall. Other guards would appear any moment, but this interim was theirs.

They ran from the darkness of the alley to where the branch of the huge Cedar of Lebanon crested the palace wall. As in the dungeon passages, Anne bent with interlocked hands and Jean stepped, reaching through the soft needles to the branch beneath. He swung himself up, locked his legs, then reached down. Anne leapt, clung to his arm, and with a heave he pulled her up. The first guards walked around the corner just as her leg disappeared into the canopy and they waited till the helmets and pikes passed beneath them before they scrambled along the branch that spanned the wall.

The gardens sloped steeply down and away from them, the tree's trunk set back from the wall, making the jump down too extreme. They were forced to crawl further along the branch to the trunk itself. There, a junction led them on, down another branch to where a second cedar overlapped. With some difficulty they straddled the gap between trees, but none of the branches were close enough to the lower ones to allow descent to the ground. If anything they were being taken higher.

'Anne!' hissed Jean. 'We have to get down somehow. If we are seen up here . . .'

His voice trailed off. She knew the danger as well as he. They would be taken for assassins, Huguenot fanatics who had attempted the life of more than one French King in his palace. Their only hope of concealment lay in mixing with the servants. They had spent most of their remaining coins on appropriate caps, smocks and an apron that barely concealed the sword strapped to his back.

She kept crawling forward, upward. This vast tree led to one more and the further they progressed, the louder the sound of the feast ahead of them grew.

'Father. I think I see something.'

He joined her near the branch end, which dipped alarmingly under their weight. He peered through the gloom.

'The wall of the palace. Can you see a balcony, or a way down?'

'No.' She turned to him and he could see well enough to note her gleaming eyes. 'But I can see a way up.'

They crawled back to the trunk, shimmied up to the next level, followed that branch out again. They came to the wall and perceived guttering, a roof sloping away beyond it.

'We can't climb onto the roof, Anne. It will be treacherous with rain. Too dangerous. Let us go back. There must be another way to the ground.'

He'd half-turned when he realized she wasn't following.

'Anne, come!'

'Father,' she said, her head angled over, 'do you hear it?'

He listened. All he could hear was the continuous buzzing of voices, some hounds giving tongue, a louder shout breaking through some steady cheering.

'I don't hear anything other than—'

'Shh!'

Then he did hear it, unmistakable, within the uproar. The deep-throated growl of a frightened animal.

'A bear!' she cried. 'A bear, Father. I knew it!'

As she spoke, Anne sprang from the branch, hands scrabbling for a purchase on the eaves. One hand slipped, but the other managed to grab hold, and she swung her legs up and scrambled onto the slick tiles.

'Anne!' he called again to halt her, but she was gone, slipping along toward the front of the building. In a moment she had disappeared.

Cursing, Jean knew he had no choice but to follow her.

The King had decided on a surprise interlude prior to the storming of the confectionery castle. There hadn't been many such entertainments lately due to the sustained demand for them and the ever diminishing supply. But while the nobility of France picked over the carcasses and sucked bone marrow from the scraps, his Majesty's chief bearward, Grillot, attended to the preparations. Before the palace, directly below the sugared walls they all craved, a pre-dug hole was uncovered, a sturdy wooden stake thrust into it and wedged tight. Thick chains ending in manacles were secured to it with iron pins. Sawdust was scattered in a wide circle with the pole as its centre.

His steward advised him when all was ready. Henri rose and there was an immediate silence – for even in their gorging everyone kept an eye on the King.

'Nobles and Ladies of France,' he declared. 'In honour of the feast of St Genesius and the visit to our court of our new Father's holy representative, Cardinal Borromeo, we have arranged a special entertainment. We hope it will give you appetite for the ransack of the sweet castle to follow. For see what stands between you and it!'

He descended from the high table, and everyone rose and crowded forward. There were bursts of excited whisperings, acclaim. They spread around the circumference of the sawdust circle. Everyone knew what it meant, everyone recognized the chain-wrapped stake at its centre. Everyone, including Tagay.

He had risen like the rest when the King did, but when he had followed the sweep of the royal arm and seen what lay below him, he had sunk down again as soon as the King left his dais. Soon he was alone, his back to the gathering crowd. He could not leave but he did not have to watch. He could drink more, attempt to achieve what he had failed to so far. All night he had remained stubbornly sober. He reached for a flagon.

He could not block his ears. As soon as the King's feet touched the ground, the signal was given and the dogs, which had been held in a dark kennel and whipped into silence, were released into the night air, pulling to the length of their chains with a chorus of deep-throated yelps. A collective gasp arose when they appeared, for these were not the hounds they were all used to.

'A gift from his Holiness the Pope,' the cardinal was saying to those near him, 'from his native land. Neapolitan mastiffs – the finest fighting dogs in the world!'

Tagay heard and, despite himself, turned. The beasts were like nothing he had ever seen. Soot grey from muzzle to back paw, they came up to the waists of the handlers struggling to rein them back. Their heads seemed to be all jaw, tendrils of salivation streaming from huge and fearsome teeth. Their shoulders and haunches were bunched muscle. Black eyes rolled in reddened sockets. Tagay saw more than one noble or lady cross themselves, for the dogs looked as if they had sprung fresh from Hades.

A different sound, deeper even than the baying, a roar of pain and confusion set the hounds yelping louder and all the nobility crying out. Tagay tried to turn away, failed, his hand reaching behind him, knocking over his full cup of wine. His eyes, like all there, were locked on the corner of the house.

With another anguished roar the bear appeared, dragging the two men who held his neck in rigid pincers. A third pulled on a thick chain wound about the animal's waist, his feet gouging trails in the lawn, while another sought to control its movements with the torches he thrust forward. The animal was big and male, its rush carrying him into the middle of the sawdust circle. The crowd gave back, ladies clutching at the arms of their escorts, the men trying to simultaneously thrust their peacock chests forward while moving their bodies out of reach. The mastiffs jerked the length of their chains, their howls doubling in volume. Somehow, and after a great struggle, the bearwards attached the bear to the stake by its waist chain. The pincers were removed and the men fell back, one tumbling to the ground as the enraged bear ran and slashed at him, his paw catching a flailing leg, tipping him over. Tagay saw that, as usual, the bear had had its claws ripped out. He was surprised to see that the bear's teeth remained. His Majesty must have noted the fearsome jaws of the mastiffs and decided on a more even contest.

Contest? There would be no contest. There would only be one loser – the bear. The spectator's joy came from seeing how long the bear could last, how many of the hounds it would defeat, in singles, pairs, threes, before the whole pack was released. Tagay could see bets already being laid, everyone caught up in the fever of it, clutching at each other in an ecstasy of excitement. When the first mastiff was let slip, a cry of release as in lovemaking rose from the crowd.

He could not look away. His mother had been of the Bear clan, one of eight clans within his tribe of the Tahontaenrat, and therefore so was he. So it was as if it were him there, tied to a stake, surrounded by snarling enemies, him who jerked up his bloody paws, who tried to grab the leaping dog and fling him to one side. He felt the teeth that crunched into the arm, felt the jaw lock, the agony of snapping bones. It was he who bent and flung the animal high up into the air, jaws rending as they released their grip. The hound flew backwards, almost reaching the crowd, bear's blood spraying from its muzzle. It fell badly, something gone in the back, but it still tried to crawl back toward the bear, front paws scrabbling, teeth snapping, till a keeper pulled it aside and, in plain sight, slit the dog's throat.

'One!' cried the crowd, as the bear crouched, fired by the pain, watching for the next of the hounds that strained and leapt. Two were released then, one coming straight for the throat, one going low, the high one buffeted to the side while the other sought to sink its jaws into the exposed belly. Its half-grip the bear tore loose, raised the animal and sank its teeth beneath the snapping jaws. When the other dog rejoined the fight, leaping on the bear's back, biting an ear, Tagay put his own hands out, as if he too were thrusting the dying dog aside, reaching up behind to grip, to throw down, to stamp on the writhing body.

'Two! Three!' they shouted and Tagay knew that it would soon be over, for he saw the King's flushed face turned in anger to the noble who had just taken his money. The King did not like to lose.

'Silence! Silence!' Henri shouted, a cry instantly taken up by his steward, his guards. Gradually, the crowd quieted, until all that could be heard was the growling of the dogs and the deep-throated *hmm hmm hmm* of the bear.

'Release them all!' Henry said softly into that silence and the crowd swayed forward to get closer to the orgy of death unfolding. The houndsmen struggled to keep hold of each dog, gripping each studded collar as they were unchained, for they had to be released as a pack. The bear stood on its hindlegs, head swaying side to side, its flanks heaving with effort, streaked in its own and its victims' blood.

It was him, Tagay, swaying there, waiting for his death, brought to bay by his enemies. He was of the Bear clan. And if he had to die, he would die fighting with that clan.

Tagay had a new sword at his side, purchased by shame. Drawing it, he stepped down from the King's high table.

Anne leant over the two-storey drop below her, her fingers splayed on the slick tiles. Jean perched a few feet away, his feet pressed against a buttress which concealed him. He didn't look down.

She did. She had to – *for it was all there as she had seen in her dream*. The nobles spread out around the stake to which the noblest creature there was chained. She had watched each hound released, turned away from the sight if not the sound of the suffering, turned back when the crowd chanted. The voices demanding silence drew her eyes again, but still she was not sure what she was looking for.

Then she saw him stand up. He'd been there all the time, she realized, separate from the mob, aloof from it, yet intricately linked to the action. She saw that now as he stood, as if he lifted a golden chain, like the one that had bound the bear of her dream, this chain linking the animal and the man over the heads of the mob. She saw his hair, blacker than hers, as long, falling to his shoulders. She saw him draw the sword, even heard it clear its scabbard in the silence that still prevailed. She saw him lift his head and, in that moment, recognized a face she had never seen.

The man stepped forward, moving toward the bear pit. Somehow she knew exactly what he was going to do.

'No!' She screamed it out, standing straight up now, swaying on the edge of the abyss.

'Anne! Get back! Lean away!' Jean hissed. He wanted to move toward her, to pull her back. But he had glanced down just the once, and found his legs would no longer obey him.

Everyone below heard her cry. All faces lifted to her. There was an instant murmuring, Henri's voice rising above it.

'Who is that? Who is that woman?'

Tagay's mind had been so concentrated on the journey he was about to take to certain death that he was the last to look. When he did, he saw the woman with the long black hair swaying high above him. He only saw her there for a moment because the moment he saw her, she lost her footing and plunged over the edge of the world.

'Ataentsic!' he shouted, as the body fell.

Jean screamed 'Anne!', his cry lost among the many. It was his voice she heard though, thinking of him as she plunged, that this was what he had always spoken of – the suspension of time around moments of death, the world a reddish cloud in which she span so slowly. She felt sad for the sadness her death would cause him. And she thought of her failure, having come so far; feeling, even now, Anne Boleyn's hand pressing into her back.

The queen for whom she was named was the final thought in her mind as her flailing arm struck the first cream and sugar turret. She was falling spine first, so it was the six-fingered hand that first encountered the puff pastry battlements, which collapsed as swiftly as any besieger's most wondrous dream. Layer upon layer gave way so that by the time the body had carved through the castle's sugared floors and ceilings much of its force had diminished. Anne's side struck the table on which the edifice was perched and it collapsed beneath her.

The collective gasp was greater than anything bear or mastiff had brought forth. No one moved, not even the animals until

Tagay sheathed his sword and ran straight through the sawdust arena, passing close by the bear which rose onto his hind legs as the man came near him.

Tumult returned, astonished voices, yelping, as Tagay plunged into the wreckage. Scrabbling through the sticky walls and collapsed towers, clouds of powdered sugar obscuring his sight, at last his hands encountered a body. Carefully, he traced her form upwards.

'Live, Earth Mother, live!' Coughing, he put one arm under her head, began gently clearing the cream with his other hand. Her face emerged suddenly, as if she had burst from a snow drift. She gasped, her eyes flickered open, unfocused, moving about. Then they settled, held on his, and it was as if he had always known them.

She struggled up through the white storm, seeking the breath that would bring her back to the world. Then, amidst all the pained sensations of her body, she felt something pressing into her back.

She felt her left arm could be broken, but her right seemed to work. Despite the pain the movement caused her, she managed to reach down and around, and pull the unravelling bandage from behind her back.

'They must not find this. No one must find it,' she said, just before the whiteness took her again.

Her limp fingers released something onto his lap. Through layers of cloth, he saw the white bone of a knuckle, the joint of a skeletal thumb. As the first of the courtiers' footfalls crunched onto the shattered sugar castle, Tagay tucked the hand and its shroud into his doublet. Then he bent and lifted the unconscious body from the wreckage.

People swirled around him then reeled back, cursing, as expensive garments were swathed in powder and cream. He strode out of it, stopping as he beheld the rank of nobles drawn up before him.

'What is she, Tagay? A Huguenot assassin dropped from the sky?'

It was the King who spoke. Henri stood at the centre of his court. Behind him, the nobility of France jostled for precedence and a view.

Tagay may have been treated as a mascot, little better than a jester, but he had been at the court long enough to know its language – and what delighted it.

'A woman, Great Father, sick with love for me. Her parents would keep us apart.'

'Well, they say love lends us wings. But is she is so desperate for your love that she tries to prove it?'

Laughter greeted his Majesty's question.

'It seems so, Father.'

'And do you love her, my Little Bear?'

Tagay looked down at the face that lolled against his shoulder. 'Beyond measure, my King.'

There was a murmur, especially from the ladies of the court. Diane de Poitiers, the King's favourite mistress, was standing just behind him. She laid a caressing hand to his neck.

'Majesty, is it not our duty, as ambassadors of love, to help our Little Bear in his plight?'

The King smiled back at her. It was well-known he could refuse her nothing. 'How fares she, Tagay? Will she survive her fall?'

'I think so, Father. But I would get her to a bed and swiftly.'

More laughter, the King leading it. 'I am sure you would, Tagay. But be gentle with her, heh? She might yet break.'

Commands were issued, stewards sent ahead to prepare a room, physicians called.

'Go now, and attend to your love, Little Bear. And we will send to inquire how the lady is later.' The King turned back to his court, raising his voice. 'Well, dessert has been overthrown by love. What a pity. But as we are discussing little bears, I believe we have another to attend to here.'

They had all forgotten in the new excitement. They returned to the killing ground behind them as Tagay went the opposite way, bearing his burden toward the palace, shrugging off the grasping fingers of the Marquise who angrily tried to delay him. As he entered through one of the great doors, he heard the hounds' baying begin anew, heard the deep-throated grunt of the chained bear.

'Die well, brother,' he said quietly. 'Die well.'

SEVENTEEN
THE GREY WOLF
AND THE BEAR

Her sleep was almost unbroken, through the night and long into the morning. Tagay had allowed the doctors to set her arm, her only serious injury, though her left side was badly bruised. Then he had dismissed them all. It was he alone who attended her when her eyes started open, soothing words accompanying the cordial or broth he fed her. Soon she'd sleep again and he would watch and wonder, eating and drinking nothing himself.

For when a goddess fell to earth, had not the hour come to fast?

It was the bell that woke him, striking somewhere within the palace. He could not have slept for long, but in that time her eyes had opened and were fixed upon him. He was at her side in a moment.

'I met you in my dream,' she said.

'And I met you in mine.' He raised the glass of cordial to her lips.

She shook her head. 'Tell me how that can be.'

Her eyes were pools of cool darkness. He had to look away before he slipped into them.

'In my land, it is said that dreams are the rulers of all life.'

'That sounds like a land where I could live.'

He looked up at her then, risking her eyes.

'Where lies this place? What is it called?'

'We call it many things. But the French, who seek to possess it, have named it Canada, which is the name we give to a big village. It lies far away, across the water, beyond the setting sun.'

'Tell me of it.'

'I have never seen it, for I was brought here inside my mother.

244

All I know was told to me by her, and by a chief who was also brought, my uncle, Donnaconna.'

'Then tell me that.'

So he did and as he talked Anne watched him. Listening to the words, to the feelings behind them. His voice took on a cadence, a rise and fall, almost as if he were singing a song of the ways of his people and of the place they lived. She took most of it in, for in his attitude to the world there was a similarity to her own, a recognition of something other that underpinned everything, living on mountaintops, in the depths of forests, in streams at twilight. Sometimes though, she found she was just listening to the way his voice sang. It was only when he spoke of the bones of his ancestors that she came fully back to her own world and its peril.

'Do you have what I asked you to keep?'

He pointed to a pillow beside hers. There, re-wrapped carefully in its cloth, she saw the hand.

'My people also keep safe and honour the bones of our ancestors.'

'She is not my ancestor. She . . .' Anne hesitated, unable to decide where to begin, how much to tell. 'She was a woman of power, who entrusted herself to my father. He seeks to protect . . . this. To hide it from men who would misuse it, abuse her memory. But it is so . . .'

She faltered. How could she explain the danger she was in? She had groped her way in the darkness, had followed the warnings of her dreams to this point. Ahead of her now, nothing was clear. Then she remembered one more thing that she could speak of.

'And I am named for this woman. We are both called Anne.'

'Anne, yes. I learnt your name, for you told it to the doctor who tended you.'

'I did? I do not remember that.'

He rose and bowed. 'You called yourself Anne Rombaud. And my name is Tagaynearguye.' He smiled, for there was confusion on her face at the string of syllables. 'I am known as Tagay. Before you were Anne, I thought you were Ataentsic, daughter of the Sun God. The Goddess who fell to earth.'

He made to withdraw his hand but she held it.

'No Goddess,' she said. 'And my father is no God. He is a man called Jean Rombaud.'

Speaking his name, she remembered him shouting hers as she plunged from the roof. She half-raised herself from the bed, but her dizziness and the firm squeeze of her hand made her settle back. It was the hand that decided her. Not Anne Boleyn's, for once. The hand of this man holding hers.

Wherever he was, her father would have to come to her.

'You! Why do you carry nothing? We'll have no slackness, sirrah!'

Jean bowed low and was rewarded with the stroke of a cane across his backside. He returned, yet again, to the site of the feast, where three other servants struggled to lift a heavy oak table. He made a fourth, heaved, and they carried it into the palace and down into the palace's depths.

It had been a long night, his disguise a mixed blessing. Every time he was within the walls and thought to slip away, another servant or steward would call him to help. The carnage of the festivities had to be cleared by the middle of the day for the King would then stroll in his gardens with his mistress. No trace must remain. So, like ants, the workers went back and forth.

In a strange way, Jean began to like what he was doing. His garb made him instantly accepted by all and the strange bulge of the sword under his apron drew no comment – there were at least three other hunchbacks among the drones. There were jokes, some laughter amidst the complaints, and a stew served near dawn. The meat was tough, gamey, and he had half a suspicion that it was bear. But it was hearty, and though his concern for Anne never quite left him, it retired to a place further back in his mind, level with the aches in his body. Also, as he worked, he listened more than he talked. Learnt of the workings of the palace, the layout of its upper rooms. By early morning he had a fair idea where his daughter might have been taken.

There was as much gossip as complaints. Much was to do with the extraordinary events of the night – the falling of the woman from the roof. He learnt of the man who had carried his Anne away, a favourite of the servant girls as well as the King. More than one, it seemed, knew him intimately. One kitchen maid, big of breast and with a sullen-looking mouth, was obviously jealous,

246

and told of the Indian's bad reputation. But another, a chubby footman named Cahusac, who had complained the whole night about his back and lifted little, defended the youth, saying that the story was like a romance from one of the broadsheets that could be found on any street corner in Paris.

When the noon bell sounded, Jean drained his tankard of beer, rose quietly. It was time to begin the search. He was halfway to the door when it burst open.

'Did I not tell you it was like a romance from the streets?' Cahusac cried, waving a piece of paper. 'Look, look! "The Pagan Prince and Wing'd Love"! It says that girl who fell is one of King Francis's bastards. The late King and one of you sluttish servant girls!'

There were boos, catcalls, as all crowded around him. Jean was drawn back.

'How could this story already be on the streets?' he asked Cahusac, who was struggling to keep hold of the pamphlet.

'You jest? There'll be half a dozen versions out by tonight. The printers work all night looking for just this sort of thing. Heh!' he shouted. 'Have a care there, you'll tear it! Let me read it. I'm the only one who can, after all.'

To cheers, he read aloud the tale as written by 'Doctor M – Physician Royal to his Majesty King Henri II of France.' It was the usual nonsense, Jean had read some of their like before. Love unrequited, the cruelty of Tagay, the native hostage spurning the late King's illegitimate daughter, till she threw herself from the highest tower in the land only to float to the ground, a miracle of angel's wings granted by the power of love, which opened the eyes of the pagan prince to her Christian fortitude and her beauty. But Jean heard all this in a blur, so stunned had he been by the subtitle:

'The Tale of Tagay of Canada and Anne Rombaud of France.'

These words now drove Jean again to the door and through it.

How could they know her name? Safety had lain in their anonymity, yet now the name of Rombaud was being bandied through the streets of the city. If it was a pamphlet now, it would be a ballad on every troubadour's lips by nightfall.

He had to find his daughter. They must be gone from Paris.

Thomas Lawley smoothed the pamphlet out on the table and looked across to the doorway of the inn where his companion kept his keen watch. Gianni had barely glanced at the text, evincing no surprise at his sister's transformation into a miracle of love. It was obvious that she held no interest for him. He was only concerned with what she had stolen and how he could get it back.

Thomas rubbed at his leg. Her bandages still bound his knee, although he had re-tied them in the complex system he'd discovered on waking in the Tower five mornings before. It helped, enabled him to move. But they were not the only legacy of his encounter with Anne Rombaud; that much was clear from the feelings he'd had on reading the absurd poetry of the love story.

He crossed himself, lowered his head, and behind the shadow of his hand he began to pray:

'Holy Mary, Mother of our Saviour, guide this, thy humble servant, in his temptations. Heavenly Father, help to make him strong in thy will alone.'

Thy will! If only he knew what that truly was. If only he had Gianni's certainty that it was all about the hand, getting it back to London before it was too late, furthering the cause of the furious Imperial Ambassador. Except he knew – and he suspected his young companion knew the same – that cause was dead. If they were indeed in Paris for the hand, it was for more complex reasons now.

Moving his lips in prayer, he tried to seek what his were.

Gianni leaned out of the doorway, spat onto the smeared cobbles. He had read the signs of his family's flight, had tracked them successfully to Paris. The absurd love story was a fortunate occurrence but he'd have found them eventually anyway. Looking at the palace gates now, he knew his quarry cowered somewhere behind them.

He watched their men moving back and forth, seeking information. Something, at least, the Jesuit had been able to muster on arrival – Imperial agents, roused by Renard's decrees. A dozen of them circled the walls, though most were here among the crowds at the main gates. All other entrances had been closed, the patrols trebled – the King had been concerned that a woman had so easily penetrated his defences. It certainly made it easier to wait and watch. The quarry may have gone to ground but they would have to break cover soon.

He had no thoughts as to why his sister had got caught up in this ridiculous romantic saga. He didn't care. All that mattered to him was that he was again within reach of the hand. This time, when he held his family's curse, no one would take it from him. No one.

Jean stood just inside the doorway of the bedroom, watching his daughter and the man who held her hand.

They did not move. They did not talk. They were simply there – Anne on the bed, Tagay on a chair before it – and Jean could only observe his daughter joined to someone as she had never been before. And there was something in his daughter's look he recognized immediately. For almost the same dark eyes had once looked at him that way, reflecting the beams of a Tuscan moon. In their daughter he saw Beck, the mother, and the love that had once been his.

Anne suddenly started and the man before her leapt up, hand on sword.

'No, Tagay! It is my father.'

Jean came forward then, taking his daughter's unbroken arm, noting the other, her pale face.

'I thought I had lost you.' He kissed her forehead. 'I have always marvelled at your powers, girl. But when did you decide that you could fly?'

'I had no choice.' She gestured to the man who stood behind her father.

Jean turned. Tagay stood motionless, arms tense at his side. 'Jean Rombaud.' The Frenchman extended his arm as he spoke and the dark young man took it, gripping along to the elbow. They held that and looked each at the other for a long moment. Then Jean nodded and turned back to the bed.

'Anne, the news of your attempted flight has spread through the city. It will not be long before they come for us and . . . what we possess.'

'Tagay knows everything, Father. He saved this for us.' She

moved her head toward the table and Jean saw the package of cloth, the familiar outline within the layers.

'Then he will know of our great need.' Turning, he said, 'Can you help us get away from this place? I fear the gates may already be watched. And I think my daughter will not be climbing for a while.'

'I can help you away from here. But where will you go?'

'I do not know. Somewhere else. I cannot think beyond that.'

'I can.' Anne had raised herself up in the bed and Tagay moved to place pillows behind her back. 'I know where we must take the hand now.'

'Another dream, child?'

'Not a dream. A certainty. Anne Boleyn's hand will never be safe here.'

'In France? Should we return to Italy then, keep it with us? I don't think your mother would like that.' He tried to force a smile, failed.

'I mean, it will not be safe anywhere in this world.'

'Then we are doomed, child. We cannot run for ever. This hand has a way of wandering. Believe me, I know.'

She looked first to Tagay, then back to her father. 'Tagay has spoken of another world. His. It is called Canada. It is a world barely touched by our ... Christian savagery. They have sacred places there too. A full moon by which to bury it. Perhaps, finally, the Queen can rest there.'

Jean was too stunned to speak. But Tagay's heart moved faster as he heard her words. For in that moment he knew she was right – and that she had fallen from heaven to bring him his great desire.

Excitedly, he said, 'We can take ship from Brittany. We can follow the sunbeams to my land.'

Jean found his voice. 'I have heard of this place. But it is not like the Spanish colonies in the Americas where there are ports, cities growing, people. The French gave up trying to settle in Canada. There's no one there!'

'Forgive me but you are wrong. My people are there.'

Jean studied that certainty, now in both the faces before him. It was hard to oppose it but he had to try. 'Even if you found a captain who had been, who could take us – and I think the last ship probably sailed when this young man was a child – do you know how much gold it would take to buy a passage?' He saw Anne's face drop. 'We have nothing left, Anne, and no way of getting what we'd need. It's impossible. Impossible!'

There was a silence. Until Tagay spoke again. 'I know where there is gold. Lots of gold. Gold that is mine by right.'

Jean looked back and forth between the two of them, saw the certainty returning.

'Father, you have always trusted me before. Trust me now.'

'And the men – my son, that Jesuit, all the Imperial agents – who probably even now wait at the gates? This may be a palace but it still stinks of a trap to me.'

'There are ways out of any trap,' Tagay said.

Jean looked between them, along the palpable link that joined them, and saw again what he had recognized from the door. Recalled other dark eyes lock with his across the decades. Beck was looking at him from beneath a gibbet, at a crossroads in the Loire. And between them, they had just accomplished the impossible.

Each carriage that left the gates was scrupulously studied. If its curtains were drawn, Gianni would find an excuse to look behind them, usually joining the beggars and pretending to seek alms, sometimes receiving a slash from the coachman's whip as reward. But each survey yielded the same result – startled ladies and blustering lords, but no guardians of the hand.

Then, at six bells, a chair came through the gates. There were two men at each of the four poles, but it was the man at its window that had Gianni grabbing at Thomas's arm.

'My father!' he whispered. Jean Rombaud's face peered between the brim of a servant's cap and the high collar of his cloak, searching the street while struggling to pull down the blind. He was still at this task when the chair swung left directly before their vantage point. His father was passing within feet of him but both Gianni and Thomas now looked beyond him to the other side of the compartment, saw long black hair spilling from beneath a white lace coif, flowing down over the shoulder of a green gown.

The blind dropped. 'And Anne!' said Thomas. He held onto Gianni's arm as the young man strained forward. 'Not here!' He gestured to the main gates, where the palace guards were massed. 'Let us follow and take them in some alley.'

'Did you see anyone?'

'Yes. And I'm sure they've seen us.'

'Good.' Tagay began stripping the lace from his hair, unhooking the stays of the dress. A sober green doublet appeared from beneath, matching breeches, with riding boots up to his knee. He donned a black cloak and wide-brimmed hat.

'How far?' said Jean.

'Not very.'

'Does that mean I can get up now?'

The plaintive voice came from the floor of the carriage. Jean looked down at Cahusac, the man who had read out the pamphlet, his fat frame wedged uncomfortably into the chair's base. The footman had volunteered to help out 'the lovers' for sentiment and the promise of a gold florin. He looked less than happy about the bargain now.

'Not yet.' Jean was stripping off his cap and cloak as he spoke. 'And put these on.'

In the wider roadways nearest the palace they made good speed, the eight chairmen taking it almost at a run, Thomas struggling to keep up. Soon, however, the rat's nest of byways narrowed and the men were forced into a halting progress. Their pursuers eased up, Gianni sending three of his men fifty paces ahead of the chair, he and the others keeping an equal distance behind.

Thomas limped up beside Gianni. 'We must not rush this, Rombaud.'

'Have you ever ambushed anyone on a street before, Englishman?'

'Well, no, I—'

'Then hold your tongue, sir.'

Gianni smiled to himself, moved slightly ahead, his eyes never leaving his quarry. He was a Grey Wolf once more on the hunt. And for a greater prize than any old Jew.

The chair had halted again, angry words drifting back to them. Tagay peered from beneath a partly raised blind.

'Rue de la Ferronerie. There's always a blockage here. Look, there is a corner ahead, a cooper's awning straddles the street beyond it. Are you ready?'

'Yes.' Jean opened the door but held it against the frame. As the chair lurched forward again he said, 'Till the rendezvous. Go with God.'

'Perhaps.' Tagay gave him a brief smile. 'And you go with the Earth Mother.' He looked out, tensed. 'Now!'

As the chair turned the corner, Jean slipped out of it. He was already beneath an awning and his knee struck a barrel, part of the stock of the cooperage. He moved swiftly into the darkened interior. From its shadows he watched as the chair moved on. The blind had been allowed to ride up and Cahusac now sprawled across the window space but half-turned away, wearing Jean's cap and cloak.

It will not deceive him for long, he thought, watching his son walk past. *Long enough, let us hope.*

He waited till Gianni had cleared his vision, counted ten. As the shopowner approached him, asking for his custom, he ducked under the awning and moved swiftly back in the direction from which he had come.

There was something wrong with the chair! Gianni closed to about twenty paces, till he could look down its right side. The blind had risen and he could still see his father's peaked cap, an edge of cloak. It took him another fifty paces before he realized.

'The chairmen!' he hissed to Thomas. 'They are walking lighter.'

'What?'

Gianni doubled his pace, grabbing his men along the way. The chair was halted up ahead, its bearers arguing with a waggoner over right of way.

Gianni closed the distance, a wolf descending on prey. His dagger was already out as he reached for his sister's door.

He jerked it open. One startled face looked at him from beneath his father's cap, above his father's cloak. But it was not his father's face.

253

'Help, help, he—!' cried Cahusac.

The third word was choked off by Gianni's hand and the dagger's point that almost touched the eyeball.

'Where are they, scum?'

The eye showed white in terror. There was the sudden, sharp smell of urine.

'Sir, sir, sir, I ... I ... I ... do not know. Please ...' the steward squeaked as the blade moved a hair closer. 'They ... they ... they say they will rendezvous later, they did not tell me where.'

As Gianni threw the terrified man to the floor, Thomas arrived. 'What has happened?'

'We have been duped!'

Gianni picked up the dress from the floor, slashing at it with his blade. Then he dropped it, pushed past Thomas, and swept his vision up and down the street.

Horses, wagons, black cloaks, brown cloaks, beggars, merchants, refuse, rats. Tiles, awnings, whips, sword hilts, black hair, fair hair, plumes, sashes. Fury, watching, shouting, laughter, shoving, limping, begging, turning.

Black cloak, black hair. Watching. Turning. He saw it all again, realized which way the man had walked.

'Go back to the palace,' he called over his shoulder. 'Try to catch them there. I am going after this other.'

Thomas watched Gianni disappear into the throng. He took a step, called, 'Rombaud!' but the youth was gone. Hurriedly he gathered the others and began to retrace their route.

It did not matter that it was not his city. There are ways of tracking game, in any forest. That one glimpse of black hair, black cloak had given him his scent even though it was a city short of neither.

This must be her pagan lover, he thought as he hurried to the corner. *Well, a brother must protect his sister's virtue, must he not?*

He changed his grip on his knife. The edge of the first building gave him a view of the next, of the figure moving swiftly around it. At the next he nearly lost him in a street of stalls, the crowd thick. Narrowing his senses down, he shut out all that was unnecessary, moved his head back and forth from the slabs of fish to the dripping carcasses of hare. It took a while but he got him again, paused at a stall up ahead, pretending to examine some item there. Gianni turned and immediately began haggling for a flagon of wine. When he'd paid and looked up the black cloak was moving round a corner.

Beyond it, the street widened, the houses growing a little larger, shops selling linens and books instead of fruit and offal. Steps led down toward the road that paralleled the Seine, the river scent ripe from the day's sun. On its banks the mansions of the rich massed. Carefully he descended the stair and looked around its buttress, saw his prey disappear through the main gate of a comparatively run-down, but still large, house.

Is this the lovers' rendezvous? he thought.

He approached the rusted gates. An old man, toothless and runny-eyed, sat just inside them. Though it was a stalker's necessity to be patient, Gianni was alone and needed information.

'Share a drink with a stranger, friend?'

The old man, startled from his daydream, blinked up at him. Gianni uncorked the bottle he'd bought at the market, thrust it nearer, saw the old man recognize and reach. He let him take a deep draft before he spoke again.

'Tell me, friend, whose magnificent palace do you guard here?'

The man muttered something, raised the bottle to drink again. Gianni took the bottle away when liquid began to spill down the soiled shirt front.

'Who lives here, friend?' His voice was harder now and the man understood that, even as his eyes followed the withdrawing bottle.

'I said! The bitch Marquise de Saint Andre, pox rot her! Doesn't pay me enough to buy such lovely wine.'

Gnarled hands reached again and Gianni let him take just another little sip.

'I thought I saw a comrade of mine enter here just now. A halbardier from the Duc de Fournay's company.'

'Eh?' The eyes were glazed in incomprehension, then cleared. A laugh like a rattle came from his throat. 'A soldier? You jest, sir. No one but Whore Boy passed me this whole day, and him only a moment ago!'

'Whore Boy?'

'Aye, sir.' A tongue ran around reddened gums. 'The Marquise's pet monkey. Brown bastard. Sticks it where she tells him to, know what I mean?'

He made an obscene gesture with thumb and circled finger. Just as he did, shouts came from the house.

Gianni leant in. 'Is there another way out of this house?'

The man, who'd been staring at the bottle, now looked up angrily. 'Who wants to know? Friend of Whore Boy's, did you say?'

'No,' said Gianni, producing a coin from his pocket, 'friend of yours.'

There was more yelling from within, then a shattering of glass, a woman's long and desperate wail. A window was flung open, an old woman's head thrust out.

'Help! Help. Stop him! Call the watch!' she screamed. 'I am robbed, ruined, oh help!'

The old man appeared not to hear. He reached for coin and wine.

'River gate, sir. Down on the path to the right there.'

Gianni ran around the crumbling wall of the house. The muddy path ran wallside to the water, making a 'T' with an even muddier pathway there. To his right, a wooden gate swung on its hinges. He looked swiftly back and forth along the river bank. Nothing! Then he looked down and saw a bootprint slowly filling with brown water.

He began to run in the direction the toe pointed, mud sucking at his feet. Soon, a bridge loomed, its stair on his left. He paused – nothing to hear beneath the vaulted wood ahead. It was almost dark now so he ran his fingers along the steps. The wet mud was on the third step up, and again on the third above that. Someone had taken these stairs at a leap not a moment before.

He reached the top in three bounds. A wagon clattered past him, spraying mud and ordure. When it had passed, on the opposite side of the bridge he saw the black-cloaked figure walking swiftly across to the Left Bank.

'I have you,' Gianni thought exultantly. He would leave no more than fifty paces between them. The pagan had stolen, was on the run and would be panicked, frightened, careless. He would not be looking for a Grey Wolf.

Fixing his eyes on the black hair swinging ahead, Gianni melded with the crowds.

Tagay had known he would be followed. He wanted it, hoped that more would seek him, less to chase Jean as he returned to the Royal Palace to collect and flee with Anne. He was disappointed when he saw just the one in pursuit, until he realized who that one was, recognizing the profile at the wine vendor's back in the street market. Almost the same profile he had so stared at as it lay on the pillow. The hair that shaded it, the structure of cheek, nose, the shape of eye, showed the kindred bond.

He thought he had lost Anne's brother, back at the Marquise's house. He'd wanted to, now that he'd led him astray, now that he had what he'd come for. Soon his pursuer would be part of a pack, for the aristocracy of Paris did not like it when one of theirs was robbed. Even . . . no, especially, if the thief was one of their former pets.

Tagay transferred the heavy leather satchel to his other shoulder, heard the clink of gold from within it.

No thief, he thought, *for this is mine, my sweat-backed labour earned it. All those purses, like the one she'd picked up . . . was it only yesterday morning? . . . from beside the crumpled beds of the so-called nobility and emptied into this leather bag.*

Tagay smiled. A woman had floated from the sky and gold was no longer heavy but light as air under an eagle's wings. It would lift him up onto the horse that waited at the rendezvous. It would waft him along a sunbeam across the Great Water to his land.

He had led his hunter through the alleys of Montparnasse, up the great hill, beyond. The fields had begun, tilled at first, gradually giving way to grazing land. Across a stretch of common, the first of the woods began. He had often accompanied the King and court here, for Henri liked to keep his Little Bear with him when he hunted and Tagay liked to run beside the King's horse, down the tree-lined paths. It felt like the home he'd only ever dreamed of. And he was fast; the King had won money on him many times. No one had ever beaten him. Somehow, he didn't think the man following him would be the first.

Tagay stopped, turned. On that open field before the woods, close-cropped by sheep and cattle, there was nowhere for Gianni to hide. He stopped too, and the two men stared at each other over fifty paces. For a long moment the only sounds were the wind and the bleating of lambs. Then, without a word, Tagay turned and ran.

The Grey Wolf of Rome was a wondrous tracker. But this was a different land and its forests belonged to the Bear.

'Read it to me again.'

'Father, I have read it to you five times already.'

'I know, but it is such a good story. And you know how I like a good story.'

Erik sighed, and raised the piece of paper into the greyish dawn light.

'"The Pagan Prince and Wing'd Love: The Tale of Tagay of Canada and Anne Rombaud of France."'

While Haakon settled back contentedly into the stone steps, Beck rose and climbed them to the wooden gates of Notre Dame. From this little elevation she could look out over some of the rooftops of the city. From here, too, Erik's recitation was just a drone in the distance, which was best for her. Where Haakon heard romance and adventure, she heard only the suffering of her kin, the danger they were in.

Are you out there as well, Jean? And Gianni? Father and son, she wondered, *which of you is the hunter, which the prey?*

Gazing now over the steeples of Paris she again felt that both her children were either near, or had been so until very recently. She had always had this sense, as if a cord still joined her to her babes, stretched out though it had been by distance and time. Once, she had had the same feeling for Jean, would look up the moment before he'd walk through the door of the Comet with a bunch of grapes and that smile. But she had lost him, sometime in the recent years, lost him in her anger, in his doubt. Although that anger had largely gone – because she had come to realize he could only do what he was driven to – she still could catch no trace of his soul nearby.

She looked down across the square before the cathedral, saw the Fugger and his daughter walking rapidly toward them. Beside them was another man, a stranger in a plumed hat and cloak. She descended the steps and met them just as they reached the Norsemen.

'News?' said Haakon, rising.

'Yes, I think so.' The Fugger leant on Maria, tried to master his breathing. 'And I was right about going to the bankers. They always know what is going on.' He turned to the man beside him. 'May I present to you my cousin, François Fugger. He has information for us.'

The young gentleman bowed, sweeping his hat from his head. He was dressed like a dandy, all lace and plumes. Yet his voice was deep and serious.

'I only know bankers' gossip. Yet when my cousin told me his need, I made a few immediate inquiries and the word that came to me this morning seemed relevant.'

He looked to the Fugger, received a nod to proceed. 'It appears a certain Marquise, patron of the native boy in that pamphlet you are holding, owed a great deal of money around the town. A bank, a rival house to ours, had advanced her considerable sums. She was due to make good on her debts with the money amassed from certain . . . ah, services.' He glanced at Maria, blushed and looked away. '. . . Services that her ward would perform. Not only did he fail to perform them, he has absconded with the money earned so far, which would have gone a little way to clearing her debts.'

Beck descended a step. 'And did your source say where he might have absconded to?'

'The bank has hired some men to recover the money. For reasons that are unclear, a large party set off, not an hour ago, for a port in the west of the country. St Malo.'

On hearing these words, Beck turned away from the rising sun, already casting the shadows of Notre Dame over the great square. Somewhere out there, to the west, were her family. She could feel again the faintest tug on the binding cord that linked them to her.

'Come then,' she said, looking down at the others, 'let us ride to the ocean. And we must ride swiftly. For I am sure we are not the only ones who have gleaned this information.'

EIGHTEEN

DEATH ON THE SHORE

'Come, my friends, let us shake hands, and toast a bargain made and the Saint's sweetest breath in our sails!'

The glimmer in Captain Ferraud's eye was a match for the gold in Tagay's hand. Yet Jean watched the young man hesitate now, something he had not seen him do in their brief but busy acquaintance. He had organized their escape from Paris with seeming ease, his money paying for the carriage and the changes of horses in both Alençon and Le Teilleul that had brought them to the harbour of St Malo by the evening of the third day. On arrival, enquiries had led them to this waterfront inn and the only two men still alive, fishing captains the pair, who had sailed with Cartier to Canada all those years before. They had interviewed both of them, and while the first, Pierre Jacquet, had proved surly, full of cautions and doubts, this Captain Ferraud was all smiles and certainties. He promised the fulfilment of the young man's deepest desire, a speedy return to his homeland.

And yet now, for the first time, Jean watched Tagay hesitate. So into that pause, Jean spoke. 'Perhaps my friend needs a little longer to consider. Will you excuse us, Captain?'

The smile faded a little. 'I will be here, gentlemen. But do not consider for long. The fishing fleet sails tomorrow with the tide and we must be with it, eh?'

The rain had returned, blown off the sea by a strong wind. They pulled their cloaks tight about them, bending their heads together to talk.

'You have doubts, Tagay?' Anne said.

'I do not know why.' He shrugged. 'This one promises me all my heart's hope, while the other speaks as if it is near impossible.

And yet . . .' He looked out to the water. 'I think we should talk to that other again.'

They found him, as before, on his caravel, which looked even smaller now as it wallowed on the rain-lashed swell, like a cork in a vat of sour wine, belying the name of *Sea Feather* painted in blue on its bow. Jacquet sat on the raised aft deck, passing nets swiftly between his fingers, checking for tears, a busy needle making necessary repairs. He was shaped like his ship, seeming almost as squat and broad as he was long. The rain ran off him unnoticed.

He grunted when told of Ferraud's response.

'There you are, then.' He spat expertly, using the wind, over the gunwales. 'I wish you a pleasant trip.'

'You do not think it will be as easy as he describes?' Jean asked.

The response was so long in coming they thought he may not have heard. 'Easy? Oh, aye, so easy. You sails a thousand leagues through the biggest seas known to man. If you're very lucky, after five weeks mayhap, you catch sight of a piece of land. You might recognize it, probably not, so you sails up and down for a week, looking for a landfall, for fresh water.' He leaned forward, spat again. 'And that's just when you've barely reached the Indies. Then maybe you've got some strength left to fish – and the fishing's fine, mark, it's why you goes, pushing against the bow, they are, leaping into these nets – so you work day and night for a month and then you sets off home before the autumn storms. Did Ferraud' – another spit – 'did he tells you how far beyond the first landfall lies the place you seek, Stadacona?'

They all shook their heads. Jacquet gave something that could have been a laugh. 'Not surprised. I recall he was lying below decks for most of that time, feigning scurvy.'

He looked up at them for the first time. 'And once you get there . . . well, there's good reason why no one's gone that far down the St Lawrence for twelve years, more.'

He stood, stepped toward Tagay, peered up at him. 'So, you're one of them, eh? Sometimes wondered what happened to those natives we brought back. You're as ugly as I remember 'em being.' He sucked at his gums, his eyes never leaving Tagay's face. 'And so you want to go home?'

'Yes.'

'In your fancy lace,' he sniffed, 'your toilet water, your groomed hair? Think you'll last a minute there before you're stripped and dangling over a flame for some savage's supper?'

Tagay's voice was even. 'Whatever my fate is, it lies there and I must go to it.'

'Oh, fate is it?'

The small eyes in the sea-scored face narrowed. The Captain studied Tagay in silence for a full minute and Tagay's gaze in return never wavered. Finally, Jacquet resumed his position on the deck, passing the net between his hands. Another silence came and they watched him work.

'How much did Ferraud ask for?'

Tagay told him. There was another snort of a laugh. 'I'll take half, for my coffin doesn't need no gold lining. Half of that left with my wife, the other half with the innkeeper of the Gannet to pay the families of my crew if we don't return. It's good wages for them but they'll earn it because I'll have to take less men to make room for you. And we might not have time to fish on the way back so our bounty will be whatever furs we can trade for. You'll both bring your own provisions and you'll both work the sails or pumps when necessary. Indeed, you'll obey my every order while at sea. Agreed?'

Jean looked at Tagay. The hesitation of the inn was gone. 'Agreed.'

'Then go. There's a chandler at the Gannet, he'll tell you all you need. Bring nothing more, for there's no room on a caravel. And take my advice, say goodbye to your lady at the inn – it's harder to sail when they're wailing dockside.'

Anne had stood beside her father while Tagay negotiated. She stepped forward now. 'Captain, you do not understand. We are buying passage for all of us.'

The needle plunged into a finger. Jacquet cursed and sucked at it. 'I thought it was for the two gentlemen. A woman on a ship is an unlucky thing.'

'Nevertheless . . .'

'I cannot do it. The crew don't like it. It makes them . . . I hires tough men, lady. Not gentlemen. Their ways are not what you're used to.'

Anne bent down, forcing the Captain to look at her. 'You

know nothing of me, Captain, nor what I am used to. I have lived my life among tough men and I come from tough stock.' She squeezed her father's arm.

Jacquet hesitated. Jean said, 'And she has the gift of healing. Better than any I know.'

Jacquet looked at them both, then at the impassivity of Tagay. He sucked at his finger again, then bent down, picking up his needle. 'Ten bells on the morrow-morn. An hour before the tide, not a moment later. My first order.'

'We will obey it as all others.'

They turned and climbed the rope ladder to the dock.

Two hours passed in the outfitting and two more over a meal. All three ate and drank well, concentrating on what would be their last big supper shoreside, talking little. Their money bought them the best of the fare the Gannet could offer as well as a room upstairs they did not have to share. They spread their cloaks over the mattress and lay down, the men on the outside, Anne between them. Soon, both she and Tagay were asleep.

Though he was as exhausted as either of them, though his body ached in all the places the carriage had thrown him as it bounced over the pitted roads, Jean could not find the rest he craved. He lay listening to the wind shriek in the harbour, heard it gradually drop to a whisper, saw the moon dancing through the torn clouds, till its bulbous, half-full shape seemed to vanquish the last of them and stand in silver solitude. It filled the room with its light and having studied, for a while, the maiden's face he had seen in that globe all his life, he turned again to the maiden beside him.

Anne lay curled with her back to Tagay, his arm a pillow, her mouth a little parted, her breathing soft. Jean remembered how he used to watch her sleeping when she was a child, the wonder of his firstborn then, that wonder still there now. And with the shadows and shapes of it moulded by moonbeams, he saw what else he had always loved about her face – the memory of her mother in it. Beck was just this age when they first came together, lying on pine boughs in the moonlight, on the umber earth, against the crumbling wall.

'Beck!' Jean whispered.

Anne stirred at the sound but did not wake. She turned again, nursing, even in her sleep, her badly bruised, strapped up arm. And, of course, there was something else in the silver light, a shape within the folds of her dress. Distinctive, to someone who had an eye for it, for the material pushed out at six points. It was mere bone now but closing his eyes to that reality, he could once more see what had been. The hand that a queen, Anne Boleyn of England, had laid upon his shoulder, laughing at his shock. The hand he took from her the same moment he took her head. The hand stolen from him at a crossroads in the Loire, returned to that same crossroads after horrors and hardships, returned and buried by the sacred glow of a full moon for the fulfilment of an oath.

Another moon, another life, another Jean Rombaud. The man who had the courage to endure those horrors, the one who had buried that hand, was gone. He had even tried getting rid of the very symbol of that man; given it away, abandoned it. But the light that fell on the bed also fell on his executioner's sword.

He reached out, touched the scabbard, and suddenly, looking once more at his women's faces melding in the silver light, Jean realized what the morrow would hold.

Smiling now, Jean surrendered to sleep.

It was a glorious day, a cloudless sky, a gentle swell, and a strong warm wind blowing off the land. The caravels roped to the dock looked like falcons on jesses, straining for flight.

They stood above the *Sea Feather* watching the seventeen men of the crew make the ship fast for the ocean. Jacquet was among them, checking every detail of provision and implement. Their own meagre goods had been taken and stowed in one of the holds below. Now they could only wait, turned inward to the land, for the ocean beyond it would beckon soon enough.

Shouting made them turn back. It came from the end of the long stone pier that bent around to nearly touch the cliffs opposite. Between the two points was the narrow gap, the entrance to the harbour of St Malo.

Anne shielded her eyes against the sun with a raised hand. She saw men gathered around an iron frame.

'What are they doing, Father?'

'Lowering the boom. It's the chain across the gap that keeps unwanted visitors out.'

The plunge of heavy iron links was a signal to the men on the boats. Those who were ready began to cast off, those who were not sped up their loading. Glancing up the dockside, Jean could see that the captain they'd rejected, Ferraud, was among the tardy.

'Come, Father. They are telling us to board.'

Jean looked to his daughter. Tagay was below her on the rope ladder, an arm reached up to support her.

'I am not going,' Jean said.

'What?' She was back beside him in an instant, Tagay joining her, despite the protests from below. 'Father! You agreed. The hand must be made safe.'

'It must. But you are its guardian now and you must decide its destiny. I can do no more.'

She made to speak. But he laid a finger to her lips and, with his other hand, drew her close.

'Hush, now, child. You know, and I know, that this is right. You know me, better than anyone else. You know I no longer have the . . . the strength for what must be done. I have used it all up. What remains may get me home, wherever that is. To your mother, at least. I have some amends to make.'

He pulled her tighter to his chest, looked past her to Tagay. 'Take her, lad. She is the dearest gift I could ever give. Help her to do what must be done, let her help you. For she is a wonder, surpassing all the wonders of the world.'

Jean gently unloosed Anne's arm from around his neck. 'Go now. Follow your visions. Let them guide Anne Boleyn to her final rest.'

Tagay reached, pulled a speechless Anne toward him. 'I will protect her, Jean Rombaud. I will give my life for hers.'

'You had better.' Jean reached to touch the sword strapped to his back. 'Or my friend and I will come looking for you.'

They descended to the boat where impatient sailors helped them aboard, then turned to ropes and knots. Soon, the *Sea Feather* was floating away from the dock, its three sails unfurling. Anne stood in the bow, tears cascading, her one good arm raised. Suddenly, it appeared to Jean that there were two Annes there, his daughter and a queen, both waving their farewells. And it was as if all his aches, his agonies dropped away, taking the pain that had sat heavy round his heart for as long as he could remember, leaving him lighter, tasting the salt in the wind, feeling the warmth of a summer sun as if for the first time. He found himself hopping from one foot to the other, and the tears that ran down his nose and chin made him smile, then laugh. He was waving like a madman, his eyes on the boat taking both his joy and his sorrow away.

It took a while, because of the noise of his heart, for the other sound to penetrate. He saw Anne, still only two boat lengths offshore, stop staring at him and look suddenly past him, above him. Her arm dropped, fingers reaching to her mouth. Then her shout joined the other shouts, the ones that were coming from the hill on the edge of the town.

Jean turned. He had no eyesight for distance, saw only shapes on the hilltop. But the voice carried well on the offshore breeze.

'They are there, on that boat!' shouted Gianni Rombaud. 'Raise the harbour boom!'

Jean saw some dozen horses, spurred by their riders, plunge down the steep hill. They were a short ride from the jetty, a short run from its shore-end to the boom's winch. He looked back to the *Sea Feather*. It would not clear the harbour entrance in time.

Sprinting for the stone steps, he reached them just ahead of the horsemen. He heard them dismounting, then their riding boots clattering off the pebble-embedded pier as they followed him along it. Stopping ten paces short of the boom winch, Jean turned around.

His son was where he expected him to be, at the front. Gianni slowed when he saw Jean turn, his men forming a wedge behind him. Ten paces away, he halted.

'Cede the ground, old man,' Gianni snarled, 'for you cannot stop us now.'

'You're right, my son, I cannot. But I can, perhaps, delay you for a while.'

As Jean spoke, he reached up behind his back and pulled the square-headed sword from its scabbard. It emerged into the sunlight as it always had done, a predator blinking into a dawn.

He glanced around. Near the shore end of the jetty, a man in a black cloak was limping toward them. Up on the hill, he could make out the shapes of another group of horsemen beginning their descent. Reinforcements to his enemy, he presumed. On the water, the *Sea Feather* was fast approaching. Not fast enough.

He looked from the ship to his son. He needed a little time.

'A man dying at a crossroads told me you may be better with a blade than me. Was he right, Gianni? Did I teach you so well?'

It was bait and Jean saw his son take it, as Jean would have taken it at his age.

'He's mine. Mine alone,' said Gianni, drawing a heavy rapier from its sheath.

He attacked fast, as Jean knew he would, with the invincibility of youth. It had been three years since they'd last crossed swords in practice and Jean could see that his son was stronger now, faster. He had not spent those years simply in prayer and penitence.

The triangular-pointed blade came at him from a running lunge, chest high, straight, a young man's attack. The square-pointed blade moved square to meet it; met air – the run was a feint, for young men know what old men think of them. Gianni's tip moved outwards and, as his back leg caught up with his front his hands joined and, double-handed, he swept the weapon over and down in a half circle to Jean's exposed shoulder. Jean had to lunge backwards, taking his body out of line, his parry a slope to guide the other's weapon away.

But Gianni had not put anything into the blow. His father had exposed his back, given ground on the first pass. Suddenly, joyously, he knew he could take him. He let his blade slide off the square tip then, jerking it to a sudden halt, he flicked it sideways. It did not have the force to cripple, but honed metal bites nonetheless and this did, into Jean's outstretched leg.

Father and son looked at the cut in shared wonder. It was Jean who recovered first, withdrew his leg, stepped back two paces, came on guard. He stood with his feet parallel now, the hilt grasped two-handed and held straight out before him.

'You have learned, Gianni. I am proud of you.'

'Pride before the fall.'

'Perhaps.'

A man limping along a jetty. Horses flowing down a hill. A boat still too far away. Gianni looked and saw it too.

'Enough, old man. Your sword or your life.'

You can only take so much from a cub, Jean thought. *Even your own.*

So he bent, dipped his finger in his wound and reached up to taste his own blood.

'Now that brings back memories,' he said, and on the last word he attacked.

Swords rose to clash, metal on metal crying like the gulls that circled overhead, while the years of anger and misunderstanding coalesced in sunlight and sparks on their blades. Two men became animal and the young stag challenged the old.

To Gianni's guards, to Anne and Tagay on the boat, it was a blur of steel as swords sped through the air, met with shrieks, screamed in parting, renewed assault and parry, feint and counterfeint. Not one watching could see who led, who followed in the dance.

The men knew. It went both ways, giving and receiving, a blow no sooner thought of than delivered.

He is good, thought Jean, *and he is now trying to kill me.*

He is still good, thought Gianni, *and once more he stands between me and my God.*

I am old, thought Jean, *and I have not done this for a while. Time sides with youth. He could fight all day while I . . . I cannot even fight until that boat passes by*

So I must do something, Jean thought.

And did.

It was a trick. An old one – simple, dirty. He had meant to show it to Gianni years ago, but the boy had run away before he could.

Just as well.

Jean did not have to pretend to be tired. But he let each parry get weaker, counter-attacks rarer, let his son's ringing blows force his own sword ever closer to his body. Parrying two-handed, his breath coming in huge whooping gasps, stepping back and back, his foot finally reached the edge of the winch. Seeing this, with a grunt of triumph, Gianni stepped in close to drive his blow hard into his father's injured thigh, and Jean's parry barely halted the cutting edge a finger's width from his flesh. Then, with sudden force, he thrust his blade along Gianni's and straight down. His cross guards brought the rapier low and Gianni had to step close to retain it. Leaving only his left hand on his sword, Jean pulled his right back into a fist and hit Gianni hard, twice, straight on the nose. Eyes watering, he reeled back, tried again to disentangle his blade and bring it up. But Jean stepped closer still, keeping the blades tight and, reaching up with the hand that had struck, he grabbed his son's left shoulder, pulled down hard, then snaked his arm around the young man's neck. In a moment their two heads were conjoined and an executioner's sword pressed at Gianni's throat.

For moments it was all each could do to breathe.

Finally, Jean spoke. 'It's over, boy. Over.'

Gianni tried to move and felt the razor edge nick his skin. He could, however, speak.

'Kill him,' he said to his stunned men, 'kill him now.'

Jean sighed, then turned again to the water. The *Sea Feather* was drawing level. Anne was reaching out to him, Tagay barely keeping her aboard. They looked close enough to touch and they were just about to pass the neck of the harbour.

Gianni had cut himself, straining against the weapon, so Jean removed it and shoved him away to sprawl on the jetty's stones. Jean knelt, watching as the tiny rivulet of blood crept down the runnels of his sword.

So much blood, Jean thought, *so much down the years.* The guilty, the innocent, the simply unlucky, their life force pooling in these same channels, long wiped away, some vestige of them yet clinging, a trace of every departed soul. Not least that of his queen, Anne Boleyn, her smile a memory now. Her blood running here, from neck, from wrist, like his son's ran now. His sword had tasted more than just its share of blood. It had tasted enough.

As his son's men came for him, weapons thrust cautiously ahead, he stood and, as he had done once on a battlefield and once in a slaughter yard and once at a crossroads in the Loire, Jean Rombaud bent, unleashed still powerful shoulders and flung the sword high up into the air. It spun in a gentle arc, rising over the bow of the boat, over the upturned face of his beloved daughter, into the sunlight. Seagulls shrieked and dived for its whirling brightness, but it plunged, square point first into the waves and was gone before any could do themselves harm upon it.

He raised his arms up to the blue sky as the first man lunged at him and, meeting no resistance, lunged on. Others followed, the sky turned red, and Jean Rombaud fell to a dozen swords.

'No!' screamed Gianni, just before the ball from a Spanish musket went past him, exploding the head of a lieutenant busy with murder. Two pistol shots followed and two more of the assailants jerked back in pain. The others paused, looked back along the jetty at the two men sprinting toward them, the sun bouncing off the weapons they carried – twin scimitars and a long-handled battle axe.

'A Haakonsson!' the Norsemen cried as they crashed into Gianni's men who scattered, desperately defended themselves, desperately died. Just two survived and only because they hurled themselves into the harbour.

She arrived as the last man fell, the smoke still curling from the muzzle of her musket.

'Tell me – do they live?' Beck panted.

'Your son does.' Haakon pointed with his axe to where Gianni still lay, clutching the thin line of blood at his throat, staring at them, mad-eyed, disbelieving. Then the Norseman began pulling at the pile of the fallen. When his body was pulled out, Beck sank down with a sob, cradled his head in her lap.

'Oh, Jean, my Jean. What have they done to you now?'

Within the sheet of blood that was his face, eyes blinked slowly open.

'Heaven so soon,' he whispered. 'That didn't take long.' Then his brow wrinkled. 'But what are you doing here before me?'

'You live! My love, oh my life! We must get you aid! Quickly ...' She turned to the others. 'Haakon! Fugger! Why will you not move?'

It was the Fugger who went to her, laying a hand gently on her shoulder. Jean's eyes flicked to him.

'How fare you, Jean?'

'I am dying, Fugger. You?'

The German couldn't help smiling. 'I am well. My Maria is safe. And your Anne – she was on that boat?'

A tiny nod. 'Both Annes. They seek their rest in a New World. Haakon?'

He could not see him, but the size of the shape that blocked the sun seemed familiar.

'Yes, little man?'

'Look to Beck, Norseman.'

'I will, old comrade.'

'Look to Beck?' she cried. 'I will look to myself, as always, Jean Rombaud. You think I need a man's protection because I am so womanly, so weak, that I . . . I . . .' Her throat tightened as the tears came.

The words were faint now, so only Beck could hear them. 'You are a warrior – and my own true love.'

She whispered. 'And you are mine.' As she bent to kiss him, the first of her tears ran from her face and onto his.

He tilted his face up to them. They were like grace falling from heaven and, feeling that grace at last, Jean Rombaud died.

She rocked him, began to keen, Hebrew words on a low note. Maria had joined her father and now the two Fuggers, Haakon and Erik turned to stare at Jean Rombaud's son.

'You don't understand.' There was a note of pleading in Gianni's voice. 'He opposed the will of God.'

'Your God, Gianni,' the Fugger said softly. 'Your interpretation of His will.'

The voice changed, hardened. 'He served the Devil in serving that English witch.'

'He served his own truth.'

'No!' Gianni howled, glaring back at the eyes before him. 'He cursed us, all of us. And only I can lift that curse.'

'And only I can help you.'

The new voice came from the limping, black-cloaked man they'd run past on the jetty.

Thomas Lawley moved to Gianni's side now, bent, helped him from the ground. 'Come away, Gianni. Come!'

Shaking off the supporting hand, Gianni made to turn. Then he looked down, saw his dead father in his mother's arms, took a step toward her. In a voice drained of defiance, he said, 'Mother?'

Beck's eyes were filled, the figure of her son appearing as if through a veil. She shook her head once, to clear her vision. When she had, she simply looked for a moment, with the glance one gives to a stranger. Then she bent again and resumed her low keening.

This time Gianni accepted the tug of the arm. The first step was hard, the second a little easier. Soon he was pulling the limping man down the jetty, away. He had seen the caravel slipping across the waves, bearing his family's curse. And he had seen other boats still tied up in the harbour.

They watched them leave, turned back to the two on the ground, to the living and the dead.

'We must bury him,' said the Fugger.

Haakon shook his head, bent to touch Beck on her shoulder. 'I have another idea.'

They were ready near sunset. They had staunched his wounds as best they could, washed his face, wrapped him in a new cloak. Erik had placed a scimitar between his hands.

'It may not be his own sword,' said Haakon as he rested a hand on his son's shoulder, 'but Rombaud was a man with an eye for a fine cutting edge.'

He bent again to the prow of the skiff they'd laid him in, using his knife to carve the last curl of a giant 'R' there.

'A rune for journeys,' he said.

The Fugger placed a flagon of wine near Jean's feet. 'You'll want a drink when you awake, old friend. It will not be as good as that from your vineyards. But it gives you something to compare your next vintage to.'

Haakon rowed; Beck sat in the stern; Erik followed in a second boat with the Fuggers. A calm sea was burnished red by the setting sun. When Haakon shipped his oars, Erik brought his vessel alongside, held the two together. The Norseman climbed over, leaving Beck holding the body.

She whispered, 'I have nothing to give you, Jean. Nothing except this promise – you will never be forgotten. We will tell your tale often and we will tell it in the courtyard of the Comet. For I *will* get it back – that I vow to you. Farewell.'

She kissed him, then took Haakon's hand and climbed over into the other boat. She looked down at their expectant faces.

'No words,' she said, 'for he was not a man of words but of deeds. And such deeds.'

She took the torch Haakon had lit for her. At her nod, Erik released the skiff which immediately began to move away. She let it drift, the tide took it and, just when they all thought it had gone too far, she stooped and threw, the shoulder that had wielded a slingshot still strong, her thirst for a target still unerring. The torch flared through the air, spinning, then plunged down, onto the straw that was his bed. It caught, instantly, and the boat, Jean Rombaud's funeral pyre, drifted blazing into the sunset.

PART TWO
NEW WORLD

ONE

HOMECOMING

Tagay crouched at the centre of the blackened circle, sifting ash, letting it fall like so much sooty snow. She had called him from the edge of this clearing that had once held a village; he'd pretended he had not heard. For what could he say that he had not said the day before and the one before that? He had promised her a New World. And he had brought her to a wasteland.

'Tomorrow, Tagay.' Anne spoke now from just behind him. As ever, he had not heard her approach, not a crack of twig or footfall on the charred earth had alerted him. He had always known how she was born of air. The first time he'd seen her she'd floated down from a palace roof. Yet wasn't he a native of this land, even if he'd never been here before?

Surely, a hunter of the Bear clan, of the tribe of the Tahontaenrat should be able to hear the approach of a white girl?

But, of course, he wasn't a hunter. He wasn't anything. All he knew in life was across the other side of the ocean. And standing in the ashes of the fourth village they had found in as many days, he wished he were back in Paris now, safely drunk, about to be shown to another woman's bed.

He stood, brushing his hands against his breeches. They could not get any dirtier; seven weeks at sea had turned their green velvet into a dull and muddied grey. Yet he could not take them off, nor his lawn shirt and brocade doublet, to dress as his mother had told him his people did in the summer, in a simple strip of skin around his waist. That would be as false as his dream of a homecoming.

At least he sensed her hand reaching for his shoulder. He stepped beyond it, out of the circle of soot, his back still to her.

'Tomorrow? You think tomorrow will be any different from today?'

Anne's hand caressed the space he'd lately occupied. 'Yes, I do. You said yourself, your people move on when the land is tired. We just have to catch up with them.'

He turned, yet still avoided her eyes. His tone was bitter. 'You've seen the fields. The earth here is rich. The corn fattens on the stalks, though the weeds now seek to choke it. These people did not move on. These people were driven out.'

She noticed how he no longer said 'my people'.

'Then we will find where they have been driven, Tagay. We will.'

Before he could muster a reply, a voice shouted their names from beyond the clearing, from the path back toward the river.

Anne was grateful for the interruption. 'Here, Captain,' she called, 'ahead, in the village.'

Jacquet appeared, moving swiftly on the makeshift crutch she'd fashioned for him when they'd first reached land. He had broken his leg badly in a fall to the deck during a storm in the middle of the Atlantic. She had set it expertly, made him a cordial from her scant supplies that calmed his impatience, sat by him in his tiny cabin nursing him through the fever that followed. He had worshipped her ever since.

Two of his crew followed him. Young though they were they struggled to keep up.

'Must you always go rushing off like that?'

He balanced on one leg and shook his crutch at them, breathing heavily. He found it hard to be angry with Anne, so he turned his venom on Tagay. 'You may think you are one of them, my lad, but you hardly look like it in your Paris finery.' He gestured at the soiled, tattered remains of Tagay's clothes. 'They are more likely to stick you full of arrows than to greet you as a lost cousin.'

'I wish I could offer them a target,' Tagay grunted before walking away, black dust rising from his footfalls, disappearing swiftly into the tree-line.

'Come back here, boy.' Jaquet hopped after him, and only Anne's hand held him from pursuing further.

'Leave him, Uncle Pierre,' Anne said softly. 'He is disappointed.'

'As I am,' said the Captain. 'How can I trade my goods if we don't find any Indians, eh? Tell me that! And if we can't trade, we have to get back up to Gaspé to fish soon. You didn't pay me enough to return to France with empty holds.'

His words were angry but the tone wasn't. As always, the touch of Anne's hand calmed him.

'I know.' She smiled. 'A little more time, eh? Soon we will all find what we seek.'

'Well, we won't here. Something's wrong in this land. When I was here in thirty-six with the Admiral, each of these places was a thriving village. If memory serves, this place was called Satadin. So see if you can get our friend back and let us push on upriver. The next village should be Stadacona and if they are not there, they are gone from this land and it's Gaspé for us on the morrow.'

While Jacquet clumped back the way he'd come, Anne followed the small path Tagay had taken into the forest, grateful that she was out of sight of either man. It didn't take Tagay's disappointment, or Jacquet's concern, to tell her something was wrong. The further they proceeded down the river the Captain called the St Lawrence, the more uneasy she felt. It wasn't her uncertainty after the seven weeks at sea, nor the anticipation of the task ahead that caused her concern. It wasn't the strange beauty of this land so different from anything she'd ever known, in its swathes of huge cypresses and cedars, walnut and spruce, its rocky inlets and towering cliffs. No, it was the one similarity with the three cities where lately she'd spent her life – Siena, London and Paris. Like each of them, this land reeked of death.

She climbed a hill through a series of stony terraces, like stairs hewn for giants, the forest thinning as she got higher. Where the hill levelled, wild grapes grew in random profusion. She found him there amongst them, his hands stripping the little green globes from the vines, chewing and spitting out tiny seeds.

He was aware of her but did not turn. Pulling a grape bunch towards her, she bit into the fruit.

'Ach! Do you not think they are too young, Tagaynearguye? Wait another month and they may be sweet.'

'And six months after that we could have wine, if we knew how to make it.' Since she spoke to him in his own language he replied in the same. 'What I would give for a glass of Bordeaux now.'

His voice had lost the harshness that the burnt village had brought to it and she moved toward him. 'I know how to make it. My father made wine that would make you think your Bordeaux was vinegar.'

'I doubt that.' He watched her approach, held, as ever, by the smile in her eyes.

'Shall we set up the first vineyard in the New World then, Tagaynearguye? Perhaps here, since you seem to like the fruit so much?'

Her hand descended to rest lightly on his. He let it lie for a moment only, then took it away. As always, the touch confused him, so he sought refuge in her words.

'Why do you call me by my full name?'

'Did you not tell me that "Tagay" only meant "Little" and the rest was "Bear"?'

'Yes. But the French were too lazy to say the whole name. And "Little" was a good name for a pet!'

'So perhaps I should just call you "Bear". Since you have returned to your native forests.'

Tagay sighed. The sun had just ridden to its mid-point in the sky, and it beat down through the thinner foliage here. His skin felt sticky under his clothes.

'I do not think I want my people to know wine, good or otherwise. Its pleasure comes at too great a price.'

'Is that why you did not drink it on the crossing?'

He nodded, waving a hand at the insects that surrounded his head like a buzzing helmet.

'Then we will make none, Little Bear.'

The heat, the insects, the taste of too-young grapes souring in his mouth. 'Will you stop using my name like that?' He saw her smile flee, startled by his sudden anger. 'I will regret teaching you my tongue if you use it to plague me like one of these biting black flies.'

He slapped at his head, ran a few paces away. The horde merely shifted with him. He began to curse, as if he were still in Paris, waving his hands in the air, shuffling now this way, now that.

Anne did not try to follow. She felt stung, as if one of the biting creatures that harried him had remained behind for her. She had spent the seven weeks on the ship learning the tongue of the Tahontaenrat. There was nothing else to do on the tedious voyage and she had always been good at languages. She saw it as a way of knowing him. But the more fluent she became, the more he had closed off from her.

'Why are you here, Anne?' He shouted at her in French now, as if his own tongue pained him.

'You know why. I am here for my father, to finish what he began. And I am here for you,' she replied, her voice low.

'For me?' Words he wanted to hear tormented him like biting insects. 'For me? And who am I?'

She began to reply but he cut her off. 'I thought I would learn that answer for myself, from the land I never knew, from my people. But that land is a pyre of ashes and my people are scattered by the winds. And I cannot even shed these clothes.' He clutched at his doublet front so violently that two of the last buttons popped off. 'Anything else I put on would be false. False! I am not Tagaynearguye. I am the French Court's little pet.'

'You carry your people there, Tagay.' She pointed at his chest. 'I know by the way you have talked of them, of the dreams you have recounted to me. I know about dreams. I know the truth of you in them.'

'Dreams?' His laugh cracked and he began scrabbling in the little leather pouch at his belt. In a moment, a small stone was in his hand. It was a deep, almost obsidian black, with a series of fine, sandy lines running up its squat, squarish shape.

'This was my uncle's dreamteller, his "Oki". He found it in the belly of a huge fish he caught somewhere near here. He was the chief of the tribe and Cartier stole him and his sister, with me in her belly, and took him to die on the banks of the Seine. If dreamtellers told true, would it not have told Donnaconna never to have left the shores of his own river?'

He was facing away from her now, looking down the vine-clad, stone terraces to the valley below. They were high enough so that in the distance the great river could be seen, shimmering in heat haze.

'He gave it to me before he died. "Take it back to the land, and use it there," he told me. Well, I'm back!'

His voice rising to a shout, he reached behind him, bending back to throw.

A hand closed over his. 'Oki – objects – have power, Tagay,' Anne said. 'Donnaconna's stone. The silver cross in my pouch that my brother once nailed to a tree in Tuscany. Above all, that which my father swore to bury, that many men covet still, the six-fingered hand of Anne Boleyn. To some, only a stone, a piece of metal, some old bones. But we know the truth of power, Tagay. You don't throw away power. Your uncle, my father, they were right. Power is to be used.'

The next village was not a pile of cinders. Fires there were, at least fifty of them, and their smoke rode the wind over the log palisade that encircled the village. Kettles, full of meat, simmered above rock hearths, in a wide cleared space where all the houses converged in a giant circle. These were made from slabs of cedar and there were scores of them, of different sizes, though a similar shape, the largest being at least forty paces in length and fifteen wide, the same in height. And every one was deserted.

'You can stop that now,' Jacquet called to Bertrand, the youngest of the crew, 'for there's no one here to appreciate your greeting.' The boy immediately lowered the flute he'd been blowing ever less enthusiastically as they had walked through the lifeless village. The fingers that had been stopping holes were now occupied with crossing himself repeatedly.

The Captain was as concerned as each of his men. 'Where are they?' he muttered. 'This place is, or was, Stadacona. I'd recognize those cliffs anywhere. Spent a winter nestled against them with the Admiral in thirty-seven. If anything, it's bigger than it was then. Someone set those pots to cook. Where the devil are they now?'

'Or what devil has taken them.' Tagay's joy at seeing the smoke from the cooking fires of his people had been ripped away by their absence, leaving an even greater desolation. 'Maybe the demon who burned the other villages first stole all life from them, as he has done here. And when he has finished eating the people, he returns to destroy their homes.'

'Enough of that talk!' Jacquet bellowed, as his men crossed themselves ever more furiously. The last thing he needed was his crew to start seeing the Devil in this. Captain or no Captain, they'd take the ship back to France on the instant.

Anne was standing slightly away from the men. 'Listen,' she said, and each laboured to pitch their hearing above the beating of their hearts. At first, there was nothing but the wind. Then something came to each of them, on swirls of air.

'It sounds like . . . wailing!' Bertrand whimpered. 'The Indian's right, the Devil's abroad.' He turned toward the river, took a step.

'Quiet!' Jacquet's head was tipped toward the cliffs. 'Sounds like cheering to me. And laughter.'

'What is up there? Do you remember?' Tagay said.

'Aye. You seem to climb for ever up those rocks and then suddenly you come out on a huge meadow.'

'My uncle told me of that place.' Tagay said. 'He called it Dayohagwenda – "Opening through the woods". My people – perhaps they are there.'

'I don't like it,' muttered Jacquet. 'What would make the whole damn village leave their cooking fires?'

'Well,' said Tagay, his face suddenly flushed, 'shall we go and find out?'

'I couldn't make the climb, not with this.' Jacquet ground the crutch's end into the earth. 'And my men won't go without me.' He thought for a moment. 'You go, Tagay. By yourself. That way, if the Devil *is* up there, he'll only get his own.' He smiled, briefly. 'We'll wait for you back at the river. *On* the river.'

He turned, walked a few paces back toward the palisade, turned back. 'Come, girl,' he said to Anne, who had not moved.

'No,' said Anne. 'I'm going too.' She halted the protest that came from both men's mouths. 'Of course I'm going. You think I've come this far to slink away? We are here to meet these people. Tagay's people. There is no other choice.'

They had, each of them, heard that tone of determination before.

'Come then,' said Tagay.

A trail, beaten by thousands of feet, led from the rear of the village, traced along a stream, then began winding up a steep slope. It was hard climbing to limbs that had only been able to stretch the length of a caravel for weeks at sea, and the sun bore down ferociously. Using his arms to pull at the shrubs that lined the path, as well as his pumping legs, Tagay pulled himself up, Anne struggling behind. As they got higher, the cries above grew louder.

They reached the summit and the noise doubled, screams bursting through the small screen of scrubby pine that crested the cliff top.

'Keep low,' Tagay turned back to whisper, 'and be ready to run.'

Through a stand of oak, the trail then plunged into a wall of shoulder high grass. The voices weaved through it, as if the shouters were just the other side of a screen.

Tagay signalled back to the last oak, whose branches stretched over the green sea ahead. Anne understood and immediately began climbing, Tagay following, letting her guide him to the foot and handholds, for he had watched her on the ship and she could go up a mast as swiftly as any of the sailors. When they reached a branch that looked solid enough, Tagay moved past and pushed outwards through the foliage.

Leaves parted on mayhem. The tall grasses reached only a few paces in and then there was a great plain filled with screaming humanity. All were semi-naked, men and women, a breech cloth and dust their only covering. A cloud of it hung above the horde that surged forward, then swayed back, men, women, children, packed so tight that many had been lifted from the ground and were borne by the press, each head thrown back, wailing to the sky:

'Ah-Ah-Ah-Ah-Ahum!' The voices started on a high note and slid down the scale, then rode up and ended in the mighty crescendo of the final phrase.

Anne found that her hand had reached into the pouch at her waist and was clutching her brother's little silver cross there.

'Are they possessed, Tagay? What agony are they in?'

Before he could reply, another tormented cry came from the far side of the field. Yet peering through the dust cloud, he could see that it was no echo but another wedge of people, letting out the same shrieking rise and fall of notes.

'Ah-Ah-Ah-Ah-Ahum!'

Silence followed, as complete and dreadful as the noise that had preceded it. Then a single, deep male voice let out a cry that conjured shapes from the ground between the opposing groups. A dozen men stood in two lines of six facing each other. Every man was naked, save for the small apron that barely covered the loins. Every man held a carved and curled stave in his hands.

Anne suddenly knew what she was watching. Her father had taken her once to a tournament of knights in Bologna. 'Tagay,' she whispered, clutching at his shoulder, 'these men fight each other.'

As she spoke, someone stepped forward from the far crowd and hurled something into the space between the two lines of warriors. The distinct clack of wood on wood came, as eight of the men merged into a solid group where the thrown object had landed. Grunts of exertion rose from the dust cloud that partially obscured them; then, suddenly, a round object burst out of the mêlée and hurtled toward the two men to the left who had stood clear of the fight. One of them flicked it from the ground up into the air with his stick, then hit it in the same movement across the field, to the men who had stood off there. A stave rose, struck; the ball – for that is what it had to be – flew upfield.

There were cries of alarm from those below the tree, screams of delight from those opposite as the warrior who had knocked the ball forward pursued it. He was heavily tattooed, blue and black lines curving around his body in wreaths of leaf and reptile shapes. Taller than the one who chased him, a shrug of hips gained him a few yards, to the further dismay of those below the oak. But the smaller man was swift and caught up, just as the taller reached the ball. Despite a vicious chop down that seemed aimed more at fingers than stick, and produced another howl of outrage from those below them, the smaller man managed to knock the ball beyond the taller one's reach. A team-mate, sweeping back, caught the ball on his stick and knocked it into the air; three men leapt, sticks high and, to agonized shouts, the ball hurtled back the way it had come, down the centre of the field.

'This is a ball game, yes, Tagay? It is not war?'

He turned, excitement in his eyes, the first she'd seen since landfall. 'It is much more than a game. War is the better word. This is Otadajishqua.'

The words were lost in the shrieking. Where the ball had rolled another group contended, more joining in as they arrived, others standing off. The ball escaped, only to be snatched back into the struggle.

Suddenly it rolled free, long enough for a stick to knock it away. Someone mis-hit it, and the small defender who had rescued it previously now retrieved it, bounced it up on his stick end and ran around a wrongfooted opponent. She could see where he was heading. She'd hadn't noticed, till then, the twin gates of two poles that faced each other at either end of the field. They were twice the height of a man, a few paces apart.

Now it was the turn of those below to let out the whoops of encouragement, those opposite the shouts of fear. The tattooed man was trying to close down the ball-runner, yet the smaller man seemed to sense him reaching out. He sped up and, as if he could see behind him, leapt, the stick thrust viciously between his pumping legs. The tattooed man fell as he thrust, the smaller man surging beyond him and, as the crowd's roar built, the ball carrier bounced the ball into the air then cracked it hard. It flew straight between the gates.

The shout that arose from below seemed as if it could lift them from the branch. The team's supporters surged forward, surrounding the players. A chant began, Tagay shouting as loud as any, and Anne recognized the one word they were chanting. It began slowly, building in volume each time. It was Tagay's own name, without the 'Little' attached.

'Bear! Bear! Bear! BEAR!' the crowd screamed.

Then, just as they had started altogether, suddenly and altogether they stopped. Only one voice continued shouting the word and then only once more.

'BEAR!' screamed Tagay into the silence, and everyone there, the supporters, the players standing or lying on the ground, all turned to look at the man standing on the end of an oak branch.

The stillness lasted for five heartbeats. Tagay knew, because he could hear his. The people stared at him, he stared back, and the only movement was that of his arms, raised aloft in the triumph of the Bear, now slowly falling to his side.

Then the world below them exploded. The crowd began to move forward as one body. A group of twenty or so older men, clad in cloaks and leggings, turned and stepped toward the tree. But those who reacted swiftest were those who had lately contested in the game. They ran to the base of the oak, their game sticks raised before them like weapons. Two had bent to the ground to snatch up bows. One of these was the smaller man who had shot the ball between the posts. The other was the tattooed warrior.

It was the smaller who spoke first. 'If these birds attack us, Tawane, I will shoot the plover with its strange plumage to the left, and you the one to the right. Through the eye. We will see whose arrow flies more true.'

The other warrior grunted. This close Anne and Tagay could clearly see the complexity of the black lines that covered him. One was a detailed drawing of a diamond-backed snake that curled up from the base of his neck, a forked tongue reaching from fanged jaws to encircle the left eye. 'Why would you end the sport so swiftly, Sadagae? Why do we not see how many arrows we can use before each die?'

As the first man hesitated, the man he'd called Tawane fitted an arrow to his string. 'A beaver skin on it,' he said. 'Look, I think they are going to attack now.'

He raised his bow.

It was then that Tagay, pulling Anne tightly behind his back, spoke. His voice wavered, belying a little the defiance of his words.

'Is this how you treat a Bear who only seeks to celebrate his clan's victory? I call that being a bad loser, Black Snake.'

The tattooed man stared along the length of his arrow, the point never wavering. 'How is it you speak the language of the people, and know my name, when you dress in the skins of the Pale Thieves?'

The exchange had allowed the rest of the people to catch up with the warriors. A huge semi-circle of men and women had swiftly formed and a group of elders had moved through to stand beneath the oak branch.

One of them stepped before the others. He was the oldest there, judging by the wrinkles on his face. But a broad, muscled chest showed through the layers of beads and shells that hung from his neck, and his grey hair was thick, oiled and set in two rolls above his ears. His raised hand brought an instant silence to the throng and he spoke slowly into that silence, his voice measured and deep.

'We know you are war chief of the Wolf clan, Black Snake. But does that give you the right to kill all prisoners for your own pleasure and deprive us of ours?'

Tawane, 'Black Snake', did not lower his bow, but his eyes flicked toward the elder. 'I seek only to end the threat of this spy, Tododaho. He may be one of the enemy who seek our lands, may he not?'

'He may. Though I think he would be a very foolish enemy to come among us and shout for the Bear clan in the game. But it is for us to judge threats together, Tawane, not for you to act alone. Lower your bow.'

For a moment, it looked like the warrior might disobey. If anything the string of the weapon drew closer to his body. Then something close to a smile came to his face, and he slowly released the string's tension.

'Tododaho has spoken. And I, of course, agree with his wisdom, famous for so many years among the people.'

Even Anne, who had struggled to follow the swift speaking of the tribesmen, could hear the measured sarcasm in the voice.

Tagay turned to her and whispered, 'Tododaho! It means "Tangled". My uncle, Donnaconna spoke of this man, as did my mother.'

Chief Tangled cleared his throat. 'Stranger, you perhaps do not know our ways. But you do not talk in low voice at our meetings. Especially when you have just been spared – for the moment – from death.'

Tagay bowed his head. 'I mean no disrespect. And it is true, there are many ways of the people that I am ignorant of. My mother, Sonosase and my uncle, Donnaconna did not have time to teach me everything before they went to the Village of the Dead.'

Whispering may have been frowned upon at meetings, but nothing could stop the buzz that arose at his statement. It only ended when a woman, as old as the Chief, clad in a heavily beaded deerskin dress, stepped forward.

Looking directly at Tangled, she said, 'Brother, if he speaks true, then he is the son of my sister, as he is the son of your brother. She was with child by him before he went to the Village of the Dead, and she was stolen with Donnaconna and taken across the Great Water. If he speaks true, then he is one of the Hunters of the Sunrise.'

The uproar that arose at this statement, contending voices mocking or approving, took a long while to quell. Finally, when a near silence had settled, Tangled looked up again to the tree.

'Young man, my neck is old and it does not like this looking up. Come down.'

Tagay and Anne descended. Such were the numbers pressing in that the crowd was ordered by the elders to move back to the game field. Soon the two of them stood in the centre of a tightly packed circle at least two thousand strong. Anne could see that sides had already formed. Those gathered around the tattooed warrior, Black Snake, had expressions of contempt, of disbelief, their arms folded before them. Others, near Chief Tangled and the woman in the dress, looked more curious than hostile. Anne was a little surprised to see the other bowman, the smaller ball player, among this group.

'Now,' said Chief Tangled, as a general silence settled, 'how can we know that you are who you say?'

Tagay swallowed, his mouth desperately dry. He suddenly didn't know what to do with his hands. As the silence lengthened, they strayed around to his back, settling finally on the pouch at his belt. He felt the hardness within it and, reaching in, he pulled out the obsidian stone.

'I am Tagaynearguye. My uncle gave me this,' he said, holding it up.

The old woman, who had stepped forward in shock, now came and took the stone from Tagay, examining it carefully. Then turning to look at Chief Tangled, she nodded. He raised his arms again and a fractured silence came.

'My sister, Gaka, recognizes the Oki. She will speak.'

There was an instant growl. Black Snake stepped forward, his eyes furious. 'Are we become like our enemies, the Tribe of the Great Hill, that we allow women to speak in our council?'

'You will have a chance to have your say, Black Snake. And we are not in the lodge house but at the celebration of the Game. Gaka was Donnaconna's favourite sister. She will know how true or false this young man is.'

To more mutterings, Black Snake stepped back.

'This is the stone that Donnaconna, my brother, took from the huge fish he slew on the edge of the Lake that Shimmers. I would never forget it. I dreamt of it for the last three days and on the fourth it appears.'

She raised it to the sky, squinting up at it. 'Welcome home, brother,' she said, then looked down again. 'You all have learnt to trust my dreams. This is a sign. A Hunter of the Sunrise has returned to help us in our danger. I have spoken.'

She stepped back. Immediately, barely waiting for a signal, Black Snake spoke. 'You see what you want to see, hear what pleases you. It is not dreams that will save us from the Tribe of the Great Hill, it is warriors like myself, of the Wolf clan and all the other clans. My enemies' scalps adorn my lodge pole. You look at me and you see a warrior. You only have to look at him to see he has not come to manhood but is still a boy. His hair is like a moose tail, unkempt and in no style.' He ran his hand down his own head, where the hair was cut into a single ridge in the centre, reaching down to his neck, the sides shaved. 'You can judge him by his woman too, who is dirty and weak-looking and who no other man would take because her hips are too thin to bear sons.' He paused and looked around the crowd, seeking and receiving approval there. 'How can he prove he is who he says? Maybe he stole this stone. Maybe he has heard its legends and comes as a pretender. We need no strangers to answer our danger. Let us kill him now and swiftly.' He glanced slowly around the crowd, then concluded, 'I have spoken.'

A babble of voices rose but it was Gaka's that topped them all. 'You too were a stranger, Black Snake, and a member of that same tribe who threatens us now and as covered in blue lines as they are. We adopted you when we captured you, as is sometimes our custom, because you were young and Small Stream needed a new husband when hers did not return from war. Even though you were ugly beyond belief and still are. And it was not a dream that Donnaconna went over the water with that Pale Thief captain. It was said that he or one of the Hunters of the Sunrise would return in our time of need. Is this not our time of need? Are we so safe that we will turn away from the favour of the Gods? I have spoken.'

Before Black Snake could reply, his ball game rival spoke.

'I am Sada, the Even-Tempered, and I favour my aunt's opinion. If this is the son of Sonosase, then he is my cousin and also of the clan of the Bear, who gained such a triumph today at the Game. So if you would kill him, Black Snake of the Wolf clan, you must first kill me. And as on the field, I will elude your war club. I will shoot between the posts of your eyes. I have spoken.'

The warrior called Even-Tempered had walked toward Black Snake as he spoke, till they were face to face, unblinking. The roar that followed his words, the biggest yet, was nevertheless silenced by Chief Tangled raising his arms.

'It is true what all speak here. It is a time of great danger and all new things must be thought of in that light. But if this is one of the Hunters of the Sunrise, who went away with Donnaconna and promised to return in our great need then we have to know it. But . . .' He stepped toward Tagay, who had followed the argument with alternating fear and yearning. 'Black Snake is right in this. You look like a boy. You have not become a man yet and we have already mourned for your death, the death of all who went to hunt the sunrise. So, before you can become one of the people, you must be born once more. You must become a man. Your clan will see to this.' Tangled lowered his voice then, but its deep richness still carried. 'And since we have gathered all our peoples to discuss the smoke that has swallowed so many of our villages, we will also discuss this matter at the great council after all the games have been played. If Tagay is ready, he will be born once more, and we will listen to his words there. If not, we will decide then. Let us go now, back to the village to feast, where the meat will be ready in the kettles. Is it agreed?'

To a universal shout of 'Ah-Ah-Ah-Ah-Ahum!' the crowd began separating out and moving back through the trees to the cliffs, the stronger carrying the elders in woven frames. Only a few did not move – Anne, Tagay, and the aunt and cousin he'd just found. Also Black Snake, who paused a dozen paces away, waited till Tagay looked, then drew a clenched fist slowly over his head as if it held a knife. Then he too headed toward the cliffs, a dozen warriors closing round him.

When the last of them had disappeared into the canopy of oak, Tagay's knees gave way and he sank onto the ground.

'It seems you have made a blood enemy, nephew.' The beads on her dress clinked together as his aunt moved around to stand in front of him.

'He likes his word to be the law.' Sada came to stand beside her.

'You saw how he resented obeying Tangled in this. If he becomes war chief . . .' He broke off and stared in the direction the tattooed man had taken, both anger and concern in his eyes.

'I thought he was already,' Tagay said tentatively.

'Only of the Wolf clan. But he seeks the office for the whole of the Tahontaenrat, the Deer people, empty now since He Who Sleeps was killed defending his village. And there are many who want him, who see his anger as our best war shield. Well,' Gaka sighed, 'we will know soon enough. For like all other matters it will be settled at the great council, when the moon is at greatest fatness.'

When it is full. Anne remembered that the moon had been new two days before.

'So that will be in . . . twelve days?' she said.

'Yes, child. So many sunrises . . .' She broke off, stared hard at Anne as if beholding some wonder, then continued. 'Twelve is the limit Tangled has allowed for Tagay to be born once more as one of the Deer people.'

'Also as a true brother of the Bear clan,' Sada said. 'I will see to both.'

'Will you also teach me to play the Game with the skill you showed today, cousin?'

It was the first time since they'd reached his land that Anne had seen even the shade of a smile appear on Tagay's lips.

The shorter warrior tipped his head back and let out a huge laugh. 'In ten days? I think you would take ten years and never learn my skill. Some people have gifts directly from the Gods. I am one and I think you must just be content to watch and wonder.'

Skilled though he was, he didn't see the blow coming that caught him on his ear. 'Arrogant dog! You get that from your father! For Tangled was a good player of the Game and knew it all too well when he was a young man.' Gaka shook her finger at him as he rubbed his ear. 'Will Blessed-by-the-Gods deign to bend then and carry me, like the moose he is, down the cliff?'

As the grumbling warrior bent, Tagay stepped forward. 'I will carry you, Aunt, if you will let me.'

She slowly ran her eyes up and down his body. 'Your knees look weak, Tagay, and the way is steep. Can you bear me?'

'I have spent a long time on a boat crossing the big water, and I am a little weakened. But I grow in strength every day.'

'You will need to grow, if you are to be born by the Moon. There is much you will need to learn and there is very little time.'

'Then let me begin now by carrying my aunt down the cliff.'

She shook her head and sighed, then moved towards him. 'I will let you, though Sada's legs look the stouter. But as we go down to the village you will tell me how a woman of the Pale Thieves comes to speak our language, although with the accent of a crow, and why you have brought her here. And you will tell me also of the Hunt for the Sunrise and of my brother, Donnaconna, and your mother, Sonosase.'

'These are many stories, Aunt, and they will take a long time to tell.'

'By the look of your legs, it will be a long journey down and so we will have that time. Come.'

Tagay bent. Sada helped their aunt onto his back. She felt so light, Tagay was suddenly conscious of her great age. But light as she was, he remembered well the steepness of the climb up the cliffs. Taking a deep breath, he took a step forward, toward the path that led, not only down to the village but to the rebirth he sought. And as he walked, he began to speak.

TWO
FIRE STICK

This New World looks even stranger upside down.

Twisting slightly, Thomas Lawley glanced down the line of seven of which he made up the end member. Three of the sailors from the *Breath of St Etienne* had sunk into a merciful unconscious ness. The one beside him, Angeleme, was still weeping, the tears mingling with the blood that flowed freely from a head wound. At the far end but one, the old sail maker, Fronchard, was mouthing prayers between broken teeth. And at the very end, the last man was using the sudden disappearance of their tattooed captors to sway and test the strength of the woven reeds that held him, like all the others, by his ankles to the branch.

Gianni Rombaud. The man whose latest action, in a long line of foolhardy ones, had led them directly to this futile death. Thomas knew he should try to suppress any anger. He didn't want to die angry. All this had still to be the Lord's will. Though he had hoped the Lord would have spared him long enough in this New World to emulate the Jesuit heroes he adored, like Francis Xavier who had gone to the East and brought the love of Jesus to the native, to the real 'Indian' of which their tattooed tormentors were just shadows.

Well, he thought, *others will follow me. Some will die but a few will eventually succeed. And this land will be claimed for Jesus.*

He closed his eyes, began to pray. He didn't even open them when laughter and footfalls on the path told him their captors were returning. He needed to concentrate completely on the word of God. Agony would force his eyes open soon enough.

'*Mea culpa, mea culpa, mea maxima culpa.*'

*

Gianni stopped swaying as soon as he heard the snapping of twigs. The blood that filled his head seemed to find an outlet through his nose and he blew it now to allow air to flow. He needed to breathe to be able to speak; and that was all he could do, for there was no escape from the Indians' bonds.

He was relieved to see that the man who spoke some French, whose intended kidnapping was the reason for the attack he'd just led to disaster, had come back with the others, equally laden down with branches of dry wood. He was a little older, smaller, had a pot belly and short legs, and his thin hair did not make the same magnificent tuft that flowed from the centre of the others' shaved heads and down their backs. His barely reached his neck.

The warriors dropped the wood directly under the hanging heads and proceeded to build a little pyre under each one, cracking branches into kindling, filling gaps with leaves and dry moss. Most chattered the while, their impenetrable tongue rising and falling in its strange cadence. One warrior was silent. Younger than the rest, less covered in blue lines and patterns, he carried a sharp, short stick and spent less time building the pyres. Instead, he went up to each of the hanging Frenchmen and stuck the stick into them in different parts of their necks and faces, obviously enjoying the flow of blood, the cries of pain. Since Angeleme was also the youngest of his party, and wept the most, this Indian spent most time by him.

Another man also did not help in the building. Gianni thought he had not been of the initial party that had captured them, though he found it hard to tell the brutes apart. This one seemed older and, by the way he was deferred to and did no work, was obviously the leader. He wore leggings of deer skin, fringed with tassels, unlike the aprons of the others. His upper body was similarly bare but the tattoos that adorned it were more elaborately patterned and made up of a greater variety of dyes. Held against his chest were two pistols. One was Gianni's own; the other had belonged to another of the sailors. Both had been fired in the lost fight on the beach.

As he watched, the leader called over the one who had some French and spoke rapidly, gesturing with the guns, which he held by the barrel, to the hanging men. The man bowed, then moved over to Gianni. The other warriors stopped fire building to watch, all save the silent one who was still delighting in thrusting his stick into the ears of the weeping young sailor, Angeleme.

'Chief want "pugh-chee"'. He imitated the sound of a shot, a ricochet. 'You say how.' He gestured back to the pistols and the Chief raised them.

'You want fire stick?' Gianni said. The man nodded vigorously. 'I show.'

The interpreter spoke rapidly to his leader. On a command, he turned back and punched Gianni in the face. 'Not show. Speak.'

Gianni blew the fresh flowing blood from his nose, then just simply shook his head.

The hand was drawn back again but a command held it. The Chief grunted something and immediately three warriors went to Gianni and cut him down from the branch. He dropped, his hands still behind him, taking the fall on the side of his face. Then the bonds of his hands were also cut. He lay on the ground, blood flowing in fire to all his limbs.

'Show!' One pistol was thrust at him, his own. He reached into the pocket of his breeches where, fortuitously, his cranking wrench had remained despite his treatment. He released the screw that held the cock down and lifted the firing pan.

'That.' He gestured to his bag that had been brought up from the beach and rifled. The packet of gun powder, spare lead balls and wadding had been thrown back inside. It was brought to him and despite the shaking of his hand he managed to get the ball and wadding shoved in and tamped down.

An idea was forming. He knew he would have just one chance or he would soon be hanging again, upside down and burning, once he had demonstrated his skill. But for his idea to work, he needed both guns.

Swallowing, he pointed at the other clutched to the Chief's chest. He saw hesitation, a calculation in the narrow eyes. He simply pointed at his own pistol again and nodded.

The weapon was handed over and, using his wrench again, he flipped the firing pan open, pretended to pass some powder between the two. Then casually, slowly, he loaded the second pistol, primed the firing pans, then used his wrench to tighten the serrated wheel against the spring on both. When the click of the wheel came to show each was ready, he took a deep breath.

Thomas's eyes had only left the loading of the guns to look at the silent warrior who was still torturing Angeleme, to draw the man's attentions to himself. All he'd received was an open-handed slap. But when he heard the click of the second pistol his gaze swivelled back. He guessed what Gianni was going to do. He knew he would need a second's distraction. So as Gianni stood, he screamed, 'Jesus, Saviour!' as loudly as he could.

For the briefest of moments, all eyes went to him. All eyes save Gianni's. They went to the man next to the dangling Jesuit, to the silent young warrior who was slowly rising, the stick he'd just withdrawn from Angeleme's ear dripping with the boy's blood.

Gianni pulled the trigger. The serrated wheel span, striking sparks off the lump of iron pyrites. They fell into the pan. It flashed, there was a roar, and a lead ball flew from the barrel and opened a hole in the warrior's face just below his left eye. Still silent, he span back against Thomas and slipped down him to the ground.

Gianni didn't see him fall because he was already turning. Stepping forward, placing the barrel of the second pistol in the forehead of the Chief, he said two words.

'Fire stick.'

For a moment, no one moved. For a moment, the silence in the small clearing was almost complete, the only sound the chafing of reed rope against tree branch as six men swayed. Gianni was surprised that the hand that held the pistol, that pressed it into the flesh of the man opposite, no longer shook. Then he remembered why. Killing for Jesus always calmed him.

Movements began. Gianni heard arrows fitted onto bow strings, the creak of wood bent back. Opposite him, the brown eyes did not waver, just returned his stare evenly. They did not look alarmed, though they'd narrowed when the barrel first touched the forehead. Now they widened again and Gianni saw something like amusement in them. He said something. Gianni sensed that the ten men whose bows were poised to send ten arrows into his body hesitated for just a moment, the tension on their bowstrings lessening just a little on an outgoing breath.

The Chief spoke again. The one who could speak French came and stood just behind his leader's left shoulder.

'Falling Day say – you sit now or you die.'

Gianni's glance never wavered. 'Tell Falling Day – only God will choose when I am to die.'

The man hesitated. 'Falling Day does not know your God.'

'He will, one day. Tell him.'

Gianni saw the smile deepen as the words were spoken. A reply came.

'Falling Day say – he chooses. He say one word and you will go to see your God.'

Gianni increased the pressure on the gun barrel, pushing it slightly harder into the forehead opposite.

'Then we will go and see Him together.'

The brown eyes narrowed, the amusement gone. Words came and Gianni braced himself as he heard the bow strings drawn back once more. When they were released and arrows sang across the clearing he nearly squeezed the trigger in what he was sure would be his last action. Then he heard the thud of arrows striking home, a wail of agony, suddenly cut short.

'No!' screamed Thomas, twisting away from the horror before him.

The boy, Angeleme, studded with barbs, quivered in his death spasm, spinning from bound ankles.

'Merciful Jesus, Saviour, help and defend us this day.'

Following Thomas's lead, suddenly all the Frenchman were crying out, prayers and exhortations reaching for Gianni, telling him what he already knew, begging him to obey on the instant.

Falling Day had merely glanced at the death throes of the young sailor. Now his gaze returned to Gianni, as level as before, as amused. He spoke again.

'Chief say – he kill your men one and one and one. Give him fire stick.'

Even Gianni felt it was hopeless now, but he couldn't let it show. So he said, 'And when he kills the last of my men, I will kill him, and I will die in the same moment.'

The small warrior began to translate but his leader cut him off with a word. Then he just stared, as if measuring Gianni, while silence came again to the glade, broken only by the sound of arrows being fitted once more onto bowstrings and the creaking of rope as the body of a dead sailor span slowly, now this way, now that.

Then Falling Day spoke and Gianni nearly closed his eyes to receive the arrows. He was glad he didn't, however, because he saw the change in the man before him, knew what he'd just said, though he spoke no word of the man's tongue.

The bows lowered and Falling Day stepped away from Gianni's gun, turning his back on the threat. Gianni kept the gun raised but did not pursue the contact. The Chief was speaking rapidly, while the translator nodded and struggled to keep up.

'Falling Day says you are a warrior and have courage. He asks if you have taken many scalps of your enemies.'

Gianni had heard the sailors' stories on the long voyage across.

'Many,' he said, lowering the pistol, 'though I am still a young dog, so Falling Day must have taken many more.'

The Chief laughed when the words were spoken back. Then a question was asked. 'Falling Day says – he is honoured to know your name, Young Dog. And he asks – will you take the scalp of the man you have just killed, though he was stupid and cruel, and there is not much honour in his death?'

'If he was so, then I will not take his scalp.'

'And will you give Falling Day the fire stick?'

The Chief had turned back to him. Once more their eyes met.

'I will. Many fire sticks. And I will show his warriors how to use them. If we can be friends.'

In reply, Falling Day reached out his right hand. Gianni moved the pistol into his left and gripped the outstretched limb with his own right and shook the Chief's. It was only when Falling Day let out an oath and the warriors around the glade began laughing that Gianni realized that the Chief had wanted the weapon. But since Falling Day followed his lead and held on, vigorously moving his arm up and down, Gianni kept shaking while, behind him, the laughing warriors set about slicing the bonds off the hanging men.

'So how is it that you speak our tongue, Hair Burned Off?'

Thomas was crouched before the hearth, coughing and trying to make out the features of the man opposite him. A woman – by the manner she tended to him and the way the Indian grunted amicably at her, Thomas assumed she was his wife – had just put more wood on the fire. It must have been damp, because smoke swiftly rose to obscure his vision even more. There seemed to be little outlet for the cloud, which joined that produced by the other half dozen fires in the long building. Around each one, women were also building up the fires and clearing away wooden bowls. While they ate, the men had been silent. Now conversations began at each one and laughter erupted at several, not least from the women who had gathered with the bowls at the hut end, where there was a porch, and some light and air. They had been busy, for Thomas had noticed that each visitor – and there had been several, come to stare at himself and Gianni – was formally greeted with a bowl of the same stew they'd partaken of, a thin gruel with lumps of fish mashed in it, bones and all. Some ate, most didn't, though each visitor took at least a sip and returned the bowl with a bow and some words that could only be thanks. Thomas had seen less courtesy in the palaces of bishops.

The man opposite had reached behind him under a sleeping platform and pulled out a small skin bag. From it, he drew a little clay cup with a spout attached. He began to fill it with something else from within the bag.

'It was many, many days ago, before I got my name.' He passed a hand over his shaven head and smiled. 'I was with a party that went for fish far, far up where the Bear is prowling in the sky.' He gestured with the stem of the cup toward the entrance of the hut, which faced onto the river. 'There were men from your tribe, they came also to fish, with their big, big canoe and their nets this big.' He stretched his arms wide. 'I went into the big canoe and fished the season, showed them where the fish ran. They came again and again. Many seasons of fish. I went in the big canoe each time. Then they came no more. But I was young and my hair was not burned off. So I learned your tongue.'

He had finished packing some of the contents of the bag into the clay bowl. Now he picked a taper from a pile beside him and, when it flamed, he put the spout to his mouth and held the taper over the bowl, sucking air in noisily. After a moment, he breathed out and a huge plume of smoke sailed across the fireplace. A pungent smell came on the breath. It reminded Gianni of autumn fires in Tuscany, but sweeter.

Hair Burned Off smiled and held the bowl out toward Gianni. Thomas saw that the younger man was about to refuse it. But he had glanced around the hearths, seen other visitors receive the burning bowls and partake with the same formality that they'd sipped of the stew.

'Careful,' he said, in a low voice and in Italian. 'You do not want to give offence. Remember – this is the man you tried to kidnap.'

Gianni changed the warding gesture to an open-handed one. He put the spout to his lips, sucked a little, coughed sightly, and made to pass it onto Thomas. But his host was not content.

'No, Young Dog,' he said, using the name that Gianni had inadvertently given himself in the clearing, 'you must do like this.' And he demonstrated with another deep inhalation. Then, placing the stem of the bowl in the younger man's mouth, he held another burning taper to it. This time Gianni sucked harder, the bowl glowed, and the next moment, a scorching ran from his throat down into his chest. Smoke exploded from him. He coughed and coughed.

Hair Burned Off laughed delightedly, a laugh echoed down the long house by the other tribesmen and women who had been casually observing. Thomas struck a balance between a deep and a shallow inhalation and managed to cough a little less. But as the plume of smoke left him, his brain surged with a dizzying power. He felt suddenly nauseous and at the same time, strangely and equally exhilarated.

Gianni seemed only to have felt the former effect. Even in the dense smoke of the fire, Thomas could see he had turned green.

'What . . . what is that?' the younger man spluttered, to more laughter from his host and more from the other occupants once Hair Burned Off had repeated it.

'You have no words for it in your tongue. We call it Oyehgwaweh. Though the men who fished with me called it "tobacco" because that was the sound they made when they coughed.' He laughed again. 'It makes thoughts better and it clears the head.'

Thomas was about to say that it had the opposite effect on him, even though he was starting to enjoy it, when Hair Burned Off suddenly stood. He was looking past his visitors to the entrance of the longhouse. Thomas turned. An older man, was beckoning their host over. He went, listened to what the elder said, then returned to his hearth. He reached once again under the platform and produced a necklace of shells which he placed over his head. Another pipe appeared then, though this one had a wooden stem the length of his arm and the clay bowl had a warrior's face intricately carved into it. A woven rope ran its length and this the Indian slipped over his shoulder.

'Come,' he said, 'we go to the Hodeoseh.'

'What,' rasped Gianni, his breath only just returning through his tortured throat, 'is that?'

'You are honoured,' replied Hair Burned Off. 'It is the – what is the word in your tongue? Chiefs' meeting, or . . .'

'Council?'

'There,' said the Indian. 'You are to hear the decision of the council.'

The longhouse of the council was double the length and width of the one they'd come from. Shields, adorned with feathers, embossed with beads, hung from the cedar-slat walls. Between them, masks of horned deer, wolf and bear shimmered in their red paint, seeming to move in the glow of the three fires set a dozen paces apart in the middle of the earthen floor. Down one side of the open space, facing the flames, at least twenty men were gathered. Some, the older ones, were weighed down with vast necklaces of shell and bead. Others, younger, had chests bared, the better to display elaborate tattoos. The elders had a variety of hair styles, some with their greying locks parted and split either side of the face, others with shanks hanging down only on one side of the head, the opposite side shaved clean. The younger were uniform, their heads hairless save for the single long top-knot, a horse's mane of it, wound and oiled and flowing down the back.

They are the warriors, Gianni thought, his opinion confirmed when he saw Falling Day among them. The imprint of a pistol's muzzle still stood out redly on the man's forehead and Gianni shuddered slightly when he remembered how close he'd come to pulling the trigger. It was only here he realized how tall the warrior was, yet he was no taller than any of his fellows. What made them appear so big was the contrast with the men who faced them on the other side of the longhouse – the rest of the captured crew of the *Breath of St Etienne.*

The crewmen looked at the newcomers in nervous, mute appeal. Though Thomas had led them often in prayer on the long voyage across the ocean, it was not their spiritual selves that needed succour now. It was Gianni Rombaud who had killed their Captain, Ferraud, when he wouldn't proceed down the river, Gianni who led them to be captured. Yet he was also the one who had saved them all, apart from poor Angeleme, from a certain and horrific death. He was their only hope now. Even Fronchard, the old sailmaker, bowed his head as the young man took his place at the line's end.

Each of the natives had a long pipe like the one Hair Burned Off was carrying. As if at a signal, they raised them and drew a deep breath through them. As Gianni and Thomas took their places, thick plumes were exhaled toward the roof, the only movement, the only sound in the longhouse, save the shallow breathing of the captives.

The eldest of the elders, whose thick grey hair was held off his face by a snakeskin band across his forehead, gestured to Hair Burned Off and said a few words. Their guide nodded and turned to them.

'Ganeodiyo, who you would call, perhaps, Handsome Lake, is the Main Sachem of the Nundawaono, what you would call the Tribe of the Great Hill, our people. He says for me to speak to you and tell you the thoughts of the council. Then we will hear your thoughts.'

When he finished he nodded again to the elder who immediately began speaking. Thomas was straightaway lulled by the cadences of the man's speech. Even though he understood not a word of it, it had a song to it, a rising and a dying fall, a flow that indicated carefully thought out ideas, eloquently expressed. When, as a young Jesuit in training, he had studied the great Roman orators like Cicero and Cato, he had delighted in the beauty of the language when some of the more gifted of his tutors had spoken it. Yet he suddenly knew that few of them could have equalled the simple rhetorical power, the verbal grace, of the man now speaking.

The translation was, of necessity, a poor and fractured

imitation. But both he and Gianni learned how they had arrived at the final crisis of a war against an ancient enemy, who lived on the fertile lands on the far bank of the great river, the starboard side as they'd sailed down. How the Great Spirit had blessed his chosen people's bone knives, war hammers and bows, and how they'd burned many of the enemies' lodges to the ground. Village after village had been reduced to ashes until now the last of this enemy – he called them the Tahontaenrat, the Tribe of the White-Eared Deer – had been driven into their last, their biggest village beneath the cliffs. The summons had been sent out to the brothers of their confederacy – for the Tribe of the Great Hill was only one of five mighty tribes joined together – and the most skilful warriors were answering the call. Soon they would have enough numbers to attack, to crush the enemy warriors, to enslave those who did not die in the fight, to take their lands both under the cliffs and all along the river.

It was the destiny of his people, sang the elder. Thomas heard the oratory rise to a peak, to a final drawn out note of triumph and, as it hung in the air like the smoke, all the other chiefs let out one cry of assent: 'Haau!'

Hair Burned Off's narration stopped on this cry, then continued as the elder introduced someone else. Another man stepped forward, as tall and muscled as any there, his tattoos elaborate. One especially drew the eye – a snake reached from the back of the neck up the face, a tongue emerging from fangs to curl around his left eye.

Hair Burned Off whispered swiftly, 'This is Tawane. Black Snake in your tongue. He was once one of our tribe, then he was taken in war, yet spared by our enemy as we have spared you. He became one of them. Yet now he turns from his adopted brothers. He helps us know their plans. He hopes to be rewarded when we conquer.'

Thomas heard the way that Hair Burned Off talked of the newcomer and noted a change in the elders.

They use this man, this spy, he thought, *but they find it distasteful. Dishonourable.*

Black Snake spoke and it seemed what he said was news also to his leaders. Hair Burned Off translated the gist of it. It seemed that the enemy were almost beaten, though some warriors still made a pretence of fierceness, a desire to resist. Too many people had arrived from the destroyed villages, were living on too little food. They were trapped and they were starving and their hope had nearly died. Then, a few days ago, something happened to revive that hope. A man arrived claiming to be one of the Hunters of the Sunrise who had gone with their great chief, Donnaconna. He had returned with Donnaconna's Oki, a powerful stone and many, especially of his clan of the Bear, believed he had come in time to save them. With him was a women of the Pale Thieves. Black Snake and his wife thought she was a sorceress. Together, they must have powerful magic, Black Snake said, for they had given our enemy new hope.

Black Snake stepped back and a silence descended, broken only by a renewed sucking upon the pipes. Then, Gianni stepped forward, Hair Burned Off following. Falling Day spoke again, briefly, saying that this man was the one known as Young Dog, who had many scalps on his lodge pole across the Great Water.

Speaking through the translator was hard, but Gianni got his meaning across.

Thomas heard in dismay how Gianni confirmed Anne as a witch, saw the horror that crossed even the calm of the elders' faces opposite. It seemed that witches were as feared in the New World as in the Old. He then heard him say that she brought with her a powerful Oki, the bones of a dead sorceress, that had caused much death in their own land. It was very important this Oki was taken back across the water, together with the witch. That was why they had journeyed here. If the Tribe of the Great Hill could help them achieve this, he would be happy to help them in return. He had many fire sticks, one for every chief there and an even bigger fire stick on his canoe. He would teach them how to use these weapons.

Black Snake spoke again. His words were only translated to Gianni and they made him smile. Then the elder who had first spoken so melifluously spoke again. His words were not translated, but drew agreement from all the other chiefs there. He seemed to summarize what had passed and, to another shout of assent, their part of the meeting ended. They were escorted outside and suddenly left, Hair Burned Off returning into the lodge.

The crew immediately gathered around, all of them shouting questions at Gianni. He stood in their midst, answering them one at a time.

'We have a pact. They will not harm us. The guns I brought on board I will trade. No, you can all trade anything else for furs or whatever you desire.'

Another clamour of questions arose. 'Enough,' Gianni shouted. Other villagers had gathered to stare, men puffing on pipes, children daring each other to approach nearest the strangers then run away. 'Let us return to the ship.'

The crew let out a whoop of relief and ran from the village chased by a party of laughing children. Thomas's knee was hurting so it took him a while to catch up with the younger man on the path.

'What have you arranged, Gianni?'

'You might not want to know.'

'I heard you at least say you needed your sister alive.'

'Yes. I think I have enough of my family's blood on my hands, don't you?'

It was the first time he'd mentioned the death of his father in St Malo. Thomas looked as if he would say something to this, but Gianni carried on walking.

Thomas struggled to keep up. 'But what was this you said about the ship's "fire stick"? You don't mean a cannon?'

'Certainly,' Gianni smiled. 'I thought we could help our new friends with the ship's Falcon.' To combat the boredom of the long voyage, Gianni had spent much time with the ship's gunner, learning how to use the small bow-chaser.

Thomas took the other man's arm, halting him. 'You would have these people kill each other more efficiently?'

'I would have them achieve their objective swiftly so we can achieve ours.'

'And if their objective is the slaughter of innocents?'

Gianni's voice was harsh. 'There are no innocents where that six-fingered hand has touched. All are tainted by it. All! And these heathens can all die, so long as that witch's legacy is returned.'

'We have already been gone two months, Rombaud.' Thomas tried to keep the anger from his voice, failed. 'Queen Mary will long have passed her crisis. So the time for the relic's use is passed also.'

'Its time is never passed. It is a weapon for now, for ever. And my family's guilt will never be purged until I lay that weapon at the feet of my Pope in Rome for him to use against his enemies, the enemies of Christ.'

The virulence of the words, the hatred in Gianni's eyes as he spoke them, halted any reply. The younger man jerked his arm away, held till that moment, and resumed his stride toward the beach.

'God help these people,' the Jesuit murmured, crossing himself. 'God help us all.'

THREE
WHITE CEDAR

Anne sat on the porch of the longhouse, shaded from a powerful sun, watching the boys at play. It was a game with javelins and hoops, the players divided into two teams along clan lines – the Wolf, Bear, Beaver and Turtle were all affiliated, cousins apparently, and lined up against the union of the Deer, Hawk, Porcupine and Snake. Yet, despite the detailed commentary by the Porcupine who sat in the space created by her legs, Anne didn't fully grasp the complex rules. Do-ne, who had attached himself to her the first day she had come to the village and barely left her side in the seven days since, had given her to understand that it wasn't her lack of language, which had improved immensely under his tutoring. No, it was probably because she was a woman, thus of a limited intelligence, and she shouldn't concern herself with it too much.

Another javelin flew, the hoop was struck, and Do-ne tried to leap upwards in joy. But his withered left leg would not support his enthusiasm. Anne had developed a sense for his sudden movements and she caught him under the arms and lifted him slightly till he was standing, without showing him that she had done so. He immediately jumped from the porch and hopped to join in the mob surrounding the victorious thrower. Though he had not played, his clan greeted him as if he had, the hugs and slaps equally fierce.

A familiar cough came from behind her, words following on its tail.

'I think you have found a husband, if you desire him, White Cedar.' She used the name they had all given her, for 'Anne-edda' was what that tree was called. 'I do not think any of mine looked at me with such love.'

Anne smiled, as she usually did on hearing Gaka's voice. They watched the boys' celebrations transform into wrestling. The beaten team joined in and a new contest ensued that seemed to have little to do with clans. Rolling in the dust, Do-ne's leg was not too heavy a disadvantage.

'If this was a village in my own country,' she said, 'the boys would not be allowed to play like that, Aunt. Their parents would be out of the houses, beating them with sticks to make them stop.'

There was a hiss of indrawn breath, another cough. 'The more you tell of your land, White Cedar, the less I like it. How can they stop children being children? How can they insult another person with a blow?'

'Children are not persons there. They are like . . .' She searched for a Tahontaenrat word. 'Possessions.'

'Here they are like persons. Only smaller.'

Women called from their porches – food was ready – so the tussles ended, the combatants drifting away to their longhouses. Do-ne's mother appeared in a doorway and beckoned him. He quickly went to her, but not before saluting Anne, indicating with a gesture that he would return soon.

They went inside their own shelter, where Gaka ladled out some stew into a wooden bowl. Reaching into the hearth she pinched some cold ashes there, crumbling them into the food. Anne did not refuse, but she wished, as always, that she'd thought to bring salt with her on this journey. Of all the tastes of her own country, she missed that the most.

One of Gaka's family, a great-niece, walked past them. 'Would you like a bowl of soup, Blue Feather?' Gaka asked.

'No, thank you, Aunt. I have to . . . meet someone.'

They both saw the girl blush. It seemed to flow right down her face and neck and on to her bare breasts. She was young, and they were still developing, but they coloured red and her nipples swelled. She was aware of it too and, raising an arm to conceal them, she hurried out.

'Ah,' said Gaka, 'and I think I know who she is to meet. He is of the Wolf clan, one of the boys who came when their village was burned out. You know how interesting a new face can seem. Well, they will make a beautiful child, if that is what the Gods want. And it is a good day to be lying by some cool pool with a handsome new boy.'

Now it was Anne who found herself blushing. 'You don't mean they . . . they are going to . . .' The older woman was watching her with a smile. 'But she seems too young.'

Gaka looked puzzled. 'She can bear a child so she is certainly not too young. And anyway, he will not be her first handsome boy. For she is very pretty, my Blue Feather. And he may not be her last.'

Anne's blush deepened. 'This is something else that is very different in my country. There, when you take a husband, he is meant to be your first – and your last.'

Gaka tipped back her head and laughed loudly, the laugh swiftly melded with a cough. Despite a cordial that Anne had made for her, the older women's throat was still raw, the cough growing worse by the day.

When she had recovered her breath she said, 'But that is like saying, "I think I will like deer meat – one day! – so I will not taste bear, or moose first." How can you know you want only one thing, for life, unless you have tried others?'

'So when they are married, do they . . .'

'When you take a husband, then it is different. You stay with him and him only. As does he with you.' Gaka paused and a glint came into her eyes. 'But at least you remember and, on nights when your husband does not please you, you can dream of bear meat, moose meat, beaver . . .'

Humour and coughing shook her again, till the tears ran down her face.

Usually Anne found she could not help but join in Gaka's laughter but a memory held her, the look in a maiden's eyes. Somewhere in this village, the man she'd followed from France was struggling to be born again. All his desire was to be part of his tribe once more, in every way. So when someone like Blue Feather, raised her eyes to him and moved them toward the forest . . .

She felt herself flush again. But it wasn't embarrassment this time, and it surprised her with the violence she suddenly felt, a fury directed at all the bare-breasted young women of the village.

The older woman had been watching her. She put down her bowl and took Anne's hands in her own.

'I think our ways are not for you, White Cedar. You came to us too late. By my eighteenth summer, I already had three children.'

'Good,' Anne said, the bitterness clear in her voice. 'So I am already too old for any man to look at me.'

'That is not what I am saying.' Gaka shook the younger woman's hands gently. 'I am saying you do not need to look for love. You have already made your choice.'

Anne looked away. 'And the man I want no longer wants me. If he ever did.' She felt warm tears cut down her face as she spoke the words she'd only thought before.

'I think your fear is making you read the signs wrongly. It is not that he does not want you. It is that he cannot want anyone – yet. Because he does not know who he is. He is like a bear cub whose mother has been killed in the hunt. He wanders in a huge, strange forest. He can see his reflection in the water so he knows he looks like a bear but he knows nothing of a bear's ways. He cannot hunt like one. He cannot sleep all the winter long like one. And he cannot choose a mate like one.'

Anne returned the pressure in the hands, gripping the older women's urgently. 'So what can I do, Gaka?'

'Wait.'

'But there is no time! Your whole nation is under threat. Tagay may be reborn one day only to go to war, maybe to die, the next. How will he find the time to know his heart?'

Gaka whispered, 'You think wisdom is only there when many moons have come and gone? I say it can come in one clear, bright moment. Tagay was born to a wise mother, part of the wisest clan. His uncle, Donnaconna was the Hunter of the Sunrise. And the sunrise takes just a moment to show us the world.'

Anne tried to smile back. 'I hope you are right.'

'I am sure I am. I am sure Tagay loves as you love. The signs are clear in his face. But if he needs one moment of power to make him realize it ... well, that is what wise old aunts are for!'

Before Anne could reply, shouting could be heard, sounding like it came from the edge of the village.

Gaka squeezed Anne's hands again, held onto them as she rose. 'Come,' she continued, 'shall we go and see what this noise is about?'

It had been a week to sap the strength of even the strongest man. And those who tested him took as of no account that he had spent so long cramped on a ship, nor that his life before at the French court had been lazy and indulgent. They knew nothing of such matters and cut him off when he tried to speak of his former life. To them, it was very simple. He was a lost member of their clan. He needed to be found. And because of what threatened the whole tribe, he needed to be found swiftly.

There was also the matter of his death. All those who had sailed away with the French Captain, Donnaconna and the other hostages, including Tagay's mother, all the Hunters of the Sunrise, were dead. Though their bones had not been wrapped in beaver skins and buried in the pit outside the village, ceremonies had been conducted, they had been mourned. Fortunately, there were precedents for the situation; warriors feared captured and killed would sometimes escape, or a hunting party, trapped by flood or fire would have to survive a winter away and return with the spring. Each of the resurrected would have to go through a ritual of rebirth.

Thus he'd spent the first night at his native village lying naked in a birch bark canoe filled with river water and lumps of deer fat. Though it was summer, the water chilled and shrivelled his skin, and he shook till he thought he'd split the frail craft apart. In the morning, every member of his clan, men, women and children, had gathered to watch him held under the water until he thought he was drowned, until the sides of the canoe were stoved in and he was spilled forth, flapping like a tickled trout, onto the river bank. Four men then threw him into the torrent, where the fat was cleansed from his skin. Then the same men – his cousin, Sada, among them – carried him, shaking uncontrollably, to a small hut made of saplings, covered in deer skins. From the intense cold he was plunged into its opposite, for large stones had been kept in the hearths all night and the heat hit his face like the slap of an open hand. More and more of the men crammed naked in behind him, till every space was filled with sweating flesh. Pipes were filled with sweet scented tobacco, clouds of it obscured even the man next to him. His shaking calmed, only for nausea to replace it, and he had to be taken outside to vomit. Gradually, though, the heat started to feel good, the tobacco making his mind conjure strange images in its smoky layers; images added to by the stories the men told, tales of talking beasts, flying men, the birth of a people, of warfare and hunting as well as the absurdity of being alive. Laughter rose on the swirls of smoke, visions shimmered in heat haze, and the day passed till, near sunset, the deer skins were stripped from the hut and the whole clan was revealed outside it. Tagay was picked up again and, along with all his companions from the hut, found himself once more in the river. When he emerged, he walked between two lines of his clan, while every man, woman and child touched him.

The sleep he had that night was deep, full of joyous dreams. It was also short. Long before dawn, he was woken by a rough shaking of his shoulder. Sada stood above him and curtly ordered him to rise and follow. About forty others – the full fighting strength of the clan, it transpired – awaited him outside the longhouse. A breech cloth was all the dress he had against the chill, that and the hide moccasins that covered his feet. Sada led them from the village and up the barely visible pathway of the cliffs, across the gaming field and into the forests beyond. They walked swiftly, silently, without pause, till morning found them high on another bare plateau.

'You are one of the Tahontaenrat, one of the Deer people again. But you are not yet a Bear.' Handing him a bow, a quiver of arrows and a small pouch with grains in it, the clan began his education.

For two days and nights, they treated him harshly. There was no time, it was said, to do anything else but test him to his limits. He was never struck, for Sada said that would be an insult to him as a person. But any failure or shortcoming would be greeted with scorn, insult piled on insult as to his skills, his manhood and his origins among the lesser, scavenging animals. And afterwards, Tagay still had to perform again whatever task he'd failed.

Each night he would sit in solitude, sometimes dozing, often awake, staring at the sky, dwarfed by its enormity, by the challenges that faced him. Sometimes, he'd weep. And often, when he did, he'd see a vision of Anne reaching out to comfort him. He wanted her touch, her soothing caress. Later though, when the tears had dried, he'd resent her part in his weakness.

Dawn of the third day on the plateau was glorious. He had stayed awake nearly the whole night, dazzled by the number of stars that shot across the heavens. And his mood of wonder continued on the journey back to the village. He even found he was joking with the other members of the party, joining in some of their tussles.

And then, at last, he discovered something at which he was better than them.

They had just arrived at the edge of the plain that would lead to the playing field. Tagay was, as usual, at the end of the line of men.

'You are slow, Tagay, your feet drag across the ground,' Otetian, the tallest of the warriors, had said. 'You are like a porcupine, you move like this.'

He squatted down and shuffled forward, his bottom raised in the air. There was laughter from the others.

'And Otetian is like a heron. Clumsy in flight and walking with its big legs like this.' Tagay impersonated the bird, his own long legs jerking forward.

There was more laughter. Otetian stepped up to Tagay. He had been one of the most provocative of all Tagay's 'tutors'.

'So you think a porcupine can beat a heron? One flap and I would be at that tree across the grass before you had got your prickly arse off the ground.' He pointed to a tree that stood about two hundred paces away.

Sada called out. 'Beware, Tagay. Do not bet him anything. Otetian has beaten every member of every village in the foot races.'

Tagay looked into the preening face of the warrior. 'Not every member,' he said, quietly.

There was a chorus of jeers. Otetian stuck out his chest. 'You would race me, Little Bear?' There was no mistaking the colour he gave to the word 'Little.'

Tagay leant in, till their faces were just a hand's breadth apart. 'I would.'

Bows, quivers and pouches were handed over. Sada stood before them, a hand on each of their chests. The others ran ahead to the tree. When they reached it and had formed a rough line, Sada said, 'On my word, fly.'

Tagay crouched in readiness. Beside him, Otetian gave a lazy grin and barely took a stance.

'Go!'

They took off together, matched pace for pace. Then Otetian began to lengthen his stride and a slight gap opened between them, with half the distance covered.

Tagay had let that happen. The man was fast and, with fifty paces to go to the cheering men, the gap between them was five paces. At twenty-five, Otetian saw a shape reach to his shoulder, then watched that shape surge past him. Despite his desperate pumping, Tagay beat him to the line by three full strides. He was surrounded immediately, hands patting him on his back, grasping his forearm. It was the first time his clan members had given him praise and Tagay revelled in it.

A voice broke into the cheers. 'So, Little Bear, you tricked me there.' Otetian was trying to keep a smile on his face and failing. 'I do not think you would be so clever a second time.'

Tagay, flush with victory, said, 'The heron wishes to race again?'

'Yes,' came the reply. 'But not such a paltry distance. Will you race to the gates of the village?'

Tagay thought. They were on the plateau that led to the game field. He could see the great oak where he'd first watched the game in the distance. They would get to it in perhaps another quarter hour of walking. The trail of the cliffs led down from the small forest there. From their base, it was a short run along the stream bank into the village, maybe another half-league.

'Yes, I will race you there.'

'And I too,' yelled another warrior. 'I am a man for that distance.'

'And I! And I!' called the others, all equally fired by the race they'd just witnessed. 'Let us go now.'

'Wait,' said Sada, his low voice commanding instant silence from the forty warriors. 'Such a race is a matter of honour. Why should not our people join in and pay tribute to the victor?' He turned to one member who had seemed less keen on the race, probably due to his stoutish stature. 'Run ahead, Ganogieh, and let the Bear clan know of what we do. When you disappear into the trees, we will be coming.'

This warrior nodded and, without further words, set off at a pace that belied his shape. As the others yelled encouragement at their departing friend Sada took Tagay aside.

'Listen well, Tagay. Otetian is fast and tireless. He is one of those who runs between villages bearing news and "the sticks that summon", when all our scattered tribe must gather. Since becoming a man, he has never lost a race. That may also be because he is rumoured to cheat.' Sada grinned. 'So watch for him on the cliff path.'

Tagay nodded and retrieved his bow and quiver from the man who'd held them for him during the first race. Each would have to carry their own during this one.

They watched the running figure recede toward the cliff-top forest. Soon he was a mere plume of dust to all eyes save for one of the younger warriors who had climbed up and balanced on the lower branches of a walnut tree, shading his brow from the sun's glare.

'He gets close,' he called down. 'Ten breaths and he will be there.'

He dropped down, took his place in the single rank of jostling men. Tagay deliberately walked up and squeezed into the space next to Otetian. The taller warrior leaned down and shoved Tagay hard, shoulder to shoulder.

'Give me room there, cub,' he growled.

'You can have all you want in a moment,' Tagay replied, shoving in return and smiling. 'For you will be watching my back.'

'Ready?' Sada raised the banner of the clan, a bear's paw thrust onto a spear, above his head for all to see.

There was one shout of acclamation.

'Then let us . . . *run!*' cried Sada, taking the first step.

He only kept the lead for a few paces. Then several of the younger warriors passed him, already running at nearly a full sprint, forming a group of some ten that swiftly moved ahead. A second, larger group coalesced about Sada, not far behind. About a dozen steps to their rear, Tagay moved a pace to his left and dropped one back. Then he simply matched Otetian stride for stride as they trailed the packs. The other man glanced at him once, disdainfully, then settled into a rhythmic tempo.

It did not take long for the front-runners to realize their error. The middle group, Sada in their lead, had caught them, the two packs merging by the time they were halfway across the plain. Only two of the early sprinters kept up, the rest of them slipping back so that even Tagay and Otetian, still trailing, overtook them, though they tucked in just at the rear and did not lose contact.

As one body, the Bear clan of the Tahontaenrat tribe ran, their moccasined feet drumming the earth, dust rising to trail from the grass tips like tendrils of smoke, the steady breaths, the occasional thump and grunt as pumping elbows collided, the only other sounds. Tagay was breathing easily, enjoying the freedom of his limbs almost as much as the collective will that drove the group on. For the time that he'd been with them in the wilderness, he'd been the object of their scorn, the focus of their efforts and thus distinct, separate. Here he was just a runner, as good as any of them.

Better! He had to be better. He was never going to match them with bow or javelin. He would never read the trails for game, or track by the stars, or know so well the ancient tales of their people. And he would never take to the field of play and shoot the ball between the posts to defeat the clan of the Wolf, as his cousin Sada had. But he could run. And, as Otetian suddenly increased his speed and began to move through the pack, he knew he could win.

Otetian's surge took him to the head of the crowd, Tagay one step behind. They passed Sada, who had set the pace till then and who grunted in frustration as he was overtaken. But Otetian was not content to just lead the field. He kept driving forward and Tagay had no choice but to match him.

The sounds of the others' exertions fell away. The trees were just ahead, a hundred or so paces off, the village trail clear. Yet Tagay still hung back. The cliff path was treacherous in places and he had negotiated it last time with his aunt on his back, his eyes focused on just the next stone, the next careful footfall. He had a feeling that Otetian would take the descent rather more briskly and he wanted to watch where the man placed his feet.

They entered the wood under the great oak. Glancing up into the thick canopy, he wondered at the changes in his life since he had first stood on the tree's branches a week before.

He had only glanced up for a moment, the beginning of a downward slope, just a few paces into the forest. Long enough though for Otetian, who had not looked at him since the running began, to hit him. He struck sharply with the elbow, straight into Tagay's mouth. The blow, combined with the pace of the running, dropped him like a shot bird. He hit the ground hard, rolling over and over, swallowing dust, his progress halted suddenly by the ridged trunk of an ash, knocking out what little wind remained in his lungs.

Hands were under his arms, he was being lifted, held, as his own legs would not support him for a moment.

'You need to watch the path, cub, then you won't have to argue with a tree.'

Sada's seven faces whirled above him. On either side warriors, drawing deep breaths, passed. Tagay shook his head again and again, though it did little to disperse the mists. Feeling something warm on his lips, he reached up. The sight of blood on his fingers brought his eyes into focus. Sada's suddenly clear face held a look of amusement. He reached out and wiped some more blood from Tagay's lip.

'Or did someone guide you into the tree's embrace? Huh? Did I not warn you that Otetian does not like to lose?'

'Yes,' was all Tagay could manage.

'Then you have one more reason to catch him. You owe him this.' Sada wiped the blood onto Tagay's hair. 'Come.'

'He's too far ahead now,' Tagay mumbled through a swelling mouth.

The smile left Sada's face. 'You do not understand. Have you learned nothing? A Bear of the Tahontaenrat does not give up. Ever. Now run!' He began moving down the path, his arms lifting and propelling the younger man.

'Besides,' he added, as Tagay flailed forward, 'you were right. Otetian *is* a heron. And long, skinny legs do not like the cliff descent. Even he will lose some speed.'

Of the next hundred steps, as many were to the side as forward. Gradually though, the strength returned to his legs and soon he was stumbling on his own. To start with he reached up to wipe the ceaseless flow of blood away from his mouth. Then he realized the movement was interfering with his rhythm. Besides, the taste of blood was the taste of anger.

By the time they reached the cliff top, they had caught up with the stragglers. The descent was narrow but, at Sada's urging, Tagay began to push past the other warriors. Some let him by easily, others seemed more reluctant and these Tagay moved aside with a shift of weight, a shoulder dipped and lifted. Sada trailed him a pace behind, planting his foot where Tagay planted his, making the same leaps down, landing with bent knee on rock shelves and shale slides.

They had passed over half the clan and were close to the bottom, the level plain ahead, when Tagay heard a slipping and then a cry. He turned to see Sada sprawled at the base of the huge rock Tagay had just leapt from. He made to return, but Sada, clutching an ankle that looked as if it was already swelling, waved him away.

'Go on. Run, Tagay, run!'

He turned back. The base of the cliff path took three more leaps, then he was running on the level, his legs wobbling at first at the renewed sensation. Soon they settled, as he did into his stride. He began to overtake the determined remnants of the clan. The youngest, who had sprinted ahead at the very beginning and who had got a second burst of power, even these were fading now, their breaths drawn in huge gulps. They had enough wind, though, to cheer him as he passed, just as the whole pack emerged from the canyon that led from the cliffs to the village.

There it was before him, the late afternoon sun reddening the wooden palisade as if with fire, shining off the wide river beyond. And between him and it, about halfway along the stream bank that flowed toward it, there was one figure. At the warriors' acclamation, the figure seemed to sense Tagay bursting from the pack who pursued him and attempted to increase his speed. But Otetian's heron legs were failing.

There were maybe two hundred paces between them, three times as much again to the palisade gate. Tagay saw movement there, people spilling out to line the pathway in, faint shouts carrying on the wind. Scent carried on it too, the cooking fires of the Tahontaenrat, of the people he had travelled across the world to meet.

His people.

He tasted again the blood on his lips, the same blood that flowed in those now gathering at the entrance to the village.

His village.

Suddenly, he knew. He was more tired than he had ever been in any chase through the hunting forests of King Henri. His chest was bruised where it had met a tree. His face ached where it had met the elbow of a warrior, the man who ran just ahead of him now, nearer with every step Tagay took.

He was maybe two hundred paces from the gates when Tagay heard the man's breath, heard it because the man who never glanced back was glancing back now. Otetian's face showed his desire to push on faster. His legs failed to act on that desire. Tagay was ten paces behind him when Otetian reached the first of the cheering villagers, five when they crossed the slat bridge over the stream. It was narrow and they took it shoulder to shoulder, elbow to elbow. Otetian didn't glance at him now, didn't attempt to raise one of those elbows for a second strike. His eyes were fixed on the gap in the palisade, just as Tagay's were. And in the few remaining paces that were left, Tagay surged past his rival and burst through the gates of his village, to the cheers of his people.

It was all blur – and pain – for a while. Faces whirled into view, appearing over him where he lay. Gaka, Chief Tangled, others he did not know but who seemed to want to befriend him now, leaning down to pound his back, making scant breaths even harder to draw. The other runners staggered in to fall beside him and Otetian. After a short time, Sada was borne in by two warriors. They laid him beside Tagay.

'So, cub,' Sada said, his voice rising above the tumult, 'it looks like you are no longer dead.'

'I do not think he is a spirit,' Otetian said, as he crawled over to them, 'for look at what his teeth did to my arm.'

He raised his elbow. There, on its end, was a distinct bite mark. 'Never mind, though,' continued the long-legged warrior, 'I'll forgive you for biting me, seeing as you are a cub and that's what they do.'

This was greeted by such a roar by the rest of the Bear clan, that Tagay did not even have to protest himself. Instead, he reached into his mouth and, with only a little waggling, produced a tooth. Handing it across to Otetian, he said, 'A bead for your wife's necklace.'

Another roar, more back slapping, so that it took a while for the boisterous members of the Bear clan to realize that they were being addressed. The village had gathered and the chiefs were standing before them. It seemed that the excitement of the race had brought them out of the council house, for the chiefs were in their ceremonial wampum beads and all clutched their long pipes.

'It seems, O you of the Bear clan, that your lost cub has been found. Is that true?'

Sada rose from the ground, balancing on one foot, and addressed the man who had just spoken, while Tagay, suddenly shy under all the attention, rose too.

'It is up to you, Tododaho, as you are our chief. But we, who have spent time with this cub, say he is fit to return to us.'

Tangled nodded. 'Then we will admit him, as we planned, in the ceremony of the moon, three sunrises from now. Meantime, he can live with his aunt, my sister Gaka, in her lodge.'

Tagay looked across to where his aunt was standing. She smiled at him and he smiled back. Next to her stood Anne and it was as if her face was divided into two parts; half was joyous for him and smiled, while the other half held a sorrow. And seeing it, he felt his own face mirror hers.

Before he could ponder this, Tangled spoke again, raising his voice so that it carried to the whole tribe who had, by now, gathered in the open space.

'My people, we were in council when news of the race reached us. We came to watch it in joy. For the truth is that it is a good distraction from our debate. We could not reach a conclusion in the matter that so troubles us.' He gestured out toward the river. 'We all know the enemy gathers. They have destroyed our villages, the homes of many of you who have now sought shelter with your brothers and sisters here under the cliffs. Nearly all of the Tahontaenrat are here and the "sticks that summon" have been sent out to the last three villages, to bring the people here for the Great Council. In our gathering together there is strength but there is also danger, for even this village cannot feed all the Tahontaenrat for long. And our council cannot decide if we should wait for this danger here, and break the enemy on our palisades as the Great Waters breaks on the rocks of the shore. Or if we should abandon this place and travel far to where this enemy is not.'

Anne had observed how, at all gatherings, each speaker was always listened to in total silence, a tribute to his wisdom, a respect for his opinion. But this last statement produced a collective moan and even a few whispers.

Tangled continued. 'We will have to deal with this matter, finally, at the feast. But in the meantime, our kettles do not have enough meat for our stomachs and we must gather more so that our feast will not disgrace the hospitality of our ancestors. So our young men must go out and hunt. We know that this has become dangerous, for the enemy encroach each day more and more on our hunting grounds. So it has been decided that each clan will not hunt by itself, but two members from each clan will go on each party. Then, if they must fight and perhaps die, no clan will suffer the loss of all its young men.' He paused and another chief handed him eight sticks, each with a different colour. 'Each of these sticks is a hunt, from the land above the cliffs where the beaver and porcupine are plentiful, to the stream of trout to the north; from the geese grounds, to the hills of the bear. This one' – he held up a stick dyed a bright, blood red – 'is for the Island of Grapes in the river. It is where the deer are abundant. But it is also close to the villages of our enemy.'

He laid the sticks down one by one before he spoke again.

'We have decided that every war chief of the eight clans will take one stick. We know that each chief will want to take the red stick of most danger, so we have made the choice for you. This is not a reflection on the courage of any clan. But some know different parts of the land better than the other. Every chief will take the stick we give them and then two from each clan will join his party. Is that clear?'

There was a universal shout of 'A-hum!' Then the clan names

were called out and Anne watched as, one by one, the clan war chiefs went to receive their commission. The Bear war chief had died defending his village. His heir, Sada, had not been formally appointed. But Sada was injured, so the stout Ganogieh took his place. In the end, there was only the red stick left, and only the Wolf clan unannounced. She watched as Black Snake, moved forward, bowed, and picked it up.

The meeting now divided, with each warrior seeking to be taken on the various hunts. Most would remain behind, as the elders required. This was not a time for the village to be undefended. But there was prestige in the hunt, honour. Anne saw many warriors jostle around each chief, a few expressing their delight, most walking away disappointed. Then she saw Black Snake move through the crowd toward the Bear clan, still gathered around Sada and Tagay.

Black Snake's question lifted his brow, the serpent tattooed around his left eye. 'Are there two Bears brave enough to join me on the Island of Grapes?'

He was immediately harangued from all sides. 'Of course,' he said, 'I would want to take my rival from the Game but . . .' He looked down at Sada's swollen foot. 'It seems you have missed your chance.'

Sada hopped forward. 'I could still run around you, Black Snake.'

The smile left the tattooed face. 'We will have to wait a while to see that. And now the tribe needs food. I do not need lame birds but warriors who can move and move fast.'

Before a furious Sada could reply, Otetian stepped in front of him. 'Then you will need me.'

Immediately there was a rush of others. Black Snake waited for the tumult to abate a little, then said, 'Otetian honours me and I accept him. But he was, after all, the loser of the race.' A raised hand halted Otetian's protest. 'Does not the winner dare to come? Or does his skill lie only in speed? Is that why he does not volunteer?'

All turned to Tagay. 'I had not offered myself because I know how many more of my clan are worthy, who have the skills of the hunt that I lack.' He stepped forward so that his face was level with the tattooed one of Black Snake. 'But I am more than willing to take the place of my cousin, Sada, and honour him.'

For a silence that lengthened, Black Snake stared deep into Tagay's eyes. 'Good,' he said finally, a slow smile returning, 'it is settled. Get your provisions, prepare your canoes. We leave when the sun is in the treetops.' And with that, he turned and headed for the river.

The Bear clan watched the muscled, coloured back moving away from them. Sada touched Tagay's arm. 'You must be careful on the island, Tagay. I do not trust this man. He keeps some secret behind his eyes.'

'I will watch over him, Sada, since I carry his mark.' Otetian raised his elbow. 'Besides, on the island I will prove this cub's triumph over me was mere chance.'

The clan split up. Other delegates went off to the gathering of their hunts, accompanied by those who must remain. Otetian said he would bring provisions for Tagay. So the young man was left, as his clan dispersed, standing alone in the suddenly emptied open space within the gates.

Not quite alone.

'So, you have your desire, Tagay.'

The voice, coming from behind, surprised him. For a moment, the words were unclear, muddied. It took him a moment longer to realize they were spoken in French.

She stood with her back to the sinking sun. Its beams dazzled Tagay, making him squint and shade his eyes. He saw the thick hair as dark as his, as long, flooded now with a light that turned it as red as an autumn forest.

'Anne-edda,' he murmured. 'White Cedar.'

She moved forward, around, so he no longer gazed into the blaze. A hand reached out but when none rose to meet it, slipped back to her side.

'They have taken you back.'

'Yes.'

'I am happy for you.'

'Thank you.'

A silence came, as awful as the stilted sentences. All those words they'd spoken after she'd fallen from the Paris sky were as nothing, mocked by this awkwardness. She coloured, hating the tone of her voice, hating having to ask. She had never depended on any man apart from her father – and he had died so they could get here. So she had no choice but to ask.

'And what of me?'

'You?' He shifted, looked away, back to the brightness. 'You are treated well, are you not? My aunt looks after you?'

'Treated well?' The tone in her voice changed. If she drew strength from her father she was her mother's daughter too and had Beck's temper. 'I am not a visitor, Tagay. Some stranger given a bowl of stew and a place beside your hearth. If you had a reason for coming here, so did I. Or have you forgotten my cause in the excitement of your own?'

'Excitement?' His voice hardened to match hers. 'This is not a game, Anne. I have come back to my family, my clan, my people. Only today was I truly born.'

'And only yesterday did my father die.' She spat the last word at him.

'He did not die for me.'

'He did. He died because I persuaded him that the only end for the cause of his life was in this New World, free from the Christian savagery of the Old. Your world. He gave his life for both of us so we could get here together and you would help me bury . . . this!'

As she spoke, she had reached into the deerskin pouch Gaka had given her. From within it she pulled the soiled wool bag. Pulling the material tight, she thrust it toward Tagay, so he could see where it pushed out at six distinct points.

He recoiled from it, took a step away. 'So you are here. In this *New World* that is as old to our people as your world is to yours. Bury it. Bury it now.'

'You know I cannot bury it till a full moon. That was this Queen's wish.'

'So bury it then. And there will be an end to it.'

'Will it?' Suddenly, her voice dropped to near a whisper. 'And what else will it be an end to, Little Bear?'

With that, clutching the hand before her, she turned and walked through the village gates.

'Anne.' He took a step after her. 'Anne, wait.'

'Leave her, nephew. Leave her alone. Unless you are going to speak the words she needs to hear.' His aunt emerged from the shadow cast by the palisade. 'Can you speak them?' she continued, walking toward him. 'Do you know what is in your heart for her?'

'Aunt.' He looked at her, then back to the direction Anne had taken, out of sight now along the stream bank. 'I do not know what I feel. She is part of another life. One I hated, one I left behind. How can I ... love her? She knows nothing of this world.'

Gaka halted before him. She coughed, wiped her mouth. 'And you, born just this moment, know so much?'

'She will not want to stay here, Aunt. I know these people. They call us savages because we do not follow their God, their ways.'

'Have you asked her if she wants to stay?'

'No.'

'Have you told her of your confusion?'

'I have not had a chance.' He could not meet his aunt's amused stare. 'I would not know what answers to give her.'

Gaka laughed. 'It is always the same with men. You think you must know everything before you speak. But often all you have to do is ask the true question of your heart. And let the woman hear it and give the answer.'

Before Tagay could reply, Otetian appeared beside the nearest longhouse. 'Tagay, come,' he called, 'the canoes are in the water.'

He took a step toward the summons, then turned back to his aunt. 'Tell her,' he said, 'tell her, when I return ... if I ...'

'Yes, nephew?'

He looked again at the impatient Otetian, at the bow, quiver and pouch he held in readiness for Tagay. Looked beyond him, to the hunt, to the dangers that awaited him on the island. To more of his New World.

'Nothing. There is nothing to tell.' He went to the waiting warrior, put the quiver on his back, the pouch to his side, took the bow. Together they ran out of sight toward the water's edge.

Anne strode along the banks of the stream, not noticing anything beyond the step before her, the one after that. In speed there was some comfort, a distance gained between her and her confusion –

or so she thought. Yet when she stopped to breathe some distance from the palisade, she realized that confusion had only come with her.

Now she looked around at a place she had never seen before. She had wandered off the main path, down alongside an even smaller stream. Where she stopped, it widened slightly, deepened, forming a small pool. It was shaded by the drooping leaves of three silver birch. The familiar trees, the gentle sound of the water, reminded her of that other glade, outside the walls of Montalcino.

'Oh, Haakon, Haakon.' Her eyes filled with water as she thought of the big, grey-bearded Norseman and those others she loved. Her mother, a widow now, needing her absent daughter. The gentle Fugger. Erik and Maria, the young lovers she envied. Suddenly, she felt so far away from everything she understood. All because she'd listened to the runes, in a place much like this one.

She looked down at the bag she yet clutched before her, felt the outline of that dead queen's bones within it.

Why must I wait for the full moon? she thought. *Here is as good a place, as good a time, as any. Why not just bury it here and have done? Then, when Uncle Pierre returns with his ship, I can be ready to leave on the instant and return to those I love, who love me.*

On the other side of the pool the trail went on into the wood. There had to be a secluded spot deep within it, perfect for such a burial. Hoisting to her hips the bead dress Gaka had lent her, she stepped into the pond to cross. It rose to the middle of her thighs and for a moment she paused to savour the feeling, the delicious coolness in the summer heat.

Something dropped into the water beside her with a loud 'plop'. She looked up hastily to the overhanging tree. Then she heard the chuckle and turned to see what at first looked like a blue snake peering from the tall grasses that lined the pool.

'I was only a boy, when the last of the Pale Thieves fled, because they were so weak and couldn't settle here,' Black Snake said, thrusting his whole face into view. 'But I remember all their women were scrawny little bitches. They did not have legs, strong like yours.'

Anne dropped the dress, careless that it now soaked up the

water. She moved swiftly back to the bank but not swiftly enough to get there before Black Snake. He stood above her, a hand stretched out.

'Let me help you,' he said gently. It was the gentleness that made her pause for she saw the coldness in the eyes, knew a sudden stab of fear. She looked away, down to the hands he wanted to take. One still clutched the remains of Anne Boleyn. She reached back to her hip pouch, slipping the woollen bag into it.

The gentleness had gone. 'What is it that you have put away so quickly?' he said. 'Could it be the Oki of the Great Witch that I have heard about?'

There was no time to wonder at what he said, where he could have heard of Anne Boleyn's hand, because he bent and pulled her, sudden and fast from the pool, one arm snaking around her, trapping hers, squeezing her chest to his.

'Yes,' he said, 'and you are not scrawny here, either.'

A hand passed over the front of her dress, fingers jabbing into her breasts. 'Yes,' he grunted again, his voice suddenly thick.

His tattooed arm was like a band of steel wrapped round her, squeezing. It was hard to get any air. She looked up into eyes that showed no pity, only a terrible desire. He began to walk backwards with her.

'White Cedar! White Cedar!' It was a young voice, a boy's, and it came through the screen of tall grass, from the path behind them. The grip loosened slightly and some air got in.

'Do-ne!' she called. In a moment, the boy appeared, hopping swiftly toward them on his one good leg.

'Get away, child.' Black Snake still held her, fury in his eyes, a beast surprised over its kill. 'Get away before I hurt you.'

The little boy stopped, but he did not retreat. 'But Black Snake,' he said, his voice quavering, 'this is where we have come to practise our javelins. See!' He raised the one he held.

The warrior, still holding Anne, took a step toward him and Do-ne limped one back, balancing the spear in the manner just before throwing. Black Snake halted, though the threat from the crippled child seemed ridiculous. And in the moment he stopped, before he could speak again, the sound of other voices came from the path and a crowd of ten-year-olds, all clutching javelins, ran into sight. They halted immediately, eyes and mouths wide.

Black Snake pushed Anne backwards. She stumbled, one foot slipping into the water at the pool's edge. He bent to her.

'There will be another time for us.' His voice was low so only she could hear. 'And your Witch's Oki, and these children, will not protect you. Nothing will.'

Then he stood and ran past the startled boys.

In a moment, Do-ne was beside her. 'I saw you leave the village,' he said. 'Then I saw Black Snake follow. He is not a good man, so . . .'

He took her hand, held it as she slipped sobbing to the ground, looking with embarrassment at his young companions as she clutched his frail body to her, rocking him, for as long as the tears fell.

FOUR
DEER HUNT

Tagay dropped more dried grass into the small hardwood bowl then blew gently, watching as the flame caught in a sudden burst of crimson and yellow. Carefully he added a few broken twigs, and when these too fired and glowed he nodded to Otetian and moved a step away, watching as the next firebearer stepped up to the crouching warrior. Otetian held the device, a short bow lying horizontally, its string wound about the top third of an upright stake whose pointed end rested in a groove on a flat piece of bark. Just above the point the stick was thrust through a lump of heavier wood. By pulling the bow up and down vigorously, the weighted stick spun into the groove causing sparks to fall on bits of grass, which, when they caught, were swiftly transferred to the wooden bowls and their kindling there.

Tagay moved away to his appointed position, nurturing his flame, marvelling at the ingenuity of his people. In the world he'd come from, flame was ever present, carefully preserved from one day to the next. Here, it was simply conjured forth when required. Lowering himself gently, he placed his back against a spruce tree, holding the bowl to his chest, blowing and feeding as required, stretching his legs out before him. He did not think there was a part of him that did not ache. The running of the day before, together with the night hours of hard paddling that had brought them to this island, had spread fire throughout his limbs as completely as Otetian's bow had brought it out of the wood.

Otetian, seemingly tireless at his paddle, had told him that they were lucky, for such a hunt would usually require more protracted effort. Several hundred warriors would take part and spend the first ten days building barriers of fresh brush stretching either side of a valley for half a mile, tapering to a narrow point – the killing zone. After the slaughter there, the deer would be skinned, butchered, the meat and hide dried before fires and packed into bark barrels for transport back to the village. But this could not be the case with their hunt for they were few, a mere sixteen hunters. There was no time to build many fences, so they had fetched old ones from their usual hunting valley further inland, repaired them where necessary. The earth had provided them with this killing ground, the slopes were steep where the valley narrowed. So they had blocked off its end with their few fences. Black Snake and half the party waited down there. Otetian headed the other half, who would fire the dry brush around them, using flame and their voices to drive the deer into the ambush. And they would only bring fresh meat for this feast.

He had also told Tagay they were lucky in something else. Though this island was traditionally the hunting ground of the Tahontaenrat, more and more parties had encountered their enemy, the Nundawaono, the Great Hill People, in ever larger numbers. Many had been slain or taken captive in recent years. But today, Otetian said, Black Snake had scouted ahead and found no sign of the fierce, tattooed warriors.

'And he should know their mark,' Otetian had reminded him, 'for he was once one of them, before he was reborn as one of us.'

The late afternoon sun slanted through the thick canopy of leaf. Tagay shifted, straightening his back, rolling his shoulders and neck, checking for the tenth time that his bow was strung to the right tension for him – he was using a boy's bow and though it was still powerful it was not the huge one carried by most warriors, which needed a lifetime's training to pull. He knew he was not yet a hunter, would just have to do his best. And he was very glad that there was no sign of the enemy. Though he had trained long hours with the sword, had even fought a few times in France, they were mere drunken brawls, entered into because of a woman and too much wine, ending in minor cuts and salvaged honour. Facing a screaming, tattooed warrior with a stone tomahawk would be somewhat different.

The file of warriors had received their fire and dispersed again. When the last was in position, Otetian swiftly dismantled his flame maker, then stood. Most could see him, as they strung out across the mouth of the valley like wampum beads on a belt. So his cry was for those at each end who could not and for those who waited up ahead.

'Ay-ee!' Otetian called and as he cried he tipped the contents of his bowl onto a pile of brush at his feet. Tagay did the same, as did each of the warriors. The dried grass caught, ran onto the kindling below, spread beyond. The wind fanned it, soon small bushes began to smoulder; here and there one broke into flames, scorching the lower branches of the canopy. Leaves curled, cones glowed. The breeze blew from behind them, so smoke pushed up the valley.

'Come!' cried Otetian. 'The deer have it in their nostrils. Come!'

He began to run, Tagay and all the warriors following. Almost immediately, there was a crashing, a large shape leaping up from a bush a hundred paces ahead. Then there were three, five, a dozen.

'Halloo!' Tagay cried, giving tongue as he would have in the royal chases near Paris. Then he listened to the cries of the Tahontaenrat around him and tried to emulate them.

The ground started to descend, while slopes on either side rose, the valley narrowing swiftly. The deer were coming clearer in sight, bunching together. There had to be fifty, at least, of varying sizes. Some, seeming to sense the danger ahead, paused, half-turned back; but the cries of the hunters, the still gusting smoke, drove them on.

Tagay and Otetian, the swiftest runners, were ahead, and getting closer together as the valley tapered. They were just a few paces apart, leaping bushes at a bound, yelling with excitement.

A huge shape lurched to a halt before them, turned. It was a big buck, its spread of antlers huge above its reddish, shaggy chest. It lowered its head as they ran at it side by side. Otetian had an arrow strung, even as he ran. He let it fly and it struck the deer's antler's, glanced off into a tree. The buck snorted, then made off, not down the valley but to the side down a barely visible path.

'Tagay. Follow it, it's yours,' Otetian cried. 'I have hunted here before. That path leads to a stream. You can kill it as it swims. Go!'

They split apart, Otetian running straight on, driving the herd, Tagay fumbling for an arrow. The path was tiny, full of roots. Once he tripped, staggered, didn't quite fall. He ran on, as the cries faded behind him.

The path narrowed still further, then widened again as it reached a small stream. This too grew larger and he was running along its banks, his feet slapping between the clear, fresh marks of hooves. Then the dense foliage thinned and he was in a clearing.

The stag was waiting at its centre. Ten paces behind it, there was a small waterfall into a pool below. The beast stood, its thick red coat heaving, plastered with mud, foam flecked. As Tagay emerged into the clearing, it snorted, turned toward the drop. He could see the animal hesitate. Then the magnificent antlers swung back and lowered.

He is a warrior, Tagay thought, *and he chooses to stand and fight.*

The arrow was notched on the string. Tagay pulled it back to full stretch, feeling the power latent within even this smaller weapon. He looked at the flint head that had been narrowed down to a tapered point, ideal for the deer hunt, for the short range kill; looked beyond it to the stag. Into the stag's eyes. It was the first deer he had seen since rejoining the Tahontaenrat, the people of the Deer. He saw now why they chose to name themselves after such a beast. He was magnificent. And trapped, his land in flames. Much like the people named for him.

He lowered his bow, let the tension in the string sag. 'Go, brother,' he said. 'We will have meat enough for our feast without you.'

The stag did not move, its eyes remaining fixed on him.

'Go!' Tagay shouted, stepping forward, waving his arms.

The stag turned, ran, bent its legs, leapt. As Tagay moved forward, he heard the splash and by the time he reached the ledge above the pool, the deer was swimming strongly downstream, toward the open water.

The sounds of the hunt, which had faded, returned to him now. He heard the human cries, some still driving the animals on, some the shouts of triumph. He heard the whine of strings released, of arrows flying, the thud of impact, the animal squeal of agony and fear. Then he heard another sound. It was familiar to him and it should not have been there. And it changed all the other sounds in an instant.

He heard the explosion of a Spanish musket.

Gianni Rombaud laid the musket down still smoking, and reached into his crossbelt to pull out the first of his wheelock pistols. His mother had taught him how to use the larger weapon and he had inherited her thirst for a target. One of these 'Deer People' had just discovered that. He hoped two more would soon find that he was just as good with a pistol.

Killing savages. They were as bad, worse, than the Jews he'd hunted through the streets of Rome. At least the Christian shared some common stories with the Jew. But these were heathen, worshipping their pagan gods. The English Jesuit wanted to bring them to the cross through Christ's love, he had even begun his mission in the short time they had spent with the tattooed ones. But Gianni knew that the cross alone was never enough. You had to wield the sword as well. Or, in his case, the pistol.

It was harder to find a target now. On the valley floor below him, it was a mass of bodies. Wounded deer, hooves flailing in the air, antlers raking the ground. Wounded men, though they did not survive their injuries for long. His native allies had shot their fire sticks to no effect, despite the days he'd spent teaching them the skill. All except Black Snake, who had found a victim for his lead ball, who seemed to have a joy in the weapon equal to Gianni's own. Now he and his warriors were down there, with stone tomahawk and bone knife. Effective, he had to admit, at such close quarters. Plus, they outnumbered these Deer People at least three to one.

He watched Black Snake run down a fleeing warrior, knock him to the ground, stab, then bend over him. A moment later, an arm was thrust upwards, a lump of flesh and bloodied hair held aloft in triumph.

Scalps, they call them. Trophies, Gianni thought. *Not unlike the collection of yarmulkes I left with the Grey Wolves back in Rome.*

He was content to watch the slaughter now. Black Snake had said that, in normal warfare, they might take some prisoners but they would not today. There must be no risk of any returning to the enemy camp and telling of his actions, not until the final act of betrayal when the Tattooed Nundawaono went to war in overwhelming strength. The last of their allies were gathering, it was nearly time. The morning after the full moon, they said. Until then, all prisoners would die.

All save one. When he'd slipped to their rendezvous in the night, Black Snake had confirmed that the Hunter of the Sunrise was with them as he had promised he would be, the week before at the camp. His men were under orders to take him alive. The Fire Stick Warrior wanted him. He had promised much for him.

Oh yes, thought Gianni. *I look forward to meeting the man who stole my sister, who made her bring the mark of my family's shame to this land. He lost me in Paris. He will not lose me here.*

Suddenly, on the fringes of the mayhem, he saw another target. This enemy had just killed the two warriors who had rushed at him. He was tall, standing proudly, waiting for more.

Pride before the fall. Gianni smiled, raising his gun.

The closer he came, the worse the screaming of deer and men. The gunfire had ceased in the time it had taken him to run back along the stream path. He could no longer make out the song of arrows in flight. But the sound of blows, given and received, was unmistakable.

He'd come at a run at first; now, with the conflict taking place just the other side of the line of brush fence they'd erected only that morning, he slowed, made for a small gap. His bow still pulled back to full tension, he swung it to the side, leaned his face into the opening.

Into a nightmare. Deer were stampeding back down the valley, fleeing the carnage. Many had arrows protruding from them, blood streaming down their flanks. Though they tried to avoid them, hooves clashed with bodies rolling over and over on the ground. Bodies of their human brothers, the Tahontaenrat, the Deer people.

A man ran into view, two warriors with crimson lines across their bodies in close pursuit, almost on him, hands reaching for his long hair braid. The man dropped suddenly, straight down and the closest pursuer was too near to avoid him, falling hard. In an instant the crouched warrior rose up, a bone knife rising ahead of him, the second pursuer running onto it, taking it in the chest.

The warrior pulled it out, turned, bent to the man who had fallen, who was struggling to his feet, jerked him up, slashed it across his throat, let him fall. Strangely, it was only when the dead man dropped away that Tagay saw the arm that held the knife, saw a distinctive ring of teeth marks on the elbow.

'Otetian!' Tagay screamed, stepping into the gap between the fences.

He turned. 'Little Bear!' he shouted, a fierce smile coming to his face. Then all time slowed as Otetian raised his knife in triumph, in greeting, before, almost languidly stumbling forward. And it was only after a hole opened slowly outwards in Otetian's side, as if some small creature was burrowing its way out, that Tagay heard the shot. Looking up, he saw gunsmoke rising from the valley side no more than thirty paces away.

'Otetian!'

He was moving forward then, time returning to its frantic speed. Another tattooed warrior ran toward the man now sinking to his knees and there was no time to think or aim. Tagay loosed his arrow and it took the man in the shoulder, knocking him backwards.

Then he was beside the stricken warrior, his arms under him. 'Come! Quick!'

Otetian rose, a hand clutched to his side, blood squirting through the fingers. He half-turned back to the carnage.

'No! Run, Otetian, run.'

He began to propel the wounded man down the valley, away, following the deer that ran and leapt before them. There was shouting behind, another pistol shot that snapped a branch by Tagay's head. After a few paces, Otetian shook Tagay off, began to run on his own, at first weaving a little, then stronger and straighter. The two men hit a stride and fled down the valley.

They did not need to glance back. Arrows flew around them, thumped into the trunks of trees, shrieked by their ears. Soon there were less and less, though the shouting continued, they were still the quarry in a chase. But the two best runners of the Tahontaenrat were gaining ground on their enemy.

'Hear me, Tagay ...'

'No talk! Run. We must get to the canoes.'

'You must get to them.' Tagay heard the bubbling in the tall warrior's throat, saw, from the side of his vision, the redness spat out onto the ground. 'I should have stayed and died there with my brothers. I only came with you to tell you . . .'

He stumbled. Tagay glanced down, saw the blood staining the warrior's breech cloth, running down his thighs.

'Tell me what?'

Otetian grimaced, then picked up the pace again. A ragged breath, blood at his lips. 'Black Snake betrayed us . . . led us into the trap . . . tell them. You must live so you can tell our people.'

Otetian slowed, so Tagay did too. From behind them, the shouting increased. 'No! Keep going. You can win this race, Little Bear . . . for you truly are faster than me.' A shadow of a smile came to the red-stained lips. 'You understand that it is only because I am about to die that I admit this.' The smile departed. 'Now go! I need my breath to sing my death song and this conversation tires me. Go!'

He stopped, turned, knife in one hand, ironwood club in the other. 'See me, dogs that skulk under the hill,' he sang. 'See me and fear. For I am Otetian, the Red Shirt of the Bear clan. Come, feel the touch of my claw.'

Tagay kept going, increasing his speed till he was running full out. He could not pace himself here. The men who followed him were not trying to beat him, but kill him.

Behind him he heard the grate of cutting bone on bone, the thump of a club striking home. There was a shout of pain, a loud cry of 'Bear', the triumph clear in it, then nothing. All noise ceased and he was running, alone and fast through a forest, down a path that led to a river. Ahead, the sun was low, its beams coursing though the foliage, lighting the avenue of spruce and cedar down which he ran. Soon he was glimpsing water between the trees and the earth under his feet was harder, studded with pebbles. In another hundred strides he burst onto the beach where they had left the canoes. They were as they had been, drawn up and inverted on the shoreline, twenty paces before him. And in the midst of them stood a man with tattoos over his body.

Tagay could not stop running now. Not even when the man snatched up his bow, released his arrow. A stone made Tagay stumble and that stone saved him because the arrow passed over his shoulder while the stumble continued. Tagay hit the man at nearly his fullest speed, a sprawling run, head hard into the centre of the man's chest. Both bodies tumbled backwards, Tagay's weight on top, shoving the man down into the shallows of the river. There was a jarring thud and the man went instantly limp under him. Looking beneath the man's head, he saw a sharp rock, thrust up like a pyramid. He used it to push himself up and when he brought his hand away, it was covered in blood.

The body floated in the shallows, bumping into other rocks. Tagay turned to the canoes, grabbed one and placed it on the water, throwing two cedar paddles into it. Then he heard the cries of warriors approaching on the path. They would be there in moments, and he would be offshore, alone, trying to paddle a craft he didn't understand; he had proved inept enough at it the night before, coming to this island.

He pushed the boat ahead of him into the water. It caught in an eddy, then suddenly shot out into the stream. As he threw himself under one of the upturned canoes, he caught a glimpse of the other one entering the main river, disappearing downstream round the fold of land that made the bay. In another moment, feet crunched onto the pebbles of the beach.

'He has killed Hosahaho. And a canoe is missing. Count them and you will see. We came with eight.'

The voice was unmistakable. The man whose moccasined feet Tagay could see in the gap between the upturned canoe and beach was Black Snake. Though he had spent years amongst the Deer people, he had retained the harsher accent of the people of his birth.

Other feet, a dozen pairs, were in view, some bare, some swathed in deer skin. But the man who spoke next had square-heeled boots. Eight weeks before Tagay had heard those boots slapping on cobble stones, for the wearer had stalked him through the alleys of Paris. And the language the man spoke was the one spoken in that city.

'He who escapes is the one you promised would fall to my knife alone. Had you not better pursue him if you are to keep the bargain?' said Gianni Rombaud.

The words were translated by a third voice. Tagay heard Black

Snake spit, then say, 'He is impatient, this Young Dog, and likes to command. Tell him what I tell the others, to make him happy.'

Black Snake then ordered four of his warriors to take two of the canoes and catch the fugitive. Tagay shrunk into himself as he waited for his cover to be ripped away. But he heard the sounds of other craft being launched on either side of him.

'Tell him that I saw this Tagay paddle and he does so like a woman and will not get far. They will catch him and bring him to your knife's edge at our village.'

The words, more or less, were rendered into French. At the same time, the canoe just next to Tagay's was inverted and its bow placed in the water.

'And where does Black Snake go?' The French came again. 'To bring me the woman as you promised? Remember, she must be brought before she buries her Oki at the full moon. Otherwise he cannot have all the gifts I promised him.' Black Snake, of all the Tattooed savages, had displayed the keenest interest in learning of the new weaponery. He had sat, silent and fascinated while Gianni brought a Falcon, one of the ship's small cannon, ashore and began to rig it in the front of a rowboat.

The translation was greeted with the sound of more spitting. 'Tell him I go to the village of our enemy, where I will still be greeted as a brother. Tell him what makes him happy – that I will capture his sister and her powerful Oki and bring them to him before the full moon. And I will persuade the people of the Deer that it is safest to stay in their palisades and wait – till all our tribe and allies are gathered and they attack the sunrise after the full moon.' The canoe was launched and Black Snake added from the water. 'But do not tell him the truth that I have seen his sister's legs and felt her breasts and hunger for the rest that was denied me. So I will take what I hunger for, and when I have done, I will kill her and eat her heart and steal her six-fingered Oki. And so I will have her witch's power. Do not tell him that, because I want to watch his face when he sees her long black hair, tied to the shaft of my war lance. And when he has seen this, when I have taken the big fire stick he has promised me, I will kill him too.'

Black Snake, the man who began to put some of his words into French, all the warriors, laughed. Tagay ground his face into the shale of the beach, using the pain of sharp stones to distract him from the terrible urge he felt to leap from his hiding place and attack. But he listened still, as the man who promised to bring disaster to all those he loved paddled away, while those who remained discussed what had to be done next. It seemed that two more of the Deer people had escaped the slaughter. They were being hunted and those on the beach would join in that hunt – for it was very important that none escaped to warn of Black Snake's treachery.

'Shall we leave someone here to guard these?' a voice asked as a foot kicked Tagay's shelter.

It was the translator who answered. 'It is better that we hunt together. Hosahaho has found out that these deer people still have antlers to gore us with.' There was a spattering of laughter. 'Let us break in the bottom of their craft so if they come back here they cannot use them. Then we can hunt them down in our own time.'

There were grunts of assent. Immediately, Tagay heard the sound of tearing bark and the next moment a rock broke through the fragile skin of his shelter, crashing into the stones a hand's breadth from his face. He tensed, looked up through the head-sized gash to the pale sky above. The thrower was just in the process of turning away, satisfied with his aim. Tagay saw fair skin, dark hair and gleaming eyes, half the face that emerged from a lace collar.

'Come, to the hunt,' said Gianni Rombaud. 'It is time I gave you all another lesson with the fire sticks.'

Eager voices receded, soon swallowed up by the forest. Tagay waited, every second that passed an agony, forcing himself to stay still. When he could stand it no longer, he cautiously emerged from under the wrecked craft. The beach was deserted.

Swiftly checked, each canoe proved a ruin. Cursing, he walked up and down the shoreline, looking out to the mass of land opposite. The quality of the setting sun's light made the forests there stand out in great detail. He could even see the outline of the taller tree-tops.

'We rowed downstream and across,' he muttered as he paced. 'It took only a few hours. Could I . . .?' He looked again, tried to will the opposite shore nearer than it was. He had always been a strong swimmer. When the King had summered in the Loire he had spent days avoiding the Marquise by traversing that great river, back and forth. But the Loire was a stream compared to the water before him, that the French called the St Lawrence.

A pistol shot carried clearly from the forest, muffled shouts of triumph, some laughter, brought to him on the wind. They were hunting down the last of his people. When they were done, they would leave the island, for they did not know he was still here. When the last canoe set out, he would be safe. Safe but trapped – and the man who had vowed to rape and kill his Anne, and then destroy his tribe, would be free to wreak that evil unchallenged.

There was no choice. Pulling the odd-shaped stone from his pouch, he said, 'Donnaconna. Uncle. Chief. Protect me now.'

He replaced the stone, made sure the drawstring was tight and the pouch firm to his belt. Then, as he walked to the water, he trod on one of the paddles. They were made of lighter wood, so that they would float if dropped over the side. It gave him an idea and, dismantling his bow, he used the string to swiftly tie both paddles across his back. When he entered the chill water, they made it slightly awkward to use his arms in an overstroke. But they supported him as he kicked with his legs.

He got offshore, the calmer water letting him go as he would. But as soon as he passed the spit of land, a current took him, pushing him downstream, away from the direction he wanted. There was no hope of swimming against it so he let it take him. At least it pushed him partially toward the opposite shore also, if away from Stadacona. When the force lessened he kicked out hard, until some other current seized him and he was able only to kick, to float with the paddles. But gradually he realized he was not getting much nearer the shore he desired, could not make headway toward it. He looked the way he had come and it was just as far. Despair grew.

A sound came, above the slapping and sucking of the waters. He sought its source and saw what he first took to be part of a tree; then, as he came closer, he realized there was a head under the interwoven branches. The antlers of a stag were cresting the water just ahead of him.

It had to be the one he'd spared! With the strength born of sudden, desperate hope, he kicked hard. The paddles resisted the water so he discarded them. Still the creature seemed to be moving away, despite his hard pulling against the current. Then a rush of water pushed him suddenly up against the animal. One huge eye, bright with panic, regarded him. He grabbed for the antlers, his hands slipped down the ridged surfaces, then held. The buck tossed its huge head, shrugged him off. He grabbed again, half-hoisting himself onto the animal's shoulders, attempting to thread his arms through the thicket of horn, to lock and hold. He got his grip, had partially mounted the beast's back, when it suddenly plunged beneath the surface of the water, taking him down just as he'd exhaled with his efforts. Water filled his mouth, his nostrils, closed over his head. His body felt instantly empty, a void of air. He tried to free his arms, but whichever way he pulled the animal seemed to twist its head to hold him, to keep them joined. As they plunged deeper, Tagay's arms lost their strength and, in doing so, slipped free. Immediately the stag kicked hard for the surface, leaving him behind.

Light was above him but it seemed such an effort to reach up to it, so he allowed himself just to float toward what he knew he could not reach. Besides, he was beginning to enjoy the way the sun's beams filled the trail of bubbles above him, transforming them into a ladder of air that his limbs were too tired to climb. At its summit, four hooves beat the water, creating new rungs.

Ungrateful beast, he thought, then smiled. An animal did not know gratitude, had no need for any such human trait. And Tagay was losing what made him human, he could feel it, shedding like a stag shed its antlers, merging into the elements that surrounded him, the green water, the yellow light of his land.

Above him, so far away, the beast continued its journey. As it went, it drew shadows in its wake, filling the sky.

Go, brother, Tagay thought, reaching up almost gratefully into the darkness. He had been born again. And all things born must die.

FIVE
WITCH HUNT

The night was still, broken only by the waves on the shore and the sharp cries of a hunting owl. The darkness was intense, for huge clouds had rolled over the sky, blotting out the waxing moon. To the north, downriver, a storm lashed lightning, thunder crashed. Gaka had told her that it was the sound made by a giant bird in the sky, flapping its wings. So far their village had escaped the rain Anne scented in the closeness of the air.

The dark was pierced only by the shifting flames of her fireplace. She had stolen a tiny ember from the hearth, carried it there in one of the bowls, nursed it with kindling then sticks. Her vigil was lonely enough without its little light. No one else had come to watch for the returning hunters. 'They will be here when they are here,' Gaka had said. But no one had her need.

Tagay! She had to tell him of Black Snake, of the danger she was now in. Gaka had warned her to be cautious. Black Snake was a war chief and highly respected, accusations against him would have to have the weight of much evidence behind them – and the word of a group of enamoured boys, who had not really understood what they saw, would not be enough.

She stared out toward the water, blind beyond her flames, listening. They were meant to be back before nightfall; all the other hunting parties had returned with their different kinds of game. Only the venison that the hunters sought on the island was missing from the full moon feast, three days away.

A dog howled in the village above her. She could just hear a faraway voice telling it to hush. A wave reached the shore, bringing a different type of sound, as if something had grounded on the shale. She called out, 'Tagay?' but there was no reply.

A sudden shriek just behind her, had her scrabbling on her knees away from the sound. Looking back in panic, she caught the shadowed outline of spread wings, firelight glimmered on talons, something small wriggling in the heart of the darkness. The owl immediately flew skywards, giving a sharp cry of triumph. She rose, taking deep breaths, trying to follow the bird's soaring shape. Gradually, her heart calmed.

The arm that went around her neck choked off any hope of sound, the weight of the body that pushed her to the earth knocking all air from her lungs.

The arm withdrew, a hand returned, forcing her head into the earth. Her mouth, open and desperate for breath, sucked in mud. Another hand reached round inside her dress, grabbing at her breasts, twisting and pulling.

She got some air, whimpered in pain. The man on her back laughed.

'I knew I would take you, White Cedar. I did not think it would be so soon. And so easy.'

Black Snake rolled her over, so she could see his tattooed face, his hand covering her mouth, his weight still crushing her. She tried to bite, caught a little flesh between her teeth. He took the hand away and, as she took in air to scream, struck her hard across the face. Her cry choked, she tasted blood.

He flipped her again so her front was once more pressed into the earth. She could barely breathe let alone cry out. Both his hands were now free to run over her body. She felt him pull her dress up, past her thighs, up further, then felt him fiddling at his breech cloth. He pulled her up off the ground so her hands were free again, but she had to brace herself to prevent falling back to the earth where he crushed her, where she knew she would faint.

'I know what you want, White Cedar,' he grunted. 'I saw the way you looked at Tagay. I will give you now what he never would. And, since he is dead, he will not be able to, ever again.' He levered himself backwards, his hand reaching up between her legs.

She let her left hand go, so that they both slipped. Her bruised face banged into the ground. Her right hand reached sideways, into flame, a different pain that she pulled to her. Cursing, he jerked her up again, banging her thighs hard into his. For a moment he had to take his own weight to steady them both. That was when she brought her right hand straight up off the ground, past her own face, over her shoulder. The burning end of the stake she clutched caught the side of his head, skittered past his eye, embedded in his nose.

The blow could only be delivered contorted, lacking a fuller force. But he reeled back with a howl, clutching at his face, and his weight shifted off her. In a moment, she was up and stumbling along the beach.

A hand wrapped around her ankle. She slipped onto her hands, kicked back with the other leg. She heard another grunt of pain and then she was running, trying to summon enough air to scream. The best she seemed to be able to manage was a whisper, as if she was held in a nightmare.

'Help! Help me!'

The beach lay just below the village but out of sight, beyond a series of huge boulders. If she could round them, she would be in sight of the guards at the palisade gates and she would not need to scream.

He was coming after her. She could hear his footfalls on the path, getting closer and closer. She didn't look back. Just as she passed the boulders, suddenly she was no longer running but flying, tumbling, rolling along the path. He was on top of her again, a blackness was filling her eyes. Then she heard another voice, different from the harsh croak of Black Snake.

'What happens here? Speak, or I will shoot you down.'

She was looking up into light, into torches held aloft.

'Help me!' she wheezed, and there was someone there, dragging her to her feet, a gate guard, and she pressed against him, while his fellow took a step toward the still prone Black Snake, raising his torch above him.

The warrior was hunched over, his face to the earth. When he raised his head, Anne could see the damage she had done. Blood ran down the side of his face, as if it dripped from the fangs of the snake. Black ash mixed with the red.

As his eyes met hers, he began to howl, an animal scream. She heard noise, then became aware there were words within it, a word she'd never heard and one she had – their word for the magic spirit that lived in all things.

'Oki!' yelled Black Snake, again and again, pointing at Anne, as more people ran from the gates, clutching weapons, more torches. Soon a crowd had gathered in the suddenly bright night, forming a semi-circle around the howling man and the woman still slumped against the guard.

The line of people opened and Chief Tangled emerged. At the sight of him, Black Snake fell to his side, and began to jerk and toss on the ground.

'What does this mean, Tawane? What of the hunt? Where are the others?'

The jerking stopped long enough for one tattooed arm to be raised. It pointed straight at Anne. Then the man spoke the word that Anne had not understood, that he had been alternating with 'Oki'.

'Ontatekiahta,' he said and fell back to the earth to shake.

Immediately, the guard who was supporting Anne against himself pushed her away. She fell toward the line of villagers who gave ground before her.

'What does he say?' She looked from one face to the next. Getting no response, she shouted, 'He ... attacked me. I ... I do not know your word for it. He wanted to take me, as a man takes a woman, but I did not want it. I had to fight.'

There was a muttering, then, the eyes shifting back to the prone man. His jerking suddenly stopped and he sat up, his eyes rolling around before settling again on Anne.

'Yes, I attacked her. But not because I wanted her like a man. I attacked her because she has cursed me. She cursed our hunt. She brought disaster to it. All the hunters are dead. All! Because of her curse.' At this, cries burst from the people, of anger, of dismay. Someone began to wail. Raising his hand again, he pointed to Anne but away from her face, to her side. 'She has an Oki there, in her pouch. It is the remains of an Ontatekiahta from her land across the Great Water. She has used it to bring her evil to us.'

Anne suddenly realized the only thing the word could mean. She screamed out, 'It's not true!' but her cry was lost in the shouts of the people. Most of them backed away still further but the two guards, on an order from Chief Tangled, grabbed her. Rough hands tore the deer skin bag from her belt, fingers fumbled for the drawstring. It was inverted and shaken upside down.

The hand fell onto the earth. It landed palm down. All could see its six skeletal fingers.

A woman, one who had been wailing loudly, ran forward and struck Anne hard across the face, another woman followed, and soon blows were falling from every side. She went to her knees, where kicks were aimed at her. So many came, she was unable to do much to protect herself.

Then, as suddenly as the attack began, it stopped. Tangled had given a command, and the women fell back. The two gate guards bent, lifted her up.

'This is not the time for justice. This is not how we judge,' he thundered, staring down any who looked back at him. 'Tomorrow all the wise men of our tribe will be gathered. We will decide this matter then. I will take her Oki for I do not fear any Ontatekiahta of the Pale Thieves. She will have no power here.'

He picked up the skeletal hand. Groans issued from all around him.

'Now, put her in the cage where the dogs for eating are kept. Watch her. Even without her Oki she may be dangerous. Do not talk to her or breathe near her. If she speaks, beat her. Otherwise, leave her alone.' He glowered at the faces around him. 'I have spoken.'

As she was picked up under her arms and dragged away, Anne caught sight of Gaka standing amongst the rest, saw the old woman shake her head and put a finger to her lips. As she went, the people followed her through the village gates, chanting the word she had not known before, that she knew, only too well, the meaning of now.

'Ontatekiahta! Ontatekiahta! Ontatekiahta!' they chanted.

'Witch! Witch! Witch!'

He had built the fire in the lee of a huge, overhanging rock, a small shelter from the rain. The worst of the sudden summer storm had passed over them, thunder rumbling away to the east now. But it had hit while he was still on the water, wrestling with the unstable craft, great spears of lightning arcing into the landfall he sought. One bolt had struck a tree, transforming it into an instant inferno, a beacon on the shore. He accepted this sign from God, turned the canoe toward its safety, for it was known that lightning did not strike the same spot twice. Also, the man he'd pulled from the river was blue-cold and since he had neither flints nor one of the native fire starters, a tree in flames seemed a good place to seek warmth.

Now Thomas stared at the youth, whose knees were drawn up to his chest, arms wrapped round them, lying under the deerskin Thomas had snatched from the village. Redness had displaced the icy blue of his cheek. The shuddering breaths had stopped. He had even begun to mumble a little, his head moving back and forth, driven by some dream; perhaps there was a fever building. But Thomas preferred that to the frozen stillness he had thought meant he had arrived too late.

'God's will,' he muttered, shrugging deeper into his heavy black cloak, as another cascade of thunder ran down the heavens. He saw more lightning strike the opposite shore, probably close to the village he'd come from. Maybe the rain was keeping them inside their lodges. Perhaps he hadn't been missed yet. They seemed to pay him little attention, while they had taken Gianni Rombaud to their warrior hearts.

The mumbling of the man across the fire grew louder. Words that Thomas could not understand but recognized as the native tongue came pouring out, interspersed with words in French, words that chilled as much as the rain. Shivering, Thomas tossed another log onto the flame.

Tagay was fighting demons in his dreams. They weighted his chest down with giant rocks, forcing the air from his body. They burned him with hot irons, slashed him with rusted swords. Then, suddenly, hands were upon him, tattooed, iron-strong, unbreakable. He was stripped, turned over, his legs were forced apart . . .

'Anne-edda,' he screamed, leaping back from the flames that burned him, from the hands that reached for him, crashing into hard rock walls. A shape rose from the other side of the fire, spreading huge black wings.

'Demon!' Tagay cried, trying to burrow back into unyielding stone, his legs scrabbling in the shale. Then, they gave way and he fell, covering his face with his arms, awaiting the touch of this Devil who had dragged him to hell.

'Tagay.' The voice that reached him was gentle, spoke in French. 'That is your name, isn't it?'

Through the crossbars of his arms, Tagay looked out at the shape that folded its wings now and sank back to the ground. The demon had a human face, with grey streaked through the black hair and beard.

'What Devil are you?' His voice quavered.

'Thomas Lawley is my name.'

'A fallen angel?'

A smile came. 'All too human. Otherwise I could raise a mightier fire than this.' He gestured to the flames before him. 'Nonetheless, it is all we have and you look cold. Come closer, friend.'

Tagay had begun to shake again, and not just with fear. But he did not move. 'Is this not hell, then? Am I not drowned?'

'It is not and you were not. Come to the warmth and I will explain.'

Tagay, shaking badly now, stumbled forward, fell. In an instant, Thomas had plucked the cloak from his own shoulders, draped it over the younger man's.

'Calm, my friend. And drink this.' He handed over a flask. Tagay took a sip, spluttered. 'Brandy? How do you have it here?'

'It is the last from the ship, the one that followed you from St Malo.'

Tagay took another gulp, a fire he craved spreading down his chest. 'How . . .?' he began.

Thomas explained as simply as he could, Tagay listening in amazed silence, his eyes widening as he heard of the pursuit across the ocean, their capture by the tattooed warriors, Gianni's part in the hunt ambush, Thomas's concern about Gianni's plans. How Thomas had followed the war party, watched the empty canoe float past, then the two bearing pursuing warriors. How he had started to paddle the other way, in hope.

Tagay took another sip from the flask. 'And how did I not drown? The stag drove me to the depths, I could not get back up.'

'It was the stag that led me to you. Otherwise I wouldn't have seen you in the water. You came to the surface and somehow I pulled you in without capsizing the boat. I thought you were dead. But I once ministered to fishermen in Portugal and knew a little of what to do. Once you had thrown up the water, you fainted. I still thought you would die from the cold.'

'But I am alive.' Tagay held up a shaking hand, looked at it in wonder. 'The gods have spared me.'

'God has,' Thomas corrected. 'And the love of Jesus Christ. He is not called Saviour for nothing. For did not He walk upon the waves? In emulation of His love, He brought me to this place. Perhaps that's why – to save you.'

'Is that why you came, Thomas Lawley? Was it not to take back the Oki of the queen?'

Suddenly, in the simplicity of the question, Thomas knew. It was like the world lit, but for a moment, by lightning, then staying on in the solid flame before him, just as this fire had. It wasn't the Jesuit cause, Christ's work, his master's desire for the weapon of Anne Boleyn's hand. All those were simply excuses to obscure, even from himself, the true reason he was there.

'In truth – I came for Anne Rombaud.'

And saying it, he knew, as if a veil had been ripped away. There it was – clear, pristine, made up of every moment he'd seen her. From the very first, when she'd floated by him, loosely tethered to a cart leaving conquered Siena; when she'd run forward to stop her brother burning heretics on Tower Green; her interrogation in that same Tower, when she'd laid healing hands upon his agony; the greater agony of watching her sail past the harbour mouth of St Malo and he thought he'd never see her again.

So few moments, such little time to effect a conversion.

But wasn't St Paul converted in one moment, in a lightning stroke, heading to Damascus?

Lightning sought land across the river and Thomas saw, in the forked flame, the truth of his confession.

The man on the other side of the fire heard the words, that truth in them. Something surged within him, similar to the surge he'd felt lying under a canoe, hearing Black Snake's plans for Anne. In these two men's utterly different desires for her, he suddenly and completely remembered his own.

He staggered up. 'Anne. I must . . . I must go to her.' He took a few weak steps. 'Where am I?'

Thomas was beside him in a moment. 'Sit, friend. I do not think you would get very far now.'

'But she is in great danger.'

'Then sit, and we will talk of how to best help her.'

Tagay allowed himself to be guided back down. Thomas handed him the flask again, then pulled, from a pocket in his cloak, some of the flat bread studded with dried fruits that the tribeswomen baked on stones. Choking on it at first, Tagay gradually managed to swallow some. Between each bite, he told the story of the threat to Anne as he had overheard it.

Thomas fought down his own immediate desire to emulate Tagay's, to take again to the canoe and paddle to Anne's rescue. He had barely made it across the river to where he was now. In the dark, with a man who had only just survived drowning, it was impossible.

Breathing to calm himself, he said, 'We must wait till the light comes, when you are a little recovered. Then perhaps we can take this boat to your village.'

Tagay was looking out to the river as if for the first time. Lightning again lit up the far shore. 'Wait,' he said. 'Are we on the northern banks of the water?'

'Yes. I found you nearly halfway across. We could not return to the island with the war party there.'

'But that means we are in the land of the Tahontaenrat, my people.' He stared upstream, as if his eyes could pierce the darkness, the walls of rain. 'We have pathways that go the length of this shore, so runners can bear messages to all of our scattered tribe. All we have to do is find the path. We can run to the village.'

He began to rise. But even the weight of Thomas's arm laid gently on his was enough to pull him back down.

'You would not get a hundred paces tonight. You must sleep and pray for strength to rise up with the sun.' As Tagay began to protest, he added, 'She is among your people, is she not? Surely she will be safe till the morning?'

Tagay nodded, reluctant. But the Englishman was right; he would not get far tonight. And he would be of no use to Anne if he died trying to find a trail in the dark.

'With the dawn then,' he said. He lay down and, as sleep took him, mumbled, 'We will run to rescue her.'

Thomas smiled, stretched out his knee, rubbed its soreness. What he needed was Anne's healing touch upon it but even with that he knew that his days of running were long past. Inept though he was with a canoe, it was his only means away from there.

Shivering, he eyed the cloak spread over Tagay with envy, then resignation. Charity was the Jesuit way, after all. Curling up on the opposite side of the fire, he thought he would be unable to sleep, driven by wonder, by his need to contemplate the words that had coalesced around his visions of Anne. But he had underestimated the effect of his exertions. Soon, two snores duetted above the snapping of flames and a beautiful, clear dawn came and went, undetected by either man.

Tagay used the last of the embers to burn the tobacco. It was still damp, despite his efforts to dry it out, and took a while to catch. When it finally did, he piled the burning shreds of leaves on top of Donnaconna's stone, inhaled the sweet fumes, and uttered a prayer.

When he opened his eyes, Thomas was before him again, having returned from the canoe.

'This was my uncle's Oki,' he said, holding up the stone with its distinctive even lines. 'His lucky spirit. I have asked for blessing upon my journey.'

'It's a similar smell to the incense we use in Church.' Thomas inhaled, then smiled. 'And has a similar effect. As for asking blessings . . . I wonder if your Donnaconna and Saint Christopher, to whom I just prayed, are so very different.'

Tagay stood. 'It is you who are different. You are unlike any priest of your faith I have ever met.'

'But I am not a priest, Tagay. I am a Jesuit. I have taken vows to my order but have never been ordained.'

'Well.' Tagay looked at the black-grey hair of the man, at the pale blue eyes, then remembered the other reason he did not think him priest-like – his words from the night before, the feeling in them when he had spoken of Anne.

'I will go,' he said. His moccasins had been sucked away in the

352

river, but his feet had hardened in the time he had been back in his land. His breech cloth was also lost, so the only covering his body had was the hide belt and the deer skin pouch that contained Donnaconna's Oki. In one hand he clutched an ash staff whose sharpened end he had fashioned with the Jesuit's knife.

'Are you sure you don't want this?' Thomas held out the small blade to him. At the shake of his head he held up the cloak. 'Or this?'

Tagay smiled. 'Are you afraid that Anne will see me naked and forget you?'

Thomas's smile in return was sad. 'I am sure she does not even remember who I am. No, I just want to help you get back to her.'

'Then let me run with nothing but my Oki and my spear. If they help me, and I am not eaten by wolf or bear, I could get there by the middle of the day. Ask your spirits to help me do that.' He tipped the shaft once in salute and disappeared between two trees.

'Go with God, my friend,' Thomas said, adding, 'and may both your Oki and Saint Christopher watch over you.' Crossing himself, he turned and made for the canoe.

Tagay followed a deer track up into the forest. In his time spent with the Bear clan in the lands above the cliffs, they had taught him to look for the smallest of paths, but even so he nearly missed it. Bending over a muddy patch, he saw the faintest imprint of a human foot, its edges blurred by rainfall. Runners, looking for any who had been scattered by the burning of the outlying villages, must have passed this way, and recently. Otetian had boasted how runners like himself could traverse half the country in a day, because they never stopped for a rest.

'Otetian,' he said to the forest. The man had saved his life, so that he could take the warning to the tribe of their betrayal. 'Anne.' The woman who had fallen to the earth to lead him to that tribe. The woman he had ignored in his quest to return to it.

Otetian. Anne.

Chanting their names under his breath, Tagay began to

run south through the forest. For the first little while, his legs were weak, making him stumble. Gradually, he felt them settle and he hit his stride, the words melding into one inside his head.

Ote-Anne. Ote-Anne. Ote-Anne.

SIX

TRIALS

The cage was one of three set near the trenches dug for human waste. Made of saplings lashed together with woven reed, it was just tall enough for the dogs it had lately contained to stand and thus not for her. They had moved the former inhabitants to the cages on either side and there had been a near continuous snapping and growling since. The dogs in these cages may have been old, or lame or simply bred for the pot, but they were still territorial.

The stench was appalling. Anne had managed to use an old bone to rake a little area clear for her to sit in. But excrement was piled up on all sides. The rains that had come in the night had done little to wash it away and the summer sun, now nearing its zenith, had returned to the new washed sky, ripening the floor she sat on, striping her through the bars in burning lines. Flies droned ceaselessly, some leaving the feast of ordure to feast on her.

No one came near her. There was no water now, for she had drunk the murky contents of the one bowl left there hours before. Once, she had looked up to see Do-ne limping toward her, flask in hand. But his mother had followed him and jerked him away, doing something Anne had never seen in her entire time in the village, beating the child as she dragged him, whimpering, by one arm out of sight.

Such is the terror I inspire, she thought.

She had wept then, silently, her head folded down upon her hunched knees. Despair took her. Tagay was dead. Betrayed somehow, she felt sure, by the tattooed man who was her accuser. And even though Tagay had turned away from her since their

355

arrival, the feeling she had since the first moment she saw him remained – the only man she could love was dead. And she was to be tried for a witch, the very accusation that had condemned the queen she had now failed. She had betrayed the cause her father, Jean Rombaud, had died for. And she, who had led him to that death, was about to die too, condemned for her visions, the arrogant belief that she had the one and only answer – to take the hand to a world where such evil did not exist. But evil was everywhere. She remembered her mother's words, the night in Montalcino when Beck had begged her not to join a quest that had already destroyed her family.

You want to stop evil, daughter? Then do not go to France to seek it out. It begins there, at our front door and it runs from there through all the world.

She had come much further than France to realize the truth of those words. And the vision of the mother she'd never see again brought more tears.

She heard shuffling steps and, through the mist of her eyes, she saw Gaka.

'Get away from me, Aunt,' she cried. 'I am lost and they will beat you for talking to me.'

With some effort, the old lady bent and finally sat on the ground near Anne.

'They will not beat me, child. They know I am so old that one blow could send me to the Village of the Dead.' She pulled out a flask and thrust it through the bars. Anne gulped the cool water down. 'And the rest follow close behind me to take you before the elders. Ayee' – she waved her hand before her face, wrinkling her nose – 'you have not chosen a clean lodge house for your rest, child.'

Anne returned the empty flask. 'What will happen to me, Aunt?'

Gaka sighed. 'It is very serious. Even if you murdered someone, you would not die for it. You would have to appease the family of your victim, with gifts, with service. Our tribe only kills its own for two causes – betrayal of the people to our enemies. And witchcraft. Usually there is no meeting of all for this, the witch is accused in secret and if the elders judge the person guilty they are secretly killed. But it is different for you.'

'Different? Why?'

'The accusation was made before the whole tribe, so you could not be killed secretly without everyone knowing the reason. And you are not one of the people, no matter how well you speak our tongue – a gift some already say proves you are a witch, for no Pale Thief has spoken like you. The tribe saw you accused. The tribe want to see you condemned. This is bad and good.'

Anne leaned till her head touched the wooden slats. 'How?'

'Bad because many of the women, especially those whose husbands went on the hunt, have already condemned you. They beat you before and want to share in your killing now.'

'And the good?' Anne asked, her voice a whisper.

Gaka smiled. 'I can be there.' She rose shakily as they heard the buzz of approaching people. A chant came.

'Heh-ah, heh-ah, heh-ah, he-hah!'

She looked down and a finger came through into the cage, just reaching the end of Anne's nose, stroking it.

'There is hope in this, White Cedar. I am one of the leaders of the Awataerohi, the Healing Circle. Many people who are sick are cured by our ceremonies, by the summoning of our Oki. I have cured many here and they respect me so they will listen when I speak for you. If I can show Black Snake is sick with some spirit and that made him accuse you falsely, then perhaps I can save you.'

'But he tried to take me by force, twice.' Anne had risen to her knees. 'Is that not enough?'

'They will say your witchcraft made him do it. It would prove his truth, not yours because everyone knows how Black Snake loves the woman who adopted him when he was a prisoner so that he would not die.'

The chant came again, louder, nearer.

'Heh-ah, heh-ah, heh-ah, he-hah!'

Then six figures ran round the corner of the lodge. Their bodies were human, streaked with ochre paint in swirling patterns. Their loins were barely covered with a thin band of hide, their backs bore each a frayed and tattered deerskin. But they had the faces of devils, were fully covered by a mask of red cedar bark – huge eyes painted above a beak-nose, a shrieking mouth with a lolling pink tongue thrust from the side, the whole slashed from one side to the other with deep black furrows. What looked like real hair hung in long shanks down either side to the shoulders. In their right hands each clutched a rattle fashioned from a turtle's shell.

'Gagosa,' Gaka said. 'The False Faces. Demon hunters.'

The masked men approached, almost in step, chanting their chant, shaking their rattles. Gaka moved aside, as the men formed a circle and danced around the cage, first one way, then the other. After three turns they stopped, all the masks lowered, painted eyes studying her. Then the False Face who had stopped closest struck the cage near her head with his rattle. Instantly, the others moved around it, levering out the pegs that held it to the ground. With the final one gone they ripped the cage from its place. Muscled, painted arms reached for her, dragged her to her feet. With a man either side and holding her tight she was half-carried, half-dragged through the village. But no one had gathered to witness her progress and the open space within the main gates, which could have held a crowd, was deserted. Only two men waited there, young men who Anne recognized from Gaka's lodge, both grandsons.

The aunt had struggled to keep up with the demon hunters. Now she sank gratefully into a chair basket that her two grandsons produced.

'I will follow. They take you to the game field. The village is swollen with all those who have fled the burning of their villages. It is the only land where all can watch.'

Anne scarcely heard the last words. The men had begun to run, her legs dragging, passing her on as each pair of bearers tired. This transfer happened more often on the cliff path, especially near the top. But those who were not doing the carrying had begun to chant again: 'Heh-ah, heh-ah, heh-ah, he-hah!' As they neared the summit, Anne heard that chant echoing from above her. Then she realized it wasn't an echo but the voices of all the Tahontaenrat, awaiting the arrival of the witch.

The giant circle was triple ranked – the children and the old sat at the front, the women standing behind them, their men at the back. When Anne emerged from the shadow of the oak where she and Tagay had first been discovered, the tribe's chorus swelled to a roar that continued as the ranks parted to admit her. The False

Faces carried her to the very centre of the circle, dropped her there, and all save one retired to squat before the rank of the elders, a solid group of some forty men.

She tried to stand, to face them, but her legs were still weak from the night spent in the cage and she slipped down again onto one knee. The one False Face who had stayed began to dance around, raising the turtle shell rattle on high then bringing it down to hover over the ground, hopping from one foot to the other, turning in half circles, gradually swooping closer and closer. She tried to look him straight in the painted face, to show that she did not fear him but he did not stay still for long, moving to different parts of her body, sniffing exaggeratedly with the huge nose, letting out long sighs of disgust.

She followed him around in a circle, pivoting on her knee. Behind him, back toward the cliffs, she saw the crowd open again and Gaka was carried into the circle. She was set down in her basket chair, then rose unsteadily on the arm of one of her grandsons. He helped her across toward Anne. At her approach, the False Face span away, still making his noises of revulsion.

'Will you tell him that he'd smell that way if he'd spent the night in a dog cage?' Anne hissed at Gaka.

'Ssh, child. Listen.' Gaka was looking past her.

Tangled the Chief had stepped forward from the throng of elders. His brow was encircled with a snakeskin braid, his grey hair combed and parted on either side of his face. Around his neck hung length after length of shells, the wampum so prized among his people, the number and size a sure sign of his status. In his right hand he held an elaborately carved and polished staff, faces both human and animal lining its length, crowned with a spray of eagle feathers. He raised this over the crowd, describing a full circle in the air. Then he recited the names of the chiefs present who had come from afar, who honoured them with their presence. It was a long list, especially as each affiliation was named, of family, clan, village. He spoke of why the summons had gone out and that important business must be discussed that day in the council. He concluded by saying that before they could discuss any of this, there was another matter that had to be dealt with. He moved forward again toward Anne. It was only when he stopped a few paces away that she saw what he'd held, till then, behind his back.

Tangled stooped and placed the skeletal hand on the ground before her.

'There it is,' he said, and there was a touch of sadness in his voice as he spoke now. 'Do not touch it, or you will die.' Anne was aware of two men raising bows behind the chief. 'Prove to us that this Oki was not brought here to do us great harm.'

As she finally forced her legs to obey her and raised herself to her feet, there was an immediate clamour. From her right, Black Snake burst out of the circle and ran towards them. He covered half the distance and then fell, but in a way Anne thought immediately was false. He crawled along for a few paces then stood again and staggered forward, groaning all the while. When he was the same distance to the side of her that Tangled was in front, he dropped to his knees, spread his arms wide and cried out, 'Do not hurt me any more, White Cedar. Free me from your curse.'

The False Face ran toward the warrior, shoving Anne to the side, his deep voice coming from beneath the mask.

'Tell us how she curses you, Tawane. How did she trap you in her snare?'

The tattooed man swayed, seemed about to fall, then straightened again. Raising one arm, he pointed along the ground.

'She came to me where I slept in my lodge. I felt her tongue touching me and I woke. She was in the form of a snake that slithered along the ground and into my ear. She said, "You could be like me, Black Snake of the Wolf clan, all powerful. Tangled is old and no longer a warrior. We need you to fight off the People of the Great Hill. Only you, who were born among the Tattooed Ones, can defeat them." So she spoke!'

'This was a dream, Tawane.' Gaka had stepped forward, her voice carrying to all despite her frailty. 'Some warriors grumbled that Tangled was old and they needed a warrior to lead them. You were dreaming their grumbles.'

There was some muttering of assent at this. Many had heard the fighting men complain that Tangled had restrained them from attack.

'No! For she came to me again the next night. She was in her own face but her body was not ugly and pale and scrawny like she is now – she took on the same beautiful shape as my wife, Gasoowano. She took off her bead dress and said, "My Oki will help us to get a son to lead the Tahontaenrat. Come, here, here!" she said, and her hand was cold like bones. But I ran away from her and her Oki.'

A woman stepped from the crowd. 'It is true. Ever since she came to the village my husband Tawane has been tormented with dreams of her. We have daughters only and she promised him a son.' She began to weep and threw herself back into the arms of her family near her in the circle.

Gaka said, 'It is another dream you have had. Let me and the Awataerohi cure you of this. It is not White Cedar's Oki that torments you, but your own.'

Black Snake spoke again. 'It was her, old woman. I know because she came a third time, not at night, and it could not have been a dream. It was the day we set off for the hunt. She led me down to the stream, and she was ugly like you see her now and she pulled up her bead dress and went on arms and knees before me and turned and said, "If you do not take me, Black Snake, and give me a son, my Oki will curse the hunt you go on. You will be the deer and all of you will die." And I said, "Not Tagay, my brother, who brought you to us?" And she said, "He will die first."' Black Snake let out a cry filled with pain. 'And my brother Tagay was the first to die and then all the others, one by one, and I only escaped because I am a strong warrior and because I did not lie with her as she asked me to do.'

There were more screams. Two of the women who had lost husbands on the hunt had to be restrained from running forward. When the uproar calmed, Gaka spoke again.

'Tagay was my nephew, the last of the Hunters of the Sunrise and he spoke to me of how White Cedar fell from the sky to help him . . .'

'She bewitched him too!' False Face had leapt before Gaka. 'Her Oki is evil, it comes from a powerful she-devil across the Great Water who has been driven out of her land and seeks to rule us here.'

'It is not true.' The argument had been building in speed, in intensity, and Anne was finding it harder to understand the sing-song voices. But she heard, clearly, the pronouncement of the queen as evil. So she said, 'This woman was powerful, yes, and a ruler. But she was a woman of honour. And men tried to take her ... Oki to do evil. My father died to save it. I thought I could bring it to the land Tagay told me of, to bury it where it might be safe.'

Her last words were drowned in the surge of noise. 'Why should we believe her words?' False Face's deep voice and shaken rattle gradually quieted the crowd. 'We have the evidence of her Oki, which she hid from us till Black Snake found it. This is the Black Snake whose lodge poles are lined with the scalps of our enemy, who used to be his people. We need no further proof of his loyalty than that he will kill his old brothers and uncles for his new brothers and uncles. But her ...?' He paused, and turned around the entire circle, taking his time, so all could see his painted eyes. 'Tagay who brought her here is dead. Black Snake who fights for us is bewitched. We need no more proof. We must smash her head, scatter her bones, burn her hair. Leave no trace of her and her witch's Oki on our land. That is my thought on the subject. Is there anyone who can disagree?'

The silence returned. Gaka opened her mouth but no words came. She looked around, shook her head, looked down, away from the young woman who stood there with the remains of a queen before her and the certainty of death in her heart.

Then a voice came, ending the silence.

'I can.'

The words seemed to float away on the wind. When they returned, they returned stronger.

'I can disagree. For this woman is innocent. And Black Snake is a lying traitor.'

Everyone in the circle looked up and down it to see who had spoken. Anne looked at Gaka who looked back. False Face stepped toward the nearest of the crowd, as did Black Snake, daring the speaker to speak again. It was Do-ne, through the tears that had come when Anne's death looked certain, who raised his eyes above them all now.

'Tagay!' he cried, pointing to a branch of the huge oak tree. And there, just where the Tahontaenrat had seen him for the first time, stood the Hunter of the Sunrise.

He had run throughout the day. He had stopped only to drink from streams and, once, to eat the dried fruit bread the Englishman had given him. There were times when his legs became like stone, others when they felt hollow, like reeds. At these times he would fix his eyes on the ground ahead of his feet and chant the name that had become one – Ote-Anne. Soon the feelings in his legs would pass and he'd feel he could run till the last sunrise.

Sometimes the path drove deep through the heart of the forest, at others he would be running along clifftops with a view of the great river. He recognized the island where the hunt had met its doom, other landmarks as he got closer. He resisted the desire to increase his pace. He could not allow that he would be too late, it would turn his legs again to reed. He had to believe he would arrive in time.

Ote-Anne.

The moment he ran into the deserted village was one of near despair. Then he remembered arriving here – *could it only be nine days ago?* The village deserted like this, his tribe gathered above for the Game.

The cliff trail hurt, his legs now feeling the leagues he had run. Voices carried by the wind drove him on and when he glimpsed human backs at the end of the forest path he thought he would burst straight into the middle of the gathering. Then a word came to him and the word slowed him to a walk. It was Ontatekiahta. Witch. He stopped, heard the distinctive throaty accent of Black Snake speaking lies. Heard Gaka's voice, then Anne's, quavering, yet determined.

He had climbed into the tree to hear more. When he had heard enough, he spoke.

Anne saw Tagay and her legs, which had kept her upright to face her accusers, collapsed again. She was on her knees, staring up, the tears that she'd held off streaming down her cheeks. Gaka was beside her but sitting, slumped down in wonder. Others were on the ground too but in terror – for most had believed that Tagay now lived in the Village of the Dead. So it had to be an unhappy soul standing in the tree, returned to seek vengeance.

After the boy, Do-ne, had cried his name, no one spoke, no

one moved except to sink to the ground. It was Chief Tangled who finally stepped forward. He was the leader both spiritual and earth-bound. If this was a vengeful spirit of the dead, Tangled would seek to return it to darkness. If Tagay was alive, he would confront the different challenge that fact, and his words, presented.

'Speak again, Tagay, or Tagay's shade, whichever you are. What is it you have to say of what we discuss here?'

'I say again – Black Snake is a liar and a traitor. White Cedar is innocent of all she is accused and I . . .' Tagay paused. 'I am no ghost but a man and alive.'

'Then come down and join our council, Tagaynearguye. Speak to us as a man.'

Tagay bowed and swiftly descended the tree, the crowd opening a wide gap for him to pass through. He walked straight to the centre of the circle, took his place beside Anne, stretching out a hand to her. She reached up and grasped it, rose. Joined, they turned to face their enemy.

Black Snake had watched Tagay's progress from the tree with the same open-jawed shock as had greeted his appearance. Only now, seeing him linked with the object of his lust and hate, did his voice return. And with it, his cunning.

'Tagay, brother!' His face formed into the unaccustomed lines of a smile. 'I give thanks to the Great Mother, Ataentsic, that you survived. I tried to rescue you when I saw you fall but the enemy were too strong.' He turned to Tangled, but raised his voice so all could hear. 'Then I remembered the danger to our tribe and how the tribe must learn of the disaster. It is only for that reason that I left the battle, to bring you the news. And to tell you of this witch's curse that led us into the trap.'

'Black Snake lies and crawls like the serpent he is named for.' Tagay's words brought all murmurs to silence. He went on. 'It was he who led the hunters into the snare and he has joined with the people of his birth, the warriors who are painted like him, to lead the Tahontaenrat into a greater snare.' He raised his arm, pointed straight into the curling snake around the warrior's eye. 'I lay hidden and heard him plot our destruction. He will lead the Nundawaono against us the sunrise after the full moon.'

Nothing could stop the uproar that followed. Warriors,

women, old and young rushed forward. Black Snake ran at Tagay screaming, 'Lies!' but the mob intervened. Clans coalesced around their war chiefs. When Tangled and the other elders had finally restored order, Tagay found Sada beside him, and he and Anne protected by a human wall of the Bear clan. Facing them, surrounding their war chief, was a wall of Wolf. Bone knives appeared in hands, war clubs were snatched from their slings.

Tangled raised his staff of office high and spoke. 'These are difficult matters. The truth of them is hidden in dark clouds of thunder. The only thing the clouds show us for certain is that a storm is coming. And you' – he gestured with his stick at both groups of warriors – 'you are our only protection against this storm. What protection will you be if clan fights clan, brother kills brother? How the Tattooed people would rejoice at that!'

The two clans looked to their leaders. Sada nodded and knives were returned to their hidden places. Black Snake continued to glare but his followers swiftly, and with some relief, also put up their weapons. They may have been members of the Wolf clan but facing them were half-brothers, cousins, friends.

Satisfied, Tangled spoke again. 'What is clear in these clouds is that two of our people have told different stories. Who are we to believe? One was not born to us but has proved himself a loyal son since he was adopted. The other is born of our flesh, our spirit, but has grown up away from our world, away from our songs and stories. But this is not a disagreement about beaver skins. It is not a dispute over reparations made for a killing. This is the life of the tribe. Are we being led to destruction by an evil spirit?' He pointed the staff at Anne. 'Or is White Cedar innocent as Tagay says? Who we choose to believe, Wolf or Bear, could decide if the Tahontaenrat live or die.' He paused and took the time to sweep his eyes over the whole circle of his people, before he continued. 'If we had more time we could debate this in council and perhaps wise minds could penetrate the thunderclouds. But the full moon is two days away. Can anyone see a solution to this?'

He looked again at all his people. Eyes averted, heads lowered. No one spoke for a long moment. Then Black Snake did.

'I have a solution,' he said. 'Let Taviscaran and Iouskaha decide who lies.'

A voice called out, 'Yes, the Twins!' Another followed it, then another, till everyone's voice was lifted, crying out the two names.

Anne saw Sada shift, unease on his face, felt Tagay's grip tighten on her hand. She shouted above the swell of noise. 'What does this mean, Tagay?'

'I am not sure. The Twins are sons of the Earth Mother, Ataentsic, but . . .' He faltered.

Sada leaned in. 'They were the first men, the only ones,' he said. 'One good, one evil. They fought and the blood from their wounds created much that you see in the world.' He raised his voice as the clamour around them grew. 'When the truth cannot be resolved between two warriors, when all argument and debate fails, they must become like the Twins. They must fight. One must die. I have witnessed it only once in my life and then I was a child.'

Anne gasped. 'Trial by combat!'

Tagay nodded. 'It seems that the Tahontaenrat share more than Cain and Abel with your people.'

Anne pulled him to her. 'Tagay! You cannot fight him. You are not a warrior trained as he is.'

Tagay turned to Sada. 'Do I have a choice?'

The smaller man shrugged. 'If you acknowledge he is right.'

'So – no choice at all then.'

'Tagay!' Anne tried to retain the hand he was pulling away. But he withdrew it, gently, and stepped forward, as Tangled finally brought the crowd again to silence.

'Tagay. Do you understand what Black Snake proposes?'

'I do.'

'And are you willing to submit to the judgement of the Twin Gods?'

Tagay looked at Anne, at Sada, at the identical look on both their faces. Then he turned back.

'I am.'

'Tomorrow then. Just before the sunrise, so that whoever is slain will die in honour of the War God, Ondoutaet, he who rises in the sun. Here on this field, before the whole of the tribe. I have spoken.'

The mob, with a shout, swept away, began to stream back to the cliff path, all save the clans who gathered around the two men. Anne was separated from Tagay by a wall of warriors. She looked for him, as his face came and went from her view. So concerned was she with keeping him in sight that she didn't feel, for a while, the tugging of her hand.

'Here,' Gaka was saying, 'here.'

Anne looked down. In her hand was another.

'I saved it from the crowd. Keep it safe.'

She looked down at the skeleton, the six fingers. The touch gave her no sense, as it had so long ago, in that distant Tower, that world away, of the person the hand belonged to. She addressed her namesake, nonetheless.

'Anne Boleyn,' she said. 'Oh, my lady. Is another man to die for you now?'

SEVEN

SACRIFICE AT SUNRISE

It was a succession of storms. The one that had guided Thomas to a lightning lit landfall and the saving of Tagay's life had passed. A clear day had intervened, bright summer's brief return. But that evening the air grew closer again, hummed and crackled with power. Thunder rode the sky, its deep explosions drawing the storm ever nearer. But somehow the rain always seemed to fall elsewhere.

Thomas was having difficulty sleeping anyway. He had returned, reluctantly, to the Nundawaono village, though his desire to paddle to Anne, to aid Tagay in her rescue, had been almost irresistible. Calm thought persuaded him otherwise, for a stranger arriving at a village going to war would be likely to achieve little except death. For now, he was better off near the man he'd been yoked to, like a reluctant coach horse.

Gianni Rombaud. However much Thomas disapproved of his methods, one thing was certain – his determination to achieve his ends was unshakeable. If anyone was going to get Anne back, it was her brother.

Throwing back the deerskin that covered him, Thomas moved out into night. The storm was coming in from the north-west, from the opposite shore. It drew him down a little path to the water. There was a smaller beach there, away from the main bay now covered with the canoes of the tribe and their gathering allies. More chance to be alone. To think. To pray.

He would not get that solitude. One boat was drawn up on this less accessible beach, a fire before it. It was the rowboat from the *Breath of St Etienne*, grounded on the shore, parallel to the water's edge but wedged up so it appeared to float on land. Crouched in its bow was Gianni Rombaud.

He had heard the footsteps, even recognized them, for the sound of European boots on the path was very different from the soft fall of a moccasin. But Gianni didn't stop in his preparations. He didn't have much time, if this storm finally brought some rain.

He had carefully measured the saltpetre, sulphur and charcoal, mixed it, wrapped it in a page torn from his Bible – God's work in God's words – then rammed it down the falcon's muzzle. Now he crammed in such pieces of metal as he could spare. Fronchard, the ship's sailmaker and gunner, had been reluctant to give him any of the remaining three-pound shot. They might need them on the return voyage. But Gianni had scavenged an impressive amount of scrap metal, dismantling the hoops of barrels, stripping an old kettle. He wouldn't use too much now. This was just practice after all.

The Jesuit halted a few paces away. Gianni ignored him, squinted along the weapon. In the sky the loudness of the storm showed the centre was getting ever closer.

'Do you really think this is necessary?'

The Jesuit's tone was calm, measured as always. As ever it annoyed Gianni but he kept his temper. He was in too good a mood.

'Necessary? Oh, I think so, yes. It brings me a step closer to my victory.'

He moved to the front of the gun raising a fire-brand carelessly near to look down the barrel.

Thomas winced. 'You'll blow yourself up.'

Gianni chuckled. 'No. Only my enemies.'

'And who are they exactly? It's become unclear to me.'

Gianni moved back into the boat, checked the grooved runners, beaten from barrel hoops, that he'd fixed onto the craft's front bench. The small weapon's wheels would run along them, allowing for its slight recoil. A thunderclap burst nearly overhead. They could feel the downward pressure. 'My enemies? Anyone who prevents me getting what I desire. Anyone.' For the first time, he looked up.

Thomas returned the stare. 'And your friends?'

Gianni shifted the barrel of the gun, lowered it slightly. Fifty paces down the beach another fire burned before some huge sheets of cedar bark, the walls of a dismantled lodge that Gianni had propped up with staves.

He grunted. 'I don't need friends. These savages are means to an end, that's all. They further God's will.'

He was ready. The thunder was so close and if rain did come, it could wet his powder.

Thomas leaned down, so he could still speak softly yet be heard. 'Why do you think you can trust this Black Snake? He has betrayed his people twice.'

'Twice?'

'The people he was born to. The people who adopted him.'

'I see. But I don't need to trust him. I have something he wants.'

'And what is that?'

Gianni smiled. Thomas nearly didn't hear the single word he said because of a thunderclap directly above them.

'Power.'

A flame applied to a touch-hole. A flash at a muzzle. A roar louder than thunder. A cedar barrier snatched away as if by God's own hand.

'Rules? There are no rules. Yes, one – kill or be killed.'

As Sada spoke, he hopped over to the bark casket where the tobacco was kept. Wiping the moisture from his hands on a deer skin before reaching in – they had been inside the sweat lodge for an hour and perspiration streamed from their bodies – he continued.

'He is taller than you, stronger than you, more experienced . . . have you ever killed a man?'

Tagay thought. 'Yes. On the island, I killed one who guarded the canoes. I didn't think. I just did it.'

Sada grunted. 'In heat like that it doesn't count. When you have time to think . . . your first takes something. Your second something less. But Black Snake has this many scalps' – he stretched his arms wide – 'and more, hanging from his lodge post. Taking another is nothing to him.'

He hopped back, snatching up a taper of wood on the way. He

sucked on the pipe, handed it across. Tagay sucked too before he spoke. He had discovered that, to his people, even the way to approach death must be conducted in calm voices, in contemplation. He had given up the choice of more sleep for this time with his cousin. In the sweat lodge, the only light came from the embers, Outside, the waxing moon rose to its zenith. The thunder clouds had moved east.

'So what can I do against this older, stronger, wiser man?'

'You can fight your fight, Tagay. Not his. No rules mean you can do what you want. You cannot hurl a spear or shoot him with an arrow. Beyond that, anything.'

Tagay coughed on a mouthful of smoke. 'So there are rules! You mean I cannot stand in my oak tree and throw acorns at him?'

Sada pulled himself up, thrust his face close to the other's. 'Listen, Little Bear, jokes will not win you this fight.'

'I am sorry. Then what will? How do I fight my fight?'

Sada settled back. 'If he is taller than you, you are lower to the ground. If he is stronger, do not try to match his strength. And if he is older, he is slower, so use your speed. You are fast, Tagay, faster even than Otetian. Use that.'

'And avenge Otetian's death.' All humour had left Tagay with the image of the man who'd died for him on the island. 'He killed him, you know.'

'I know.' Sada's voice was low, hard. 'I believe all you say about him. But for the tribe to believe you must kill him. For then it will be the judgement of the Twin Gods.'

There was a scratching at the deer skin flap, a voice outside calling, 'We have the armour, Sada.'

'Good.' The warrior rose, reached for the crutch that Anne had fashioned for him. 'We will choose you a fine weapon. But first, you must plunge in the river. If you *are* to journey to the Village of the Dead, you do not want to arrive stinking like a beaver in the spring.'

'I thought you said no jokes.' Tagay rose and followed the limping man.

The last deer hide strap was tied into place. The clan member stepped back to study the result.

Tagay lifted his arms, jumped to the side, swung an imaginary war club. 'It is still tight. It constricts me.'

He was encased in slats of yew, each two fingers in width, linked together with cords. One plate of them covered his torso, a skirt of them covered his groin and thighs. Smaller panels protected his arms and legs.

'No, Sada, I cannot move in these. I thank you for the idea but . . .'

'Tagay, if he catches you and hits you with his war club and you do not have this armour to protect you, you will be dead.'

Tagay was fiddling with the straps. Others of the clan came to help him. 'I think, if he catches me, I will be dead anyway.' The chest and back slats were pulled over his head. 'I may keep this one that covers my fighting arm. And this.' He picked up a small, round shield from the ground. Made from curled slats of kilned cedar bark, it was of a shape and size near to the steel bucklers he had practised with in France. It had two straps, one to push his forearm through, one to grip with his hand.

With many disapproving grunts the rest of the armour was stripped off.

'And what will you hold in your fighting arm, Little Bear?'

An array of clubs had been laid out in a line. They were all similar, hewn from ironwood. Some had a grooved stone bound with twisted hide into their heads, while others were carved from one piece of wood, their ends a huge ball. They were all heavy.

'What will he use?' Tagay asked.

Sada pointed at one of the all-carved ones. 'Except his will be twice the size to go with his strength.'

Someone said, 'It should be half the size to go with his manhood.' While they all laughed, Tagay came to the end of the line and saw something different.

'What is this?'

The weapon was the same length as the clubs but not as wide, oval in cross-section. Red stained grooves ran parallel down each brown side. At its tip was a hawk with carved eye and sharp beak while its butt end had a fish. Just above that was a rawhide handgrip, sewed with sinew.

But what really drew Tagay's eye was the blade that thrust straight down just behind and beneath the hawk's head.

'Steel,' he said. He ran his finger down the rusted dullness. 'How can that be?'

He knew his people had little of it. The blade had been taken from a knife and fixed into this club with a rivet and a circular nail.

Sada grunted. 'Choose another, Tagay. No one knows how to use that club. No one knows where it comes from.'

'I know.'

The woman's voice was behind them. They turned to see Gaka there.

'It was your father's, Tagay – Hasdaweh, who was Tangled's brother. He made it from a knife that he traded for a fur with the first of the Pale Thieves. It was said he killed a thousand enemies with it, though he and Tangled had nearly as many legends about them as the Twins.'

She came forward as she spoke, stooped before Tagay. 'When your mother was taken with Donnaconna by the Pale Thieves the next year, your father lost all heart to live. He died on the next war raid. Tangled brought back this. I do not think that anyone has used it since.'

Tagay took the weapon again from Sada. When he'd lifted it before, it had felt good to his hand, lighter than the ironwood clubs with their heavy heads, a beautiful heft. He practised a slashing stroke, then a strike down. With its cutting edge and point, it felt a little like the swords King Henri had ordered him to train with.

His father's weapon. It felt perfect. But he found he couldn't state that, or anything else, because something had moved into his throat. So he simply nodded his choice and tried another cut through the air.

She followed the light of the reed and tallow torch, though the moon was still bright enough to see the beach path by. But the torch was held aloft by Do-ne and it obviously gave the boy pleasure to have the title and function of 'lightbearer'. He would not leave her side, even though it was known that Black Snake was locked into the seclusion of his clan. He was the protector of White Cedar, all knew that, and it gave him a status the limping boy had never had among his young peers.

When they reached the shale of the beach, Anne called him to stop, let her eyes relax from the glare of flame, scanned the beach. When she located the glow ahead, she turned back to the boy.

'You must leave me here, Do-ne. I must go on alone. Just a little way.'

He shook his head.

'Please, Do-ne. I will not go far. There is someone I must see. Just up there.'

'Then I will wait just down here,' he said, falling onto the ground, planting the torch end into the ground. 'And if you call me I will come. I have this.' He pulled a small bone knife from his belt.

'Good.' She bent, touched his head. 'I will return in a moment.'

Her feet slipped on the pebbles and, though the moon was bright, she still managed to trip over some larger stones. But the noise did not matter. He whom she sought would be expecting her anyway.

She followed the glow of embers to its source. Tagay was sitting cross-legged, facing the water. Before him, some kind of club was laid out. She could see the scroll work down its side, the hawk head, a blade beneath. Beside it she saw the striped stone, Donnaconna's Oki. She stood silently and watched as Tagay dropped tobacco into the flames. It glowed, caught, and a sweet scent rose from it.

'Who do you burn it for, Tagay?'

'Everyone. Everything. Myself.' His voice was calm.

'Do you also burn it for me?' She hated that her voice could not match his, heard the hardness in it.

'For you?' He paused, thought. 'Of course, for you. I fight for you.'

'Do you?' She knelt beside him. 'Then don't. I don't want another man to die for me.'

'Thank you. Are you so sure that I will die?'

'He is a warrior, trained from birth to kill.'

'And I am not. It is true. But I am a warrior's son.' He leaned forward, ran his fingers gently up the shaft of his club. 'And I come from a warrior people. Besides, I have no choice. You heard. They will kill you as a witch.'

She reached to either side of his head, turned him. 'Listen to me. You do have a choice. You have a choice whether to live or die. Uncle Pierre promised to return with the full moon. There are canoes here, right here. We can take one, hide, wait for him.'

'Creep back to France while my people are massacred?'

'If you die they will be massacred anyway.'

He turned fully around to her, his voice now urgent. 'And you, White Cedar? What of your quest? The hand you must bury.'

She reached behind her, pulled the hand from its pouch. The moonlight made the bones glow green, as if they were possessed of a sickness.

'This?' Her disgust was clear. 'This is a collection of bones, of a woman who died twenty years ago. I will drop it into the ocean on the voyage back.'

'You could have done that on the voyage across.' He reached forward. One hand touched her chest, the other rested on her head. 'You know, you heard it in here, Anne, and here, the voice that told you that you must bury it, just as she who gave it to your father asked for it to be buried. Safely, by the light of the full moon. Two nights from now.'

'And if you are dead by then?' Her voice had become a whisper. 'Then none of it will happen, for I will be dead too.'

'You may not be.' Tagay came onto his knees. 'There is something I didn't tell you about the hunt. They used guns there to kill my people.'

'Guns?'

'Pistols.'

'But how?'

'I think,' he sighed, 'your brother gave the pistols to them.'

'My broth . . .'

It felt as if she'd been struck. She fell back, sat on the beach, her knees drawn up, her forehead lowered onto them, scarcely breathing. He let her stay that way for a while, then reached forward again, nearly touched her hair.

'You could go to him now,' he said, gently. 'Take one of the canoes. It is dangerous but less dangerous than staying, perhaps. He is your brother. He will not turn you away. Especially if you take him what he seeks.' He pointed at the skeletal hand she still held. 'You say your family have sacrificed enough. If you believe it, then give this to your brother. Let him take it back across the water. Let him take you with it.'

Anne rose, stumbled slightly, then stood straight. Reaching back, she put the hand away in the pouch, replacing it with something else.

'This is all I will give to my brother.' She lifted the tiny silver cross so Tagay could see its glimmer in the moonlight. 'I found it in a tree in Tuscany. It was a gift to him from our father, in the days when we were all still happy. Gianni placed it in the branches, hoping some day to take it back.'

She turned, took a couple of steps up the path, stopped. 'You are right, Tagay. You have your task clear before you. And Gianni's coming here reminds me of mine. So I tell you this, in a way our mother, both Gianni's and mine, would have told you: Black Snake? Kill the fucker.'

Then she was gone. Her feet slipping on shale meant she could not see his smile, nor hear his reply. But he said it anyway.

'I will try, White Cedar. Believe me, I will try.'

The torches were placed at intervals of a dozen paces around the perimeter of the field. Between them, the entire tribe of the Tahontaenrat had gathered, every man, woman and child, from babies on their carry boards to the eldest in bark chairs. They came from the village below the cliffs and from every village the length and breadth of their country; yet they mustered, not by village, but by clan. Every member of each clan was hungry, for the influx of refugees had sorely tested the reserves of food. But no one was any hungrier than the person standing next to them, for what they had was shared out equally according to the custom of their people. Yet it was quite unlike the time when Tagay had first beheld the gathering for the Game, when voices had risen, solely and in unison like a thousand geese in flight. Now the people were silent. Not even the newborn cried out though they all seemed awake, as watchful as their parents.

He waited at one end of the field, behind the posts through which Sada had shot the knot ball. Around him, the Bear clan massed, some nearest him commenting on, or fussing around, his armour – or lack of it. Most were simply staring toward the far end of the field where, behind their own posts, the clan of the Wolf stared back.

While his aunt, Gaka, finished the painting of his body in swirling red patterns, Sada was the most fussy of the Bears, bending over Tagay's arm, checking and rechecking the straps of the forearm guard, cinching the straps to make sure each cedar slat overlapped perfectly. The buckler's hand grip was next, reinforced with more stitches of hide thread.

While he was pushing the bone needle through against the skin of a hand that seemed made of wood, another clan member ran up and whispered something in his ear. Sada just grunted and carried on with the stitch.

Tagay said, 'What are the odds now, cousin?'

Sada looked up, shock on his face. 'Odds? This is a ceremony, Tagay, as well as a fight. It is part of the religion of our people. We do not bet on our Gods' favours. If you had been raised amongst us, and not among people who have no religion, you would know that.' He went back to his stitching, putting the thread end in his mouth.

'Sada?'

'What?'

'The odds?'

The warrior spat to the side, while keeping the thread in his mouth, a difficult feat. 'Eight beaver skins to one,' he grumbled. 'It was only five at nightfall. But then you appeared this morning with no armour.' He put the final stitch in place.

Tagay kept the smile on his face, but inside his stomach flipped again. He was glad he'd already vomited up the soup they'd forced upon him an hour before. He would not want to increase the odds by vomiting again now.

He looked behind him. A faint light shone in the east. The swollen moon was bathed red.

As if washed with blood, he thought. *Someone is about to die.*

There was a shifting from his clan, a murmur. Tagay saw four torches moving to the centre of the field. A man walked beneath them wearing full wampum, bearing a pipe in one hand and a carved staff in the other. The drums, which had kept up a steady pulse, stopped.

'Tangled.' Sada rose. 'So. It begins.'

'People of the Deer.' The Chief's strong voice, honed by the rigours of speech-making in council, carried easily to every part of the field. 'It is a day I never thought I would see, when all of the Tahontaenrat were gathered together beside the lodgepost of our Gods. This is something to praise, when village gathers with village like this, clan from afar merges with clan nearby, families, long separated, re-unite. This is a thing of joy to me.'

There was a universal shout then, the communal cry, 'Haauu'. When it died away, Tangled continued. 'But it is also one of sadness. Because we do not gather for celebration, we draw around our hearths because of danger. Many of our people have been killed, many lodges burned. We have been driven out of the hunting grounds, here and here, here and here.' He raised his staff, pointing to the four winds. 'These are matters we will discuss, today in a great council. But first we are called here to witness the battle of the Twins, Taviscaran and Iouskaha. They fought in the beginning of our times when the earth was a flat plain of nothing. The blood they shed formed many of the things of our world. I do not think this strange that now, in this time of greatest danger, the Twins are called to fight again.'

Once more there was the cry, 'Haauu', stronger than before. Tangled let it reverberate around the field and die away, then spoke again.

'We know what these two have said. One of them lies in the deepest part of their soul. One of them dies today to prove the other truthful. But this is not the Game, when clan gives knocks to clan and one side or the other rejoice. Let no one think it is and let no blood feud make us fight ourselves. There will be fighting enough for our people in the days to come. Remember that this is not a Wolf fighting a Bear. This is the fight of the Twins. Let them decide.'

Tangled's voice soared to a high note and he raised his staff. 'Haauu' came the cry, louder and longer than before. When it died away, the drums began again and Tangled moved back to his position with all the other chiefs.

Sada went to Tagay. 'Kneel,' he commanded. Tagay knelt and Sada moved behind him. He felt his cousin tying a moosehair band around his brow.

'It is my own, the one I wear to war,' Sada said. 'Many enemies have looked at it and died. I think this Wolf will be the next.'

Tagay rose. His legs felt suddenly strong, as if the band around his head was raising him up somehow. 'Bring me my father's club,' he said.

It had been hidden in a bear skin, safe from eyes that would carry the information back to Black Snake. An ordinary club had been exposed to sight. The members of his clan all felt that Tagay's opponent would be surprised, as they had been, by the choice of weapon.

Tagay swung it, felt its good balance. Sada took the younger man's finger, pressed it against the cutting edge under the hawk's head. No trace of dullness, of rust now. It had been well-honed and cut him instantly. Startled, Tagay sucked the blood from his finger.

'Better you draw blood first than him.' Sada smiled.

They moved out onto the field to the murmuring of the crowd, many surprised by the young man near naked in his breech cloth, wearing only a guard on his fighting arm, carrying the smallest of shields in the other; surprised also by the slender weapon in his hand. The other Bear members had come with him to the edge, but only Sada was allowed further. He limped beside Tagay, using a stick. They halted twenty paces before their posts.

The murmurings doubled, the drums increased their throbbing pulse, when the Wolf ranks parted and Black Snake strode forth. He had always been a big man but the full slat armour he wore made him appear like a giant. It covered him, from the cedar bark helmet, to the shins swathed in single slats. He walked steadily forward then stopped the same distance before his ranks as Tagay was before his. As he walked, he swung his war club. It was, as predicted, a huge single piece of carved ironwood. Tagay could see the heavy ball end.

He felt his heart pounding, was sure that all could hear it as clearly as he could. If Sada did, he gave no indication.

'Listen to me, Tagay,' he whispered, making a show of checking the forearm straps. 'His armour is good, but it is weak here and here.' He touched Tagay swiftly at the armpit and knee. 'Also, it is heavy and he was never the fastest beast in the forest to begin with. So keep moving around him, make him chase you. Do not stand and trade blows, for he will kill you quick. No one cares if you look brave. We only care that you win.'

The drum beats that had built and built as they walked forward now stopped suddenly as Tangled stepped forward, holding his staff out by the end as if dividing the field in two.

'One more thing. I know this may not seem the best time to talk of my prowess at the Game. But you remember how I scored that final ball that gave the Bear clan its great victory?'

Tagay, whose eyes had been fixed and glazed ahead of him, now looked down. 'What? What are you saying?'

'The final ball! I feinted high and went low. And I beat Black Snake on the outside. Remember that!'

With those words, Sada turned and walked back to the ranks of the Bear.

Tagay stood, uncertain that his feet would move if he commanded them. To steady himself, he swept his eyes around, taking in the entire extent of his tribe. As his eyes reached the huge oak tree, he saw a shape up on the branch.

'Anne!' he murmured. 'White Cedar.'

Raising his club toward her, he slowly lowered the tip to the ground. Then he began to walk down the field.

She watched the weapon swept down, raised her hand to return the salute. She didn't know whether he'd seen it, but she kept waving anyway as he began to march toward his opponent. From her vantage point, looking down, it seemed like a small boy was approaching some giant striding from the pages of a myth. Tagay looked frail, all too human with the vulnerability that implied. The figure that marched toward him was alien, implacable, monstrous.

She had never been religious, unlike her brother. But she knew Gianni believed, fervently, passionately. So she pulled his little cross from her pouch, raised it before her, trying to release some of the prayers he had poured into it, held like breath somewhere in those shining planes. Half-forgotten sentences came from a world so far away. Yet she didn't care. For Tagay needed all the help he could get.

'Mater Dei, Memento Mei.'

Mother of God, Remember me. Remember him!

The hardest thing was resisting the urge to rush forward. Walking seemed a difficult action to control; in running there would be less time to think. Still, they were approaching each other fast enough. Tagay could soon hear the man's steady breath. It reminded him to take one of his own. Then he heard the first of the man's words.

'Little Bear.' The emphasis was on the first word, the tone derisive. 'Child! Come to the Wolf. Come and be suckled.'

Twenty paces, ten. At five, Black Snake stopped, so Tagay did as well.

'Little Bear.' The voice was low now, the words meant only for him. 'You will die knowing your woman will lie beneath me, and then beneath every Wolf, before we kill her. You will die knowing your aunt will be murdered, your clan destroyed, your people enslaved. You will die knowing that you failed to save them. And that knowledge will haunt you for ever in the Village of the Dead.'

And then the man whom Sada had said was slow proved he wasn't.

It was the sound of the club that Tagay reacted to, not the blur of slatted wood that ran at him. It whirred through the air, as if it already shattered bodies on its journey. He turned, just, and the wind of the passing almost bruised him at side of head, at shoulder and hip. A cry came from around the field as he lurched sideways.

Black Snake had put so much into the first blow that he followed the heavy club down, embedding its head in the soft earth. Yet it took only a moment to jerk it out and bending, he swept it upwards diagonally off the ground, the blow aimed at the knee. Tagay thrust his shield out, angled, as he remembered his teachers telling him to do years before with the buckler. But the angle wasn't enough, the club caught him hard, splintering wood, sending him reeling again. Black Snake was up and following in a heart beat.

You are faster, Sada had said. The words came to him now and he moved, ran from the man approaching him. He *was* faster.

Black Snake halted. 'Coward!' he bellowed, shaking his club before him. 'You dare not stand and fight. It was how your father fought, I have heard, how he died – with an arrow in his back, running from the foe.'

Until that moment, Tagay had only thought about how to avoid the next blow, how to keep away from his opponent. Now, with a vision of a man he'd never met, and that man's war club in his hand, his mind came clear. When Black Snake rushed at him again, he still ran. But there was less distance, the gap small enough, luring Black Snake to chase.

The club descended. This time Tagay stopped, ducked into the blow, raising his own club. The blow landed, but glanced off Tagay's forearm guard. It hurt but not enough to stop him lunging after his opponent's back, stabbing with the wooden point. It was nothing, for it was not a killing part of the weapon and it caught Black Snake harmlessly on his shoulder armour. But it was the first attack he had made, and the crowd greeted it with a shout.

Black Snake laughed. 'The flies are buzzing here today,' he said.

Tagay, who had moved again just out of an arm's reach laughed back. 'They are waiting to lay their eggs in your wounds, Tawane. Or is it your smell that draws them?'

He did not think such a jest would sting – or perhaps it was the defiance – but it caused the tattooed face to cloud. He ran forward again, the club whirring like bees around a hive, cutting the air as if air was solid. Tagay retreated but didn't run, dodging blows, deflecting some on shield and arm guard. But for every blow that fell, he returned a thrust back, always with the point, always high, near the neck, at the under arm, stabbing the cedar, till the hawk beak began to splay and splinter.

The noise had built in the crowd, shouts and groans issuing from either end, from each side, according to the nearness of the blows, the giver or the taker.

On each strike, Black Snake grunted, a huge exhalation. He was breathing heavily while Tagay's breaths came lighter.

Maybe, he thought, *maybe I can do this.*

It was the flicker of confidence that nearly betrayed him. He had outdistanced Black Snake again, but his lunge at the neck took him off balance. The tattooed warrior saw it, stepped in, the war club rising in a great arc from behind him. Tagay was too far forward, too late to dodge. He raised his shield and the ironwood fell hard into its middle, shattering it.

Everyone saw. Anne leaned forward, witnessing one doom,

anticipating in it her own. Sada started forward with a curse. Wolves howled in triumph; neutrals looked for the decision of their Gods.

It felt like his arm was as broken as his shield. He managed to scramble away, as another blow plunged into the ground by his head. But the mud caused Black Snake's foot to slip and Tagay rolled onto one knee, shook away the remnants of his shattered shield. The two men, both breathing heavily, faced each other again.

'The Bear . . . has lost . . . a paw.' Black Snake gestured to the arm already swelling. 'Kneel before me . . . one blow . . . and all your hurts will be over.'

He came forward again, his own shield raised high to fend off what he knew would be Tagay's last and most desperate attack. And, lunging from his crouch, Tagay's point did indeed rise up, aiming, so it seemed, for the blue snake that held the warrior's left eye in its fanged mouth. Black Snake's shield rose even higher over his forward foot, to counter, to deflect. The club was lowered to the ground poised to bring over the killing blow.

But Tagay's weapon did not hold true to its course. Instead, as he rose from the ground he pivoted on his front foot, throwing his battered left arm out and around, using it to spin him. His father's weapon he dropped down and, for the first time, he used not the point, but the blade. Falling, his eyes fixed on the target, just before his back reached the ground, Tagay thrust the hawk's head between the front and rear guards of the slat armour of the lower leg. He landed, using the full force of his fall and a cocked wrist to rip the blade outwards, severing the flesh and tendons behind the knee.

He kept rolling, his face sliding into the wet earth, hearing but not seeing the club once more thud into the ground behind him, hearing but not seeing the crowd because of the mud lodged in his eyes. He rolled up, spat, wiped a hand. His vision cleared.

It was Black Snake who was on one knee now, trying to force himself up. But the leg wouldn't work and he kept sinking down. Then he used the club like a crutch raising himself onto one foot.

All sounds disappeared for Tagay. The crowd gone, grunts and insults gone, even the tide of blood that had pounded so in his ears receded to nothing. The only thing he heard, because it wasn't a sound but a memory, were the words of Sada, telling him where the two weaknesses in his opponent's armour lay. And having found the one, Tagay stepped forward now to seek the other.

Tagay ran around the raised shield. Black Snake lifted the club from the ground but in doing so his slashed leg collapsed. As he fell, Tagay found what he was looking for. With a wide blow, he drove the blade between two more plates of armour, burying its length in the muscle that joins shoulder and arm.

Then sound returned in a rush, the rush of people running onto the field, screams of triumph, of shock. A smaller circle formed around the two combatants. Black Snake lay on his back, one leg twisted, blood seeping through the slats of his armour, pooling in the mud. Tagay sank to the ground, but was pulled to his feet immediately by Sada. His cousin's placid face, which so rarely showed any emotion, was cracked with wonder now, with joy.

'Feint high, take him low, take him on the outside.' The man laughed. 'Good advice, eh?'

He was one of the few to display any passion. Most seemed to think that what Tagay had done was normal, everyday. Like the tall, thin elder who pushed his way through to them, nodded at Tagay once, before turning to Sada.

'My grandson will come to your lodge and collect the beaver skins.'

He turned and walked away, barely glancing at Black Snake. Sada was doing his best to look small.

Tagay finally found his eyes. 'You bet against me, Sada?'

The smaller man looked embarrassed for a moment, then shrugged. 'That man makes the finest beaver cloaks in the village,' he said. 'I thought one of them would keep me warmer next winter than my memory of you.'

Tagay laughed. It felt a strange sensation, wonderful and new. He looked above the crowd to the oak tree. The branch was empty.

Are you coming to me, White Cedar? he thought. Then a gap opened in the crowd and Tangled appeared, followed by the other chiefs. The space widened to accommodate them.

*

She was trying to reach him. When he'd fallen that last time, she'd known he was finished. She did not see his crippling blow struck home, because she'd looked down to the silver cross on the branch before her.

It is over, she'd thought, *all over*.

At the great shout, she'd forced her eyes up again, to testify to a brave man dying, as she had watched her father die only two months before. It was the least and all she could do. And she'd looked up just in time to see the miracle – the monstrous warrior on his knees, Tagay up and moving in again, Black Snake falling to another cut. She'd snatched up the cross, replaced it beside the hand in the pouch, dropped from the branches of the oak as if she was stepping down one stair.

It was while she was running toward the gathering crowd, looking left and right to seek some gap to bring her to him, that she saw what at first appeared to be a mere bundle of deer skin abandoned on the ground. She looked away, back to her desire. Then something stopped her, perhaps the sparkle of torchlight reflecting in the elaborate pattern of beads on a dress.

Gaka was lying on her side. When Anne reached her, turned her, she saw that the old woman's face was distorted, turning a blueish shade. Her left arm was clamped rigidly to her side, while her right flopped and banged into the ground, scrabbling in the dirt as if seeking a hand-hold on the earth. The eyes were rolled back under half-opened lids.

She was getting no air! Her jaw was locked so, grabbing the grey-haired head into her lap, Anne forced the mouth open. Gaka had swallowed her tongue. Anne reached in. It was fortunate that Gaka had lost most of her teeth, because the jaw bit down on her fingers. She grabbed the tongue, pulled it back up. Looking around desperately, she saw a small stick on the ground nearby, grabbed it, laid it on top of the tongue, let the mouth close around it.

'Do-ne!' The boy had stayed at the base of the tree during the fight. Now he hobbled up, his eyes wide as he looked at the writhing body.

'Stay with her. Try to keep this in her mouth. I will get help.'

She had to reach Tagay. The crowd was still forming up ahead. She reached the rear of it, began to push her way through.

'The Twins have made their judgement, Tawane,' Tangled said. 'Do you abide by it?'

'I do.' Black Snake grimaced as he pulled himself up from the ground into a sitting position. The blood that had flowed down his back onto the ground now ran from his chest, bubbling between the cedar slats, staining them a deeper red. 'It is as the Little Bear has told you. The Tattooed people gather their allies from all over the world. The sunrise after the full moon will see them here, burning your lodges down. It is the end for the Tahontaenrat.'

The muttering that had been continuous during his speaking now broke into shouts. Tangled quelled it with a raising of his staff. 'Is that why you betrayed us?'

'I returned to an older loyalty, that is all. I despised myself that I did not die like a warrior when you captured me, because I was so young and weak. I lied to myself for the many summers since. But then I saw the strength of the people I was born to, while the Deer people grew weaker. I wanted to be strong like them again.'

Once more, Tangled quieted the crowd. 'And now?'

'Now I wish to die like a warrior as I should have before. I wish to sing my death song so you will all see that my people have courage beyond your courage, strength beyond your strength. That is my wish.'

'And you will have it.' Tangled lifted his staff and pointed to the east, where the sky was lightening. 'The God of War is coming to us in fire and we will send him your soul to greet him. If we had time we should prepare you for many days, so you and he would both have much honour. But by his swift coming and your life flowing in red upon the ground I do not think we have that time.' He turned now to his people, to the warriors who had gathered at the front. 'Release his soul.'

The people spread back but not far, creating a space of about fifty paces in length, thirty wide. The drums that had beat during the fight started up again now, and the crowd began to chant 'Heh-Heh-Heh-Heh-Heh'. The torches were brought in, placed around at intervals, though the growing light was rendering them unnecessary. Yet their fire was needed for a different purpose now.

Sada came to Tagay, handed him a smouldering stick, took him to the end of the two lines that had formed, facing each other, twenty warriors in each. Black Snake was stripped of his armour and, naked, his blood spreading in a red web over the blue tattooed body, he was dragged to the entrance of the lines, forced to stand.

'Do as I do,' whispered Sada. Then he stepped up to Black Snake and said, 'You look cold, Tawane. Let me warm you.' And he thrust his flaming, sharpened stick into the blue tattooed ear.

Black Snake did not scream. He roared, 'I am Tawane of the Nundawaono. Hear my death song!' and he began to stagger down the lines.

Tagay thrust, at the same time as the man facing him on the other side of the line. Their brands were pushed into flesh, but Black Snake did not turn, or acknowledge the pain in any way. He limped down the gauntlet, receiving the fire and jabs, singing his song through clenched teeth. He fell twice, forced himself up, dragging his useless leg behind him and on.

Somehow he reached the end of the line. When the last stake had been pushed home with a cry of, 'You bleed. Let me stop the flow!' he was thrown down, his hands stretched out to logs on either side, other logs brought crashing down on them with full weight crushing his fingers. He screamed then, but just his name, and fainted. Water was thrown over him, and he sat up. Immediately, he began to sing again.

'The Black Snake steals across the ground, enemies run or fall into his jaws.'

They crushed his feet then, as his hands had been. Revived once more, he was tied swiftly to a stake, new thrust into the earth, his face toward the growing light.

Drumbeats, chanting, smoke, burned flesh, blood. Every sense stretched with the taste of death, the scent of it, touching mortality, breathing the beyond, glimpses of hell. Tagay let Sada lead him, did as Sada did – stabbed, scorched, crushed. Flames ran up limbs, a snake curled round an eye socket, now empty and oozing. Nothing outside the flaming circle, only the flesh before him, strapped to a stake.

The writhing body went limp, dangled from its bonds. Sada stepped in, put a hand to the wreckage of a chest, an ear to what had once been a mouth. The drums dropped to a mere caress of hand on skin, the chanting to a whisper.

'He is close,' Sada announced. 'He seeks the Sun God.'

'And see where Ondoutaehte comes for him. See!' Tangled raised his staff again, pointed to the east. All the people turned, just as the ball of flames that was the sun, the Sun God, burst from the forests, a ball spun up by some huge hand.

They greeted it with a cry. 'Heh-heh-heh-heh-heh!'

Sada placed a bone knife into Tagay's hand. 'The head and then the heart,' he whispered and walked away.

He was still moving in the blur of his senses. As he stepped up to the stake, his approach somehow made the mass of broken bone and lacerated skin raise his head. Sounds came from somewhere in his throat. Sounds that could have been 'Tawane of the Nundawaono.'

'And I am Tagaynearguye, and my people are the Tahontaenrat.'

He raised the knife.

He had never scalped anyone before. But he discovered he knew how.

He had never cut out someone's heart. But he found he knew that too.

Turning to his tribe, he lifted each bloodied, full hand. 'Heh-heh-heh-heh-heh!' he shouted into the sunrise.

'Heh-heh-heh-heh-heh!' his people shouted back.

Then he looked down. Straight into the horror-filled eyes of Anne Rombaud.

EIGHT
ANDAC-WANDA

He sat exactly where he'd sat only the night before. Once more, his father's war club was before him, though it was frayed and battered now. Once more, embers burned tobacco for his Gods, for his Oki, the bright, striped stone given to him by his uncle in another time, another world. He looked out on this one now, which he had become part of again, and marvelled. The slanting rays of a setting sun had turned the river to a cascade of polished gems. Seeing that sparkle, a memory came, of a young child in France when Jaques Cartier, the great Captain, had returned from his last failed attempt to set up a colony here, in this place he called Stadacona. He had brought thousands of what he thought were diamonds back, to be his fortune. They had proved brittle, worthless pebbles and Tagay recalled how he and his fellow hostages were mocked with the phrase, 'as false as a diamond in Canada'.

Tagay looked out now, to the waters of the surging river, to the huge forests lit by the setting sun, and knew that Cartier had left the true diamonds behind.

But how long will we keep them?' he thought, as a shadow ran the width of the river with a cloud passing before the sun. From the banks to his left, two more canoes were pushed into the water, and twelve warriors began to move rapidly toward the canoes that floated ten boat lengths offshore. But the Tattooed warriors only let them get so close before they paddled swiftly ahead of them. When the Tahontaenrat gave up the chase, the enemy craft returned to take up the same position, to resume their observations. The game had been going on all day and both sides seemed to be enjoying it. But Tagay knew it was no game.

The People of the Great Hill were seeing that their quarry remained trapped where they were.

Another shadow fell on him and he thought it was the sun hiding again because he had not been aware of any footfalls on the pebbles of the beach. So he was startled by the voice.

'Is your arm broken?'

He squinted up. Anne stood with her back to the sun, a silhouette, her long, black hair etched in flame. The beauty of it caught him, just as the diamonds on the water had.

'No, it is hurt but . . .' He rose as he spoke, looking down at the leaves wrapped tight around his forearm by Sada, soaked in some distillation of herb that cooled the bruised flesh. So it was only when he was standing and had shaded his eyes from the sunlight that he saw her face.

She wore the same look he had seen on it at dawn as he stood with a man's heart in one hand and his scalp in the other.

He felt a blow, like a war club falling, but inside him, in his chest. He reached his good arm toward her. 'White Cedar . . .'

'Don't!' She pulled her hand back, held it up, awkwardly high. 'Do not touch me.'

'What is wrong?'

'Your hands.' Her eyes left him, stared into a memory. 'What they did to him!'

He felt a stirring, first of anger, then something else as well, a need to explain. 'My hands helped him to die.'

'They tortured him till he died.'

'Helped him to die as he chose.'

'He had no choice!' The eyes were back on him now, hard as the voice.

'He did!' His voice matched hers. 'He could have stayed on the ground, I could have cut his throat like a beaver in a snare. What honour would there have been for him in that? What stories to tell in the next world? You saw him, how he hardly cried out, how he sang his death song to the end.' He stepped closer. 'It is the same as your father.'

'My . . . father?'

The look she gave him made him wince but he pressed on. 'You told me how his enemies chained him to a wall, broke his body. He chose that. It is the same.'

'No!' As she thought of Jean Rombaud, tears came, ran down her face. 'My father was keeping faith with his queen, with the oath he had sworn. They tortured him to get information.'

'Then that is their cruelty, Anne. We do not do that for . . . information.' He spat the last word. 'We helped a man prove his courage. As the men who killed your father helped him. I saw Jean Rombaud before, in Paris, in St Malo, how afraid he was! A proud man, afraid. It hurt him, here.' He touched his chest. 'You know this, Anne.'

'He had suffered much . . .'

'Yes!' He leaned forward, eagerly. 'But I saw him at the end. He was no longer afraid. He chose to die. Like a warrior.'

'It is different,' she said, fiercely. 'How can you say it is the same? My father fell to a dozen swords, in battle. Even though I hated Black Snake, hated him above all men . . .' She faltered. 'Jesus save me, what you did to his eyes!'

'Jesus,' he said. 'Your Sun God. Your Son of God. He chose this death too. I heard the tales. Whipped, nailed to a stake, stabbed. Singing his song, so he could live for ever with his father in the heavens. So all his people could live. Jesus. Your father. Black Snake. This is how warriors choose to die.'

'So you would have me watch you die that way?'

'No. But if I do, know that I die as I choose. Like a warrior of my people.'

He reached out once more to her. She moved back immediately, taking several steps down the beach. In a new voice, flat, uninflected, she spoke and she did not look at him. 'Your aunt is dying. Will you come?'

He knew only that Gaka had been taken sick, no more. 'Yes. I will come now.'

'Let me go ahead and prepare her.' She began to move away up the beach.

'Anne!' He came after her. 'Wait.'

Her hand halted him. 'Don't,' was all she said before she walked rapidly around the boulders and disappeared.

He turned back to the water, but the light on it gave him no pleasure now. There was a wall between him and Anne and every day, it seemed, one of them added another stone to it.

Whatever I do, I must make sure she is safe. So when the 'Sea Feather' returns, Jacquet can take her back to France.

The thought made him suddenly, deeply sad. Then he heard feet crunching on the beach pebbles again.

She has come back, he thought joyfully. *Speak to her the words you need to say.*

Sada came limping down the beach. 'What is wrong, Tagay? You do not look like the man who has eaten the heart of his enemy.'

'There is something I need to do.'

He made to push past but a hand on his chest halted him. 'There is. You are summoned to the council.'

Tagay looked at his cousin in surprise. 'The council? But I thought it was just for the chiefs and elders.'

Sada grunted. 'It is, in normal times. But these are not normal times as you can see.' He pointed over Tagay's shoulders to the water, where the enemies' canoes had circled back again. 'Besides, Little Bear, as war chief of your clan you should be there.'

'What are you saying, Sada? The sun has boiled your head. I am not a war chief.'

'And who holds that office for the Bear clan?'

Tagay thought. 'He was killed, wasn't he, defending one of the burned villages? And his successor will be named tomorrow, at the feast of the full moon.' Tagay smiled. 'You are his successor, Sada.'

'You are right and you are wrong and you are right and you are wrong. I can see why you would be confused.' Sada lowered himself onto the ground. 'I must sit, because my leg, which I twisted helping you win a race, still hurts. Ah!' He began to rub at his ankle. 'And that is one of the reasons you are right and wrong. I should be war chief. But when one is appointed, it is customary that he should go immediately to war. The war waits,' he pointed again to the water and the circling canoes, 'but this prevents me going to it. The Bear clan gathered after the death this morning, while you slept. It is decided. You will go in my place.'

Tagay fell down beside his cousin. 'You *are* mad. All of you. There are many far worthier than me. I am not even trained in the Tahontaenrat way of war.'

'No. But you are favoured by the Gods. And that is better than any skill.' Sada reached across, placing a hand on Tagay's shoulder. 'You won the judgement of the Twin Gods and killed your enemy. You carry Donnaconna's Oki. Your father was a war chief of great skill as was your uncle, Tangled. Above all, Tagay, the dream tellers of our people have long spoken of the Hunter of the Sunrise who would return when we had great need of him. You are that Hunter.'

Sada had brought a large deerskin bag with him. Now he reached into it.

'This is the wampum belt of our clan war chief.' He stretched the lengths of beaded cords out toward Tagay.

'Sada, this is madness.'

Without replying, Sada draped the beads over his neck. 'Now, you are to be called by his name in council, which has been passed down from chief to chief since the deer first came from the forest. That name is Tonessah. It means 'One Who Guards'. This,' he said, pulling a long piece of carved wood from the bag, 'is our pipe.'

He handed it over, despite Tagay's protestations.

'And this is "The Arrow That Flies True". It is the first one you shoot into the ranks of our enemies.'

'Sada.' Tagay tried to speak.

His cousin was rising to his feet. 'There will be ceremony later, but now there is no time. You must go to the council. They have deliberated long and still have found no answer.'

Tagay looked at the pipe in one hand, the arrow in the other, at the beads hanging from his neck. 'What will I say there?'

'Maybe nothing. Maybe you will just be silent. But maybe the Gods, who love you, will speak to you, here!' Sada tapped him on the chest. 'Listen for their words.'

And with that, the limping warrior led his war chief from the beach and through the village to Tangled's lodge, where the council sat.

'Your nephew sends word,' Anne said. 'He has been summoned to the council. But he will come soon.'

She looked again, in the faint hope that her words would cause a reaction. But the right eye that gazed up from behind its half-closed lid was still static, while the left one remained where it had settled after her attack above the cliffs – rolled over and down, as if seeking something on the tip of her nose.

Anne touched the left hand, curled into a claw above the beaver skin. It was cold, despite the warmth of the lodge, the fire heavily banked only a few paces away.

'Gaka. Aunt.' She squeezed the hand, which stayed lifeless to her touch. It felt like the hands of the dying always did, barely clinging to this side of the veil. She thought of Guiseppe Toldo, the old carpenter whom she had helped on this journey, that other lifetime, in Siena. Then, her hand had been support, to ease his passage through from this plane to the next. But here, her hand was trying to pull Gaka back.

'What will I do without you, Aunt?'

She pressed the old woman's hand into her own forehead, began to murmur, words in a mixture of their languages, seeking to be understood yet to understand herself also, speaking of her fear. And of Tagay, of the dreams she'd had of him. Dreams collapsed in blood now, in a heart pulled beating from a dying man's chest.

She thought it was her, the agitation she felt spreading through their joined limbs. But then she felt the hand in hers contract, heard a rattle in the throat of the woman she held, a sound she had heard so many times before.

'No, Gaka, no, don't leave me,' she cried out.

Then she heard the whisper.

'I have had a dream.'

'Gaka!' Anne bent, saw light in the one eye that looked straight out at her.

'Do not fear, child,' Gaka whispered. 'I have been to the house of my ancestors. A feast waits for me there in the Village of the Dead. Such a feast. But they told me it was not quite ready, that I must have patience, go back and wait a little longer. That there was something I had to do first, here. A gift I had to bring them.'

She coughed and Anne ran to get some water. The old woman spluttered, some of the liquid running down her chin.

'Rest, Aunt, rest,' Anne said gently.

'Rest? No, child, if I wanted rest I would have stayed at the feast my ancestors are preparing for me.' She tried to raise her head, but sank back with a sigh. 'Is your little shadow, Do-ne, here?'

The boy rarely left Anne's side. Now, on hearing his name, he came up to his great-aunt's bed, staring with undisguised interest at Gaka's rolled over eye.

'Do-ne,' Gaka said fondly. 'You must do something for me and for White Cedar. You must go to the council. You must take a message to my brother, Tangled. Tell him' – and here she reached out and took Anne's hand with her good one – 'tell him I have had a dream. And tell him that I request andac-wanda.'

The boy's eyes widened and he looked between the two women. 'But, Aunt . . .'

'Go, little one. Tell them.'

He looked as if he would speak again. But then he turned and limped from the lodgehouse.

'What have you asked him to do, Aunt? What is this "andac-wanda"? Is it a powerful medicine.'

'Oh yes, child. One of the most powerful.'

'Will it make you better?'

'Perhaps. But the medicine is really for you.'

'And that is my thought on this matter.'

The war chief of the Turtle clan bowed toward the centre of the circle and then returned to his place, accompanied by the voices of his peers chanting, 'Haauu, Haauu, Haauu.' By this, his third hour in the debate, Tagay was able to distinguish the level of support within those chants. These were muted, merely polite. The Turtle's desire to retreat to the clifftops and fight from there did not receive much support.

Despite the desperate nature of the situation under discussion, every speaker was listened to in silence, allowed to have his full say and each speech went on for some time, full as each was with the rhetorical flourishes, the delight in wordplay that Tagay had discovered was the essence of every Tahontaenrat debate.

As the Turtle chief sat, Tangled rose again. As overall chief, it was his duty to sum up the arguments put forward so far, incorporating the last one, and to call upon the next speaker to make his. As the subject debated was war, it was those chiefs, rather than the civil ones, who had spoken. Seven of them, one for each clan. Only the war chief of the Bear clan had remained unheard.

Tagay shifted. The wooden floor was hard and his limbs ached still from the fight. He watched as Tangled went to the centre, smoke trailing him like morning mist rising from a pool. He felt dread, a hollowness in the stomach, as he knew his turn had come, knew he was expected to put forward, not only his own view but that of the Bear clan as Sada had expressed it to him. The problem was only partly his nervousness at having to speak. It was mainly that his clan was as divided as the chiefs within the lodge. And a decision, Tagay had learnt, had to be unanimous. Consensus must be achieved, or a final decision would need to be put off. And that, in the present crisis, was unacceptable. The time for discussion, like the life of the Tahontaenrat as they had known it, would end with the coming of the full moon.

So Tagay strained forward through the smoke, watching Tangled, listening to his detailed summation. The options were to fight here; to fight on other ground; or to flee, either inland or upriver and into the country where their brother tribes already lived. Each option had its own merits and special problems. Hence the deadlock.

What had Sada said to him? '*Listen with your heart*'. Tangled's sonorous voice drew him. His heart, which had been beating loud in his ears, slowed and he heard what was behind the even tone of the chief's summation. Tangled wanted to go, to join their brother tribes who dwelt near the Big Lakes. Others had told how there was plenty of room there, good hunting and fishing, fertile land for their crops, all far beyond the reach of the Tattooed people's war clubs. But how did you move a whole people, men, women and children, the old and the new born, along the river when their enemies' canoes were thicker in the water than spawning salmon in a stream? When they would be overtaken as they fled?

'And that is my thought on this matter,' Tangled concluded. 'Does anyone have an answer for this?' He turned to Tagay, addressed him by his hereditary name. 'Tonessah. Only you have not spoken. Can we hear your voice?'

The ritualistic words were succeeded by the sounds of the chiefs sucking deep on their pipes. As all eyes turned to him, he sucked deep too, as he had learned to do in his time there, and as his mind moved, what he saw before him changed. Figures emerged in the haze, drawn from memory, a voice from a time before. From when his Old World was young, as those who taught him there in France said the world of the Tahontaenrat was young. And the voice was of a monk, Brother Raymond, a gentle man filled with learning and the love of all things ancient, who had told the lonely boy stories of a world of heroes, of Troy and Greece, of Hector, Theseus, Jason. And there, before him in the lodge, heroes from those stories strode from the smoke. Huge bronze helms crowned in horsehair plumes rested on their heads, giant shields painted with stars, a leaf-bladed spear in one hand, a double-edged short sword at their belts. Two mist warriors clashed, he could hear the ringing of metal on metal, see the plunging spear strike home, hear their cries.

Another story came, of a Greek tribe, their land invaded, outnumbered, desperate. A small band of their warriors painted themselves as white as smoke so they could tell friend from foe in the deepest part of the night, and they went into the enemy camp where they lay dozing after their feast and slew them in great numbers, and in that slaughter saved their people.

So Tagay rose and told the tale as he remembered it. Told the council of the Tahontaenrat the story of the Ghost Warriors.

'Let the tribe embark on the river. At the same time, let me lead across the water eighty warriors, daubed in white, ten from each clan. We will destroy their canoes where they sit on the beach, so that our people can pass in safety to the lands of our brothers.'

He paused. The smoke had cleared, taking the Greek heroes away. His knees suddenly felt weak. 'That is my thought on the subject,' he remembered to say, just before he took his place again in the circle.

For a long moment, there was silence. Tagay unsure now of what his heart had told him, waited for the ritual of politeness, the acknowledgement of his views and the inevitable moving on to the opinions of wiser, more experienced men.

Then the silence ended in a roar – 'Haauu! Haauu! Haauu! Haauu!' – and the elders were all on their feet, those nearest to him pulling him up as well.

Tangled came forward again. 'The Hunter of the Sunrise has spoken well. This is a warrior's answer to our problem. We cannot sit in our lodges and wait for what comes, like the wolf caught in a snare waits the singing of the hunter's arrow. We must go out and prove who we are. For are we not the Tahontaenrat?'

Another cry of, 'Haauu!' greeted him. And more punctuated his speech, and the speeches that followed, as the chiefs debated no more but decided who would do what. Many men would be assigned to the building of the rafts necessary to ferry the entire tribe. Women would prepare the dried meat and the corn meal that would have to last the journey to the land of the Big Lakes. And several of each sex would be assigned a final, essential task.

'For they will continue to prepare the Kettle, the Feast of the Dead,' said Tangled. 'We cannot leave the bones of our families, all those of our tribe who have died since the feast three summers gone by, to be picked over by the dogs of our enemy. The Kettle will be held, as we planned it, under the full moon that rises above us tomorrow night. And after each family throws the bones of their relatives into the pit, they will go to the water and board the rafts.'

The details were discussed only a little longer, each clan leader, for peace and war, knowing the area of their responsibility. 'Is there anything more?' Tangled announced.

The chiefs all looked around at each other. They were eager to be gone. Then the flap of tanned hide that covered the entrance to the lodge was thrown back and one of the warriors who guarded it and had brought tobacco or water when it was needed now came in. He went up to Tangled and whispered in his ear.

The chief raised his arms. 'There is yet one matter,' he said. 'Though it needs no debate. Gaka, my sister, mother to some of you here, grandmother and great-aunt to many of our people, is sick. She has had a dream. All here know the power of her dreams, for many times has she helped the people with her visions. Now she has seen the only way for her to get well in this life or to journey in safety to the life beyond. So she asks for andac-wanda. She asks for it tonight, for her need is urgent.' He paused, and a slight smile came to his face. 'Tonessah, who she still calls by his nephew-name, Tagay, is asked to lead the ceremony.'

'But I know nothing about this.' Tagay saw all in the lodge turn to him, each chief with the same, slight smile that remained on Tangled's face. 'What is this andac-wanda? How will I know what to do?'

'It is . . . magic. And I think you will know.' The smile widened as he saw Tagay's puzzlement grow. 'Come with me, nephew.' Tangled stretched out his hand. 'Come and you will see.'

The evening star sparkled in a sky half-orange, half-blue. As Tangled led him from the council lodge across the central open space of the village, the chiefs scattered to their clans. Each cluster of people immediately began to buzz, messengers running from the groups to bear the news to the lodges where the evening meal was being prepared. Before Gaka's lodge, his home since his arrival, Sada awaited him with the rest of the Bear clan.

Tangled thrust Tagay through their ranks to the lodge entrance. 'I will tell you when I come back,' he said curtly, before throwing back the skin that covered the doorway. But before he could push the young man inside, several young women ran out, each looking up to meet Tagay's eyes, then colouring and looking swiftly away. He heard them say, 'Andac-wanda' to the waiting men. There was the sound of indrawn breath but the falling skin cut off further reaction.

It was as dark as ever in there, as murky, the one hole in the ceiling a poor exit for what the hearth fires produced. Tangled led him through to the end where, on a raised platform, Gaka lay. She was propped up now, lying on and wrapped in many skins, both beaver and bear.

Tangled flopped down beside her, took her hand, then spoke, his voice gentle. 'How are you, sister?'

'I am better if you have brought me who I need.' She squinted up, her one eye fixing in the space before Tagay. 'Is that you, nephew?'

Tagay felt tears in his eyes. In the short time he had been there, this woman had been his family. 'I am here, Aunt.'

'Sit beside me.' She motioned with a gnarled hand. 'There are things we must talk about.'

As he sat, Tangled rose. 'I will return, sister, with the moon.'

'You will take care of everything?'

'I will.' He sighed. 'It is not as if I have anything else of importance to do.'

He left. His aunt's gnarled hand seemed to be searching for something on the skin before her. Tagay took it, pressed it to his lips.

'I cannot see you so well, Tagay. But I remember your touch. Did I tell you that when I first held you in my arms it was like holding your father again.'

'My father?' Tagay raised his head. 'You . . . and my father?'

'You know it is our way. A maiden may choose many until the day she chooses just the one and marries him. And your father was one of the best looking young men I knew. I thought, for a little while . . .' She sighed. 'But it was always my sister, your mother, Sonosase, whom he loved, who loved him, even as children.' She squeezed Tagay's hand. 'But sometimes I remember him, his hand like your hand, his skin like your skin. And I remember these things well because he and I were called upon. He and I were andac-wanda. As you will be. For I saw you in my dream, when I journeyed to the lodge of my people in the sunset.'

'Will you tell me what this is, Aunt?'

She began to cough. He swiftly raised a flask of river water to her lips. Much splashed down her, but she swallowed enough and her spasm passed.

'You know how it is with our people. We live altogether here, so close, and it gives us much comfort to hear the breathing of our family around us in the night. But we do not hear anything else. Because we sleep, we eat, we tell our stories here yet we do not come together as man and woman within the lodge. We go to the woods, to the banks of river and stream, in the land above the cliff. It is a thing for two people alone. It is our way.'

Tagay said, gently, 'I know this, Aunt.'

'Well, know this also. There is one time, and only one, when we do not seek the quiet place away from others' eyes. It is in a time of need, when a dream tells one who has visited the world of dreams that we need a special Oki, a special power, and that power can only be made by a man and a woman, together here, before the lodge. The calling is 'andac-wanda'. Your father and I were called, once. Now I call you. Tonight.'

Tagay flushed, his hand suddenly hot in hers. 'Aunt!' he stuttered. 'I am honoured to be chosen. But you are unwell. Should this not wait till you are better?'

The one eye regarded him, searched his face. The silence that followed lengthened, as he felt his colour grow, the sweat forming on the skin that touched hers. Then, suddenly, Gaka began to laugh, coughing and choking at the same time. More water finally calmed her, but the merriment did not leave her.

'Oh, Tagay. You poor boy! You thought I . . .' She laughed again. 'No, nephew, though there was a time when a handsome young man like you . . . and I . . . but no matter.' She used his hand to pull herself up from where she had sunk down in the bed. 'No, nephew. You are called and a woman is called also.'

The relief mingled with a different feeling, which brought a further flush to his face. He had seen many of the unmarried girls of the village, many who were beautiful. His mind and body had been distracted by all the conflicts of returning to this world. But he was a man who had always loved women. When he spoke, his voice was lower.

'And whom have you chosen, Aunt?'

'She waits behind me, Tagay. Can you not see her?'

The raised platform on which his aunt lay was almost flush against the walls of the lodge. There was the slightest space created by the gap between them. Peering into it now, he saw a shape that must always have been there, a shape that, as his aunt finished speaking, rose from the shadows.

'Tagay,' she said, 'Little Bear.'

He was surprised, for just a moment. And then he wasn't.

'Anne,' he said, 'White Cedar.'

He stood by the deer hide blankets that were, in turn, piled over a bearskin. It lay on the floor, not in the very centre of the lodge but down near the end, below and before his aunt's platform. But the lodge that had been empty when they talked earlier was now full of men and women, their faces emerging or disappearing according to the swirling of the tobacco burning on their hearths. They swayed and chanted, 'Heh-heh-heh-heh-heh', the rhythm dictated by the tortoise-shell rattles that Tangled and his fellow chiefs were shaking at the other end of the lodge.

He was wearing only a breech cloth. His body had been painted with lines of red river mud, swirling patterns of stars, of animals and birds. His head had been partially shaved, the hair left long in the middle, curled and oiled, put up into a long tress, held in a deer skin band.

His hands shook. Mouth dry, he licked his lips repeatedly, watching the entrance of the hut, waiting for the quiver of the deerskin that would show she was about to appear. He had started with every arrival, as each member of the lodge made their entrance, moved to their place, took up the rhythm of the chant. But it had been a while since the last. And his shaking was growing.

When he'd seen her before, he'd only had time to whisper, in French, 'You don't have to do this,' and she'd only had time to reply, 'I know,' before the maidens of the lodge swept in, swept her away. The men had come for him then, taken him to the river to bathe, used the mud there to draw the elaborate patterns and symbols on his body. He knew that if such a thing were possible in France he would have been surrounded by men making obscene jokes, commenting on the night ahead, disparaging his anatomy. But the men of the Bear clan, when they talked, talked of war. Mostly, they sang their songs. No reference was made to what lay ahead of him that night, for it was sacred.

A flourish of rattles, the chant ending on a high note. Then silence, save for the wind outside the lodge and the crackle of fresh tobacco thrown on the fire.

And then she was there. Her hair was pulled back, set high as well. And her body was painted too. He had never seen her like this, for she had been clothed as a Frenchwoman when they'd met and had worn bead dresses since her arrival in this land. Now, she was dressed like any other maiden of the village in the summer, with just a short shift around her waist that scarcely reached to the middle of her thighs. Beads hung down them from a wampum belt. Around her neck, more lengths of river shell hung, concealing, but only a little, her nakedness.

Anne had meant to stride in unafraid, head high, like a princess. But when the deerskin was flung back and she saw him there, she suddenly had to raise her arms, cross them before her, as protection, as concealment. Only a gentle prodding made her step forward. More of a stumble, she thought, ungraceful as that. She was suddenly unsure if she could remember how to walk.

In a moment, she realized she must have, because she was standing before him and the rattles that had ceased on her entrance had begun again, as well as the chanting. In those sounds, it felt as if there was less attention on her. She could at least breathe, though she couldn't bring down the barrier of her arms, had indeed lost the ability to move them at all.

He stepped in to her, close, so she could smell the river on him, a clean, good scent that transcended the tobacco smoke. There was something else too, as good. The scent of him.

'Anne,' he said, 'we don't, you still can . . .'

He'd had words before, words he'd stored up in the time he'd waited there, words to excuse her, to release her. He'd even formed a plan – there was a pile of skins to lie beneath, they could hide there together, movements made, sounds, enough to satisfy the watchers.

He'd had a speech. And it vanished from his mouth and mind as he saw the beauty of her, a beauty he'd recognized once and had lost somehow.

She'd wondered if she could go through with it. Had decided for and against it with every long minute that had passed since Gaka had told her of her dream. Now, as she looked into his eyes, she saw in them what she'd first seen when she'd woken in the royal palace in Paris and he'd been by her side. And all the darkness between them since, the misunderstandings, the pain as he searched for himself in this world, vanished.

In their silence, the chants and the rattles once more built under their thoughts. Then;

'You don't . . .'

'I've never . . .'

They both stopped as they started, together. They both laughed. And the sound of the laughs, hers to him, his to her, chased away all the other sounds.

'I've never . . . loved anyone else,' she said. 'No man has ever . . . I've never wanted to be with anyone.'

'Then it is the same for both of us,' he smiled. 'For I have never loved anyone either.'

'I thought, in France . . .'

'That wasn't me. That was someone else. I think . . . I think I was only conceived when I saw you fall from the Paris sky. I was only born when I returned to my tribe.'

He swung his head to either side, raised his arms to gesture to those who chanted in the smoke. She saw the way his body moved, how it had grown even in the short time that he had been there. She reached out then and touched him, on the big muscle of his back. He turned at her touch and she kept her fingers there, dropping her other arm away. His eyes lowered to her breasts and when she saw him shudder, she felt happy and excited, in a way she never had before.

'I do not know what to do,' she said.

'I know,' he replied and he took her hand and laid her gently down onto the skins.

'Do not think of the people,' he said.

'What people?' she said and smiled.

Even though the others seemed far away, their chanting felt near, surrounding them. The rhythm of it took them both and though there was a little pain to start, it receded swiftly, diminished by the strange, the wondrous sensations that their bodies' joining was causing her. And the chants changed as she did, becoming more urgent, and soon, as he moved in different ways inside her, as his hands stroked and caressed her in ways she could never have guessed at, she found she was chanting too, and her cries and then his rose to mingle with the sounds above them both. She gathered in the smoke, the rattles, the rhythm, the way they moved, until her whole body rushed to a point where everything was one.

There was no moment in the night they were not together, asleep, or awake and moving again, joined by the sounds around them that did not cease.

It was the morning light streaming through the vent in the roof, falling on her face, that woke her. She was on her side and he was curled around her, so that they still touched, at every part of them that could. She moved and he groaned but did not wake, so she

404

slipped out from under him. Gentle snores came from mouths that had chanted all night.

Then she remembered what all the magic had been for. And she ran the few paces up to the platform.

Gaka was on her back, her eyelids half open. The one eye was still rolled over, the other stared straight out.

'Oh, Gaka, oh Aunt,' Anne cried, slipping down beside her. Then she noticed two things. The smile on Gaka's face, and her hand, the one that had been bent and twisted by her sudden sickness. It was open now as if, at the end, she'd reached out for something. And resting in that hand, was Anne Boleyn's.

NINE
GHOSTS

The full moon did not have the sky entirely to itself. Columns of cloud rolled across it, as they had all day, so that land and water would be suddenly concealed or as swiftly revealed. The clouds pressed down, holding in the day's heat. The air crackled, filling every nostril with the promise of rain.

The heat was fiercest at the entrance to the lodges for fires burned before each of them, huge pyres consuming all that was thrown on them in moments. It was flesh that burned, but not such as would delight the stomachs of the hungry. For each family had gone to the graves of their dead, all those who had stayed above the earth since the last Kettle, three years before. They had taken them down from their platforms, out of their bark coffins. They had stripped them of the beaver skins that had covered them and, if there was flesh still on their bones, that flesh was purged in a crucible of flame. Then the bones were raked from the ashes, washed, and wrapped again in fresh beaver skins.

Gaka's relations attended to her body differently, for she was of the most recent dead. As soon as it was discovered, her body had been curled up, chest to knees, hands clasped before her face. Now she lay on a bear skin robe close to the fire as if asleep. Anne sat right beside her, enjoying the heat on her near-naked skin. One hand rested on Gaka's shoulder, marvelling at the intensity of the dead woman's smile.

Something moved through her hair. She reached a hand up, thinking it must be another of the giant moths that had gathered around the firelight. But her brushing fingers encountered others and she lifted her head . . . to a vision that only the presence of so many dead could have conjured up.

She scrambled away, a cry caught in her throat. He followed her, his white hands raised toward her in a gesture of calming.

'I am sorry, Anne,' Tagay said. 'I did not know how to come to you.'

Her breath returning, she studied him. Every part of his body was whitened, except for his face and even that had streaks of the dye across it, five parallel lines the width of each cheek. His breech cloth, even his hair, was covered in the same compound, the stickiness of which she discovered as she raised her hand to it.

'Ugh! What is it?'

'A mixture of river mud and shavings of a special rock, ground to powder. Oh, and we each put blood into it, though I think that was more ceremonial.' He laughed as she tried to wipe her fingers on his chest, increasing the amount she had. Then she laughed too, and wiped them in lines across her own face, a faint mirror of his.

His laughter stopped when he looked down at Gaka. He was silent a moment, studying her. 'She looks content,' he said.

She took a sticky, white hand in hers. 'She begins her journey smiling. Is that not a lesson to us all?'

'It is. I hope to have a similar smile on my face when I start on mine. And probably thinking about the same thing, the last thing she saw.'

He looked down at her, hoping that she would join him in a memory of the previous night. But the look on her face was sad.

'Do not make that smile too soon, Tagay.'

'Not for twenty summers. More,' he said quickly, but not quick enough to stop the tear that formed in one of her eyes. He reached up to her face, stopped the tear as it ran down her cheek, raised it on a finger's end, watching it catch and hold the firelight.

'You promise?' Both her hands clasped his. 'When these painted lines are wrinkles?'

'I promise.' Then she pulled him to her, careless of the paint, needing to feel his body against hers. Their skin touched and a heat came that had nothing to do with the proximity of flames.

They held each other till they became aware of other sounds around them. The families of the lodge were gathering the last of the bones burned cleaned, wrapping them in skin bundles. Two women came for Gaka and began to fold the edges of her blanket around her. From the far side of the open space, they heard the shiver of tortoise-shell rattles, the first soft chanting of, 'Ha-eh-eh, Ha-eh-eh.'

Tagay shivered, muttered, 'I must go.' He half turned, then hesitated, turned back. 'There is something else. You must take this.'

She looked down. There was now a dark centre to the whiteness of his hand.

'Donnaconna's Oki.' She pulled her hand back as he lifted the smooth stone toward her. 'I stopped you throwing it away once. I told you then, it is power. Why do you seek to give that away when you need it most?'

His voice stayed soft. 'We do not take Oki over there. Only weapons.'

'Tagay . . .'

'I have prayed to it, burnt tobacco for it.' He hesitated, and she could see the struggle within him. 'I do not want to lose it in a fight.'

It was an excuse and they both knew it. He wanted it to survive, even if he didn't.

For a long moment they stared at each other across the stone. Then her hand closed over it and they held it between them. 'I will keep it for you. But only for tonight.'

She took it and he sighed. Then, looking down at the paint that daubed her, laughed. 'It is difficult to clean off.'

'We will clean it off together,' she replied fiercely, 'when I give you your Oki back. At the rendezvous.'

'At the rendezvous.'

Bending to the blanket at his feet, he said, 'Goodbye, Aunt.'

'I will see to her, Tagay. I loved her too.'

'I know.' He hesitated. 'Anne, I . . .'

'I know. Go on. Go! I will see you at the rendezvous.'

He walked swiftly away toward the river. She watched him until he was out of sight. Then she dropped the Oki into her pouch, and bent to help Gaka's nieces lift the bundle of skins that contained their aunt. Together, they joined the procession from the village and up the cliff path that led to the Feast of the Dead.

Still the thunder would not come. The air was agitated, the wind building in gusts and sudden short rushes, then dying away to a heated stillness. Changing directions too, bearing sounds to where they lay on the beach. It would blow from behind them and they would hear the tortoise-shell rattles, and the cries of, 'Ha-eh-eh, Ha-eh-eh.' Then many of the warriors would turn into the wind, sending muttered prayers toward the sounds, for all had relatives who were beginning their journeys that night to the Village of the Dead. And they all knew that, all too soon, they could be following them on that journey. But when the wind switched and blew into their faces from the water, other sounds came to them, faint but unmistakable. On the far shore, the Tattooed people were holding a feast of war.

Tagay turned his head, looked down the beach to either side. Though the moon was hidden, the ghost warriors were easy to see. Eighty of them, ten from each clan but all intermingled, each clutching their bows and quivers, their war clubs and knives, their own protective Oki of stones, sticks, bones. The ten nearest to Tagay were his guard – older, more experienced fighters. The rest were younger, full of the crazed courage of youth. These also were mainly bachelors, with no families dependent on them in the village.

A hand pulled at his elbow. Nishane, an older member of the Beaver clan, whose scars testified to his history in war, gestured to the water. Carefully, Tagay peered through a little gap in the foliage that hid them. At first, all he could see was what he'd seen in the hour or more they'd waited there – the river glittering or dull depending on the position of clouds and moon, and still maintaining their position against the flow of the stream, the enemy's cluster of five canoes. There were two men in each and every so often a new craft would appear as a replacement, the one relieved taking back the same message to their camp – that their Tahontaenrat prey were feasting in their village.

Nishane drew Tagay's attention to other movement in the water and he could now make out the shapes that drifted with the stream toward the enemy's canoes. Shapes that to most eyes would appear merely as branches of old trees that had fallen into the water. But as the moon suddenly appeared, Tagay could make out the darker shapes at the heart of the floating wood. Not all the warriors of the Deer people had painted themselves as ghosts.

Some had found black mud, darker rock powder, though they had still bound it with their blood.

The canoes began to separate to allow the branches to pass between them, a paddle stretched out to fend off a collision. And it was when the paddle reached into the leaves that ten black shapes disengaged themselves from the five, floating trunks. From being stationary in the water the canoes were suddenly all moving agitatedly. Then four of them flipped over, flailing bodies falling. A bone knife that had been covered in mud flashed clean in the moonlight. Cries carried, swiftly cut off as water filled mouths.

One canoe had survived. Tagay could see the two warriors in it, frantically turning the craft toward their own shore, thrusting their paddles into the water, striking at hands that tried to hold them. A paddle was seized but the canoe broke free and immediately began to surge away. Drawing breath now, its occupants began to shout. But the wind was in their faces, bearing the sounds of their tribe's feast.

One of the other canoes was righted. Two black shapes slipped into it and paddles immediately dipped into the water. The pursued were several canoe lengths ahead but they had only one paddle between them. The gap was closed, the boats merged into one shape. There were grunts, a howl of pain. Then, as the moon hid again, silence. And the five canoes, all righted now, began to pull strongly for the Tahontaenrat shore.

Eighty silent, white figures rose as one from their hiding. The canoes grounded, and ten black shapes leapt out, pulling their craft higher. One of them was limping and it was this shape that made his way straight to Tagay.

The only part of Sada that could be seen clearly were his eyes and his teeth, these because they were bared in a smile.

'First blood, War Chief,' he said, dropping something wet at Tagay's feet.

Tagay looked down. Even in the half light he could see the scalp, the hair pulled up into a single top knot. There was even a trace of a tattooed line curling down from it.

'First blood.' He raised his arm, turning to either side so all could see. Instantly, the white figures began to pull larger canoes from their hiding place into the water, six or eight figures climbing into each of them. From behind them other, unpainted men appeared, laying logs along the beach down which they began to roll rafts.

'Are you sure I can't come with you, Tagay?' Sada's eyes gleamed up at him.

'We talked of this, cousin. Your leg was good enough for swimming, not for running along a beach, dodging arrows.'

'It is true.' Sada reached down, rubbed his ankle, then bent and picked up the scalp. 'I just wanted a few more of these for my lodge post.'

'Then I will bring some back for you.' Tagay looked around, saw that his war party was all embarked. The canoes floated just offshore, all save one nearby. At its prow, Nishane held two paddles. 'And you have made me a promise.'

'I know. White Cedar.' Sada grinned up at him. 'I heard that you were so tireless at the andac-wanda that the Gods came to chant by the hearth and envy their new rival.'

Tagay smiled. 'Watch for her, Sada.' Then he headed to the water.

'I will. And later we will smoke pipes together in our new lodge near the Big Lakes and you will tell me the story of your feats this night. Night after night, season after season after . . .' He faked a huge yawn.

Tagay laughed, then moved down the beach. When he'd climbed into the canoe, he lifted the paddle high so all could see it. As it rose, the moon appeared again in a rent of cloud as if summoned by him.

Glowing in its light, the Ghost Warriors set out across the water toward the village of their enemy.

The song ended. Thirty pairs of feet thumped down together on the dense packed earth, the deer-hoof rattles at each knee shaking in unison with the force. The leader, who had been crouched in an attitude of attack, now swung his club high into the air using its trajectory to pull him up. As the weapon reached for the sky he let out the war whoop, starting high on a note then running down to a moment's pause before reaching again for the same note but louder, wilder. As his cry finished, every dancer took it up. 'Ah-aaaaa -Ah,' burst from thirty throats.

Then the drums came with a slower beat, and the dancers

walked to its rhythm around the huge circle of people. Since no one strode forward to make a speech – and there had been many in the hours of the feast – Thomas took the opportunity to move across the circle to Gianni. It would have been rude to do so while the war chief, Falling Day, the man who had first captured them, declaimed the glory of their tribe.

'Will they have any strength left for their dawn battle?' Gianni gestured to the dancers.

'From what I've seen of them, they could dance all night and still fight all the next day.' Thomas lowered himself onto the ground beside the younger man. 'But these are only a few. How many warriors do you think have gathered here?'

'It is difficult to say. Six hundred? Seven?'

Thomas nodded. He thought it might be even more. The allies of their hosts had been coming, in smaller and larger bands, for the entire time they had been there. Through their interpreter he had learnt that those who came were of different tribes yet bound with the Great Hill People in a confederacy of five nations. It was always hard to tell time with them, everything was just 'before'. But their own tribe had been the last to join the compact, the Hodenosaunee, as it was called. And they had been members for at least twenty summers, it seemed.

'Do you still hold to your plan, Gianni?'

'I do. And do you still hold to yours?'

'What choice have you left me?'

The younger man looked over at him. 'The choice to wait here till the battle is over and I return. With the hand of the witch.'

'And with your sister.'

Gianni coloured. 'Yes, of course. With my sister as well.'

Thomas started to speak again, but there was no point. The younger man would never be dissuaded. He had been very disappointed when Black Snake had failed to return with what they sought. But reasoned argument – that the hand was lost this night of the full moon – was only met with a grunted, 'Then we will make her find it again.' Thomas knew that the hand was still Gianni's obsession. So Anne had to be his. He need not tell her brother why.

'Remember, Jesuit, you will have to look to yourself. I will not take care of you over there.' Gianni gestured to the far shore, just visible as a shadow in the moon-hidden night.

Despite his training in calm, something in Gianni's arrogance could still prickle Thomas. 'And how many battles have you fought in, boy?' he said.

'Well, I . . .'

'Exactly. I know you have killed in alleys. You know all about the knife in the dark. But I was storming breaches when you were chasing chickens on your farm! So you look to *yourself*.'

As the two men glared at each other, a whoop from the war leader, immediately answered by his dancers, signalled another round of the dance. Gianni rose. 'I will go see to my gunpowder and leave you to your prayers.'

The drumbeats doubled as Gianni walked away.

'Well reminded,' Thomas muttered to himself. From where he sat he could see through the dancers and between a gap in the lodgehouses and the trees to the river. It was lit by the sudden appearance of the moon and black shapes moved on its surface, like insects on the surface of a pond. He struggled up and onto his knees and, as another war song started, began his prayers.

'Holy Mary, Mother of God, hearken to my pleas. Keep safe your daughter Anne. Holy Jesus, Blessed Saviour, listen to . . .'

'Ah-aaaaa -Ah.' The war whoop rang out again and again, drowning the words of his prayer, even in his own ears and heart. 'Ah-aaaaa -Ah.'

'Ha-eh-eh, Ha-ch-ch.'

The last group of the procession had arrived from the village. They were from one of the destroyed villages and they took their allotted place at the circular pit's edge. The women laid out the bundles of presents that they had managed to save from the destruction of their homes, supplemented with gifts from their relatives and clan fellows in Stadacona. The men of the group clambered up onto the wooden platform that had been erected around one half of the pit. There they attached the bundles of skin that contained the bones of their dead to poles and wedged these so they reached out above the void.

Anne stood with the people of Gaka's lodge, their aunt's body still wrapped in skins at their feet, as were all the other bodies of the recent dead. The pit she stood above was at least two large men deep and perhaps five across, its floor completely lined in beaver robes.

As the cries of the last of the arrivals died away, Tangled stepped forward and raised his arms. Drums murmured lightly under the words that followed.

'You are all welcome here, both you who have brought your dead and those you have brought who continue their journey this night.' He reached behind him and was handed a large wooden ladle. He stretched it out over the pit. 'Let us give them our gifts, so that their journey to the next village will be easy and they will have many feasts on the way.'

He dropped the ladle. Instantly, from all around the pit, utensils were thrown in, kettles, bowls, sieves and trays, pipes and mortars and deer hide bags. When the last of the gifts had fallen, Tangled spoke again.

'Now, let us feast our relatives.'

Immediately, food was produced, bowls of stew ladled out from kettles, dried deer meat handed around, roasted fish on skewers. The Tahontaenrat sat and ate and talked as if they had all the time in the world.

Anne felt it was her, and her alone, who could not eat, was the only one who looked back now beyond the village, over the water. Toward their men, the other ghosts at this feast.

At last the thunder came, in the wake of a stab of lightning that cut down in jagged lines to strike the high country, lighting the white-daubed warriors as if they were shards of its power. And the roll that followed coincided with the sound of their canoes grounding on the beach. It was like a small shoal of fish joining a huge host of them, for the canoes of their enemy were drawn up rank on rank, hundreds and hundreds, from little two-man craft to boats that could hold twenty. On and on they stretched, from water's edge to the first trees.

They had sent one canoe in first, men of the dark mud who had swiftly killed the two men who watched the water. They came to Tagay and reported now.

'They are holding their feast in the open space at the centre of their village,' one said.

The other added. 'This path here leads to it. It is the only one to the beach, but four paths join it up ahead to the different gates of their palisade.'

'Which gate lies closest to the forest?' Tagay asked.

'The west,' the first man replied. 'Low bushes run almost up to it.'

Tagay spoke swiftly to the clan leaders. The plan had been decided before they set out, it just needed refining now. The ten youngest men were to stay on the beach and destroy the canoes and the more solid rafts. Ten more, who were the best archers, would go to the crossroads of paths ahead and wait for the swift return of the rest – sixty of them, who would enter the village by the west gate. Tagay knew it would only be a matter of time before a Tattooed warrior came across them on the beach and raised the alarm. He didn't want to be trapped there by overwhelming odds. The only way to get enough time to do the job was to create panic at the feast fires of their enemies.

To the sound of cedar bark splintering behind them, they set off from the beach. Twice they saw pairs of men coming their way, twice a dozen arrows sang through the night. At the crossroads of the four paths, the ten dispersed through the trees, some to climb, some to take advantage of a slight rise of ground where they planted arrows tip down in the earth before them.

Tagay led the remaining men west at a gentle run. Within a minute, they were crouched in bushes before the palisade gate. It was closed and would be barred on the inside. Two points glowed atop it, showing where the night guards sucked on their pipes. From beyond them, came the cries of the feast, the never ceasing beating of drums.

At a signal, each man slipped an arrow onto a bow string. Tagay strung the one given him as war chief by Sada, the Arrow That Flies True. The best archers may have been left behind at the crossroads but of the sixty arrows that were given flight, more than enough struck home to send the two men reeling backwards, their pipes a crescent of sparks in the darkness. Pale wraiths moved forward, throwing hide lassoes over the palisade posts, then climbing swiftly up. A moment later the gates swung open and the warriors of the Tahontaenrat were inside the stronghold of their foe.

They gathered just within the gateway. Tagay knew that they would not have much time before discovery and the fight that would follow. They would kill silently for as long as they could do so. They would spread through the camp in their groups of ten and try to wait for his signal.

'Our people should now be embarking on the rafts,' he said. 'Soon our wives, our children, our parents, our sisters and brothers will be past us and on their way to safety in our new lands. We only have to stay and hurt them here a little, to give our brothers on the beach time to destroy their boats. Listen for the cry we discussed, the call of the crane, for when I, or if I am killed, one of my ten, give it, then it is time to run for the beach. Do not stay for scalps and do not stay too long to prove your bravery. It is already proved by being a Ghost Warrior. I want us to sing the song of this night together to our grandchildren in the new lodges our people will build.'

From sixty throats came a grunted assent: 'Haauu.'

'Good then.' Tagay smiled. 'Let us now honour our ancestors.'

The village was more organized than the random construction of the Tahontaenrat. The four roads from the four gates led straight to the central open space. With arrows strung they ran down this west one, groups of ten wheeling off every twenty paces or so to spread through the narrower alleys between the lodges. Tagay and his ten ran directly down the path and when they came to within fifty paces of its end, when they could clearly see the backs of the people gathered, a huge circle of warriors, women, children, all facing inward to the dance, only then did they peel off left, to shelter behind the biggest hut. There, one of the warriors produced a wooden bowl he'd carefully sheltered all the way across. Embers tumbled from it, lighting some dried straw. Dipping a special arrow, whose tip was wrapped in a cloth steeped with deer fat, he lifted the bow, pulled back the string . . .

To any in the circle who looked up, it could have been a shooting star. That's what Thomas thought at first and he wished on it, as he had on many a cloudless night as a youth in Shropshire. But no star he saw there ever fell into a tree. And none was followed, a few seconds later, by twenty, forty, fifty more. Most rose into the sky in flaming arcs and plunged into the roofs of houses which immediately began to burn. Some fell into the circle of dancers. But the drums continued for a few beats more, the dancers leapt and chanted, and it was only when their leader seemed to swallow a shot of flame and fell suddenly to the ground that Thomas, and everyone else, suddenly realized that something was very wrong.

Or maybe it was the cry of, 'Tahontaenrat' that broke in from outside their circle. Or the sight of the running ghost, the first of many, who burst into the middle of the circle swinging his huge war club, striking down another of the dancers and running out the other side. The circle surged inwards on itself, and screams were heard from those nearest the outside, from those who were dying first.

Many of his men struck at any bodies that came near them, be it child, woman or man. But Tagay sought a warrior for his first encounter and soon had him, a huge and tattooed brute who had seized a war club from the porch of the nearest lodge and now ran at him. The blow was raised from on high and swept down, down to where Tagay had been, thumping into the earth. Lunging to the side, Tagay cut with his father's club, the blade's point slicing down into the giant's foot. As he howled in pain, Tagay jerked it hard, pulling the blade out. The warrior fell and Tagay lunged low again, the metal biting into the exposed neck. Leaping over the body he saw a white warrior holding off three of the enemy with swings of his club. Tagay joined, cutting high for a face, ripping low for a leg. Flailing limbs fell around them and, when the heavy war club crushed a skull, the two Tahontaenrat were suddenly alone.

Flames crackled. The roofs caught swiftly, burnt in moments and collapsed inwards in a volcano of sparks. The heat was ferocious near them. Between the infernos, warriors fought, flame lit. The open space had cleared, the crowd streaming away, crushing those who fell. For a strange moment of clarity, Tagay felt the first fat drops of rain that had long been promised, striking his face.

'This way,' he yelled to the other warrior. He could see a bigger fight developing down the east road, where some of the enemy had rallied and many of the Tahontaenrat had chased them. They ran down the avenue toward the mêlée.

At first, Gianni thought it was merely a different form of dance, louder, noisier than even the ones before. Then he heard the devouring sound of fire and with that the screams took on a different meaning. He had just finished cleaning and loading the second of his pistols. Lowering the pan cover on it, he thrust it into his belt next to its twin and, picking up his sword, stepped from the lodge.

Into mayhem. The deerskin opened up a world of horror. Ghouls chased through the streets, clubbing at the backs of tattooed warriors. Sheets of flame rose to the west and the smoke from an immense burning immediately stung his eyes. Thunder rode the air, and tipping his head up for a brief moment, he felt the first heavy raindrops. As yet another man was chased down and slain before him, it felt like blood falling from the skies.

His sword was out. Whoever they were, these white ghouls were killing, if not his friends, then the people who promised to get him what he desired. So, as yet another of them ran past, pursued by his demon, Gianni took the sword in a double grip and sliced parallel to the ground. The blade bit into the white-painted neck, cutting off his war whoop with his life.

To his left, some of his allies had rallied. Their cries rose with their clubs to challenge the invader. A skirmish of twenty men developed, blows fell, shields clashed. He stepped toward the fray, looking for an opening. Then, behind him, he heard running steps. He turned, drawing one of his pistols. Two white warriors were ten paces away. Aiming at the nearest one, he pulled the trigger. The ball erupted from the barrel, smoke partially obscuring his view for just one moment. The next it had cleared, enough for him to see the first warrior on the ground and the second running at him, a slim, curving club swept high and back.

To shoot, he had put his sword into his left hand, so he was forced to parry wrong-handed. Also, he'd expected the shock of one of the heavy balled war clubs. This one cut at him, like a sword, and he only just got his blade between it and his flesh. But the weapon was lighter than his and the warrior wielding it had pulled it back, struck again. Gianni felt something push into his hip bone, grating there. It took him a moment to realize that he'd been cut.

418

'Sacred Jesus!' he cried and it was those words that made Tagay realize who it was he was fighting. Till that moment, he had just reacted, seeing his comrade fall to the pistol shot, leaping on to avenge him. Now he noticed the face, lit by the flames of a burning lodge. He had seen it before, through the broken skin of a canoe. And once before that, in the back alleys of Montmartre.

'Gianni Rombaud,' he said and, in saying it, he hesitated. Long enough for the other man to reel back, switch sword hands and return his stare with an equal measure of disbelief, then with fury.

'Tagay.' He attacked on the word, his long blade cutting the air. Tagay knew he couldn't take a blow to his own weapon, the metal would shatter it, so he ducked and feinted, let the man push him back.

Gianni tripped on the body of the man he'd just killed. He skittered onto one knee but his last lunge, point to chest, had pushed Tagay back so that he fell too, onto his back. He was up in a moment but it only took that moment for the Italian to pull his second pistol from his belt.

The fight behind them rounded a corner. Suddenly, though screams and flames still filled the night, they were alone.

'Now,' Gianni said, squinting along the gunbarrel, 'what have you done with my sister?'

The rain had begun to fall just as the last few bundles of bones were dropped into the pit. The families moved away as each package disgorged its contents, as last prayers were uttered, last tears shed. They moved slowly at first, then swifter as the men who led them to the water urged them on. By the time the last of them left, the rain was heavy.

Only one family remained, along with the men who stirred the bones together in the pit with long paddles, mixing the bones of the Tahontaenrat into a common grave. Anne watched two of the nieces, helped by little Do-ne, now pull back the skins, revealing Gaka to the rest of the grieving relatives.

'My sister was happy, at the end.' Tangled spoke from beside her. He had moved down from the platform where he had directed the ceremony. Taking his wampum belts, he knelt and laid these carefully down now beside the body. He spoke words to her, words for her alone. When he rose, he turned to Anne and said, 'Is there anything you wish to give her?'

Her throat was thick. 'I have nothing . . . nothing except . . .' She felt in the pouch at her back. She touched two objects there. The silver cross of her brother . . . and the hand of Anne Boleyn. And with that touch came memories, flashes of moments, presenting in her mind like a series of living paintings. That first moment when she had touched the hand in the Tower of London and she had sensed the lost queen so near, disturbed from her rest once more by the desires of evil men. Other moments: a rune-vision of destruction and redemption in a grove of silver birch; another hand with the red brand of a murderer sitting in a casket; a bear tied to a stake in a palace yard and the man who was also a bear pulling her from the wreckage of a sugar castle; her father's sword sailing over the prow of her ship with the strength of a courage re-found. Finally, a memory so recent not even a sleep had come between her and it – of waking beside the man she had spent the night loving and rushing to see the woman who had made that love possible. That woman, Gaka, had died with a smile on her lips – and a six-fingered hand clutched in hers.

And then Anne knew! Suddenly, there could be no doubt. Gaka had spoken to her, even after she had died. She was willing to take the hand on, to bring rest to both the Annes. This was the gift the old woman had spoken of, to be brought to the Village of her Dead.

Bending swiftly, she placed the skeletal six fingers in the hand of the one who lay there. 'Thank you,' was all she said. Stepping back, the rest of the family came forward, with their gifts, their words of parting. Then this last body was tipped over into the pit where the men with paddles blended the flesh with other flesh, other bones, finally pulling the finest beaver skin robes over the surface of the entire area. These were stretched tight, pegged down, sand and earth piled in on top.

'Come,' said Tangled, tugging gently at her arm. 'The last of the rafts waits for us. Come.'

Tagay stared down the muzzle of the gun. Strangely he felt no fear, seeing his death waiting there.

'Your sister is safe and beyond your reach. And so is the thing you desire, that has drawn you across the world.'

Gianni tipped his head. 'And what do you think that is?'

'The hand of the queen. The hand you killed your father for. It is buried. Anne will have buried it by now.'

The mention of his family's names made him feel strange, a void that spread from his stomach, filling his chest. He didn't like the feeling so, to disperse it, he reached for his ready anger.

'Oh well,' he spat, 'she'll just have to dig it up again.'

He squeezed the trigger. The flintlock wheel struck a spark which fell into the gunpowder pan. Tagay waited for the explosion and the pain that would follow it, raising his club in futile defence. But the rain had got heavier, much heavier so the powder produced a wisp of smoke, a sound like a sigh, and nothing else.

Tagay breathed out. 'Misfire.' He smiled. 'Happens all the time.'

With a roar, Gianni threw the pistol at him, brought his sword again into his right hand. Then the noise of fighting that had all but disappeared returned in full measure, as ten Ghost Warriors burst round the bend of lodges. Striking at their backs were a greater number of their enemies. Then, as suddenly, more of the painted appeared, Nishane at their head. The three groups collided just where Tagay and Gianni faced each other at a sword's length. Both men were swept up in the crowd, swept apart.

'Come, Tonessah.' Nishane was beside him. 'We have seen the fire arrows in the sky from our village. The last raft is on the water.'

At Tagay's nod, both men threw back their heads and gave the cry of the whooping crane. It was taken up by those around them and turning, the Ghost Warriors ran yelling just ahead of their enemies. In the open space, more white figures joined.

Gianni managed, with shouts and blows, to halt some of the pursuers. 'This way,' he screamed. Half a dozen, who had tried to master the fire sticks, followed him at a run down to the other bay.

The Tahontaenrat were chased out of the main gate of the

village and ran into the forest. At the crossroads, a flight of arrows from skilled men stopped the pursuit.

'The beach! Now!' Tagay yelled.

Bare feet sounded loud on the forest floor, as the shouts and the roar of flames faded behind them. Exhilarated by their success and the number of the Tahontaenrat who had escaped – he hadn't time to count but many white warriors ran through the trees around him – Tagay led his party to the beach. If he had purchased enough time for his men there to do the task they'd been set, if the war canoes and rafts of their enemy were destroyed and the last of his people were on the water, then they had saved the tribe. Now he could save himself and return to the love he had found. To Anne.

They ran from the trees. The rain had stopped, the clouds rolled away to torment some other part of the earth and the bloated moon was right above their heads, its beams lighting destruction – for everywhere lay the shattered hulls of the Hodenosaunee war fleet.

'To the water,' Tagay shouted and warriors ran past him and started pushing their own craft into the stream. He stood with Nishane and the other experienced men who had survived, five of them in all, each with a bow in hand, facing the forest from where the enemy would come. It was not long before the first war cry was heard, before the first arrow passed close to their heads.

'Go now, Tagay,' Nishane shouted. 'We stay.'

'No! We all go,' the younger man replied, raising his club toward the forest path. It was as if he'd conjured a tattooed warrior from the green depths with it, who burst out screaming, his own war club flailing. An arrow through the chest cut off the sound. But more whoops came to them from the fringe of trees, deeper shadows within the shadows, massing.

'They will shoot the last of us from the beach. So, go now!' Nishane took Tagay's arm and shoved him hard toward the water.

'How can I leave you?'

Nishane smiled. 'You have learnt fast, War Chief, since your return. But you have not learnt everything. The elder stays to help the young man escape. It is the way of the Tahontaenrat. So – go!'

He shoved again, just as another arrow passed between their

faces. Tagay stumbled down the shale. Canoes were pushed from the shore and one of them had but a single pale shape in it. He waded through the shallows and pulled himself on board at the front. The young warrior handed him a paddle and they both began ply them. Behind, the war whoops of the enemy increased to a frenzy. But above them, he could hear Nishane's voice, singing his war song. 'I do not fear death. Those who do are cowards and fools. I am Nishane of the Beaver clan. Taste my war club.'

Then the song was lost in the song of clubs through the air, the grunts of blows striking, the cries of pain. Tagay was at the front and he drove his paddle hard into the water. They were pulling well from the shore, when on an instant it became much harder. He looked back and his companion, whose name he had not known, a member of the Hawk clan, was staring at him, paddle raised across his chest. Tagay saw the arrow head poking through the neck and then, a moment later, a surge of blood streamed down the white of his chest. The Hawk fell forward, half over the edge of the canoe.

Tagay, seeing he was dead, somehow managed to get the body into the water without capsizing the frail craft. Glancing back, he could make out a frenzy of warriors on the beach, dancing around and on fallen white bodies. As he watched, the last of their own canoes were launched from the beach, surrounded by tattooed warriors. And to his left, from around a point of land, came another boat, a larger, darker shape.

He began to paddle, a frenzy of strokes. Ahead, the others of his tribe pulled away, the distance between them growing fast. He was just one, and he had not mastered the canoe, but for a while, his desire leant him strength and skill. For a while, he even managed to pull ahead of his pursuit as their arguing voices, jostling for precedence in their craft, faded behind him. He drove hard along the path of a moonbeam. But soon he heard the unmistakable sound of other paddles, getting closer, closer. And another sound, something that should not have been there. Wood grinding on metal.

There was a dark shape ahead on the water. He began to make for it, he didn't know why and it was only when he got near that he realized his mistake, realized where he'd led his pursuers. And when he was close enough to see, he was close enough to hear her voice, crying out.

'Tagay! Tagay! Come!'

Anne had watched the canoes bearing the white warriors go past them. Even at a distance and with only the moonlight to see by she knew that none was her love. She'd prayed that maybe she'd missed him, that he had preceded her, was waiting for her upstream at the rendezvous. So many had escaped the attack, why not him? Then she'd seen the lonely craft and those that closed on it remorselessly. And she'd known.

There was little those few on the raft could do but steer with the current. But the canoe's occupant, having hesitated, now drove straight toward them, the enemy a scant fifty lengths behind.

'Tagay,' she said, her hands reaching out as he fell aboard. But he turned immediately, bow in hand toward the pursuit. Beside him, the three others put down their paddles and grabbed weapons. Do-ne hopped on his withered leg, clutching a bone knife before him. Tangled stepped beside him, a javelin in his hands.

'Come to my arms, Coyotes, tattooed scavengers. Feel the kiss of my war spear,' the old chief cried.

Then something spat flame from the larger of the pursuing vessels, and the air filled with screams and flying metal. Something struck her, high up on the head. As she fell she saw a man's back, white painted, and a muscle that she'd run her fingers down in another life. Something was wrong with it, something protruded from it that shouldn't have, breaking its beautiful symmetry. But darkness came before she could see what it was.

TEN

DEATH SONG

The world was washed clean. The thunderclouds had long since passed away, leaving the sky to itself, an immense and nearly undisturbed expanse of blue. Only against the far shore were there threads of darkness, rising up from the forest. She had heard the tattooed warriors around her talk of how their village had been almost destroyed in the fight. But it did not concern them. They would build their new village here, a clifftop fortress in a conquered land.

A gentle breeze touched her, still hot with summer but within it the hint of something else, a finger of coolness within the caress. Autumn coming, the recognition bringing her a memory, of Montepulciano, the grapes as they would be now in her father's vineyards, fat globes of fruit fast approaching their moment of transformation into wine. There were grapes in this land too, though there the similarity ended, the sweeping river valley, the huge pines and maples so different from the slopes and the cypresses of Tuscany. Except for the oak, the one that she had sat in twice, that she looked at now. That tree could have been in the forests near their home. She and Gianni could have climbed one just like it.

The memory was chased away by the crack of a ship's cannon, the third in so many minutes. Uncle Pierre had kept his promise and returned for her the day after the full moon.

Too late! For now she looked again at the man standing at the edge of the covered pit, dwarfed by the tall warriors around him, for he was smaller of stature, like his father. Next to Gianni stood another man, leaning on a stick, a black cloak wrapped around him despite the heat, the man she'd last seen in the Tower of

London, in another world and time. If she hadn't felt so numb, she might have been surprised at the sight of him. And at Thomas Lawley's feet, a boy with a withered leg crouched terrified. The only other survivor of the raft, Do-ne.

The head of the dying man in her lap rolled, blood bubbled at his lips and at the rent in his chest where the shaft of jagged metal still protruded. It looked strangely like a length from a barrel hoop. She knew she could not pull it out without killing him; it was too near his heart. So she just wiped the blood from his wound, from his mouth. Tagay murmured, something she couldn't catch.

She realized someone had asked her a question. 'What?' she said.

The black-cloaked figure limped toward her. She remembered that in another world she had bound this man's leg.

'Anne,' said Thomas, gently. 'They need to know – what became of the hand?'

'The hand?' She raised hers, brushed hair away from her face. He saw the jagged cut near her temple where metal had struck her a glancing blow. 'Oh, *that* hand.'

'Where is it, Anne?' Gianni had moved beside Thomas, his voice a harsh contrast to the Englishman's. 'It is your last chance for redemption. Give it to us.'

'Redemption?' Before she could answer further, a weak voice came from her lap.

'It is beyond your reach, Gianni. It has begun its journey to the Village of the Dead. Your queen travels with other spirits, now. Leave her be.'

Anne looked down. It was the first words she had heard Tagay speak since they had been brought to the cliff top. She'd feared she might not ever hear that voice again.

'Oh, my love,' she said, rocking him. She had whispered to him what she had done with Anne Boleyn's legacy. She'd thought he'd been too close to death to hear.

'*Other spirits*?' Gianni straightened in sudden understanding. 'It's there, isn't it? With the bones of all the other savages. There!' His finger jabbed toward the smoothed over earth of the pit.

He didn't need an answer. He turned. 'Then we will dig it up.'

Thomas said, 'It's impossible, Gianni. There will be hundreds of bodies down there.'

'Impossible?' he screamed. 'It was impossible to cross the world, do all that I have done. And now I stand with only this little earth between me and my salvation?'

He fell to his knees at the pit's edge and began to scrabble in the dirt. Hands like twisted iron grabbed him, hauled him back. The face of the interpreter, Hair Burned Off, appeared before him.

'Falling Day asks what you do?' He gestured to his chief who stood, arms folded, on the other side of the pit.

'It is buried, here, what I seek. The mighty witch's Oki. Help me. Help me!' Gianni tried to brush off the hands that held him, to throw himself forward and burrow straight down to his desire. But his own loss of blood, from Tagay's cut to his hip, had weakened him. And the warrior's grip was unbreakable.

Falling Day talked rapidly and the interpreter nodded, then spoke. 'He says that if the witch's spirit was here then she is gone now. She is with the dead and it is the dead who must fight her. Those buried here were our enemies, yes. But we do not disturb their burial place.'

'No! Don't you see? We must . . . we must.' Gianni started to sob, struggling against the hands that held him.

Thomas was at his side in a moment. 'Rombaud,' he whispered fiercely. 'It is over. Do not show them any emotion. They kill men for weakness.'

The chief spoke rapidly again. Anne heard and understood the words, before they were translated. Tagay too, and he tried desperately to raise himself up on his elbow.

The interpreter said, 'But Falling Day knows this woman is a witch too. So we will kill her now, before she can do us any harm.'

A spoken command and Gianni was released to fall forward, while Anne was seized, dragged to her feet, Tagay's weak fingers reaching for her, losing her. One man pinned her arms, a second moved before her with a knife.

'Wait!' Thomas didn't know where the speed, the strength, came from. But he was beside Anne in a moment, his stick striking the knife from the hand, a blow knocking the warrior who held her aside. He placed himself before her, braced himself, as arrows were notched, strings pulled back.

Another guttural command. The weapons eased, slightly. Words were spoken and the interpreter came up to him.

'Falling Day asks why you help her, Black Robe? Is she not a witch? You said your gods, as ours, hate such bad Oki.'

If ever Thomas had needed his Jesuit training it was now. He breathed deeply, calmly, and looked straight into the war chief's eyes.

'No,' he said, calmly. 'She is not. She is a Dreamteller, that is all.'

'But this man is her brother and her brother say she is witch.'

'Her brother lies.' Thomas raised his arm, pointed at Gianni. 'He wants her Oki, her power.'

Everyone there turned to look at the prone man. Gianni knelt, hands muddied with earth. He stared back but not at them, his eyes wild, unfocused.

Then his sister stepped from around the black cloak. She had something in her hand and she threw it before her brother.

Gianni looked down. A little cross with double bars had fallen on its end, landing upright in the earth of the grave. With trembling fingers he reached for what he saw. But it was not until he touched it that he knew for certain what it was.

A groan came, a memory – of his father's rough hand running through his hair, handing him this piece of silver. Then another, of tears falling onto its shiny surface as he nailed it to a tree. And a third memory, of his father's sword raised in the air, an inverted crucifix on a harbour wall.

He looked up. Anne was staring at him, and in the darkness of her eyes, he could see Jean and Beck staring back. His father as he'd been, fighting him, dying because of him. His mother on the pier, cradling her husband's body, giving her son the look she'd give a stranger. He looked past Anne's eyes, past the memories, to the silent, tattooed warriors.

Heathens.

Suddenly, it was all so simple. A calm came over him, a vision of bliss eternal.

And he said, 'He is right. I want her Oki. I lied to you. *I* am the witch. It's me you want, not her.'

The words were translated. Hands hauled him upright.

The interpreter was before him, doubt on his face. 'You know what you say? You know what happens to a witch?'

The calmness had not left him. 'I know.'

Anne cried, 'No, Gianni. No! It does not have to be this way.'

'It does, sister. These pagans . . .' He looked around him. 'They will have their blood sacrifice.' He paused and then he suddenly smiled, sadly, shyly, like a boy she'd once known. 'Not so different from me, then.'

Before she could speak again, she heard a groan from behind her. She turned just as Tagay was dragged upright and she heard the chief say, 'He is a brave warrior, the leader of the Ghosts who fought us. We will honour him with a brave warrior's death.'

Behind her they stripped Gianni of his clothes and he let them, unresisting. Thomas went to him, laid a hand upon his shoulder, bent his head. Their lips moved in murmured question, in response. Tagay was near naked anyway, his body streaked both red and white. She ran to him and, at a nod from the chief, the men who held him up let him go. He slumped forward into her arms. His eyes were open.

'Anne,' he said. 'White Cedar.'

'I cannot . . . cannot let them . . .' Over his shoulder she saw warriors forming the lines of a gauntlet. Flames had been kindled, sharpened stakes thrust into them.

'What did I say to you, after Black Snake?' Tagay whispered. 'That if it came, I would also choose to die this way. Like a warrior. I am only sorry that I am so weak . . .' Blood bubbled again at his mouth. 'I will not sing my death song very long.'

She pulled him hard against her body, her arms reaching around him, keeping him upright. 'And did I not say to you that I would not watch you die?'

He nodded. 'You did. So go. Let the Black Robe take you. Uncle Pierre stays his boat for you in the river. Let me die – but without your eyes upon me. Just remember: for ever, you are my love.'

Somehow she kept her voice calm. 'And you are mine. And you die a warrior of the Tahontaenrat, as you always dreamed you would.'

She turned his face toward the sunrise, reached around him,

found what she sought. Her fingers closed over jagged metal. It cut her, but she jerked it upwards anyway, then pulled it from his body. He gasped, his eyes widened, she felt his blood pour over her hand. She tucked the piece of metal into her pouch, where it clinked against stone – Donnaconna's Oki, Tagay's Oki now – then lowered his lifeless body to the ground. She began to walk, looking straight ahead, through the press of warriors that opened for her, toward the cliff path. She did not look around, though she heard the steps of a limping man, and a limping boy, behind her. As she passed under the oak, the drums and the chanting began. And she listened to a death song, unsung till then in that New World – Gianni's voice, beautiful, clear, rising in the first notes of the *Te Deum*.

'Die well, my brother,' she said, her own voice still strong. 'Die well.'

EPILOGUE

The sound of the flute accompanied Thomas in his dawn search. With a strong wind bellying the *Sea Feather*'s sails, there was time now for music; and Do-ne, under the tutelage of the old fisherman, Gaspard, had progressed rapidly from the ear-piercing shrillness of his first lessons. Four weeks at sea and he could carry, and carry well, half a dozen tunes.

He found her at the prow of the ship. It wasn't hard, the ship was small, even for a caravel. But for the first month of the voyage he would always go straight aft if he wanted her, because each day she would be there, looking back, weeks after the last giant pine had disappeared. Then, yesterday, he'd found her at the bow for the first time, her eyes as fixed on the horizon before them as they had been on the one behind. When he asked her what she scanned for, when they were yet some weeks from any harbour, she had simply said, 'My future.'

She smiled when he sat beside her, then returned her look ahead. He was content to stare with her until he felt her gaze once more upon him.

'This suits you.' She leant toward him to pull at the blue material of his shirt.

'I hope so,' he said, 'because it's undoubtedly the most expensive shirt I've ever had – if you figure that the robe I gave Gaspard for it cost me twenty scudi in Milan.'

She laughed. 'Then I think you were cheated. But my father always said the Bretons were the masters of that art. Then again, he was from the Loire.'

'It was worth it just to hear you laugh,' he said.

He was sorry he said it, because the words chased the fragile smile away and she returned her look to the horizon. But when he placed his hand on hers, as he had for the first time the day before, she did not withdraw it. Her fingers even tightened on his and he sat there, immeasurably content.

Will she come with me to Shropshire? he thought. *Is that what her hand in mine means? Or is mine in hers and she will lead me?*

He thought then of another hand, another Anne he'd once held and he shuddered as his memory compared bone to flesh. His mind moved back again to that night in the Tower, a mere . . . *six months before?* When he'd gone to violate a grave and found . . .

What? It didn't matter. A path. God's paths, always mysterious, no map could ever mark them. Leading here. And the miles and the pain in between, what were they after all? A route to this contentment, to holding the hand of the only woman he had ever loved.

Leaning back against the gunwale, he sighed and closed his eyes.

She heard his sigh, turned to study his face, its lines, its fringe of grey-black hair. He was a kind man, this Thomas Lawley and that, she had discovered, was a rare quality in this world. But she'd observed that such kindness often came to men who had experienced much sadness, as he had, as her father had. Tagay had not been allowed the time to grow kind but she knew he would have, if only they had been granted those years together. But his fierceness had been what he needed to fulfil his destiny. So she hoped that his son, whose first stirrings she had felt within her, would have the best of all the men from which his life sprang. The gentleness of this man dozing beside her, to whom she was now linked. Tagay's fire. And through her, perhaps some of her own father's courage. For though he had faltered along the way, Jean Rombaud had triumphed in the end.

Yes, she thought, *let me teach my son the true meaning of courage, as both his father and grandfather had learned it: to be afraid, yet still leap into the darkness.*

The notes of a flute rose from the ship as Anne Rombaud, named for a queen, turned her face again toward a new, old world.

HISTORICAL NOTE

Queen Mary died, childless, after a protracted illness and careworn life, on 17 November 1558.

Elizabeth, having survived all the plots against her, was crowned on 12 January 1559. She married no one.

Simon Renard, 'the Fox', lost his power with Mary's death. He died in 1571.

Philip of Spain, having failed in his wooing, sent his Armada to invade England in 1588. It was famously defeated by daring seamanship and dreadful storms.

The Tahontaenrat were the last to join the Huron Confederacy, the Wendat, in 1610. For several decades the Wendat, allied with the French, thrived and dominated the fur trade. Yet they were not strong enough to defeat the Iroquois, mainly Mohawk and Seneca, who conquered them in 1648–9.

The Hodenosaunee, or Iroquois Confederacy, eventually became six nations and grew powerful, usually siding with the British against the French in the wars of the next centuries. Their power only started to decline when the united front cracked, four tribes staying with the British, two joining the American Revolutionaries in 1776 – one of the subjects to be dealt with in C.C. Humphreys' next novel, *Jack Absolute*, available in Orion hardback from January 2004.